TALL, DARK, AND TEXAN

Tall, Dark, and Texan

Jodi Thomas

JOVE BOOKS, NEW YORK

THE BERKLEY PUBLISHING GROUP
Published by the Penguin Group
Penguin Group (USA) Inc.
375 Hudson Street, New York, New York 10014, USA
Penguin Group (Canada), 90 Eglinton Avenue East, Suite 700, Toronto, Ontario M4P 2Y3, Canada
(a division of Pearson Penguin Canada Inc.)
Penguin Books Ltd., 80 Strand, London WC2R 0RL, England
Penguin Group Ireland, 25 St. Stephen's Green, Dublin 2, Ireland (a division of Penguin Books Ltd.)
Penguin Group (Australia), 250 Camberwell Road, Camberwell, Victoria 3124, Australia
(a division of Pearson Australia Group Pty. Ltd.)
Penguin Books India Pvt. Ltd., 11 Community Centre, Panchsheel Park, New Delhi—110 017, India
Penguin Group (NZ), 67 Apollo Drive, Rosedale, North Shore 0632, New Zealand
(a division of Pearson New Zealand Ltd.)
Penguin Books (South Africa) (Pty.) Ltd., 24 Sturdee Avenue, Rosebank, Johannesburg 2196,
South Africa

Penguin Books Ltd., Registered Offices: 80 Strand, London WC2R 0RL, England

This is a work of fiction. Names, characters, places, and incidents either are the product of the author's imagination or are used fictitiously, and any resemblance to actual persons, living or dead, business establishments, events, or locales is entirely coincidental. The publisher does not have any control over and does not assume any responsibility for author or third-party websites or their content.

TALL, DARK, AND TEXAN

A Jove Book / published by arrangement with the author

PRINTING HISTORY
Jove mass-market edition / November 2008

Copyright © 2008 by Jodi Koumalats.
Cover illustration by Jim Griffin.
Cover handlettering by Ron Zinn.
Cover design by George Long.

ISBN: 978-1-60751-110-6

JOVE®
Jove Books are published by The Berkley Publishing Group,
a division of Penguin Group (USA) Inc.,
375 Hudson Street, New York, New York 10014.
JOVE® is a registered trademark of Penguin Group (USA) Inc.
The "J" design is a trademark belonging to Penguin Group (USA) Inc.

PRINTED IN THE UNITED STATES OF AMERICA

TALL, DARK, AND TEXAN

CHAPTER 1

JESSICA ANNE BARTON TUCKED HER DAUGHTERS INTO bed, wrapped a quilt around her shoulders, and tiptoed down the winding stairway to her desk in the corner of the bookstore. A month ago the two book-lined rooms would have been warm from fireplaces left smoldering. A month ago she would have looked forward to the next day.

But not now.

Now she had no future. Not in Chicago. Maybe not anywhere. If she didn't plan very carefully, she'd lose the only thing that mattered to her: her children.

Since that first night when she'd been thirteen, cold and homeless, Barton Bookstore had been her refuge. Eli Barton caught her sleeping between the stacks and had put her to work in exchange for food and a cot in the attic. Three years passed before he married her, not out of love or even kindness but simply because he couldn't run the store without her.

Eleven years and three daughters later, nothing had changed. At dawn she would once again be homeless, and Eli, her rescuer, her husband, her jailer, would be buried.

She settled into an old desk chair far too big for her thin frame. Her life within these walls had crumbled. While a bitter March wind made the eviction notice tap against the glass at the front door, Jessie dug in the bottom drawer for her one hope. When she found the bundle of letters from Texas, she gripped it tightly. Whispering Mountain Ranch had always seemed a make-believe place she visited only in her dreams.

But this time, the dream had to be real, for now it was her only hope.

Grabbing a piece of paper, she scribbled a note and signed her dead husband's name. As she wrote Teagen McMurray's address on the envelope, Jessie whispered an apology for what she was about to do to this friend she'd never met.

By dawn she'd have her girls dressed and walking toward the train station. Eli's family hadn't invited her to his funeral. That hadn't mattered, for she knew as soon as the coffin was lowered they would be coming to claim what they considered family property: the store, the modest bank account, the children.

They would be searching the house while she and the girls boarded a train heading west. It would be a long, costly journey, first the train, then a boat from New Orleans to Galveston, then a stage almost three hundred miles across land barely claimed. In two months they would be in Texas. The stage would drop them off at a town with no name except Anderson's Trading Post. There, they'd wait for a man she'd never met to help them.

If McMurray was the kind of man she prayed he would be, she'd probably end all peace in his life.

And if he ever found out the truth about what she was about to do, he'd hate her a day longer than forever.

CHAPTER 2

Texas, 1856

TEAGEN MCMURRAY WRAPPED THE CUT ON HIS HAND with his handkerchief and used his teeth to help tighten a knot as he drove the buckboard to the front of Elmo Anderson's Trading Post. The injury looked more bothersome than dangerous, he decided.

Glancing at the sun, he wondered if he would have time to check the property lines before nightfall. The gash would wait, but safety at the ranch couldn't. If horse thieves came in fast, he had to be ready. The kind of men who stole horses had little regard for property lines or who they might have to kill to get what they wanted. He needed his brothers, but they were too far away to help. This time he'd have to stand alone, at least until the men he'd hired as extra guards arrived from Austin.

He looked around at the growing town behind Elmo's place, trying to guess if some of the recent residents were responsible for the broken posts and downed fence on his land. Anyone could have noticed his brothers leaving and decided the time might be right to rustle a few head. From the looks of some of the gunfighters and drifters settling in around Elmo Anderson's place, Teagen wouldn't be surprised if someone watched him now.

He would have preferred to ride into town on horseback. It meant far less time away from the ranch. But this was the first Saturday of the month, and he had Martha's list in his pocket.

His housekeeper would not be happy if he made it back with half the order, so he'd hitched a team. The matched bays belonged in front of a fine carriage, not a work wagon, but they needed exercise, and a trip to town would have to do.

Climbing down, he checked the rigging. He wanted to hurry, but care of the horses always came first. Eli Barton's letter was already three months overdue. Teagen could wait another few minutes before he handed over the grocery list and walked back to check the mail that was always tossed into the back corner of the trading post.

Two men in buckskins walked past and gave him a nod. Teagen returned the greeting. Everyone in town knew he didn't go in for small talk. He might have managed the huge Whispering Mountain Ranch for almost twenty years, but he called no one in this settlement friend. In fact, except for the trading post, Teagen had little use for the town that seemed to be growing like grounded bindweed.

Of course, if he was counting people who should stay, he'd have to add Mrs. Dickerson, the only schoolteacher around, to his list. She'd been bombarding her way into the McMurray brothers' lives since the winter after their father died fighting for Texas independence and their mother passed away giving birth to their sister Sage. Teagen and his brothers had burned the bridge separating their land from the rest of Texas in order to hold on to what was theirs. Teagen, the oldest, had just turned twelve when he became the head of the family. No one came to help or bothered to check on them. Except Mrs. Dickerson. She'd sent notes out with every food delivery the boys picked up at night from Elmo's back porch, and with every note came assignments and books the boys should read.

Teagen tied the reins to the brake, remembering how she'd given him an address of a new bookstore in Chicago. He'd waited three years before writing. At first just books came, then slowly a few letters a year, Teagen formed a friendship with the bookstore owner. The past ten years the letters had arrived regularly. One every fall, another near Christmas, and one in March accompanying the new spring catalogue.

Except for this time. It was well into June, and he hadn't heard from Chicago.

Teagen walked into the shade of the porch, removed his hat, and wiped his forehead on his sleeve. It would be after noon before he returned, and he had two days of work to finish before nightfall. The splintered post had not only cut his hand, it delayed him. Martha would be so mad about him being late with her provisions, she would probably abandon not speaking to him in favor of nagging him to death.

"Morning." A pretty little lady in black drew his attention. Her voice held a hint of a northern accent that marked her instantly as an outsider.

For a second, he glanced to his left and right, thinking she must be greeting someone else. Town folk never talked to any McMurray except his sister Sage.

But this stranger, sitting on Anderson's porch, just looked up at him and smiled.

Three little girls, stacked like leaning dominoes, were sleeping beside her on the bench. "Morning," he managed, gave her a quick nod, and moved on.

Almost smiling at his newfound friendly attitude, he stepped inside the post.

"Teagen," Elmo Anderson yelled from across the length of his store. "You got the list?"

Teagen reached in his pocket and tugged out the list of items Martha had dictated to him at breakfast. It was shorter than usual, since both his brothers and their wives were gone. Even Sage had left to visit Travis and Rainey in Austin. For three weeks he'd eaten his meals alone with a book propped against his coffee cup. A few times he'd had to remind himself he preferred the silence while he read. He'd reread several novels and journals and knew he'd be wishing for company if the new shipment didn't come soon from Barton Books.

Before he could ask, Anderson volunteered, "That letter you've been expecting from Chicago finally came in on the stage, along with that widow and three girls on the porch. She's been waiting for someone all morning." He flipped Teagen the letter and went back to work.

She was not his worry, Teagen thought, as he opened the envelope. One page tumbled out. Teagen frowned. He'd hoped for a long letter from his friend.

Four lines were boldly written on the page.

To my dear friend Teagen McMurray.
In this my last will and testimony
I leave you my wife and children.
I know you'll take care of them.
—Eli Barton

Teagen looked up to see if someone was playing a prank. But no one ever played jokes on him. Anderson and a stock boy were the only two in the store, and they seemed busy collecting supplies. If they had any idea what had been in the letter, neither showed any sign of it.

Reading the message again, he frowned. This had to be some kind of trick. It was obviously his friend's handwriting—he'd know Eli's signature anywhere after all the years—but when Teagen heard from Barton Books in December, Eli had said he was well. Why was he now sending something that sounded like a will?

Teagen tried to remember what Eli had written at Christmas. Something short and to the point, talking only of books. At the time Teagen had assumed Eli was busy, but now he wondered if he could have already been ill, maybe even dying.

He flipped the envelope over. No postmarks. "How'd you say this letter came in?"

"On the stage," Elmo answered. "The lady out on the porch handed it to me."

Not wanting anyone to know his business, Teagen folded the letter, stuffed it in his shirt pocket, and walked outside.

The woman in black and three sleeping little girls hadn't moved. He took a closer look. They all looked exhausted, their clothes travel-dirty and worn.

Maybe it was coincidence they waited here, he thought as he stepped closer.

The woman stood, using her bag as a pillow for the child who'd been sleeping on her leg. She wasn't tall, not even to his shoulder. Teagen had the feeling she stood on her tiptoes to face him. He'd seen rabbits braver than her. Dark circles shadowed her huge brown eyes.

Before he could figure out how to ask a total stranger who she was, the little lady said, "You're Teagen McMurray, aren't you?"

He nodded slowly, afraid to make any fast moves because the poor woman looked like she might cry. In general, he had no idea how to handle women, and this one in particular seemed even more of a puzzle with her northern accent and big, frightened eyes.

She blinked as if she could push away fear. "You're bigger than I thought you would be."

He didn't know how to respond. Hard work had put two hundred pounds on his six-foot frame, and he saw no need to explain. Better to get things straight right away. "There's been some mistake, miss."

"Mrs.," she whispered. "Mrs. Eli Barton. My husband told me to come to you if something happened to him. He died of pneumonia over three months ago."

"I'm sorry to hear that." Teagen felt far more sorrow than he let show in his words. "I considered him a good friend."

She stared. Grief wasn't new to her, he guessed, so it no longer held a sting.

The letter scratched against his chest, but he didn't pull it out. Teagen was not a man who could be talked or bullied into anything. Not even by a friend's dying words. "How can I be of service, Mrs. Barton?" he said coldly, already drawing lines in his mind as to how far he would go to help Eli's widow. Teagen had seen far too many con men in his life to trust anyone except family. Money for the stage back to Austin and the fee for a few nights in the hotel seemed appropriate. Maybe, if she needed respectable work, he could ask around. Mrs. Dickerson might help her find employment.

For a second he thought he saw pain flicker in her brown eyes, and he almost wished he'd asked more softly. But a gentle tone would die from lack of use in his mouth.

"If it wouldn't be too much to ask, could we stay a few days with you, Mr. McMurray?" She hesitated as if she'd practiced her speech and wanted to remember it exactly. "We've been traveling for weeks and need somewhere to rest until my relatives from California can reach us."

A weight lifted from his shoulders. If all she wanted was a way station, he could provide that, even if it wasn't something he'd ever done. This was a special circumstance. This was the widow of his friend. "When will they be coming?" he asked before committing.

She looked at him again with those sad eyes. "Soon," she whispered. "I'm sure they are already on their way. A week or two at the most."

"I could see you to the hotel. You'd be comfortable there."

She reached out and touched his arm so quickly he didn't have time to step back. "Please, if you've room, may we stay at your ranch? The girls have been boxed up on smoky trains, airless hotels, and stagecoaches for so long. We've found most places on the way here to be noisy and not always friendly to children."

Teagen couldn't argue. He'd rather camp outside a town than go into a hotel and sleep where the air smelled of sweaty bodies, and arguments drifted through paper-thin walls. He glanced at the three sleeping girls, then back at their shy little mother. How much trouble could they be? "Of course. If you like. I've got the room."

She collected her things while Teagen loaded up her two small trunks. It crossed his mind that Whispering Mountain wasn't on the way to anything, certainly not California. She should have traveled with wagons to Santa Fe and waited there or taken a train from Chicago to the East Coast and then a ship to California. But, he reasoned, a ship around the horn might have been too expensive and, with three children, a hotel in Santa Fe would not be easy to find.

The letter scratched through the cotton of his shirt. It had almost sounded as if Eli had given Teagen his family to keep, not just to watch over for a few days. Teagen told himself it was not too much of a favor to ask. After all, if the truth be told, Eli was his only friend. To everyone around, he'd always had to be solid as a rock, but there had been a few times over the years when Teagen had written out all his thoughts and problems in letters to a man he'd thought he would never meet.

Anderson shoved the last box of supplies into the buckboard and turned to stare. "You taking the lady home, Teagen?" If gossip had a crusader, it would be bald-headed, round-bodied Elmo Anderson. He was worse than a two-headed magpie.

"Yes," Teagen answered. He shoved the widow's box deep into the bed of the buckboard.

"To Whispering Mountain?"

The petite widow straightened as she carried the oldest of her three sleeping children in her arms. Her glance told Teagen she also waited to make sure he wouldn't change his mind.

"Yes," Teagen echoed. "Appears I'm going to have company for a few days."

Anderson's stare reminded Teagen of an openmouthed catfish.

Mrs. Barton stepped forward. "If you could move a few of those boxes, I think my Emily can sleep next to the supplies. She's very tired."

For the first time Teagen really looked at the child. She was thin with skin as pale as milk and hair so blonde it was almost white. Nothing about her appeared healthy. Teagen didn't look away as he spoke to the store owner. "Bring out a few new blankets. We're running short at the house anyway. She can sleep on them for the ride back."

Anderson, always happy for the sale, hurried toward the store. "Any particular kind?"

"Blue," a tiny voice shouted. "Em loves blue."

Teagen looked around at the other two children. The one closest to him must be the youngest. She had a round face with her mother's eyes and auburn hair so curly it looked like a bush.

"What's this one's name?" He indicated with his head as he began moving boxes in the wagon.

"That's Bethie." The middle child stepped forward. "And I'm Rose. She likes red."

The wee one waddled toward him. "Red, red, red."

Teagen frowned down at the one who said she was Rose. She was thin, like her sleeping sister Emily, but her hair hung in long black braids. As he watched, she caught the back of her baby sister's dress and tugged, keeping Bethie from toppling off the porch.

"Why don't you both go with Mr. Anderson and pick out a few colors you like? It doesn't matter to me."

Rose's dark eyes danced with excitement. "Really?"

"Really." He fought down a smile. The baby reminded him of a cherub, but in the middle girl he saw a hint of himself in the way she watched out for her siblings. She hadn't told him her favorite color, only Emily's and Bethie's.

Rose glanced at her mother for approval. When a slight nod came, the children ran into the store.

Teagen waited, trying to think of something to say, trying not to stare at how Mrs. Barton looked in the sun. She had fair skin as though she spent little time in the open air, and her hair was tied back beneath her bonnet. The wisp of a strand he could see looked brown. Not pretty or shiny, but just a dull medium brown.

He turned his attention to the sleeping child. "Emily, Rose, and Bethie," he mumbled.

Mrs. Barton smiled. "And I'm Jessica, but everyone calls me Jessie."

Teagen nodded silently, accepting her offer to allow them to be less formal. "You're welcome to stay and rest," he said. Judging from their clothes, she could use a few days to wash as well. "But we're not used to company." That had to be the biggest understatement he'd ever managed. "Whispering Mountain is a working ranch."

"I can pay you—" she began.

"No." He felt insulted at the offer. "Martha always cooks far too much anyway, and we've got empty rooms."

Anderson returned with Bethie on one arm and three blankets tucked under the other. Rose followed, tying her bonnet as she walked. She looked quite the proper little lady, having finished her shopping. Like a well-trained lady, she hid a yawn behind her hand.

As Elmo Anderson spread the blankets out, he shook his head. "In all my days I ain't never seen you have company out to your place. None 'cept a Ranger now and then. Times are sure changing when the McMurrays welcome strangers on their land."

Teagen didn't comment. He took the sleeping child from the widow's arms and placed her gently atop the blankets. Then, without asking, he lifted the one called Rose from the porch and carried her to the wagon. She didn't make a sound as he lowered her in beside her big sister. She was already asleep by the time he pulled a blanket over her shoulder.

When he glanced back at the chubby one circling round the porch like a wobbly top, the widow said, "She better ride between us on the bench, or she'll either fall out of the wagon or wake the others."

Teagen agreed and offered his hand to the widow. When she hesitated, he said, "I'll help you up, Jessie."

Awkwardly, she gathered her skirts. "Thank you, Teagen."

He rested his free hand at her waist to steady her and was surprised at how thin she felt. Even through the layers of her traveling jacket, he swore he could feel her bones.

When she was seated, he turned to catch the cherub bumping into things as she now circled round and round like a drunk.

Bethie rocked in his arms, laughing as he lifted her. He carried her to the wagon. Just as he set her on the bench, she patted his cheek with a sticky palm covered in the remains of a piece of rock candy.

Teagen frowned and tried to rub off the sugar, but it seemed permanently tangled in his three-day-old beard. When he frowned down at her, the child smiled at him.

He growled.

Bethie giggled and reached for him again.

Only her mother's grip kept her from tumbling off the bench and landing on the floor at their feet.

CHAPTER 3

JESSIE LEANED BACK AGAINST THE HARD WOOD OF THE wagon bench and tried to breathe. She'd made it to Teagen. After almost three months of struggling to hold on to three children and be alert to danger and try to find food and sleep with one eye open, she'd finally made it to Whispering Mountain.

That predawn morning when she'd left the bookstore, she convinced herself Teagen McMurray would be her sanctuary from harm. Now in this wild country, she wasn't so sure.

She tried to find a good thought among her worries. Even though Teagen was none too friendly, he *had* agreed to take her in. Without the letter he might not have done that. She hated that the letter was a lie, and the fact that it was only one of many didn't make her feel much better.

She glanced over at the big man driving the wagon. He seemed coldhearted, but she'd read his letters and knew he worried about his little sister and the ranch he owned. He looked all granite on the outside, a man chiseled from stone. A man who'd written he'd never open his heart to a woman. A man who'd been her only friend, and he hadn't even known it.

She tried to smile at him. "What happened to your hand?"

He didn't smile back. "Nothing," he answered without glancing at the makeshift bandage.

Surely, somewhere in him there was room for a little kindness. At least she prayed there would be, because if Teagen ever raised his hand in anger like Eli used to, he'd kill her with one blow. If he didn't prove to be the man in his letters, at least maybe she could buy enough time for the girls to rest while she decided her next step.

Jessie tried not to think of the times she'd been hurt by her husband's thoughtless words or drunken swings. Eli hadn't meant it. In fact, most of the time he hadn't even remembered when he sobered up. Deep down Jessie knew Eli tried. He'd never said he loved her, but he had been considerate each time she was pregnant, making sure she didn't work too hard and that she had plenty to eat. As soon as each girl was born, he'd gone back to his drinking, showing no interest in the girls or in the store his parents set up for him.

She took a deep breath and pushed memories of Chicago far back in her mind. Somehow, out here, she'd make a new start. Because of Teagen's letters, she had read every book she could find about the West. Looking around at the rolling hills and wildflowers growing along a road, she couldn't help but wonder where the wildness was. Except for the man beside her, all she saw appeared tame, harmless.

Closing her eyes, she listened. Silence. Peace. She heard the soft clop of the two horses traveling on dirt, a bird calling in the distance, the jingle of the harness. The freshness of this place washed over her like a gentle rain.

"Jessie?"

One word pulled her back.

She watched as Teagen tugged on the reins, then handed them to her when the horses stopped. Without explanation, he stepped down from the wagon and grabbed a canteen beneath the bench.

"What is it?" All the wild stories she'd read about Texas tumbled into her brain.

A hint of a smile lifted one corner of his mouth when he looked up at her. If she hadn't known it was impossible, she would think he read her mind.

"There's a stream just beyond the trees. I'll get you and the girls some cool water."

Jessie nodded, trying to decide what he wanted her to do with the reins. Hopefully nothing. She'd been born in Chicago and considered herself an expert at dodging wagons and carriages, but she'd never driven one.

Bethie wiggled off the bench and tried to reach one of the horses' tails.

Smiling, Jessie realized these animals must be part of the Whispering Mountain breed of horses Teagen so often described. "The finest in Texas," he'd written. Somehow those bold words penned with such obvious pride always made her smile.

The horses shifted, pulling the wagon with them as they moved into the grass beside the road.

"Stop," Jessie ordered. "Be still." She tugged at the reins, but the animals didn't seem to notice.

Bethie plopped down in the floor of the wagon and began to cry.

Jessie dropped the reins on the footboard in front of her and reached for her daughter. With the shift of the wagon, the horses moved forward again pulling it off the narrow road and onto the incline leading down to the creek. Holding Bethie tighter, she fought to stay on the sloping bench.

"Stop!" she shouted at the horses, but only succeeded in making the baby cry harder.

The horses moved farther as if they hadn't heard her yell. The right wheel rocked into a hole, almost tipping the wagon. Supplies shifted, bumping into her sleeping daughters.

Suddenly all three girls were crying and screaming. Jessie reached for the reins just as they slipped away. She turned to order her older daughters to jump before the wagon rolled, but as she formed the words, Teagen was suddenly standing at the side of the wagon.

He walked right past her and the screaming children, patted one of the horses on the shoulder, grabbed the leather harness and turned the animals back toward the road. In seconds all was righted.

Retrieving the reins, he tied them around the brake while she climbed down the other side and ran to the girls in the back.

Rose came first, her tears already finished. "Where are we?" she asked. "What happened?"

Emily mumbled behind her. "Horses."

"It's all right, Rose. We're fine."

Teagen joined them behind the wagon and offered to help Emily. The seven-year-old backed up into the boxes.

"I'm not going to hurt you, child," he said. "I'll give you a hand down."

Frightened, Emily didn't move until Jessie stepped in front of Teagen and lifted her to the ground. "She's afraid of strangers," Jessie whispered. "She'll warm up to you when she gets to know you."

Teagen shoved his hat back and shrugged. "Most folks don't."

She fought a grin. He'd said the words so honestly she had no doubt that he thought them to be true.

"Girls, I'd like you to meet Mr. McMurray. He's a friend of your father, and he's offered to let us stay with him for a while."

Jessie almost laughed. Rose and Emily looked like she'd just introduced a monster to them. "He's taking us to his ranch. No more trains or boats or stagecoaches for a while."

Rose looked up at him with interest. "Do you have more horses and a cow?"

"Yes." Teagen knelt down to the five-year-old's level. "Lots of cows and a few goats, pigs, and chickens and a half dozen barn cats."

Rose nodded as if he'd given the right answer. "What are their names?"

Teagen frowned. "Who?"

"The cats? Cats all have names." Her head nodded, sending her long braids dancing. "It's a fact, Mister."

Teagen considered her for a minute and finally answered. "I haven't had time to name them. Could you do it for me? That can be your chore. Everybody on a ranch has to have a job."

She let out a long sigh. "I guess, but it's hard to think of the right name for a cat. Pigs are easier, and that is a fact."

To Teagen's credit, he seemed to take the problem seriously. "Then you'll have your work cut out for you. We'd better get going." He settled Rose just behind the wagon bench, telling her she could stand if she held on with both hands or sat on one of the trunks.

When he turned to Emily, she backed away, and Jessie picked her up.

As Jessie hiked her skirt a few inches and began to climb up, Teagen's hand braced her back. She froze midway up and looked at him. "Thank you."

He seemed to understand that she meant more than a thanks for the help up. "No problem," he answered back in the same low tone she'd used. "You should have told me you didn't know how to handle a wagon."

With her foot on the step they were at eye level. "I know." For balance, she placed her hand on his shoulder. "Would you have time to teach me? It seems a skill I need to learn."

He studied her before he finally said, "I'll make time. A woman able to handle a team will come in handy on the long trail to California."

She looked away, and the moment between them was gone. Taking her seat, she straightened her skirts as he circled the wagon. Maybe it had been her imagination, but for a heartbeat in time she thought she'd seen the Teagen she'd written to for years in his eyes. The man who cared and worried about people, not this cold, indifferent man who seemed bothered that they'd interrupted his day.

Before they started again, she gave each of the girls a long drink of water, then used the last of the canteen to wash Bethie's hands.

"I'm ready," Jessie said when she realized Teagen was sitting, his foot propped up on the footrest, waiting.

He lowered his boot and made a sound that set the horses in motion.

Fifteen minutes later when she asked him to stop, he didn't say a word. He simply climbed from the wagon and handed the girls to her. Emily allowed him to lift her down, but she didn't look at him.

"They have to . . ." She had no idea how to tell him.

"To see to nature's call," he said. "I know. I have a little sister. She was almost grown before we could make it between town and the ranch without stopping."

When they returned, he didn't smile but helped the girls, then her, back onto the wagon. Jessie tried to think of something to say to him. Suddenly he seemed a total stranger to her. She could almost quote every word he'd ever written in his letters, yet she didn't know him. Didn't even know the color of his eyes.

Blue, she finally guessed. Blue-gray, like the winter sky in Chicago.

They crossed a bridge, and Jessie knew they were now on McMurray land. Teagen had written that he and his brothers had burned the original bridge when their father died. Burned it so no one could take their property while they were still boys.

"Are we on your land?" she asked, already knowing the answer.

"We are," Teagen answered. "You can see the house from here."

"Thank you for letting us stay." Jessie felt safe, truly safe, for the first time since her parents died.

Teagen looked over Bethie's head. "We might have only known each other by letters, but I considered Eli my friend. I'm doing this for his sake."

Jessie nodded and looked away. How could she tell him that Eli Barton had never even known Whispering Mountain or Teagen McMurray existed? She'd written the letters. She'd been his friend.

Only, if she told him, she had a feeling all she'd be to him was a liar. If he believed her now, then he'd realize she'd lied in the letters. If he didn't believe her about writing the letters, he'd think she was lying to him now. Either way, she'd lose.

"It's a beautiful place," she said as the ranch headquarters spread out beneath the hills. "So beautiful it takes my breath away."

"The Indians call this place what translates to Whispering Mountain, even though folks that have seen the Rockies say those are hills not mountains. The Apache believed the hills will whisper a man's future to anyone who dreams on the top of the mountain."

She studied him. "And you, Teagen McMurray, do you believe?"

He shook his head. "I'm living the life I was meant to live. My brothers married and enjoy traveling away, but my heart draws its beat from this place. I wouldn't survive long anywhere else. Sometimes I think it's more that the land owns me than I own the land."

Jessie smiled. His words reminded her of his letters, almost poetic when he talked of his ranch.

As they neared the wide ranch house with barns and corrals on either side, he added, "My housekeeper will be surprised to see company." He hesitated a moment before continuing, "She's not too friendly to strangers. Hell, in twenty years she hasn't warmed up to me yet."

Jessie laughed nervously. The wagon pulled up in front of a white porch wide enough to set a dining table on. A woman with silver streaks in her hair stood tall by the back door. Her blue dress and starched apron left no doubt of her identity.

Teagen climbed down. Jessie and her daughters didn't move. She'd told the girls they would be staying at a ranch, but even she had no idea it would be so grand. Just the house was four or five times bigger than the bookstore and their living quarters above.

He carried the first box of supplies and set it on the porch near Martha's feet. When he turned for the second box, Jessie heard Martha say matter-of-factly, "Did you pick up a wife and kids during your morning shopping, Teagen? Buying them would be the only way a man ornery as you would ever find a family."

Her words seemed to have no effect on him as he turned and walked back to the wagon. He grabbed the second crate and carried it to the porch before he answered, "No, I just invited them to stay awhile."

Martha's mouth fell open as she watched him walk back to the wagon. "You invited company?"

Teagen raised his hands to Jessie.

She stood and allowed him to lift her down.

The girls followed her lead, Bethie giggling, Rose curious, and Emily looking like she might cry at any moment. They circled around Jessie's skirts as if the dusty wool of her traveling clothes would protect them.

Teagen grabbed another box, then motioned for them to go ahead of him. She had no choice but to walk directly toward the stern woman in blue who looked more like she belonged as a prison warden than in a kitchen.

"Martha." Teagen set the box down with a thud. "I'd like you to meet Mrs. Barton and her three daughters."

The matronly housekeeper's eyes narrowed. "Barton, as in Eli Barton of Barton Books. The fellow who sends all them books from Chicago."

Jessie nodded. "My husband died almost three months ago. We've had a very long journey to get here, and I hope we won't be too much trouble." Touching each of her daughters, she added, "This is Rose, and Emily, and Bethie." She expected questions, but to her surprise, Martha smiled.

The housekeeper opened the door and said, "You all must be tired. You can wash up back here in the mud room, and I'll fix you something to eat."

Jessie felt like she might kiss Miss Martha. "Thank you," she managed.

Bethie, at the mention of food, wrapped her hand around two of Martha's fingers.

"No thanks needed," Martha insisted. "As the housekeeper, it's my pleasure to welcome you." She looked down at the child now holding her hand. "I make the best biscuits and gravy you ever ate. Bethie, is it?"

Bethie nodded, and Jessie felt a twinge of guilt. The girls hadn't eaten since yesterday.

As she moved into the cool shadows of the mud room, she saw clean towels stacked beside a huge tub. Neatly folded clothes were in long columns against one wall, and buckets for water hung on pegs near the door.

She heard Martha yell at Teagen, "We'll be needing water before you disappear." About the time buckets clanged, she added, "What'd you do to your hand?"

"Nothing," Teagen snapped back.

"Well, I'll be seeing about that 'nothing' as soon as you come in. The blood's already spotting through that handkerchief, and you know what that means."

"I get pie?" Teagen guessed.

"No." Martha snorted. "It means more laundry for me. I know there's no use trying to tie you down and doctor you now, but you'd better make it in before nightfall."

"It'll wait until I get the work done today. Don't lose any sleep waiting up."

"I won't, but you doctor it right," Martha ordered. "Do you hear me, Teagen?"

Jessie smiled. They sounded angry, but she had a feeling there was real caring in this argument. He might be a man in his early thirties, but Martha had known him long enough to at least try to order him around.

CHAPTER 4

WHEN TEAGEN FINALLY TURNED TOWARD HOME, THE dying light of a summer sun reflected off Whispering Mountain. He'd spent most of the day in the saddle covering the ranch and checking every pasture. Twice he'd seen tracks that didn't belong to McMurray horses. Whoever planned to raid the ranch was being careful, taking no chance of being caught in daylight. That kind of precaution could mean only one thing. When the raid came, it would be a big one.

Like an animal feeling a storm coming, Teagen raised his head slightly and listened. He could feel trouble riding the wind, and he planned to be ready when it came.

For twenty years, since he'd been twelve, Teagen's primary goal had been to protect the ranch and his family. He felt weary and, with none of the family home, he half wished he could let down his guard. But, deep down he knew he never would . . . never could. This ranch was all the family he had near.

Most of their land was open range where horses could run full out, fenced only by the rocks bordering the hills and the river's edge. Some of the canyons had been blocked off to keep in bred mares and horses Tobin was working with. The McMurrays trained some of the best riding horses in the state, and a matched pair of carriage horses went for top dollar. There were outlaws who'd risk their lives to steal them.

Teagen frowned and headed for the creek. Tobin, his brother who swore he'd never leave Whispering Mountain, was in Washington, D.C., with his new wife and baby. The kid who claimed he'd never wear anything but moccasins was probably dressed in one of those fancy suits with tails and dancing around a ballroom floor. Marriage made men do strange things. Even Travis, who was only a year younger than Teagen, had put down his gun and Ranger badge for the love of a woman. All his fights of late had been as a lawyer in the courtroom.

Teagen was the last. The only brother who'd never marry, which suited him just fine. He didn't trust most people, and women were a total mystery to him. Plus, if a man married, there was always the possibility that children would appear. The last thing Teagen wanted was kids. His adopted nephew they called Duck was all right, but little girls, like the ones visiting, were nothing but pestersome. The small one called Bethie seemed to think he was some kind of toy bear to pat on; the oldest, Emily, was afraid of him; and that middle one, Rose, never stopped asking questions.

When he reached the creek, Teagen stripped off his gun belt and clothes, then dove in without remembering to take off the bandage around his hand. The wound had bothered him all day. He'd soak it in a mixture of turpentine and baking soda when he got home, but for now he just wanted to wash a layer of sweat and dust off before he turned in for a few hours' sleep.

As he swam in long, steady strokes around the pool of deep water, he thought not of what he'd accomplished but what he hadn't completed. Ranch work was never done. Trouble was so close he could smell it. He'd be up while it was still dark making his first round before breakfast.

Climbing from the water, he slung his hair like an animal and laughed, thinking he wasn't far from the bear little Bethie claimed him to be.

After tugging on his trousers, he rode the short distance home shirtless and shoeless. The night air felt good as it dried his body. He'd bathed in the stream every summer of his life and wondered if people who lived in towns had any idea of what they missed.

A few minutes later, he'd let his horse out into the corral and stepped soundlessly into the back space off the kitchen that everyone called the mud room. He didn't need the light. He knew where his clean shirt and trousers were. None of the McMurray men wore long johns in the summer, despite Martha's constant preaching that wool next to the skin prevents illness all year long.

His shelves of clean clothes had always been the first row by the door. Shirt on top, pants next, and then socks.

Leaving his boots by the door, Teagen pulled on a clean pair of socks and stepped into the kitchen. The lamp on the table burned low, casting shadows across shadows. He knew his dinner waited in the warming box above the stove, but he needed to doctor his hand first. Martha had a firm rule about going to bed with the sun, and there had to be a serious crisis for her to break any of her rules. So he'd do his own doctoring tonight.

When he set the medicine box on the table, he sensed someone near more than saw her. Teagen turned slowly and noticed Jessie in the shadow of the doorway leading to the rest of the house. Her hair was tied back with a ribbon, and her white nightgown made her look like an angel come to watch over him. He recognized the robe she wore as one of his sister's and knew Sage wouldn't mind her borrowing it.

"I thought you'd be in bed." He frowned. The dark circles beneath her eyes made him wonder if she ever slept.

She took one step into the room. "I told Martha I'd stay up and doctor that hand. She was worried about infection setting in."

Teagen didn't bother to say it was nothing again. No one seemed to have heard him the first two times. He simply sat down and laid his hand, palm up, on the table. "All right, I'm all yours."

She came close and untied the knots on his wet handkerchief. Her hands shook a little, and he wondered if she dreaded seeing the wound or if it was his nearness that frightened her. Most people he didn't much care if he frightened or not, but for some reason he didn't like the idea that she might be afraid of him.

He tried to think of something to say. "How was your day?" Teagen felt bad that he hadn't given much thought about the widow and her chicks since he'd dropped them off. He'd spent some time remembering his friend, Eli, and how there would be no more letters to look forward to, no more long ramblings about problems he faced on the ranch, and no more eager questions from Eli. It occurred to him that the bookstore owner had never mentioned his family. Had they been too precious to talk about to a stranger, or too insignificant to mention?

"It was very nice," she answered, pulling Teagen back from his guessing. "We bathed the girls and washed their hair. Then Martha let them help her make blackberry pies while I had time for a real bath. Then we had to wash Bethie all over again because she made such a mess. And . . ." She drew in a sudden breath.

"What?" Teagen asked, realizing he'd been looking at her hair and not really listening.

"Teagen, you're hurt. The cut is still bleeding, and there's a piece of wood in your palm."

He tried to tug his hand from her grip. "It's—"

She held tightly, her small hand circling his thumb. "Don't you even think of saying it's nothing. This needs taking care of right away. Don't move; I'll get a bowl of hot water, and we will deal with this before you have an infection. I can't believe you let it go this long."

"Bossy little woman, aren't you, Jessie." Her temper warmed the paleness from her cheeks.

She didn't bother to argue. The widow simply went to work cleaning the wound and applying salve. She had a gentle touch.

"You know what you're doing." He leaned back in his chair, the wound already feeling better than it had all day.

She didn't look at him. "Eli often came home with cuts and bruises."

Teagen frowned. "I wouldn't think owning a bookstore would be hazardous work."

"It wasn't, but drinking in the pubs seemed to be."

Teagen had trouble mixing the images of a drunk with the words in Eli's letters describing books he just read. Maybe she was just doing what some wives do, painting her man in a bad light. He'd heard men do it, so he supposed women did the same.

"Do you drink?" she asked, her big eyes flashing to his.

"Yes," he answered, thinking of the one drink he usually managed to have with his brothers whenever they came to-gether after being separated for a time. "But I've never suf-fered an injury from it."

She smiled at him then. "Do you need a drink for the pain? I'm about to dig a splinter the size of a sewing needle out of your palm."

"No," he said, hoping he was telling the truth.

She began to work. "Tell me of your day, Teagen. It'll take your mind off what I'm doing."

Teagen placed his other hand over his forearm, holding his injury still as she poked into damaged flesh. "I think there is someone riding onto my land at night. If the broken fence is any indication, it's someone trying to steal several horses. The way we have the ranch set up, it would take a while to move a herd off our land fast. But if they cut the fences ahead of time, they could do it in one day . . . or one night. It's been a long time since we've lost even one horse."

He paused, took a slow breath, and tried not to think of the pain.

"Like the boy Roak did over a year ago."

"You know about him?" Teagen was surprised Eli had shared his letters.

She nodded and continued doctoring his hand.

"No." He thought of the kid he'd caught trying to take a horse. The boy had escaped and ended up doing them a great favor last year. Roak wasn't like the band of thieves he'd been born into. Drummond Roak would always be welcome on the

ranch after what he did to help Tobin's wife, and he had promised never to try to steal another McMurray horse.

"It's out," she said as she leaned against his leg and placed
the splinter on the table. "I can't believe you put up with that
all day."

Teagen didn't speak. His hand could have fallen off, and he
probably wouldn't have noticed. Every sense he had seemed
to be warming to the feel of her leg pressing against his.

She didn't step away as she cleaned and wrapped the
wound.

Teagen finally found his tongue and managed to tell her of
what he'd discovered—the tracks, the cut fence—but he
didn't tell her of the danger. Let her believe only the loss of
horses worried him. She didn't need to be frightened.

As she wrapped his hand, he felt her soft touch on his skin.
When she tied off the bandage, he started to stand, but her
hand on his shoulder stopped him.

"I'll get your dinner. You just hold still."

Teagen almost argued that she didn't need to wait on him,
but he thought she'd leave if he objected. The sudden realiza-
tion that he wanted her to stay awhile shocked him.

She set his plate and silverware in front of him, and for a
moment the room seemed crowded with silence.

"Do you need something else?" she finally asked when he
made no move to eat.

The words seemed to fight their way up his throat. "Sit
down and have some pie. There's more here than I can eat." He
couldn't bring himself to ask for company, but if she wanted to
stay, he wouldn't mind.

He expected her to tell him how tired she was, but she
pulled a chair out across from him and cut a slice of pie no
bigger than a bite.

He ate in silence, then asked the only question he could
think of. "How did Eli die?"

Jessie straightened as if she were a witness on the stand.
"He passed out in the snow one night. By the time I found him
the next morning, he was half frozen. I tried everything, but

pneumonia took over. His family blamed me for not letting them know, for not taking better care of him."

Teagen had a feeling there was far more to the story, and he wasn't sure he wanted to know it all. It seemed enough that Eli had been his friend. Teagen figured if Eli sent Jessie to Whispering Mountain, he wanted him to be on her side. "What did they do?"

"They came and took him to the hospital, but he died two days later. With the girls, I couldn't go visit him, and I wasn't allowed to attend the funeral. When his mother came by, not to tell me he'd died, but to make sure I knew I couldn't come even to the gravesite, she said she wished I'd died and not him."

"But why run? Why come all the way here?"

Her brown eyes met his. "Because they wanted to take the girls away from me, and they have the money to do it. Eli's mother told me I was being selfish wanting to keep them when she could give them the best of everything, but I saw what else she gave Eli, and the price was too high. Without love, the money doesn't matter."

He found himself admiring her. "So you wouldn't let them take the girls?"

"Not as long as I'm breathing. They couldn't name one of the girls' birthdays, yet now that their only child is dead, they want the part of him left alive."

Teagen refilled his glass with milk and offered her one. "I'm glad you came here," he said, surprised that he meant every word. "They'll never find you here."

She smiled. "I agree. It was the first place I . . . I mean Eli thought I should go if something bad happened. Thank you for letting me stay."

The rest of the meal Jessie told him of all the funny things the girls did trying to make pies. At one point Bethie was stumbling around with an unbaked pie crust drooping over her face. "Martha laughed so hard I thought she might faint."

"Martha laughed," he echoed, then urged her to continue.

Jessie told him of their adventure to the barn to find the cats and how Rose had started her list of names.

When she cut him a piece of pie, Teagen asked if this was the crust that had been on Bethie's head. Jessie smiled as if he were kidding.

He liked her smile and didn't tell her that Martha wasted nothing. His question hadn't been a joke.

She touched his arm as she asked if he minded that Martha moved his things downstairs and gave two of the upstairs rooms to her and the girls. The housekeeper had also transferred Sage's clothes and personal items to the third bedroom upstairs so when his sister returned home her room would be ready.

"No," Teagen said, more aware of her touch than what she was saying. "All the rooms are the same. It makes sense that the upstairs become the girls' and the downstairs be mine." He also knew he could leave early without waking anyone if he were downstairs. Since he was the only McMurray here, he had to pull double duty to guard the ranch.

They walked through the rooms to the stairs. Teagen showed her the study lined with books.

She smiled when she saw them. "My father once said that a man who owns a dozen books is a rich man." Running her fingers along the shelves of volumes she whispered, "You're very rich indeed."

Teagen didn't argue. He also saw this room as a treasure, and he was proud she understood. "You're welcome to borrow and read whatever you like while you're here."

She turned to him. "Thank you. I've read all of them, but revisiting them will be like calling on an old friend."

"All?" He doubted.

She nodded.

"Then we'll talk more about them later."

Jessie laughed. "Is this going to be a test or a challenge?"

He thought about it. If he had a right to ask her questions to make sure she knew the books, she should have the same right. "A challenge."

She agreed. "Tomorrow night, after I get the girls to bed, we'll begin."

"I look forward to it." Teagen was surprised at just how much he meant the words.

As she climbed the stairs, Teagen thought again how he didn't mind her being here. In fact, he'd enjoyed the meal more than he had in a long time, and the idea of discussing the books sounded interesting.

Halfway up the stairs, she turned. "Good night, Teagen."

"Good night, Jessie," he said and watched her disappear before he went to what was now his bedroom. Having her visit here would be quite pleasant, he decided.

At breakfast the next morning he reconsidered.

The seven-year-old, Emily, refused to eat anything and cried silently every time anyone talked to her. Rose, who'd just turned five, insisted on bringing in the half-wild barn cats, who darted through the house like furry cannonballs. And Bethie, sweet little Bethie, wanted to sit in Teagen's lap while she ate and spilled oatmeal on his shirt. Which wouldn't have been so bad, but she wanted to play with the mess while Martha cleaned up.

Jessie tried to corral her batch of troublemakers, but Martha thought it was all very funny. If Teagen didn't know better, he'd swear she'd found the bottle of whiskey he kept stashed in the library. The old housekeeper seemed delighted to have the children around.

When he finally managed to pry free of Bethie, Teagen went outside and almost ran for his horse. He'd already made a predawn round, but it was time for another. Suddenly a chance encounter with rustlers didn't seem all that bad compared to the chaos at home.

"Bye, Mister," Rose said from the porch.

She waved, and he touched the brim of his hat. Rose had her mother's brown eyes, Teagen thought. Of the three girls, she'd be the one to grow up to be a rare beauty.

As he turned the animal toward the back of the house, planning to ride up on the hill for an overview of the place, he saw Jessie. She stood several yards away in the weeds beyond the garden.

He walked his horse closer.

Her head was down, almost as if she were in prayer.

Ten feet away, he realized what was happening.

Jessie Barton was throwing up.

CHAPTER 5

JESSIE HEARD SOMETHING MOVING THROUGH THE TALL grass and turned in time to see Teagen swing off his horse. Straightening, she wiped her mouth as she fought down the need to vomit again. She thought the weeds were high enough that no one would notice. She'd been quiet.

"What's wrong?" he snapped. "Are you sick?"

"It's nothing." She raised her hand, hoping he wouldn't come closer. "I tried to get far enough away from the house so that no one would see me."

He grabbed his canteen and held it out to her. "To hell with anyone seeing you. What's wrong?" The worry in his eyes didn't match the anger in his tone.

"You know," she said and then realized he probably didn't. "It's morning sickness, that's all."

Teagen shoved back his hat and stared at her. "What kind of sickness comes only in the morning?"

"Didn't your sister-in-law have it when she was pregnant?"

"No." He thought a moment. "I don't know. What does her being pregnant have to do with you tossing your breakfast? You can't be pregnant. You've been widowed for three months."

Jessie closed her eyes, wishing the sun would stop swirling in the sky. "Yes, I'm afraid I can. If I'm guessing right, I'm almost to my fourth month."

She couldn't believe she was telling a stranger her secret. No one knew. When she ran from Chicago, she hadn't even suspected.

He offered the canteen again. "How long have you known?"

"A month, maybe a little longer. I've never been regular and . . ." Jessie realized what she said and added the heat of embarrassment to nausea. No woman in her right mind would admit something so private to a man.

If he understood a word she'd said, he showed no sign. "Here, drink some water. I'll walk you back to the house. It might help if you got out of the sun."

She nodded and took a long drink. "Promise me you won't tell anyone."

"Who would I tell?" he asked, still looking at her as if he were seeing someone dying.

"I'll be all right," she managed. "Don't worry about me. I'll be past this part soon."

"We don't have a doctor in town, but I could ride to—"

"I don't need a doctor. I'm not sick. I'm pregnant." She almost added that she'd had this disease enough to know there would be only one cure.

She started back toward the house. He fell into step beside her. "Sure, okay," he said. "If your people come soon, you can deliver the baby in California. If you're four months, you've still got five months to go, right?"

She didn't answer. Her first child had come a month earlier than she'd thought. If she was counting months, she'd guess she had less than five to wait.

"How often do you do this?" He glanced back to the weeds.

"Most mornings. But once it's done, I feel better."

"Good." They reached the house. "Should you go in and lie down or something?"

"No," Jessie said. "I'll be fine. Don't worry about me. I've kept you from your work long enough." She stepped inside and let the door close behind her.

Leaning her back against the wall, she prayed he followed her advice and left. How could she have ever gotten into such a mess? When they ran from Chicago, she really hadn't thought her plan through. The loss of Eli, the closing of the store, the threats from her mother-in-law to take her children, it all piled up until the only thing she could think about was getting away. In her mind, the one place of safety had always been the ranch described by a man she'd never met. How could she have been dumb enough to expect Teagen to welcome a woman and three children he never knew existed?

No. Correction, three and a half children.

During the journey, when it had crossed her mind that there might be no Teagen McMurray or he wouldn't be the man he appeared to be in the letters, she'd said she would somehow find a job and make it just fine on her own. The girls were almost big enough to watch over one another, and surely there were bookstores that needed employees, even in the West.

Only now, she was pregnant again. Once Teagen figured out that there were no relatives coming from California, he'd probably ask her to leave. She might have enough money to live until the baby came if she could find someplace cheap, but how would she ever earn enough to feed four children?

Jessie closed her eyes, refusing to allow tears to fall. She'd find a way. Maybe she could stay here a little longer than he'd offered. If she helped Martha, Teagen might not notice how much trouble she and the children were.

She thought of the letter she'd written to him before she left Chicago. She'd been such a fool to think he'd take her and the kids just because she signed Eli's name.

"Mom?" a voice whispered. "What's wrong?"

Jessie looked down at her oldest, Emily, whose eyes had seen far too much sadness in her seven years of life. "Nothing, dear," Jessie whispered. "I'm fine."

Emily's stare didn't look like she believed a word.

Jessie hugged her, remembering back when she'd been nineteen and thought the birth of a child would make Eli love her. She'd spent her first pregnancy thinking that once the baby was born, he'd stop drinking and stay home, his family would accept her, and they'd have a life outside the bookstore walls.

But it hadn't happened. Eli had asked about her a few times during the pregnancy, griped when he thought she looked too thin. He even closed the store a few days near the end so she could rest. But the day she delivered, he'd been gone to the pub. She lay frightened and in labor for six hours before the baby crowned, then she delivered Emily alone.

"Mom?" Em pulled away. "That man scares me. Mister frowns at me."

Jessie brushed Emily's almost-white hair off her forehead and kissed her. "I'll tell him to stop," she promised. "Now, let's help Martha with the breakfast dishes."

Emily didn't budge. "Are you sure he won't hurt me?"

"I'm sure," Jessie whispered. "If he does, I'll flatten his head with one of those skillets Martha keeps hanging near the stove."

Emily's thin body relaxed. "Promise?"

"Cross my heart." Jessie hugged her oldest. Of the three girls, Em was the only one who looked like Eli. His hair had been more sandy-yellow than white-blond, but his eyes had been the same shallow-water blue.

As they walked to the kitchen, Jessie took a deep breath. She was finished running and hiding. It was time she learned to stand on her own two feet and take care of herself and her three daughters. Her children deserved something better than growing up in fear and worry.

No . . . make that four.

CHAPTER 6

TEAGEN WORKED WITH THE MARES IN THE SOUTH PAS-
ture all morning. He noticed a few looked close to dropping a
colt, which reminded him of Jessie. There was probably nothing the same between delivering a baby and a horse having a
foal, but still, he couldn't help but think about it.

First, Jessie was too thin, far too thin to be eating for two.
Next, she had to rest more. Running after three kids in her
condition couldn't be easy. She might only be with him a
few days, two weeks on the long side, but maybe he could
pay Eli back for listening to his problems all those years by
taking good care of his wife while she stayed at Whispering
Mountain.

When Teagen rode home, it was late as usual. He washed up
in the mud room and changed into fresh clothes, then stepped
into the kitchen. Jessie was there waiting for him.

"You should be asleep," he snapped, then frowned when
she jumped.

"Jessie?" he said in a lower tone, fearing she might still be
ill. "Is something wrong?"

When she raised her gaze to him, he thought he saw something different in her eyes. Determination, maybe. A strength
he hadn't seen before.

"I took a nap with Bethie today," she began. "I waited up to
check your hand and to have supper with you. It doesn't seem
right that you should have to eat alone every night."

Teagen tried to hide his surprise, but he was sure he failed when she smiled at him. He sat down as he had the night before and let her change the bandage on his hand. The cut no longer bothered him, but he found himself welcoming her nearness.

"It's much better. One more day of the bandage, I think." Jessie cleaned the wound and applied more salve. "Tell me, how was your day, Teagen?" she asked as casually as if she'd said the words a thousand times.

He told her all he'd done and enjoyed the way she leaned against his leg as she worked. When she finished the dressing, he stood and helped her move the food to the table. Without being obvious, he took his time eating, hoping she'd finish her plate. When she pushed it aside half eaten, he shoved it right back. "Finish it."

"I'm full."

"Finish it. You're far too thin."

She glared at him. "Don't bully me, Teagen. I'm not your problem."

"If you're under my roof, you *are* my problem," he snapped.

Before he realized her intent, she was up and halfway to the door.

She made it to the hallway before he caught her. For a second, when he whirled her around, he thought she'd fight him. As if facing a wild animal, Teagen's instincts kicked in. He dropped his hand and took a step backward.

Then Teagen McMurray did something he'd never done in his life. He said he was sorry.

She stood in the shadows facing him like a tiny warrior ready for battle. Neither of them moved as his words slowly registered, and she relaxed.

He retreated toward the kitchen. "I didn't mean to frighten you. I do think you should eat more. You've got the baby to consider."

"And you know a lot about pregnant women?" she said as she took one step in his direction.

He dug his fingers through his hair. "Nothing at all. But, if you'll come back and sit down at the table, I'd like to learn."

She didn't move. "Why?"

"Because while you're here, I want to help if I can. Plus, I've got two sisters-in-law who plan to double the McMurray clan. I don't even know what to ask them except, 'How are you feeling?' and I can promise you, women in the family way get real tired of hearing that."

He took another step toward the kitchen. "How about we have dessert, and you answer a few general questions? I'd consider it a real favor."

She followed as he moved back to the kitchen. "All right." She shrugged. "But no ordering me around, Teagen. And no grabbing me and trying to drag me back."

"I wasn't grabbing or dragging. I just wanted you to stop."

"Then say, 'Jessie, stop,' the next time you want to talk to me."

He held out her chair for her, and they resumed their seats at the table. "All right. I'll try that." He frowned, guessing that getting someone to stop couldn't be that easy. "Only you have to be honest with me about this pregnancy. You have to tell me what's going on as long as you're here. That way I'll know what to do if trouble comes."

"Trouble won't—"

"Don't even say it, Jessie. My mother died giving birth. I was almost twelve. If she'd told me what to do, I might have been able to help. She might not have bled out all alone after the birth. Tobin was guarding the house because he was in-jured. By the time he fired signal shots and I made it back, her blood covered the bed. I had the others wait on the porch while I cleaned it up myself. I didn't want them to have that memory."

She nodded, understanding. He might have shielded his brothers, but the memory still lived in him. "All right. I'll tell you what you need to know. I'll tell you everything, but don't start looking at me as if I'm going to die. I've done this alone three times . . ." She swallowed and raised her chin. "But, in truth, it would be easier to have a friend nearby."

"Then that's what you'll have."

"Yes, I'd like that. I'll answer your questions the best I can."

He set the pie on the table. "First, dessert."

She smiled. "A little piece."

He cut her twice what she'd had last night and shoved the plate toward her, then grinned when she didn't shove it back.

They ate in silence. Teagen figured that he'd better be careful. She was skittish like a horse that had been hurt or damaged in some way. If he planned to help Eli's wife, he'd be wise to walk softly for a few days until she learned that his bellowing and angry snaps were just a part of his manner and nothing personal.

He could live a long while without seeing the anger again in her brown eyes.

As he finished his pie, his thoughts turned dark, remembering how she said she delivered three babies alone. Hadn't Eli been there? They lived in a big city. Couldn't she have gone to a hospital or had a midwife with her? Teagen decided not to ask those questions, for he feared he'd learn things he didn't want to know about his only friend. All these years he'd thought of Eli as a gentle kind of bookworm who loved dreaming about living the life Teagen lived. Not once had he thought of Eli as a drunk or a fool.

"Shall we move into the study?" She stood with a grace he liked watching.

He lifted his coffee cup. "Sure."

When they crossed into the hall once more, he was careful not to follow too closely. When they reached the study, he shoved a few windows open to let in the warm night air, while she lit the lamps on either side of the fireplace. She took the small rocker his sister liked, and Teagen sat in the leather chair across from her. For a few minutes neither spoke. He couldn't put his finger on why, but he felt comfortable with her, almost as if they'd known each other for years.

She rocked forward. "If you've no objections, I'd like to propose a format to our discussions."

Teagen frowned, trying to guess what she was talking about.

She continued, "I'd very much like to talk about the books." She smiled. "Partly because it's been weeks and weeks since I've talked to an adult about anything. Partly because Martha and I agree you could use some polishing with your skill in conversation. But mostly because I think there is a chance that you love them as dearly as I do."

He wasn't about to comment on that statement. He guessed Martha had suggested the polishing of his nonexistent conversational skills. That woman had been trying to change him since the night he'd picked her up at the stage station. He was twelve and she in her late twenties. There had been no doubt that she would have left the ranch in less than a week if she hadn't loved baby Sage at first sight. The three older boys had never been more than a bother, and sometimes a project, to her.

"So." Jessie rocked back in her chair. "Here is my plan. We set a book on the desk to discuss each night when the conversation slows. We'll each start the way people do, talking about this and that. I'd like to know more about your ranch, and you want to ask about my pregnancy. We should be able to talk at least a few minutes before one of us picks up the book. I'll try to be as honest as possible about my condition if you'll tell me the truth, good and bad, about running a ranch. Once that's finished, we'll move on to the book and end the discussion on a subject we both like."

"Fair enough." He liked that she was a woman of order. The few women he'd tried to talk to seemed to have the concentration of a stringless kite.

She stood and circled the room. "Where should we start?" Her fingers tapped along the spines of the leather-bound books.

"How about tonight we talk about books in general?"

"All right."

She sat, pulled off her shoes, curled her feet under her, and began to talk about her love of books. Teagen heard the titles and the comments of all her favorites, but the story she really told him affected him far more. As she spoke, he saw a little girl surrounded by loving parents and a small library where her father read to her every night. Then, when they were gone, he saw a half-grown child hiding in a bookstore, escaping her life by reading. And last, he saw a lonely woman trapped in a store with only books to keep her company.

When she stopped talking, he bent forward and told her of how he used to feel if he spent one minute reading that he was somehow cheating the ranch. As he grew up, he learned no matter how hectic life got, books offered peace.

She agreed, then both fell silent. Finally, she said, "Ask your questions now, Teagen."

He hesitated. Their time here in the study had been so relaxing, he didn't want to spoil it, but he had things he needed to know. "Does a woman know when it happens? Did you know?"

She laughed. "No. Most women don't know exactly when it happens, but, looking back, I do. I think it happened the night before Eli fell ill. We didn't . . . mate that often. When we did, he always left upset, and I knew he wouldn't be back until morning."

Teagen tried to remember her exact words because he knew it would be days before he figured out what she meant. "Eli didn't enjoy the act." He said the words out loud before he realized it.

Jessie looked down.

Even without much light, he could see he'd embarrassed her. But before he could say anything, she added, "Eli tried to be a good man. I think it bothered him greatly that he came to my bed and didn't love me."

Now she made no sense. Jessie didn't seem a woman who'd be hard to love. A man was honor bound to love his wife. Teagen had a feeling he'd be stepping too far to say more.

"Can you feel the baby?" He tried for what he hoped would be an easy question.

"No," she answered. "Once I feel it move, I'll be halfway through."

"Oh." Teagen studied her. "What makes you sick in the mornings?"

Jessie shrugged. "The smell of bacon mostly. We walked past a street vendor in Galveston a few weeks ago who was serving up bacon wrapped in bread. I threw up in every alley for half a mile."

Teagen smiled. "No wonder you're so thin. The food you get when traveling isn't fit to eat, and without being able to camp out, your choices are so limited. I'd rather eat jerky and hardtack than stop off at some of the stations the stages use."

Jessie laughed. "I can just picture me trying to 'camp out' with three girls. Even traveling with a bag of food wasn't easy with our trunks to shift from place to place."

He almost said that she should have had a man to help her. But her man had died. From the few things Teagen had heard, Eli didn't seem to be there when she needed him. "It must have been hard on you, Jessie."

"We managed." She sighed. "Emily and Rose could handle the small trunk if we moved slowly. I could carry the other if Bethie held on to my skirt." She smiled. "Most of the time other travelers lent us a hand, and once we settled on the train or the boat, we circled into our own little space."

"It couldn't have been easy." He thought of what the months must have been like for her.

"I took care of the girls."

Teagen studied her. "But who took care of you?" He could almost see her with the girls huddled around her. How many nights had she gone without sleep so she could watch over them? How many times had she passed her food to the girls? He couldn't help but wonder.

He stood and offered her his hand. "Speaking of taking care of you, I'd better walk you to the stairs."

She didn't object. Taking his hand, she let him tug her to her feet, then she pulled away, only accepting his assistance for a moment.

As they left the study, he asked, "What food can you eat that doesn't make you . . . have to visit the weeds?"

"Apples," she said, starting up the stairs. "Some days that is about all that seems to want to stay down."

Halfway up the steps, she turned and smiled. "Until our talk tomorrow, Mr. McMurray?"

He knew she was making an effort to civilize him. He bowed his head slightly. "I'll look forward to it, Mrs. Barton."

After she disappeared, Teagen walked out onto the front porch and lit a long, thin cigar he'd saved for a week. He liked this time of night when all the earth seemed to sleep. The night sky hung on a few clouds, and the moon offered only a sliver of light.

When he took a long pull on the cigar, he looked across his land. Nothing moved, not a sound out of place, but Teagen knew he wasn't alone. He sensed it on his skin.

His first thought was that Jessie had tiptoed downstairs to tell him something, but even with her light weight, the stairs would have creaked.

He turned slowly as if doing nothing more than watching the night.

A tall form leaned against the last post on the porch where shadows doubled over one another.

The figure didn't move. Teagen let out smoke and studied the silhouette: taller, a little broader in the shoulders, and a gun strapped to his hip as if it had been there since birth. Only one person could make it onto the ranch without even the horses in the corral noticing.

"Roak," Teagen said simply with the cigar still between his teeth.

The shadow pushed away from the pole and walked toward him. "Nice of you to finally come out." The young man passed through the light drifting from the study window. "I didn't want to come in and take a chance of waking the women, but I thought you and that lady would never stop talking."

Teagen remembered the time a year or so ago when he'd caught the boy trying to steal a horse. The wild kid had fought violently, almost getting the better of him. Now he knew he could still take Roak in a fair fight, but he doubted the boy knew how to fight fair. He'd grown up in an outlaw settlement deep in the hills. Wolf packs had more rules than Roak's people.

"Is this a social call, Roak?" Teagen tossed his cigar off the porch. "I figured when we gave you that horse, we'd never see you again."

Roak shoved his hat back. "That makes two of us. I went down on the border for a while. Moved cattle for the army. Even did a little scouting. Thought I might leave Texas and head on over to New Orleans, but when it came time to get on the boat, I couldn't do it. There were things in Texas that I'd miss."

Teagen watched him closely. "We both know you're not here on a social call. What's on your mind?"

Roak passed one of the porch chairs. His long, thin fingers brushed the wood as if seeing if the chair would rock. When it did, he backed away and rested against the railing. "I figure you know there's an outfit meaning to steal a herd of your best." He said the words so casually no one would have thought the two men talked about something that might mean life or death.

Teagen widened his stance. "Your group?"

Roak shook his head. "I'm not with any group, haven't been since before you caught me on your land. I tried to tell you, but you never seemed in a listening mood while you were trying to bash my head in."

"I'm the one with the scar in my scalp," Teagen reminded him.

Roak's hand waved the comment aside. "About the gang coming your way. These outlaws make the people my ma lived with up in the hills look like a church settlement. These men are bone-bad. The kind of bad you don't want near your land."

"How is your ma?" Teagen asked, knowing that he'd never heard a word about Roak's mother. As far as he knew, the boy had been wild and alone all his life.

Roak shrugged. "She died drunk years ago from what I heard. Once I could outrun that bastard she lived with, I never went back to check on her."

Teagen moved into the shadows between the windows. He had no idea how much the kid knew, but if he were guessing, he'd say Drummond Roak knew close to everything going on in these parts.

"So, why'd you come out here and risk me shooting you to tell me something I already know?"

"Hell if I know." The boy sounded young for the first time, reminding Teagen that he was still a few years from being out of his teens. He'd had to grow up fast to survive, but he hadn't been the only one.

The boy shifted, resting his hand on the butt of his gun. "You and your kin spent more time trying to kill me than any one family I know. If I had any sense, I'd ride as far away from this mountain as I could get and let you deal with the bucket full of meanness coming your way."

Teagen realized how much alike he and this kid were. After a moment of silence, he asked, "I got some coffee still on the stove. Want some?"

Roak's head jerked up as if he smelled a trap, but after a short hesitation, he said, "I might if you got any of them cookies your housekeeper makes. I can still remember them from when you tied me up in the barn and all your womenfolk tried to feed me to death."

Laughing, he showed Roak the way to the kitchen. "We had other things on our minds at the time, as I remember. We figured you'd stay put in the barn."

"I seen a play in Houston, in a fancy bar, that had less acts in it than your barn did while I was your *guest*."

Teagen poured the boy the last of the coffee and set the jar of cookies on the table. "Nothing's changed around here. I've still got my hands full of women and thieves."

Roak ate the first cookie whole, then mumbled around it as he chewed. "You're not kidding, McMurray. Everyone in town knows your brothers are both gone. What kind of fool lets them both leave at the same time and then invites a widow and three kids to stay with him?"

Teagen had little defense; in fact, he agreed with Roak. He was a fool. "Tobin and his family left first for Washington, D.C., then Travis got called into Austin for a trial. He lives there more than he lives here these days." He didn't add that a few old Rangers were riding in from Austin to help him out.

Once they were here, he'd no longer be alone. No sense filling the kid in on anything he didn't know. "Don't tell me you're here to offer to help guard the place?"

Roak laughed and dug out another cookie. "Of course not. That'd ruin my reputation as a gunfighter. I just thought I'd tell you what I know about this gang of cutthroats. When they come it will be at dusk, and they're planning to ride right over the bridge. They figure alone, you can't stop them. Maybe you'll get one or two, but then they'll take you down and have a free pass to take all the horses they can find. You're too far from town and too mean to have any neighbors who could hear shooting and come to help. So, the way they look at it, they've got one man between them and a fortune in fine horseflesh."

Teagen had never heard of such a bold plan. "Where'd you hear about this?"

"From one of the men who's scared 'cause he knows he'll be riding in front when they storm the bridge. He got drunk one night in a bar not even the cowhands will hang out in. The more he drank, the more he talked." Roak looked up. "By the way, you owe me for the whiskey I had to buy to get all the details."

"Take it out in cookies, boy."

Roak's words came fast and deadly. "I'm not a boy."

Teagen raised his hands. "All right. Fair enough. I have no plan to fight with the *man* who brings me a warning." He watched Roak closely. "By the way, why did you really come out here to warn me?"

Roak grinned. "I thought Sage might be home by now. I hear she's due back any day."

Teagen fought down a laugh. The kid was sweet on his sister and had no idea that he was out of his league. Sage was not only three years older and far more educated, she'd want nothing to do with a man who wore a gun. "Even if she was here, Roak, she wouldn't want to see you."

Teagen's words didn't seem to bother Roak. "I know." He shrugged. "I just like knowing she's home and safe." He winked and offered a wicked smile. "When I get a little older, she's going to be crazy about me; you wait and see."

"I doubt it. She's sworn off men. The Ranger she fell hard for a few years ago in Austin is dead, and she claims she'll never love any man again. Swears she'll be an old maid and live with me."

Roak nodded as if he'd heard this promise before. "Which is why I have to warn you. I can't have you losing the ranch while she's gone."

Teagen returned the coffeepot to the stove and added, "All right, kid, I'll take—"

He turned back to the table to find Roak gone. He'd left as silently as he'd come without even stirring the air.

Teagen swore when he realized the thief had also taken the jar of cookies.

CHAPTER 7

J ESSIE WOKE LATE AND KNEW THE GIRLS HAD ALREADY
tiptoed down the back stairs. Even Bethie had learned to crawl
her way down one step at a time. Jessie dressed as fast as she
could and ran to make sure they were all right and not getting
into trouble.

She couldn't help brushing her hand along the wood. If
houses had souls, this one must have a strong one. In the two
days she'd been here it seemed to have cradled her, making her
feel welcome and protected. Even if today were the day she had
to leave, Jessie would never forget the warmth of this place.

When she stepped into the kitchen, she let out a long-held
breath. All three of her daughters sat at the table. Emily and
Rose wore Martha's aprons tied around their necks. Bethie's
borrowed apron had been tied to the chair as well. They all
smiled at their mother with bright syrup grins that tickled her
heart. The three looked nothing alike, but they were all hers.

"Morning, Mom." Rose lifted her fork and smiled. "We're
having pancakes with raisin smiles for breakfast."

"Great." Jessie came closer, almost dreading the first smell
of breakfast. "What else?"

"Cinnamon apples." Martha turned from the stove. "Teagen
McMurray has decided we have far too many apples in the
storage shed. He told me he wanted apples at every meal from
now on."

Jessie smiled.

Martha continued to fret. "That man would drive a sane

woman to drink. He's had the same breakfast for years. Biscuits, sausage or bacon, eggs, and gravy. Now all of a sudden, this morning he comes in and says he doesn't want bacon or sausage. He says he doesn't even want to smell it cooking. I swear if he wasn't already over thirty, I'd mail order him a bride to watch over him and take some time off. But, with my luck, I'd never find a woman to marry a man who has spent twenty years stewing in ornery."

Jessie tried to defend him. "Apples don't sound all that strange. Maybe he just wants a change."

"Oh, that is not all." Martha waved her wooden spoon. "He seems to have eaten the cookies, jar and all. When I asked him about it, he didn't even deny it."

Jessie laughed as she poured a cup of coffee. Now *that* she couldn't believe. "Well, the girls will help you make more. They are great cookie makers."

"I can't, Mom." Rose shook her dark braids. "I've got to start naming the pigs today. My work around here is never done. I've finished with the cats and the goats, but today I have to start on the pigs, and they keep moving around, so it won't be easy. You can't just give a pig any old name. I have to find just the right ones."

"Help!" Bethie cried and kicked her legs, turning the table into a drum.

Jessie glanced over at her youngest, who'd poured so much syrup on her pancakes her fingers were stuck together with huge pieces of pancake clinging to both hands.

"Mommy," she cried. "Help."

Both Jessie and Martha dropped what they were doing and ran to her aid.

"Morning." Teagen stepped through the back door just as Bethie managed to pull her hands apart and sent the pancake flying.

Teagen growled and looked around the room.

All three of her daughters froze and watched as he slowly reached up, pulled the pancake piece off the side of his face, and ate it.

Emily started to cry.

Teagen frowned at her and took a step toward her.

Emily broke into huge gulps of half screams, half sobs.

"Stop it!" Jessie yelled at Teagen. "Stop it right this instant."

Teagen glowered in confusion when he figured out she was yelling at him. "Stop what? I'm not the one screaming my head off. That honor goes to your oldest."

Jessie stepped in front of him and lowered her voice. "Stop looking at her with that look."

Teagen appeared to be chewing on words to keep them from coming out. Finally, he managed, "This is the only look I have, lady. I may think for some reason it's raining pancakes in this kitchen, but you're the one who's crazy."

Jessie didn't back down an inch. "Stop frowning at Emily. It frightens her."

To everyone's surprise, Teagen turned around and stormed back through the door. "Martha," he yelled. "I'm taking my breakfast on the porch."

"This ain't no boardinghouse!" the housekeeper hollered back. "If you can't stop scaring that child, you can go without breakfast."

Jessie stood at the door and watched him swing into the saddle and disappear in a cloud of dust.

For no reason at all, she began to cry. Tears ran silently down her face. She'd managed to drive Teagen out of his own home. He'd already been up for three hours doing chores, and now he'd go until noon without any breakfast.

She heard the kitchen return to normal behind her. Bethie was eating, probably getting more on the floor than in her mouth. Rose asked Martha how she got all the pancakes the same size, and Emily had stopped screaming.

All was normal, except Teagen was gone. Resting against the doorframe, she watched until the last of the dust he'd kicked up vanished. She saw herself as a mighty warrior when defending her daughters, but this time, this one time, she may have rushed to the battle call too fast.

Wiping her tears aside, Jessie turned to Emily. "Finish your breakfast, Em, and we'll start your lessons."

"All right, Mom." The child showed no sign of having ever been upset.

"And, tomorrow, when you see Mr. McMurray, if you feel you are about to cry or scream, I'd like you to leave the room."

The seven-year-old teared up. "But Mom. He—"

"He did nothing but walk into his own house, Em. He's been kind to us, and you've paid him for that kindness by screaming and crying."

Jessie could almost hear her oldest daughter's mind working. For the first time she realized Emily had controlled her with tantrums for as long as she could remember. When she'd been tiny, Jessie had often given in to Emily's demands because Eli hated any noise in the bookstore. Somehow she'd believed if her child were perfect and silent, Eli would love her. By the time Rose came along, Jessie knew it would never happen.

Moving around the table, Jessie hugged her firstborn. "I'll be here ready to fight if someone tries to bother you, but you can't just pick a person and scream every time you see him."

"He'll hit you like Father did," Emily whispered.

"No, he won't," Jessie answered, remembering how Emily had once been in the kitchen during a fight she'd had with Eli. He'd been determined to leave. She'd been just as determined that he'd stay. The argument had ended when he knocked her out of the way. Jessie had only been bruised when she'd fallen, but Emily had cried all night long.

"Oh, Em, we're going to find a place where we'll be safe. You don't have to cry or scream anymore. You don't have to be afraid."

Martha set Jessie's plate down beside Emily's. "Your mom is right about the McMurrays. They're a tough bunch, but in all my years here, I ain't never seen one of them hurt a woman. In fact, from what I've seen, I think they see little girls as some kind of rare treasures that seldom come along. You should see the way Tobin and Travis almost carry their wives around on pillows."

Emily looked up at the housekeeper. "You have never seen Mister get mad and hit his sister?"

"Nope, and believe you me, Sage did some crazy things growing up. I love her dearly, but there were times I thought she could use a spanking. None of the boys would hear of it." Martha took the empty seat at the table. "When she was growing up around this place, if the truth be told, she was as wild as them. They'd ride in at full gallop and pass her off from one to the other. When I made them stop, she cried so hard she made herself sick."

Jessie ate her stack of pancakes as Martha continued. "When that girl weren't no bigger than Rose, she could outrun the wind on horseback, and she'd be laughing all the way."

"I want to do that," Emily said, propping her elbows on the table. "I want to ride a horse."

"Me too," Rose said with a hint less determination.

"Well, you'll have to ask Teagen to teach you. I don't know how to ride, and I'm guessing your mother doesn't either."

"Would he if we asked?" Emily, her shyness forgotten, looked directly at Martha.

"Maybe, maybe not. If you made him cookies and didn't scream when he walked into the room, I'd say you'd have a good chance."

The two girls looked at each other and nodded once as if making a pact.

Jessie downed the last of her milk and wondered if Teagen had any idea of what waited for him when he got home.

While the girls helped clear the table, Martha whispered close to Jessie's ear, "You feeling the need to visit the weeds this morning?"

"No." Jessie studied the older woman. "How'd you know about that?"

"There ain't much that happens between dawn and dusk that I don't know about. I'll put some salt crackers on my grocery list. I've heard they help for women who have upset stomach in the morning."

Jessie was trying to decide whether to tell Martha the truth or lie, when the housekeeper got up and went to help the girls wash the dishes. Apparently, Martha hadn't needed her to explain.

Teagen didn't come in for lunch. Martha told Jessie that it wasn't unusual for the men to eat jerky and hard biscuits when riding in wasn't convenient, but Jessie still had the feeling he might be avoiding her family.

When he didn't return for supper, she got worried. The girls had played hard all day and were ready for bed, but she found herself wandering from room to room, waiting for Teagen's return.

The McMurray house seemed huge with its wide dining room and a great room with one group of chairs turned toward the fire for warmth in winter and another group facing the windows. There were no frills or pictures on the walls. What looked like an Irish tartan and a strand of Indian beads hung above the fireplace. It was a home built like the man who owned it: solid and strong enough to weather anything.

At sunset she walked out on the porch. The last light of day disappeared along the mountain ridge. Jessie looked in the direction of the bridge and to her surprise saw what looked like an Indian encampment.

"Martha!" she screamed. "Martha, come quick."

Several moments passed before Martha, dressed for bed, stepped out of the house. "This better be important. I like my head hitting the pillow as the world turns dark."

"It is. We're being invaded."

Martha squinted out in the direction Jessie pointed. "You're right. I'll get the guns, and we'll shoot them all."

"But I can't fire a gun." Jessie panicked. "And I'm not sure I could shoot anyone, even if I knew how to pull the trigger."

Martha laughed. "Well, I guess we'll just have to let Teagen's grandfather stay then."

"Teagen's grandfather?"

The sound of a horse riding in made both women turn. Teagen circled the barn and headed toward them. When he was ten feet away, he reined his horse in but didn't climb down. He seemed to stare at the two of them a minute, then raised his hat. "Martha, shouldn't you be in bed?"

"I should," she answered. "But the yelling woke me."

"Emily again."

The housekeeper shook her head. "Jessie. She seems to believe we're in danger of an attack."

"We are," Teagen admitted. "I heard a band of raiders planned to storm the bridge, so I asked Grandfather if there was any chance he'd send a hunting party to camp out for a few days."

Martha laughed. "I know your grandfather has a strict rule about interfering with McMurray business, but the raiders couldn't know that. Any outlaws would be fools to try to cross that bridge now, so I guess I can sleep easy. Which is past due." She turned to the door.

"I'm sorry," Jessie said as Martha passed. "I didn't know they were McMurray relatives."

Martha glanced back from the threshold. "It's all right, dear."

Teagen nudged his horse closer. "Martha, I was wondering." His words sounded stiff. "Would you leave your door open? If the girls cry or come down, they'll have to pass your room. I'd like to take Jessie over to the campsite so she'll know there's nothing to fear."

Martha smiled. "Are you asking me for a favor, Teagen Mc-Murray?"

"I guess, I am."

"Well then, I'll do it. Only because you asked nice and didn't yell at me." She disappeared into the house.

Jessie laughed. "I think there has been enough yelling for one day." She walked to the edge of the porch where she could almost touch Teagen's horse. "I'm sorry about the mess at breakfast. You must be starving."

"No, I ate at my grandfather's summer camp when I rode up to talk to him. The old man is funny. If I ask him for support or advice, he acts like he doesn't understand, but if I tell him my problem, he finds a way to help."

"He sounds like a wise man."

"He is." Teagen offered his hand. "If you'll come along with me for a short ride, I'll show you the camp set up down by the bridge."

"I don't know how to ride. It might be dangerous. It's late. The girls—"

Teagen laughed. "When you're out of reasons to say no, we can start." He maneuvered the horse a few inches closer. "You won't be riding alone. You'll be sitting here in front of me. It's no more dangerous than rocking in a rocking chair. Martha will look after the girls if they wake, and the best time to see an Apache village is at night when the fires make the place glow."

Jessie had never done anything adventurous in her life. When she'd been thirteen and Eli hired her, within months she was running the bookstore. There were always things that needed doing, or the weather was bad, or one of the girls was sick. Except for Sunday afternoon walks, she'd never had a single adventure. And now, Teagen offered her one that she could fold away and cherish forever.

She stepped closer and touched his shoulder. He carefully circled her waist and lifted her up in front of him. The horse shifted. Jessie let out a little cry of fear, and Teagen laughed.

"I've got you," he whispered against her ear. "I'm not going to let you fall."

His arm pulled her against the warmth of his chest, and they began to move. "It'll take longer to walk the horse, but I don't mind. Just relax and enjoy the night."

Jessie wasn't sure relaxing was possible, but she did plan to enjoy tonight.

They talked about the ranch and what had happened during the day. Teagen told her about Roak's visit and didn't ask questions when she seemed to know all about the boy. Jessie reminded herself that the letters from him that she'd treasured had been addressed to Eli. She made a point to mention that Eli sometimes shared a few lines of Teagen's letters.

She wished she could call them her letters. She wished she could tell him they had been her own private treasure. A hundred nights, when loneliness kept her awake, she'd tiptoed to her desk in the corner of the bookstore and lit one lamp so she could read his words, his thoughts, his dreams.

As they moved closer to the campfire lights, Jessie noticed they both lowered their voices. In a funny way even out here in the open, she felt very much alone with Teagen.

"Is it all right to ask how you felt today?" He broke the silence.

"I feel fine. And you'll be happy to know that I ate like a pig all day."

His arm squeezed slightly. "I can tell you're getting fatter."

"Martha made apple pancakes, applesauce, and apple pie today. Tomorrow she promised more cinnamon apples." She shifted slightly so she could face him. "The big excitement of the afternoon was one of the hens had chicks hatch out. The girls loved it. By the time the birds were all out of their shells, Rose had tried to name every one. It took me an hour to convince her she couldn't bring them in the house."

Their faces were so close she could feel his breath on her cheek. Suddenly she became very much aware that their bodies touched from shoulder to leg. She knew she should turn away. This wasn't proper to be so close to a man she barely knew. But it felt so right. He felt so warm.

The memory of what life had been like with Eli invaded her thoughts. They'd been married over a year before he came to her bed in the attic. He hadn't said a word. He pulled her covers away, lifted her nightgown to her waist, and lowered his body on top of her. Jessie closed her eyes and shivered with the cold until it was over. When he left, he hadn't pulled her gown back or returned the covers, but Jessie didn't care. She lay shaking until the cold numbed her body and she no longer felt the pain. Eli never spoke of what had happened. He set a pattern of climbing the stairs once or twice a month. In all those years, through winters and summers, Jessie never felt anything but cold when he touched her.

"There's the night guard." Teagen turned loose of her for a moment while he waved.

A man with very few clothes on stood and waved back. Teagen reined the horse so they circled the camp. Firelight made the place seem enchanted. The tepees glowed in the night, and tiny embers drifted into the sky as if dancing toward the stars.

"How many are here?"

"A dozen men and a few women. Most of these braves are young and unmarried. Once married, their wives travel with them until too many children keep them back at the main camp.

"This is more a holiday for them than work. My grandfather knows I'll cut a couple of head of cattle out of my herd for them to take home."

"How long will they stay?"

"A week maybe. By then the men I've hired should be here. We'll just wake up one morning, and they'll be gone, tents and all."

They circled the camp twice. One couple sat talking by a fire, another man seemed to be checking the line of horses, but most of the men must have retired for the night.

"Martha says you're half-Apache," she whispered.

"Yeah, but I don't feel it like Travis and Tobin do. Maybe because before I was twelve I stepped into my father's role. I even grew into his clothes. The Apache are my mother's people. Both my brothers spent time at the camps, but I never had the time. There was always too much to do here."

No sadness or regret lingered in his words. Teagen had simply done what he had to do, but she couldn't help but wonder: if he'd been allowed to be a boy for a few summers longer, would he be a different man? Eli had always been treated like a child by his parents, and he'd crumbled into a bottle. Teagen had grown up too fast, and somehow he'd hardened to stone.

She laid her hand over Teagen's arm. If only to her, he didn't seem as unyielding as the world thought him to be. She knew the Teagen of the letters, the one who worried and bragged and loved this land. "Thank you for bringing me out here. It's like I stepped into the pages of a book for a little while tonight."

"You're welcome." He turned his horse toward the house, now only a spot of light in the distance. "You must be ready to get back. It's getting late."

"No," she said without thinking.

She couldn't see his face beneath the shadow of his hat, but she knew he was studying her. Finally, he said, "There's a place behind the house where you can see almost the whole ranch. Would you like to see that?"

"Yes, please."

As they rode toward Lookout Point, Jessie wondered why Martha thought Teagen was so impossible to get along with. To her, he'd been kinder than anyone ever had.

She rested her back against his chest, thinking that if he ever found out she'd written the letter and signed Eli's name, she'd probably see the hard side of Teagen. The lies she'd told him seemed to be piling up. She couldn't stay here forever and wait for relatives who weren't going to show up. When she'd stepped off the stage, she'd told herself she had to find a place to rest and think. Now she had to find the courage to face her lie.

A few more days, she almost whispered aloud. Let me stay in this place for just a little longer, then I'll be stronger.

CHAPTER 8

Teagen didn't say a word as he guided the roan up the rocky slope to where a ledge provided the perfect viewing point. Jessie seemed relaxed in his arms, moving with him as the horse shifted with the climb.

He knew he shouldn't be thinking about her as a woman. She was the widow of his only friend. She was pregnant. Hell, he thought, in a few weeks she'll be headed out of here and on her way to California with her own people. He'd never see her again. By the time she finished mourning Eli, she'd be so far away he'd be lucky if mail reached her.

Teagen might not know her well, but he'd bet his horse she wasn't the kind of woman who'd consider a friendly roll in the hay before she left. And, he decided, neither was he. Early in his twenties he'd danced a few rounds with the kind of women who cuddle up easy and then didn't remember a fellow's name come morning. He discovered that no matter how interested he might have been after a few drinks at night, he couldn't wait to get away the next morning.

"Cold?" he asked more gruffly than he'd meant to.

"No." She patted his arm. "I'm fine." Leaning her head against his shoulder, she added, "The stars look so bright here."

It never occurred to Teagen that the stars wouldn't appear to be the same anywhere. The only town of any size he'd ever been in was Austin. With four thousand people running around, he didn't remember having time to look at the sky. Funny thing, he'd been born here, born beneath this sky, and in a way he thought of it as his.

"My father used to bring me up here at night." The horse slowed as they reached the edge of the shelf twice again as high as the ranch house. "We'd come up here, and he'd tell me about his dream for this place. About how we'd raise the finest horses ever and how his sons and grandsons and great-grandsons would leave their mark on this piece of Texas."

Teagen could never remember talking so much, but once he started, he couldn't seem to stop. "The night before he left, he brought all three of us up here. Tobin was only six. He fell asleep and almost tumbled out of his saddle. We all knew our father was leaving the next day, and he'd be gone until the fight for Texas was over. But he didn't talk about leaving us. He talked about how much he loved this place."

Teagen felt her fingers brushing across the muscle on his forearm as if she were brushing away pain. "Did he tell you he loved you?"

"He didn't have to."

Jessie nodded. "I know what you mean. I was thirteen when my folks died too. When the fever got bad, my mother kept saying she loved me, but my father's last words were that he was sorry. He only lived a few hours longer than my mother."

"What do you think he was sorry for?" Teagen couldn't help but ask.

"For leaving me, I guess. We never had much, and when they got sick, all we had disappeared. I'd been selling the fur-niture to buy medicine for weeks. We leased a place, and the only reason we stayed was because the landlord didn't want to come into the apartment with them down with fever."

"What happened when they died?" Teagen told himself he didn't want to know, but he had to ask.

"I sold everything we had left to pay for their burial. Then I lived there awhile alone. The neighbors would invite me in to eat, but most of them had more kids than they could raise al-ready. The landlord finally came around and told me I had to clean the place up and then he'd take me to the orphanage. I didn't want to go, so I ran away. For a while I slept in the park, but when winter came I knew I'd freeze, so I started hiding in the bookstore about closing time. Eli was usually so busy it was easy to slip in at night and out before he opened. The place was a mess with boxes of books everywhere. Then, one morning he caught me."

Teagen waited. He wouldn't ask what happened, but he didn't plan on moving until she told more.

Jessie looked up at him, her huge eyes filling with moonlight. "I thought he'd turn me over to the police, but he offered me a job. Meals, if I cooked them, and a cot in the attic if I worked in the store. The arrangement was good. It gave me a safe place to stay, and it provided him with the freedom to leave. Eli loved two things in his life: books and whiskey. As long as the store was open and running, he had both."

Watching her, Teagen wondered why she didn't add herself to the list. This was the second time she'd mentioned Eli not loving her, but he must have cared about her. He'd saved her from starving and given her a place to sleep. He'd married her.

She shrugged so slightly Teagen felt it more than saw it. "On summer nights in the attic, I used to open the windows to the roof and look out at the night sky, but the stars never looked so big. Raising her hand, fingers wide, she whispered, "It's almost as if I can touch them."

Teagen watched her. She had to be in her mid-twenties, she was a mother, a widow, but there was such wonder in her. She reminded him of a blind person seeing for the first time.

When her hand came down, it rested once more on his arm as if that was the place where her touch belonged. "If I lived here," she breathed deep of the summer night, "I'd come out here every night."

"I do." He didn't add that it was part of the security routine all the McMurray men practiced. From this point they could see any campfires on their land.

She twisted so she could see his face clearly. "Could I

come here again with you? Not every night, but just sometime before I have to go?"

"Of course." The thought that she'd be leaving soon returned. Teagen frowned. "How long do you think before your relatives come?"

He felt her entire body tense.

"Not long. A few weeks, a month maybe. I didn't have time to wait for their answer before I left Chicago."

It occurred to Teagen that her relatives might not have gotten the letter. The mail wasn't always dependable, or they could have moved. Or, in a land as wild as California, they could even be dead.

Teagen turned his horse back toward the house. They rode in silence for a while before he said, "If they take much longer than a month, it'll be too late to start the trip back across the Rockies before winter. The journey's going to be hard enough with three little ones in the summer."

She didn't say a word, and he guessed he'd frightened her, so he added, "If they don't come by August, you'd better stay here until spring."

"You'd let me?" she whispered as they neared the corral gate.

"It'd be safer for you and the girls." He swung down and reached up to help her. "By spring you'll be recovered from the birth. Staying here might be your only logical choice."

She came so easily into his arms he gave no thought to resisting. Wrapping her arms around his neck, she pressed her body against his even before her feet touched the ground. "Thank you," she said against his ear. "Thank you."

He held her close, feeling her tears against his shoulder. Neither said another word, but he got the point. She must have been worried sick about her relatives not getting to her in time. The thought of being heavy with child and having to cross almost twice the distance she'd already come would be a troublesome burden.

After awhile, she stopped crying and pulled away.

"I'm sorry," she managed with a little laugh. "Tears seem

to be spilling out of me at every turn. I'm not like that usually." She brushed his shoulder as if she could dust away tears. "I'll try to make myself useful while I'm here. Now that I know I'll be welcome if they don't make it, I can relax. But I want to help out while I stay. I'm not much of a cook, but I can sew and knit."

Teagen stepped away to unsaddle his mount. He wished she'd said she could shoot rather than knit. Outlaws are seldom stopped by knitting needles. But he didn't want to hurt her feelings, so he said, "You've already been a big help. You've managed to keep Martha so busy she hasn't had time to pick on me. I swear, when Sage is gone, she bristles like an old porcupine in a hailstorm. Nothing I do, including disappear, makes her happy."

"When is Sage due back? The way Martha talks about her, I can't wait to meet her."

"She should be back anytime now. She wanted to drive her own team home, but I wouldn't let her. Sage thinks she can do anything a man can do, and the only thing that usually keeps her from it is when all three of us gang up on her."

"Her three big brothers?"

"Right." Teagen let his horse into the corral. "She rode down with Travis and his wife. Travis will be tied up at the capital for at least another month. Sage can't stay tame that long, so I wasn't surprised when she sent word that she'd be coming home. Since we all vetoed her driving, Travis will put her on the stage in Austin."

"You all thought it too dangerous for her to come alone."

"Of course it would be. A woman alone would look like an easy target, and there's no telling how many bodies she'd leave along the road to prove that she wasn't."

Jessie laughed. "So, you weren't worried about her, just the poor robbers."

Teagen took her elbow and started toward the house. "You don't know my sister."

"I can hardly wait." Jessie matched her step to his. "You love her lots, don't you?"

"Of course I do." He slowed. "But she cried for an hour one time when we were target shooting, and Travis made her shoot a rabbit. Imagine what she'll do if she has to kill half the outlaws between here and Austin."

Jessie took the first step on the porch and turned to face him at eye level. "But you think she would go ahead and shoot them if need be."

Teagen winked at her. "I'd bet on it."

CHAPTER 9

TEAGEN LAY AWAKE HALF THE NIGHT. HE COULDN'T believe he'd told Jessie she could stay as long as she liked. When he brought her home from the trading post he'd figured it would be a week, two at the most. Now, if her relatives were delayed for some reason, it could be months.

Strange how the notion of having company for that long didn't bother him near as much as he thought it would.

He looked up at the ceiling of his first-floor bedroom and thought of Jessie sleeping above him. She had no idea how her light touch affected him. Teagen wasn't a man anyone got that close to. Except for Sage hugging him good-bye a few times a year when one of them left the ranch, or one of his brothers slapping him on the back now and then, no one touched him. He made a habit of staying far enough away from folks in town that he never had to bother with shaking hands. He'd always considered unnecessary contact a nuisance and thought of himself as strong enough to do without it.

But Jessie touched him like they were old friends.

About the time he fell asleep, he'd finally made up his mind that he'd have to tell her to stop such nonsense. They weren't friends; they hardly knew one another. Even the little time they'd spent alone probably hadn't been proper. She was newly widowed, and he had no plans of ever offering more than already given.

The next night after supper, when she entered the study for

their talk, Teagen couldn't remember what it was he'd been going to tell her.

She curled up with her feet beneath her skirts and rocked. "How was your day, Teagen?" she asked. "I was up getting the girls to sleep when you came in and ate supper."

"Fine." He settled back in his chair. "Rose visited the barn this afternoon."

"To check on the cats." Jessie smiled. "She has her rounds with all the animals. I've never seen her so happy, even if Martha wouldn't let her name the chickens. She told Rose it was because chickens are too dumb to remember their names if they had them, but she told me she didn't want Rose naming them because she didn't like the idea of cooking Philip or Victoria for dinner."

Teagen laughed. "Martha's got a point."

"I know, but Rose has so much fun. Eli wouldn't let her have a pet, but she visited the print shop's watchdog every day, and the lady who lived across the street let her play with her two cats. Sometimes, I swear, I can see her as an old woman with cats and dogs all around her. She loves animals so."

"I guessed that," he admitted, "but she came out to the barn to ask if I'd let her and Emily see one of the horses up close."

Jessie tilted forward. "What did you say?"

"I said they should wait until Sage comes home. Sage would be the one to teach them to ride."

"Fair enough."

"But I did put them both on an old mare we have named Glory."

Jessie was off the rocker and on her feet in a blink. "You shouldn't have." Her fists rested on her hips as she faced him. "They could have been hurt. Emily must have been scared to death. I'm surprised I didn't hear her crying."

Teagen watched her closely. He should have been insulted at her lack of trust, but all he could think about was how protective she was of her girls. He wouldn't be surprised if she took a swing at him. Just the thought of it made him smile.

Jessie glared at him as if she questioned his sanity.

Teagen's smile turned into a laugh. "Now calm down, little mother. I just walked them around the corral. Glory is too old and gentle to scare anyone." He almost patted her shoulder, then reconsidered. "They were in no danger, and besides, it wasn't Emily who showed fear, but Rose. Emily cried when I set her off the horse."

"Really?"

"To a five-year-old, a horse can look awful big. Rose was ready to get down after we circled. But Emily asked if she could hold the lead rope, and when I showed her how to pat Glory's neck, she rubbed her face against the mane the way Sage used to do. My sister used to say she was giving Glory a horse kiss."

Jessie sat back down. "I wish I could have seen that. It seems like Em's been afraid of everything since the day she was born."

"Not of horses." Teagen relaxed, glad Jessie had finally settled. "She asked me if I'd let her ride again tomorrow. She was shy, wouldn't look me in the eye, but she wanted it so badly I could hear her voice shake."

"You don't have time."

"I'll make time." He hesitated then added, "Martha and Sage have been after me for years to slow down and take a few minutes to do something besides work. Maybe they're right." He thought about it a minute and added, "But Em will need a proper hat to ride. As fair as she is, her skin will blister in an hour. Tell Martha to add one to the grocery list." When she didn't correct him, he added, "Might as well make it three wide-brimmed hats, though I doubt you'll be able to keep one on the little one." Before Jessie could argue, he added, "Did Bethie stay out of trouble today?"

Jessie shook her head. "We worked in the garden this morning. She found the only mud hole and looked like she must have rolled in it several times before we noticed. Martha made her undress on the porch before she'd even let her in the mud room."

Teagen fought down a smile. "I know how she felt."

He watched Jessie carefully, thinking she didn't look so

tired tonight. "It's cool outside. Would you walk out with me before you turn in?"

"I'd like that." She stood and reached for her shawl. "Is this one of the 'things besides work' you plan to do?"

"It is." Teagen stood and offered his hand. He'd looked forward to seeing her all day long. One more day, he thought. One more evening talk before she goes.

He'd caught himself watching the bridge, not for outlaws who might be fool enough to storm the place with a dozen Apache just on the other side, but for Jessie's relatives. He didn't like the idea of anyone coming for her just yet. He told himself she needed more time to rest, but in truth he knew he was the one who needed more time.

They stepped off the porch and walked toward the dots of campfires near the bridge. He tucked her hand in the bend of his arm and slowed so that she didn't have to hurry. "Life must seem pretty dull out here compared to Chicago?"

"No," she answered. "We made bread today. I haven't done that since my mother was alive. Because I had to open the store at eight, and I never closed before six, there was little time for me to bake properly. Now and then I managed a pie, but it was easier to trade the baker a book for a month's supply of bread."

"Did you do a lot of that, trading?"

"More than you'd think. Many of the merchants didn't read, but they had children, and the measure of a wealthy man lies in the width of his wife and his bookshelf."

Teagen laughed. "So you traded books for supplies with shopkeepers who couldn't read."

She nodded. "It made counting the till at night easy, and Eli, if he knew, never seemed to mind."

Teagen was glad it was too dark for her to see his face. He couldn't help but frown. How could Eli own the store, live with her, and not know what was going on? Teagen didn't want to think about it. He refused to ask.

The sound of a child crying drifted through the night. Jessie turned around a moment before Teagen figured out where it was coming from.

Emily stood on the porch, hugging herself but too afraid to step out into the night. "Hello," she cried. "Is anyone out there?"

Jessie let go of Teagen's arm and ran to her. "Em, I'm right here. What is it? What's wrong?"

Emily looked past her mother at Teagen. Her face seemed as white as the moon in the glow of the study windows.

"It's all right, Em. I'm right here." Jessie reached for her, but the girl pulled away.

"No," she insisted. "I came to see Mister."

Teagen took a step closer. He knew the girls called him Mister and had decided that was as good as any name. "What is it, Emily?" he asked, making a true effort not to frighten her.

She looked at him with a mixture of fear and hope. "Would you take me to say good night to Glory?"

Jessie began the word *no*, when Teagen cut in. "Of course, but it'll be dark out near the barn. Real dark until your eyes get used to the night."

She reached up to him in answer.

Without another word he picked up the thin little girl and settled her on his arm, then offered his hand to Jessie. "You want to come too?"

She shrugged. "Why not. The barn is as good a way to walk as any."

Teagen felt Em's little arm wrap around his neck while Jessie laced her fingers in his.

They walked past the barn to the corral. Teagen whistled, and the palomino lifted her head, then came toward him. "She was my mother's horse," he said. "So she's very old."

He sat Em on the top railing as Glory stretched her neck over the fence. "Tomorrow night when you come to say good night, Em, bring a piece of a carrot or apple. Glory loves that. If you bring her a treat, she'll walk over to meet you every time, hoping to get more."

Emily brushed the mare's mane. "I will." Then she did what she'd done that afternoon; she wrapped an arm around the horse and pressed her face against the warm hair.

Jessie squeezed Teagen's fingers. When he glanced in her direction, he thought he saw tears in her eyes.

They stood for a while, then Teagen lifted Emily back on his arm. "Glory and you both need your sleep now. After you eat your breakfast in the morning, I'll saddle her for you and let you ride her around the corral."

They walked toward the light of the house. In the blackness between the barn and the porch, Emily snuggled against Teagen's shoulder and whispered, "Thank you, Mister."

"You're welcome," he answered.

He set the child down on the porch. Without a word, she bent close and kissed his cheek, then ran back into the house.

Jessie stepped onto the porch and smiled. "I'd like to thank you also."

"Good night, Jessie." Teagen stayed on the ground, knowing he still had to make rounds before he turned in, but before he could turn away, Jessie leaned down and kissed his cheek.

"Good night, Teagen," she said as if she'd repeated the words a hundred times.

Before Teagen could think of what to do, she vanished.

CHAPTER 10

Teagen MANAGED TO EAT BREAKFAST THE NEXT morning without being hit by flying food or having Bethie spill something on him. The girls now felt at home, and after four days of good food and plenty of sleep, they were as fun as puppies to watch. Rose seemed only to know how to talk in questions. Emily still didn't look like she wanted him around, but at least she didn't cry. And Bethie giggled and played with everything she touched. This morning she wielded a wooden spoon and had great fun doing so until she whacked Rose in the head, and Jessie took the spoon away.

Bethie would have cried, but Martha handed her a long, thin biscuit she'd rolled in cinnamon and sugar before baking. The tiny girl giggled with delight. Within seconds her face was sparkling with spices.

Martha served hot biscuits covered in fresh butter and honey alongside scrambled eggs made with cheese. He thought of asking where the meat was, but he'd much rather do without than see Jessie bent over in the weeds again. They raised pigs for food and, at this rate, he'd be selling them soon.

When he got the chance to talk to Jessie, while Martha took the girls to wash their hands, he asked, "You all right?" He didn't want to add that she looked tired.

"I'm fine," she answered. "Martha said you'll be going into town to pick up supplies and meet the stage."

Teagen hadn't heard anything about supplies. Martha only gave him a list once a month, but with the extra guests she may have thought of something she needed, so he played along. "Right." There were a few things he wanted to pick up.

"Could I go too?"

"If you like." The idea of spending a few hours alone with her sounded good. He tried to keep their visits at night short because she needed her sleep and he had rounds to make. But the drive over and back would give them lots of time.

"Thanks. The girls will love it."

Teagen reached for his hat, not allowing her to see his disappointment. Of course a mother would want to be with her children. He felt guilty for even thinking she would have wanted to come along with just him.

"The girls will love what?" Rose asked as she ran into the room.

"A ride back and forth from town," Jessie announced as the others joined her. "Teagen has to go in for supplies, and I thought we'd join him."

"Not me," Rose said. "I don't have time. One of the cats is going to have kittens, and I can't leave. If it happened while I was gone, I'd never forgive myself."

Teagen rested against the doorjamb and smiled. He swore little Rose already sounded just like Mrs. Dickerson, the schoolteacher who'd lived across from the trading post for years. Maybe schoolteachers really were born.

Emily started to cry. "I don't want to go without Rose."

Martha shook her head. "Bethie might miss her nap if she goes to town. She'd better stay with me. And Emily can help me put up jelly." Martha patted Em's head. "She's the best helper I've ever had."

Emily stopped crying.

Jessie looked disappointed. "Well, I thought it was a good idea."

"You go on," Martha said. "I'll watch the girls and without them you can travel faster. I'll give you the list of supplies while Teagen brings the team around."

Jessie ran from the kitchen. "I'll need time to get ready."

"Take all you need," he answered, having learned from his sister that it never paid to hurry a female.

Teagen walked out, happy for once to follow orders. He never dreamed something as simple as going into town would be such a debate. As he got the team ready, he decided he shouldn't have been surprised, half the time Sage had trouble making up her mind about things. For Teagen, it was a question of what needed to be done; he never really considered what he wanted to do.

Glancing toward the barn door, he noticed Rose, her arms full of cats, heading to the house. Women, even the tiny ones, were strange creatures. The five-year-old was afraid of gentle Glory but dragged the half-wild cats around as if they were her dolls. He wouldn't be surprised if he returned to find them all dressed up in clothes.

Emily came out while he waited for her mother. Teagen didn't waste time talking; he knew what she wanted. He sat her up on Glory's bare back and showed her how to control the horse just by her movements. Glory was so well trained and sensitive to the slightest guiding that she moved easily when Em directed her.

When Teagen pulled her off, Emily cried, not wanting to leave, but her tears seemed more sad than angry. He promised her they'd ride again when he got back from town, and she seemed satisfied.

"Thanks, Mister," she said with her head down. Then she turned and ran back to the house.

Teagen didn't know what he thought about a creature so afraid of everything around her, but he did like the way she loved Glory. That he could understand.

Thirty minutes later, Jessie was finally ready to go. She and Martha had a long discussion about what color of thread to buy even after he'd helped Jessie in the wagon. Teagen waited in frustrated silence. When Jessie climbed back down to kiss the girls good-bye again, he didn't say a word. When she spent five minutes beside Martha looking at the clouds gathering to the north and wondering if it might rain, Teagen waited without comment.

When she finally settled in beside him, he'd calculated that he could have been halfway back from town by now if he'd left without her after breakfast. A few dark clouds covered the sun, making his mood even darker than usual.

They were across the bridge and on the road when she finally said, "Are we making this trip in silence?"

"I hadn't planned on it," he answered without looking at her.

"Are you mad about something?"

"No." The word came far too fast to be true.

To his surprise, Jessie laughed. "You are. You're like a big angry bear. Well, if you're trying to frighten me, Teagen, you're far too late. I know you too well."

He started to say she didn't know him at all. A few walks, a few minutes of conversation at night didn't mean she knew him. But she thought she did, and that he found very interesting. "If you know me so well, you should know why I'm mad."

She patted his arm. "Oh, so you lied; you are mad."

He forgot what they were talking about. She'd leaned so close that their bodies bumped together as the wagon rocked. With a tug on the reins, he stopped the team and faced her. It was time to have the talk he'd been putting off. She couldn't go on patting on him and touching him and lacing her hand in his. It wasn't proper. She was a widow, and her touches made his thoughts go in directions he shouldn't be heading with a woman like Jessie.

"We need to talk about something, Jessie," he began.

"All right, but Martha packed a lunch. Maybe we should wait until we stop to eat." She rested her hand on his shoulder as she searched behind the bench. "I thought we'd eat it on our way back, but if you want to stop now . . ."

"I'm not hungry," he said.

Her breast accidentally brushed his arm as she straightened. "Me, either, but it does smell good. Martha is a fine cook."

He closed his eyes and took a deep breath. He wanted to talk about her touching him, but suddenly this didn't seem the time when it came so natural to her and he guessed she didn't mean anything by it. She'd probably be embarrassed if he even mentioned it.

Teagen made a decision. He'd endure the touching for her sake. After all, he didn't want to make her feel bad about something she seemed to think was so natural. And he knew he couldn't bring himself to say "breast" in front of her.

He urged the horses on, knowing that all this talking to himself was a lie. He wasn't mentioning it because he liked her touch and didn't want to do one damn thing to stop it. "You're right, we'll talk after we pick up the supplies."

She slipped her hand between his arm and chest. "Good idea. We never seem to have enough time to talk." After a moment of silence, she added, "You know why Martha insisted you go to town today?"

He slowed the team as they made a bend in the road. "I know. She thinks Sage will be on the stage. She's done it almost every week. If Sage doesn't get home soon, we'll have enough supplies to last us through three winters. I wouldn't have left today, but the Apache will see no one crosses the bridge."

They drove on awhile, then she surprised him by asking if he'd teach her to drive a team. When he passed the reins to her, he placed his arms around Jessie, talking her through what to do. He laughed and she squealed all the way to the trading post. By the time he showed her how to pull up the team, his arm felt quite comfortable around her.

Once inside, his good mood continued as they picked out the supplies Martha needed and added hats for the girls. He tossed in more items he noticed that Jessie might need while she picked out just the right color of thread for Martha's latest sewing project.

Shouting drew him to the porch while Anderson figured up his bill.

A boy of about ten rode bareback on a horse that had a

rope tied to make a crude bridle. He yelled as he came closer. "Help!" He sounded out of breath. "I got to have help!"

Teagen lifted his rifle from the wagon and noticed several other men did the same. If trouble followed the boy, they needed to be prepared.

The boy seemed to jump from his horse while at full speed. "You got to come," he said to the nearest man. "You all got to come help."

Teagen lowered his gun when he saw no one following the boy.

"What is it?" Teagen was aware that even though the kid's panic looked real, it might be a trap.

The boy tried to talk and gulp air at the same time. "The stage has been hit. Folks are hurt back about six miles from here." He crumpled to the dirt, exhausted and frightened. "Some of them are dead. They got to be. There is blood in the road."

Teagen's fingers gripped around his rifle and he looked over at the barrel-chested trading post owner. "Anderson?"

Elmo Anderson didn't need Teagen to say more. "My horse is tied just off the porch. It's not a McMurray horse, but you're welcome to it."

Teagen nodded his thanks and headed for the mount. He glanced at Jessie as he passed.

Her face paled, and a cool wind whipped loose strands of her hair across her cheek. He couldn't help but think she looked too young to be the widowed mother of three.

"Stay here with Elmo until I get back," he ordered.

She looked like she might faint, so he lowered his voice. "You'll be safe here, Jessie. Wait for me."

She nodded once, then ran to help Elmo with the boy.

The kid looked at Teagen. "You one of the McMurrays, mister?"

"Yeah," Teagen said as he and several others prepared to ride.

"I thought so. Your sister is on that stage."

Teagen was gone without hearing more. He rode as fast as

he could up the road with the other riders at his heels. In his mind only one fact kept rolling around in his head: Sage was on the stage.

It seemed like forever before he caught first sight of the stagecoach. It was turned on one side with the door open and pointing toward heaven. Luggage lay scattered around. One box had come open, and paper blew out of it a few pages at a time.

He slowed and moved closer, barely noticing as rain started plopping down in huge drops.

Two men lay in the dirt. One had a pool of blood circling his head. The other's body lay twisted like a broken toy. Both looked dead.

The horses had been unhooked from the stage and grazed at the side of the road as if nothing had happened.

When he drew closer, he saw an older woman sitting on a piece of luggage. Her hands covered her face, and he could hear her crying. Sage was nowhere in sight.

Teagen rode past the bodies and the woman. He couldn't help the dead, and the woman looked in no danger.

A young man in a store-bought suit stood with a Bible in his hand. He didn't seem to be comforting the crying woman or praying for the dead. His eyes were glazed over in fear. Blood dripped from a wound on his forehead, but he didn't seem to notice.

He stared at the riders in panic. The crying woman looked up also but just stared. Fear floated in their eyes, yet they seemed incapable of doing anything to protect themselves.

Charlie, the blacksmith, rode just behind Teagen. He yelled that they were here to help. The woman started to cry louder, and the city fellow yelled, "Praise the Lord."

Ignoring them, Teagen jumped from his horse. "Sage!" he yelled loud enough to spook the horses. "Sage!"

"What?" came an answer from behind the stagecoach.

Teagen watched as his little sister stepped into the open. She raised one bloody hand and shoved her hair away from her eyes with her wrist. Her dress was covered in dirt and blood.

His heart stopped. She took one look at him and smiled, kicking it back into action.

"Thank God, Teagen, you're here. I've got two outlaws dead and the driver wounded bad."

He walked toward her. "Are you hurt?" He brushed the blood off her forehead.

"No. But we need to get these people to town. The driver may die if I don't get that bullet out and the bleeding stopped. Help me get the wound wrapped tight." She lifted her skirt and ripped away a section of her petticoat.

Teagen shouted for the others to right the stagecoach.

He followed her and saw why she was having so much trouble. The driver outweighed her three times over. Teagen lifted him off the ground as Sage wrapped a gaping wound in the center of his chest.

"Where's the man riding shotgun?" Teagen asked as they worked. He knew it wouldn't be the dandy quoting scripture from the other side of the road.

"They shot him first," Sage answered. "I saw him fall about half a mile back. If the bullets didn't kill him, the fall probably did."

Teagen heard the stage rock back onto its wheels, and the others began to hook up the team as Sage finished with the bandage.

He shouted for help to lift the wounded driver into the coach.

Sage followed, giving them orders to be careful.

"The woman over there is in shock, I think, and the preacher, her son, never had to face anything like this. They're from back East."

"He's wounded," Teagen commented.

The Yankee stared up at the rain now as if each drop fell just to bother him.

"I know. He hit his head getting out of the coach."

Teagen looked around as she continued, "They came at us from the front. Hit the shotgun rider first, then the driver. I killed two before the rest backed away. The horses were running wild and tried to make this curve too fast."

The young preacher walked in their direction. He must have decided Teagen was the head of the rescue team since he rode in first. The thin man removed his hat and explained, "They were ordering us to stop, sir. Maybe if we had, they would have simply taken our money and left." He pointed at Sage. "But this woman pulled a gun and started shooting."

Teagen didn't like the preacher, but he explained, "If you would have stopped and stepped out of the stage unarmed, all of you would be dead right now. Who does the boy who rode in to tell us about the attack belong to?"

Sage answered as she climbed into the coach with the wounded man. "His folks have a place not far from here. They heard the shots and sent him to check. He wanted to go get his ma, but I told him to ride for town. I wouldn't have been surprised if the bandits decided to turn around and try again. If his folks had come, it might have only meant more people hurt or killed."

"Are you out of lead?" Teagen knew the answer. If she hadn't been, there would have been more bodies on the ground.

She nodded. "I wasn't traveling as well-armed as I should have been."

"And you?" Teagen looked at the preacher.

"I don't carry a gun," he answered. "And neither does my mother."

The men from town were saddling up. A few headed farther down the road to look for the guard; the rest flanked the stage.

"Can you drive this stage?" Teagen asked.

"No," the preacher answered.

"Then get your mother and climb in." Teagen tied his mount to the back. "And hold on. It's going to be a fast ride."

He glanced in at his sister, sitting on the floor of the stage with the driver's head in her lap. "You ready?" he asked.

"Get us to town, Teagen."

He climbed up and took the set of six reins between his fingers. With a pop of leather, they were off. He took care but rarely slowed. Teagen knew how to drive a team, and he had also ridden in enough coaches to know that the rocking motion wouldn't change all that much from one speed to another.

When he pulled up to the trading post, Elmo directed him to the hotel. There, several men helped unload the driver onto a table in the parlor. Sage took over. She'd delivered enough babies in the area that most folks knew having her around was as good as having a doctor. Some said she got her gift from her Indian blood, but right now no one seemed to care; they were just ready to help.

Teagen walked the stage to the barn and turned it over to one of the hands, then headed back to the trading post. His wagon was still out front, but he saw no sign of Jessie. Or anyone else. Everyone in town seemed to be standing in front of the hotel talking about what had just happened. When Teagen approached, he heard Charlie saying, "That McMurray girl saved all their lives. There's no telling how many of them she shot. We found two bodies."

Teagen passed through the crowd looking for Jessie. He overheard one man say that the ground was covered in blood. Another said they'd all be dead if it hadn't been for Sage McMurray.

He spotted Elmo. "Anderson, you know what happened to the little widow I left in your care?"

The old man nodded. "The last time I saw her, she was carrying in supplies to Sage."

Teagen moved to the entrance. He told himself he just needed to check on Jessie to make sure she was fine, but he knew it was more. After seeing all the blood, he knew the sight of her would calm him.

Before he could reach the door, men rode in with the guard who'd served as shotgun rider.

"He's alive!" one shouted as several men gathered around to lift the wounded man down.

"Get him inside," another hollered.

Teagen found himself backing to the edge of the porch to make room. The bad news was, ten men stood between him and the entrance. The good news was, he could see the street. If Jessie were anywhere besides inside the hotel, he'd see her.

"How's Sage?" A low voice came from below Teagen, just off the porch.

He looked down to see Drummond Roak standing at the corner of the hotel.

"Fine, Roak. What are you doing here?"

"Came to check on my girl."

Teagen almost laughed. "She's not your girl."

"I know, but she will be." Roak flicked a chip from the piece of wood he whittled. "Was she hurt? I heard one guy say she had blood all over her."

"No. It wasn't her blood. She's trying to help the driver, but I don't think there's much hope. He had a bullet in his chest." Teagen watched from the livery to the trading post. No little widow.

"She stopped the attack," Drum interrupted.

"That's what I hear." He glanced down, but the wild kid was gone. "Nice talking to you, Roak," Teagen said to no one.

CHAPTER 11

FOR TWO HOURS JESSIE STOOD NEXT TO SAGE AND OF-
fered any help she could. She'd taken care of little scrapes and
even sewed a few stitches, but nothing like what Sage McMurray was doing to the man who lay still as stone on the table. The
girl couldn't have been a year out of her teens, but she knew
what she was doing. Her hands were steady and her voice calm
as she talked her way through each step as if reciting a lesson
learned from a book.

Another man, in no better shape, lay a few feet away. The
barber and what looked like a dance hall girl worked on him.
Their voices were loud and broken with swear words. Their
patient died within minutes, but he left most of his blood behind. The barber yelled for someone to come in and take the
body to the undertaker, then he said he'd had enough blood
for one day and left. The dance hall girl agreed with the barber
and didn't stay around, though she did turn a curtsy in Sage's
direction at the door as if she thought it proper.

Sage smiled at her but didn't ask the girl to stay. Then her
eyes met Jessie's, and she knew what Sage silently asked.

"I'll stay," Jessie answered. "Just tell me what I need to do
to help."

Sage nodded and went back to work.

Blood made the floor slippery but Jessie couldn't leave
Sage alone, so she stayed, offering what help she could.

The hotel manager had given them both huge aprons, or
their clothes would have been a complete mess. They hadn't

talked of anything except trying to save a life, but Jessie felt like they'd bonded. She already knew she liked Sage just from the way Martha and Teagen talked about her, but she also saw why they loved her so much. Where Jessie was shy and always hesitated, Sage stepped in like a general ready for action. There was something about her that drew all around her.

When Jessie could think of no other way to help, she washed blood away until her hands chapped.

"A few more stitches, and we'll have him patched up," Sage said, the exhaustion filtering into her voice.

Jessie ran her hand along the driver's arm. At first it had been hot, then clammy, and now cold. He hadn't made a move in twenty minutes.

She felt for a pulse at his throat. Nothing.

"Sage," Jessie whispered, "I think he's dead."

"No," Sage snapped. "He's lost a lot of blood. His breathing is just real shallow. He's fainted." She began wrapping the wound.

Jessie opened one glassy eye. She'd seen death's stare in both her parents' faces and knew it well. "No. He's dead."

Sage kept wrapping, refusing to admit defeat. "He lived through the fall. He'll live through being shot." If determination could have kept him alive, Teagen's sister would have saved the man.

Jessie watched Sage fight for a life that was already lost. The girl moved faster and faster as if racing death. Finally, she slowed and gulped in air as if she'd finished a long run.

Taking her hand, Jessie forced Sage to face her. "He's gone. There's nothing else we can do."

Sage looked very young. She took another deep breath and nodded. "I know. I thought if I didn't admit it that it wouldn't be true." She took off her apron and covered his face so gently it almost made Jessie cry.

Jessie hugged her. "You did your best."

Sage stiffened. "I know, but this time it wasn't enough. I'll go tell the others." She pulled away and walked toward the front of the hotel.

Jessie didn't want to see the faces outside. Washing her hands one more time in the cold water, she fought down sobs. She turned and ran out the side door, needing to breathe air that didn't smell like blood.

When she stepped outside, she saw Teagen's rig parked in the shadow of an old cottonwood near a barn. Gentle rain didn't give her pause as she ran across the muddy street to the tree. The dark clouds made the world seem in twilight.

She was almost to Teagen's wagon when someone caught her from behind.

For a second she fought, then she heard his rough voice whisper, "Jessie, it's me."

She collapsed into the solid feel of Teagen and let the tears she hadn't had time to cry fall.

He held her firmly against him, so tight she could feel his heart pounding next to her own. Wrapping her arms around his neck, Jessie buried her face beneath his chin. She needed to feel someone alive. She needed to know that a part of her didn't die on that table in the hotel. And Teagen was there just as he'd always been in her dreams. A hundred times over the years she'd clutched his letters and wished he'd hold her as he was holding her now.

Slowly, the tears stopped, and her breathing grew normal. The comforting smell of him calmed her, erasing the taste of blood in her throat. The warmth of him passed through their clothes and eased the muscles she'd held in check for hours.

His big hand cupped the back of her head as she pulled away enough to look at him. "Jessie," he asked. "Are you all right?"

She nodded, liking the feel of him touching her. "I'm fine, but the man died. Sage fought so hard to save him."

"No one expected him to live. You and Sage did the best you could do to try."

"Sage said it wasn't good enough," Jessie whispered, rubbing her cheek against his chin. "If I'd known more, maybe I could have been more help."

His arm at her waist tightened. "You did your best. I'm proud of you."

She gulped back a cry. No one had said they were proud of her in so many years she'd forgotten how a simple compliment could make her feel.

His hand at the small of her back moved up along her spine, and she relaxed with each stroke. Her body pressed closer into the wall of him. She felt herself melting into him.

"Jessie," he whispered against her ear as he lifted her off the ground in his hug. "Jessie, don't cry."

She thought of all the losses in her life. Her mother and father, Eli, her home, and then the bookstore. Through it all no one had been there to hold her, to give her something as simple as a hug.

When he lowered her down, she pulled an inch away. "Thank you," she managed.

"For what?" he said, his hand still stroking her back.

"For being here when I needed someone."

He didn't comment. With his hands at her waist, he gently lifted her onto the bench of the wagon. "If you'll wait here, I'll go see if I can find Sage."

She nodded and watched him walk away. The feel of his hands were still on her body, and she breathed in the scent of him with each breath. He'd done nothing to welcome her nearness, but she had a desire deep down inside herself to be close to him. Maybe she'd had it from the first time she'd read his letters; maybe it came when they met. She didn't know. But the ache was something basic. Something she'd never felt before.

Jessie closed her eyes and sat perfectly still. The old tree sheltered her from the rain, but the wind carried the cool moisture to her hot cheeks. She relaxed and let her mind drift on the breeze without any real thought.

A woman's voice drifted in the air, pulling her back. Jessie opened her eyes and saw Sage standing at the side of the barn with a tall man dressed in black.

"I'm fine, Drum. Stop worrying." Sage sounded angry.

"You've been through a lot, Sage. Hell, you killed two men today."

"Thanks for reminding me," she snapped. "I also couldn't save another, so I guess you could say this hasn't been my day."

"I know what you need, Sage." He gripped her arm. Judging from his size, he could have easily pulled her any direction he'd wanted, but the tall man just held her.

There was no humor in Sage's laughter. "What? You, Drum? You think I want you? I don't think so."

The stranger moved closer to Sage, but his words still drifted to Jessie. "One day, it'll be me you need, but if I know you at all, I'd say right now you need to ride."

He tugged Sage toward a magnificent black horse tied a few feet away. "I'll let you ride Satan home."

She hesitated. "What's the price?"

"None. I just love seeing you ride. I'll be right behind you on one of Anderson's nags."

Sage tilted her head. "No you won't." She took the reins and swung onto the midnight horse. "You'll never catch up."

With a real laugh, she charged out of the barn entrance and was gone.

Jessie heard the man in black swear and run for a horse.

CHAPTER 12

TEAGEN SAW HIS SISTER STREAK THROUGH THE RAIN on a black demon mount that could have only belonged to Drummond Roak. He stormed across the road as Roak came out of the barn.

"Did you loan her your horse?" Teagen yelled above the thunder.

"Yeah. You got a problem with that?" He mounted and pulled in the reins on an animal ready to run.

Teagen's hands balled into fists. This kid had been a thorn in his side for too long. "Yes, I have a problem with that. In case you didn't notice, it's raining. There are outlaws out there robbing people on the road, and she's on your horse, which is the wildest mount we ever tried to train."

Roak didn't seem bothered by Teagen's ranting. "She can outride either of us. No outlaw is going to catch that horse, and I plan to be right behind her if you'll stop yelling at me."

Teagen opened his mouth to continue, but Roak shot off after Sage. He stood staring in the direction they'd gone. The kid was as wild as his sister. If Roak had been a few years older, they'd either be courting or killing each other. Sage was probably already home, and much as he hated to admit it, she handled a horse as well or better than any of the McMurrays.

He glanced at the wagon and saw Jessie still sitting on the bench, shivering. Suddenly, Sage and Roak were forgotten. They could take care of themselves, but Jessie was out of her world. All that had happened today must have scared her to death.

Walking over to her, he tugged his oil slicker from the box beneath the seat and circled it around her shoulders. "You all right?"

"Yes," she answered, but she was a poor liar.

"You hungry?"

She nodded. "But it's raining too much for us to stop along the way home. I was looking forward to the picnic, but we'll have to eat it when we get back."

"Come here," he ordered. "We'll try the next best thing to a picnic."

Hesitantly, she scooted across the seat. He lifted her and carried her to one of the new buildings that had a café sign over the door. As he walked, he admitted, "I've never eaten in town, but maybe it's time I gave it a try."

When they walked through the door, everyone in the small place stopped talking and stared. He knew nobody in town liked the McMurrays. He'd always preferred it that way. No one but Mrs. Dickerson had even tried to help them when their parents died, so he had little use for townsfolk. He'd never understood people who favored huddling up in smelly settlements when there was so much land in Texas. Hopefully, Jessie would just think this was a town of idiots and not question the reason they stared.

He walked to the only empty table and sat her down. "Coffee," he said to the waitress in what he thought was a normal tone, but she jumped, then darted like a frightened deer.

A minute later two hot cups of coffee sat on the table. Jessie smiled. "The service is good here."

He glared over her shoulder to the waitress cowering behind Jessie's chair as if she expected him to pull his gun and shoot up the place at any moment.

"Do you want something to eat, Mr. McMurray?" she managed in a voice with an Irish accent that reminded him of his father.

Teagen frowned. He had no idea what to order. Finally he said, "Two plates of food and two desserts if you've got them."

The girl was gone so fast he decided she must be part rabbit.

He looked around. No one in the room talked. A few stared openly, but most tried to act like they weren't watching Teagen's every move. Most were wet enough to be dripping puddles around their chairs, so they must have been part of the crowd who'd waited in the rain to see if the stagecoach driver lived.

Teagen waited. He didn't plan on talking to Jessie with half the town watching and reporting. He smiled, thinking of his brother Tobin, who talked so little that folks thought him unable to speak.

A woman old enough to be a grandmother stood, pulling Teagen back from his thoughts. She walked to their table and ignored Teagen completely as she faced Jessie.

"Missus." She held her wrinkled hands in front of her as if she planned to pray. "I want to tell you what you did in the hotel today was a brave thing. Most of us, man or woman, couldn't have dealt with the sight. We've all known Miss Sage has a gift, but you. Well, you stood like a soldier beside her. We could see you from the window."

"Thank you," Jessie whispered.

The old woman wasn't finished. "You didn't know him, but Dodge was a good man, and you paid him respect by washing the blood off his face. Now, when his mother sees him she won't have that memory to try to forget."

Several others in the room agreed. The woman moved away, and conversation started at the other tables.

"I'm not brave," Jessie whispered as the girl set two plates before them.

"You'll do." Teagen shoved her plate closer to her. "Now eat."

She looked up, a little of the color back in her cheeks. "An order?"

"A request," he answered, wondering what difference it

made. She was hungry. She needed to eat. Why would it matter if he ordered or asked?

They ate in silence. Teagen didn't like all the noise of the place once everyone stopped staring. It was like having dinner in the middle of a migration of magpies. He hated the food. The beef was tough and oversalted. The potatoes didn't taste like Martha's. The carrots were boiled until they had the texture of mush.

Still, he ate slowly, hoping Jessie would clean her plate.

She'd barely made a dent in the food when she shoved it away.

He didn't dare shove it back. The last thing he wanted to do in this place was make a scene.

The girl picked up the plates and delivered a bread pudding for dessert. It was passable, but when he noticed Jessie eating, he set his spoon down. When she finished her pudding, he traded bowls.

She looked up in question.

"I'm too full to eat it," he said. "I must have eaten too much of that mule meat."

Jessie smiled at his joke.

He almost winked at her. She understood. He took a deep breath. So much for folks not thinking he had a sense of humor.

She finished off his pudding while he paid the bill. The room grew quiet again as they walked out. Teagen didn't touch Jessie until they stepped into the rain; then he swung her into his arms.

She laughed. "I can walk."

He didn't know how to tell her that sitting across from her all that time and not touching her had been hard on him. He'd almost offered his hand when they stood, but he knew there would be more talk if he had. It didn't matter what anyone in town said about him, but he didn't like the idea of them talking about Jessie.

The rain had slowed to a drizzle so slight it seemed to hang in the air. She cuddled close to him as he drove home. Neither one said a word.

As they neared the bridge, Teagen slowed. He wasn't sure what had happened on their journey, but somehow the two people who crossed the bridge this morning were different. No words had passed between them, but he knew she felt it as strongly as he did. Something had changed between them. Something good.

When they made it back to the barn, Teagen helped her down and held her to him a moment longer than necessary. In many ways it had been a terrible trip to town, but in a few small ways, Teagen didn't want their time alone to end.

She thanked him when he turned loose of her waist and took one of the boxes. They walked to the house in silence, but not the kind they'd left this morning feeling.

Sage looked like she had had time for a hot bath. She greeted them at the door wearing trousers and a plaid shirt. "Come in, come in. We've all been wondering what happened to you two. It's not like Teagen to wait out the rain."

When Jessie passed, Sage whispered, "I didn't know you were our houseguest, but I couldn't be happier. It will be wonderful to get to know someone I already admire."

"I feel the same." Jessie placed the box on the mud room table and headed back for another, but Sage stopped her. "Oh, no. You stay here and get cleaned up. I'll help Teagen bring in the supplies." When Jessie hesitated, she added, "You've got three girls in the kitchen dying to see you."

Teagen smiled at the gentle way his sister had manipulated Jessie. He set his boxes down and hugged Sage. "Glad you're back," he said. "I knew you wouldn't be able to stay in Austin long. It's too much of a cage for you."

She knocked his hat off and laughed. "I had to come back. You've gotten the place in all kinds of trouble since I left."

"Martha told you about the threats."

Sage nodded. "And about the widow. You were right to bring her here. I can't imagine how hard it must have been to travel across the country with three little ones."

"She's braver than she knows," Teagen agreed.

"Is that a compliment coming from you, big brother?"

He frowned. "No, it's a fact."

"Now that sounds more like Teagen." She tugged him toward the kitchen. "Come on in. Martha made an early supper, and I invited a guest."

"Not that preacher?" Teagen could barely stomach the dude. While two men lay dying in the hotel, he complained to everyone who would listen about his head wound that was no more than a scratch.

"No, not the preacher, but that might be a great idea. He and his mother were very pleasant before the shooting started." She laughed. "You should have seen them when I pulled my guns from beneath my skirt. I thought his mother would faint. She was more upset about seeing my underskirts than about the shooting. When I started firing, she screamed after each round like some kind of crazy echo in the coach. Now, I'll be lucky if they speak to me again."

Teagen followed her though the kitchen door. "If not the preacher, then who?"

A man in black stood a few feet into the room, his gun still strapped on his leg. "Me," Drummond Roak said with a silly smile on his face. He didn't even have the sense to act like he wasn't eavesdropping.

Teagen felt his fist balling up, but the noise of laughing little girls warned him that this was not the time or the place to be rid of the bothersome Roak. "Fine," he managed to say. "Have a seat."

Roak straddled a chair and looked at all the food Martha had spread on the table. The girls were in their chairs, Bethie tied up with apron strings as usual. Teagen guessed Jessie had already hugged her daughters and disappeared to clean up.

Everyone but Teagen seemed to talk at once. Sage told them of her trip to Austin and managed to leave out the problem on the way home until after the girls had vanished to look for a missing cat that had accidentally been left in the house.

Then she leaned forward and told every detail. Roak listened without comment. Teagen asked questions, then lectured her on being better armed next time.

"If I carried any more, my guns would outweigh me."

"One more wouldn't have hurt," Teagen snapped.

"How was I to know the two people with me were traveling unarmed? Paul even told me he's never carried. Imagine that."

"Paul? Who's Paul?" Roak asked between bites.

"The preacher," Teagen answered before Sage could.

"Yes, the preacher." Sage turned to Roak. "The one who I'm planning to invite to dinner as soon as he and his mother settle in."

Both men said *no* at the same time, then stared at one another as if they couldn't believe they agreed on something.

Sage gave them no time to add their opinions. "He's a good man, and I'm finished with men who wear guns. I'm thinking my next beau should be a preacher man. He's not that bad-looking, and his mother says they're from 'good' people back East."

"He's not for you," Roak grumbled.

Teagen frowned. He agreed with the boy again. Something must be wrong.

Sage stretched across the table until her nose almost touched Drummond's. "How would you know? I happen to be looking for a man of peace."

Roak shook his head. "If you hadn't been armed this morning, you all would be dead, and we wouldn't be having this conversation. Those good people would be starting to smell about now."

"Maybe. But I'll not bury another man I love. Paul's the kind of man a girl can grow old with."

"He's not for you," Roak said between closed teeth.

"And you know who is?"

"Me." Roak stood. "I'm the right man for you."

Teagen shoved his chair back, feeling the tension between his shoulders relax. Finally the boy said something he disagreed with. The world was back to normal. Before Roak or Sage could say a word, Teagen offered his hand to Drummond Roak. "Thank you for seeing her home. Stop by again sometime."

Roak stared at him as if he smelled a trap.

Teagen continued, "Do you need me to saddle your horse?"

"I can saddle my own damn horse." Roak took a step to the door. "Tell Martha thanks for the supper."

Sage frowned at Teagen. She might have been arguing with Roak, but she didn't approve of Teagen almost kicking him out.

"I'll see you out." She followed Roak.

Teagen sat down, trying to understand why, if the boy was such a bother to Sage, she cared one way or the other that he practically asked Roak to leave.

Jessie came down the back stairs and looked around the empty room.

Teagen didn't like the way she tilted her head as if already assuming he'd done something that ran everyone off.

"Where . . . ?"

Teagen acted like he was more interested in his coffee than her. "Martha's with the girls in the main room. Sage is walking Roak out like the boy might get lost between here and the barn."

Suddenly Jessie laughed, and her laughter lightened his mood. He smiled up at her. She was doing it again, reading him like a book.

She poured herself a cup of coffee and sat down before she asked, "Do we need to work on your conversation skills, Teagen?"

"Probably." He shrugged. If anyone else in the house had even suggested such a thing, he would have snapped their heads off, but not Jessie. He could talk to her, even joke with her.

She placed her hand on his arm. "It's been a long day."

He agreed. "And it's not sunset yet." He noticed the redness of her knuckles and without a word reached for the bottle of lotion and began rubbing it into her chapped skin.

She didn't pull away but rested her small hand in his. Neither of them spoke until he finished and looked up.

"After I put the girls down tonight," she whispered, "would you take me back up to look at the stars?"

"If you want to go." He didn't need her answer. He could see it in her brown eyes.

Rose darted through the kitchen. "Where's Jeanie-Peanie?"

"Who?" Jessie pulled her hand away from Teagen.

"The yellow cat. She's always running away. I think she wants to go to California."

Rose was gone before they could ask more.

Teagen studied Jessie. He started to say that the cat could go, but he didn't want to talk about California, because when he did, he'd have to talk about Jessie and the girls leaving.

Emily hurried into the room and dashed past them without a word. Next came Bethie, clapping her hands as she waddled. Before she could cross the room to follow her sisters, they circled around the mud room and were heading back the way they came. They were out of sight by the time Bethie could stop her forward motion and follow.

Jessie laughed. "Are you sure you don't mind us staying?"

"I don't mind at all." He stood and reached for his hat. "I'll be back in a few hours."

She smiled. "I'll be waiting."

CHAPTER 13

DYING SUNLIGHT TURNED THE HORIZON RED, AND the wind tasted of rain as Sage followed Drummond to the barn. He was long and lean and would be dangerous in a few years with his good looks and fiery attitude. If he hired out as a gun, he'd be the kind of man Sage wouldn't speak to on the street. The kind that mothers pulled their children inside when he passed. But not now. Today he was just a kid trying to do what was right.

Putting Drum in the same room with Teagen was like caging a cougar cub with a bear. She should have known better than to ask the boy to dinner. To Teagen he'd always be a horse thief, even if he had saved Tobin's life last year.

Too bad Tobin wasn't here to stand guard between the two of them. She'd done a lousy job, getting into an argument with Drum. In truth, she admired the kid for making more of himself than most of the offspring from the outlaw camp. Drum had cleaned up. His clothes were well made and his gun as good in quality as any Ranger strapped on. He'd worked, at least long enough to buy the clothes and a weapon. And, to her surprise, he'd trained Satan beautifully, allowing the horse's spirit to remain wild and free.

"Where you headed?" she asked as Drum checked the cinches on Satan.

"North," he answered without looking at her. "I'm just here for a few days, a week at the most. Talk is that the forts to the north are in trouble. I might sign on as scout. There's fairly good money in scouting if you can stay alive."

Sage nodded. "Staying alive sounds good." She remembered how much of a boy he'd been last year when Teagen had tied him up in the barn. Now, in a little over a year, he seemed more a man. She'd have to stop thinking of him as a kid. "Thanks for letting me ride Satan." Stroking the big stallion's neck, she added, "He's a great horse, and you were right; a ride was exactly what I needed."

Drum twisted the reins in his hand. "You're not really going to start seeing that preacher, are you, Sage?"

"Why?" She looked up at him. In his black clothes and hat he was already old enough to frighten some people. "You planning to shoot him if I do?"

"I was thinking about it."

Sage laughed and bumped her shoulder against his. "You don't have to worry. I don't think he'll speak to me again. Besides, I've told you before: I buried the only man I'll ever love on that rise over there." She looked in the direction of her parents' graves, focusing on the Ranger's headstone just beyond. He belonged there because, if he'd lived, they would have been buried on the spot together after years of marriage. "His eyes promised me forever, and he died on me."

"Not every man is gonna die on you, Sage."

"How do you know?"

"I wouldn't." Drum brushed her cheek with his knuckles.

Sage jerked away. "You're not old enough to make such a statement. You, Drummond Roak, are already well on the way to living by the gun. Look at the way you wear that weapon, hung low like you'll need to draw it fast. You'll be lucky to stay alive long enough to finish growing."

Anger finally flashed in his eyes. "I'm almost seventeen, Sage. I think I've finished growing. But *you're* turning into a hard old maid. When I come back, you'll probably be pulling your hair back in a bun and wearing those ugly blue dresses

Martha always wears. In five years there'll be no telling the two of you apart."

"Well then, maybe I'll start stepping out with the preacher. Since I'm already long in the tooth, I may not want to let him slip by."

"He's not man enough for you." Drum reached for the saddle horn, pinning her between him and the horse. "One of these days you'll figure it out."

Sage jumped toward Drum as Satan danced restlessly. "Good-bye, Drum."

He twisted and circled one arm around her waist before she could act. With an arm far stronger than she'd thought possible, he pulled her against him and lowered his mouth to hers.

After a quick, hard kiss, he said, "Good night, Sage."

Before she could think of the stream of swear words she needed, he swung onto Satan and rode full-out toward the bridge. The Apache between the ranch and the bridge would let him pass. They might not know him, but they knew horses. If he rode a McMurray mount, he must be trusted.

Sage walked back to the house, trying to wipe the feel of him off her mouth and swearing that if Drummond Roak ever tried that again, she'd shoot him. He might have grown this past year, but he was as wild as ever. She'd say he was raised by coyotes, but that would show little respect for coyotes.

When she reached the porch, she glanced toward the bridge. If he headed north she'd probably never see him again. The settlers outside the fort were having a hard time staying alive.

She laughed suddenly. If he stayed around her, she'd probably have to kill him. Who knows? Maybe the north country would be healthier for him.

CHAPTER 14

TEAGEN TILTED BACK IN HIS CHAIR AND WATCHED THE morning circus. It was hard to believe Jessie and the girls had been on the ranch three weeks. He enjoyed the racket of breakfast and the quiet talks in the evening. He'd miss them when the relatives showed up from California.

This morning, Bethie was busy painting her oatmeal into the table. Emily sat waiting by the door with her hat in her hand, because she knew as soon as Teagen finished his coffee, he'd let her ride Glory. And Rose stared at him with her elbows propped on the table, asking her usual morning questions.

"Do you think it's going to rain, Mister?"

"Nope," Teagen answered the same question he'd answered for over a week. The rain worried Rose because Martha told her that chickens were too dumb to come in out of it. Martha had said they just stand watching the rain until they drown.

"Would you help me build a little porch onto the chicken coop?"

Before Teagen could answer, Sage walked into the room. "I'll help you when I get back. I've got to ride over to the east pasture and check on a few mares first. Should be back in an hour or so." Sage grabbed a biscuit and glanced at Emily. "You want to ride over with me, Em?"

Silence.

Emily stared, her blue eyes full of hope, at her mother.

Jessie turned from the sink and looked not at her daughter but at Teagen.

He knew what she wanted. She wanted him to answer, because if she said a word, it would be no. They'd talked about it a few nights ago, and she'd told him she was always afraid to let her daughters try anything for fear one would get hurt.

Teagen stood. "Em, you want to go?"

"Yes, sir." Shy little Emily couldn't even look him in the face.

"Will you listen to everything Sage tells you to do?"

"Yes, sir."

"And wear your hat?" The child was so fair she'd probably sunburn through the hat.

"Yes, sir."

He knelt, hoping she'd look at him, but she didn't. "Now you're old enough to ride outside the corral, you should know one of the ranch rules. If trouble comes, or if you hear three shots, ride hard and fast back to the house. It's easy to find because it's at the base of a mountain you can see for miles. If anything happens, I want you to remember the rule."

Sage touched the child's hair. "Don't worry, Emily, nothing ever happens around here."

Emily glanced up at Teagen. "I'll remember the rule," she said.

"Then you can go." Teagen doubted she'd ever need to know the rule, but he didn't like the idea of her not knowing, just in case.

She looked up, and he saw her rare smile. "Thank you," she whispered.

"Well, come along." Sage winked at Teagen. "If you're old enough to ride, you're old enough to saddle your own horse. Then we've got riding to do."

A few minutes later Teagen stood with Jessie on the porch and watched his sister ride out beside Emily. He leaned close to Jessie. "It's all right. Sage won't let anything happen to her. Em has been riding the corral long enough. It's time."

Jessie turned and pressed her forehead against his chest. "I know," she whispered. "I just wish they could stay the same age forever and never grow up."

He put his arm around her shoulder and thought about how easily she came to him. Every night now after their talks, she'd kiss him on the cheek or hug him lightly. He was growing used to the feel of her near, and he didn't want to think about her leaving soon. They'd been in his life three weeks, and much as he hated to admit it, he'd miss them when they left.

"How long?" she whispered, and for a moment he thought she was reading his mind; then he realized she was watching the girls ride away.

"An hour, maybe a little longer because Sage is riding so slow." He dropped his arm from her, letting his fingers slide down her back. She had gained a little weight and didn't feel so thin. Next time he caught Martha alone, he'd thank her for constantly making all the things Jessie loved. If Jessie ate more than a few bites of something, it usually appeared on the table again.

"We could ride out to the pasture tonight if you like. You'll see it's all tall grass. With the full moon it'll be light enough for you to watch the same horses they're seeing today." He thought about adding that even if Em fell off, she wouldn't be hurt, but he didn't think he needed to mention the possibility.

"I'd like that."

Fine, curly hair brushed against his hand a moment before sticky fingers grabbed his thumb. He shifted and lifted Bethie. "I have to go." Handing the baby to her mother, he added, "I'll not be back at noon. There's too much work to do."

"All right," Jessie answered. "Sage and I thought we'd take the wagon into town and buy material while the girls are down for a nap."

He realized he'd never seen her in anything but black. He thought of suggesting she buy something in a color, but somehow that sounded too personal.

He touched the baby's cheek but looked at Jessie. "Be careful."

She smiled at him. "Worry more about Martha here alone with the girls. As soon as they are up from their naps, they'll run her ragged."

Teagen agreed and stepped off the porch. He rode hard all day, thinking of the evening when he'd take Jessie out to the east pasture. It wasn't all that special to see, but they'd have an hour alone. He found he enjoyed their time together more each night. Often they talked about the girls. Sometimes they'd argue over a book. Jessie had not only read all of them, she remembered them. Now and then he told her of the problems with the ranch and felt it was almost like writing Eli again. Twice she'd talked about the baby growing inside her. He'd learned more than either of his sisters-in-law had shared about their pregnancy.

Teagen rode the fence line looking for more damage but saw none. Whoever planned to steal the horses had either given up the effort or was biding their time until the Apache left.

Turning his horse toward home a few hours earlier than usual, he told himself that he had work to do in the study before supper, but in truth, he wanted to be back. He wanted to hear about Emily's ride and inspect Rose's chicken porch. And, if he were being honest, he'd have to admit that he wanted to see Jessie.

She had a way of doing little things that settled into his mind. Maybe they'd share a few minutes of coffee on the porch alone, or she'd whisper something she thought was funny so only he could hear. A few days before, they'd laughed over Bethie playing in the mud around the well. When he'd caught Jessie's eye, she'd winked at him.

Last night Sage had invited the preacher to dinner. The women had made a fuss, but Preacher Paul hadn't noticed. He'd brought his mother along, who seemed to be taking inventory of the house. The only thing good about the dinner was laughing about it with Jessie after everyone else had gone to bed.

He kicked his horse, suddenly in a hurry to be home.

Teagen knew something was wrong even before he made it to the corral. The wagon that Sage would have driven to town hours ago had been pulled to the house and left in the sun. Sage would never leave the horses like that, and Martha always insisted on the supplies being brought in at once.

Teagen galloped straight to the porch, his thoughts full of worry that something could have happened to Emily during her ride or to Sage and Jessie on their way home.

Before he swung down, Jessie was there.

"What's wrong?" He could see tear streaks on her cheeks, and her eyes were wild with fear.

"It's Em," Jessie cried. "She must have woke up from her nap and found us gone. We think she saddled Glory and rode out to meet us, but Sage and I never saw her on the road back from town."

Sage hurried from the barn and joined them. "I'm changing horses. The Apache said she crossed the bridge about an hour after we left. We should have seen her. I've covered the road from here to town. Now I'll go the other direction."

He looked at Jessie, fighting the need to pull her against him. "Don't worry. We'll find her."

The little mother didn't look like she believed him, but she nodded.

Teagen rode to the bridge and tried to track Glory's prints. He wasn't the tracker Tobin or Travis was, but he could follow a fresh trail. Sage rode beside him, watching for trouble while he climbed down again and again to study the tracks in the fading light. The road between their place and town was well traveled and fairly safe, but anyone turning the opposite direction at the bridge would be in open territory within a few miles. Any farmhouses would be few and far between. The ranch nearest the bridge had been abandoned for years so, if Emily looked for help, she wouldn't find any.

The ground turned rocky, making tracking impossible.

"I should have told her not to ride alone," Sage complained. "I should have warned her of the danger and not just told her how much fun it was. I should have—"

"Stop," Teagen cut in. "We'll find her."

"It'll be dark in less than an hour." Sage yelled Emily's name.

No answer.

"We'll find her." He thought of the frightened little girl

who couldn't even look him in the eye. "I'll find her," he whispered, knowing that he'd stay out all night if need be.

They moved on slowly, not sure what direction would be best. It looked like she turned around once, twice, three times. She must have been panicking. At one point she rode off the trail, and he couldn't tell which way she'd turned. Since Sage hadn't crossed her path coming home, it made sense she headed in the wrong direction at the bridge, but Teagen could find no tracks after the first mile. He should have added a second rule this morning. A rule that said never cross the bridge alone.

A little after dark, they saw a campfire in the trees. Teagen signaled Sage to be careful as they walked their horses toward it. He guessed if the campsite were Indians, they'd already heard the horses. If it was an outlaw gang, they'd be lucky to get away without shooting. Sage would be as good as either of his brothers if firing started, but he didn't want to think about what might happen if the fight came down to fists. Most of him wanted to tell her to turn around and go back, but a small part knew his life might depend on having backup.

He'd also bet she wouldn't leave him, no matter how loudly he ordered. Sage had always thought she was one of them, a full partner in the running of the ranch.

As they crossed through the trees and spotted the camp, Teagen took a long breath and relaxed when he saw only two men by the fire. From the way they had their gear stowed and their horses staked, they were traveling, not raiding.

"Hello the fire," he called.

Both men reached for their rifles but didn't take aim.

"State your name and purpose?" came the answer.

"Teagen McMurray, and I mean you no harm."

To his surprise both rifles lowered. "Come on in, Mr. McMurray. You're welcome to share our coffee."

Teagen frowned, suspecting a trap.

Sage pushed forward. "They must not know you if they're welcoming you," she teased.

They both kept their guns ready as they walked in. The fire

was small, and from the looks of it the men only had coffee boiling. He saw no hint of food or game.

From twenty feet away, Teagen recognized both men. They were Rangers that Travis had introduced him to in Austin. Tattor Sims, somewhat of a legend for never being wounded in more than a dozen fights, and Dolan Hatch, who lost his family twenty years ago and swore he'd never settle anywhere until buried. Travis had said to call on them if Teagen ever needed guards. It had been so long since he'd sent the letter, he'd almost forgotten about asking them to come.

Teagen moved closer. "Sims and Hatch, welcome. I expected you sooner, but I'm glad you're here tonight."

"We would have arrived yesterday." Sims stepped closer. "But we ran into a bit of trouble on the road and had to talk a couple of horse thieves into changing occupations before moving on."

Dolan laughed at Sims's choice of words but said nothing.

Teagen nodded at Sage, and they lowered their guns. "This is my sister, gentlemen. Sage, these are the guards I hired, Tattor Sims and Dolan Hatch."

Sage stepped forward and offered her hand to each of the older men. "You could have ridden on in tonight. You weren't far from the ranch."

Sims shook his head. "We didn't think it would be a good idea to ride in after sunset. We figured tomorrow morning would be soon enough." His watery-blue eyes stared at Teagen, then the old man lifted one eyebrow. "You got trouble already, don't you?"

Teagen figured Sims had been around long enough to smell trouble. Dolan hadn't said a word, but Teagen didn't miss the fact he watched every movement. If he were guessing, Teagen would say no one ever got the jump on Hatch. Maybe the two men's talents had kept them alive long enough to turn gray.

Sims had an easy, friendly manner about him, but Teagen remembered Travis saying once that Tattor Sims was lightning-fast with a gun. Now he looked more like a kindly grandfather than a gunslinger.

Sage explained about Emily being lost. The old Rangers listened as they collected their gear.

"I've already checked the road to town. She has to have gone this way unless she struck out across open land or somehow crossed back over the bridge unnoticed."

"What kind of horse is she riding?" Sims asked.

"The best, a McMurray horse," Teagen answered. "But the palomino's old. The mare wouldn't do much more than a walk unless something spooked her."

Sims spoke his thoughts. "Some outlaw might knock the kid out of the saddle and take the horse. Or a few might even capture her to use in trade. There are those who'd pay good money for a little white girl."

Teagen didn't even want to think about that possibility. If it were true, Emily could be miles away by now, probably headed toward Mexico. They'd never find her.

"If my horse gets the chance, she'll turn toward home," Sage said. "She's old enough to want her stall when it gets dark."

Teagen motioned for Sage to climb up, then he turned to the Rangers. "The riding won't be easy at night. We'll go back to the bridge and spread out. If she fell off, she'll be on foot and frightened. We have to find her."

No one argued. They rode back to the bridge.

Teagen could see the main house. It had to be after ten, but every lantern in the place was lit as if calling to Emily. He thought he could make out Jessie standing on the porch, her arms folded over her chest like she always did when she was worried. Part of him wanted to ride in and tell her everything was going to be all right, but with each hour passing, he grew more uncertain. If Emily had stepped down or fallen from Glory, the horse might have returned to the barn. At this point, seeing Glory would offer some hope, but they both seemed to have vanished.

He searched the dark yard to the left of the ranch house. If anything had happened since he and Sage left, Martha would have fired off three shots and lit the wash fires beside the house. She'd keep them burning high until they saw the signal.

Sims pointed with his head toward the tepees. "You got company?"

"Family," Teagen answered. Since they knew Travis in Austin, they knew the McMurrays were part Apache. He and Tobin looked like their father, but Travis favored their mother's people. "Some of the men from that camp are riding the ranch land just in case."

"Good," Sims said simply. "How about we ride in and get lanterns? If the kid sees a light, she might find us."

Teagen was so tired and worried he hadn't thought of lanterns. "You're right. We'll ride in. Sage and I will fill lanterns, and you men eat a bite. If I know Martha, she'll have food waiting." If they had no food at their campfire, he could pretty well guess that they hadn't eaten all day.

When they rode back to the house, Teagen only took a minute with introductions, then he went to saddle fresh horses and get the lanterns.

He wasn't surprised when Jessie followed him. "Can I help? I have to do something."

He looked into her brown eyes, wishing he could ease a little of the pain he saw there. "We'll find her."

"I know." She worked at his side, filling every extra barn lantern. By the time they'd finished, the Rangers were back at their horses, still chewing their food. Sage handed him a roll stuffed with a slice of ham, but Teagen knew he could never get it down. All he could think about was Emily, frightened and alone out in the dark. Even if she hadn't been kidnapped, she was lost and maybe hurt.

They mounted. Jessie tied the last of the lanterns on when Dolan Hatch stood in his saddle and said calmly, "Someone's coming."

Teagen looked toward the bridge. He saw nothing in the darkness for a moment, then, with everyone frozen, he heard what sounded like a low hum.

All stood ready.

A black horse and a rider dressed in midnight slowly materialized out of the shadows. Drummond Roak was riding easily as if he carried something with great care. His head bent low, he hummed what sounded like a lullaby as he cradled his charge.

Jessie was the first one to break and run toward him. Teagen followed on horseback. They reached the kid at the same time.

"Evening," Roak said with a smile. "I found this little one down by the creek near town and remembered she belonged to you."

He lifted his coat to reveal a sleeping Emily in his arm. "Came with me when I told her I'd take her home, but she was so scared, she cried herself to sleep. She kept saying she had to get back to the mountain 'cause it was a rule."

Carefully, he handed her down to Jessie.

"Thank you," she whispered as she hugged her daughter. "Thank you so much."

Roak shoved back his hat and smiled. "You're welcome, Widow Barton. She told me she was riding to meet you and Sage, but when she passed the place where Mister had refilled the canteen, she decided to get a drink. Apparently no one told the child how to tie a horse up. She's been wandering around looking for Glory."

Sage kissed Emily's cheek. "Thank the Lord she's safe." She looked up at Roak. "What about my horse, Glory?"

"I thought I saw her grazing about a quarter mile downstream. I figured she'd be all right till morning."

Sage patted his leg. "Thank you."

"You're welcome, darlin'."

Teagen felt like a weight had been lifted off his chest. "Would you like to come in, Roak?" He tried his best to say it like he meant it.

"No. But I will bring that old palomino back come morning, say around breakfast time."

"You'll be welcome." Teagen meant the words. This was the second time Roak had helped the McMurrays, and he owed him friendship, no matter how much the kid irritated him.

Jessie thanked Roak one more time, then took Emily inside. Martha followed, fretting over the child as if she were Em's grandmother.

Roak looked down at Sage. "Since you're already saddled, how about riding with me to the bridge?"

"All right." She smiled. "But don't get any ideas."

They were halfway to the bridge with Teagen still wondering what Sage had been talking about. He turned to the Rangers. "Well, it wasn't as long a night as we feared. I'll show you to the bunkhouse and let you settle in. Tomorrow, at dawn, I'll explain everything."

Sims grinned. "Sounds good. I'm looking forward to sleeping on a bed. The ground gets harder every year."

Hatch offered to take care of the horses.

As Teagen walked to the bunkhouse Sims said, "Travis told us you were having trouble. We've done this kind of thing before. Between the three of us there won't be a time when someone isn't watching over the ranch."

"Four," Teagen said. "Sage will do her part."

"I should have figured that," Sims agreed. "All the Rangers know about her. We were real sad when Mike Saddler died. He was a good man, and from the way he talked about your sister, I know he planned to offer marriage."

Teagen looked off toward the rise in the land where three bodies lay. "We buried him here," he said. "I think it's where he would have wanted to be. Travis told me once that Mike said the best he could hope for in life was a woman to cry over his grave. I guess he got that."

"We all liked him."

Sims scratched his week-old stubble. "By the way, how'd that rider get past those Apache down at the bridge?"

Teagen shrugged. "He was riding a McMurray horse. I guess they figured he was one of us."

The old man nodded as Teagen opened the door to the small bunkhouse. The place was rarely used because the McMurrays never hired men they didn't know well. Most were Rangers Travis had served with.

"There's a stove and coffee for the making."

Sims seemed far more interested in the bunks lining each wall.

"You're welcome to eat breakfast in the main house tomorrow, but if I know Martha, she'll have it on your porch as soon as she sees you're up and around. Once things settle down, Martha will have your supper waiting in here." Teagen knew, like most men who live ranging, they'd prefer to be alone. Here they could have an evening whiskey and a smoke without womenfolk to complain. "After breakfast she'll have a sack with enough food to last you until supper."

"Sounds mighty nice." Sims smiled. "It ain't often we get three meals a day. Better watch it, McMurray, or we'll find reasons to stay."

"The work's hard. You'll be in the saddle from dawn to after dark. But the food is good." He thought of the meal he'd had at the café with Jessie. "Better than you'll ever get in town."

"So I've heard." Sims smiled wide enough to show a few gaps where teeth had been.

Teagen had talked all he could manage. If Sims planned to chat, he'd have to do it with Hatch. He said good night and walked back into the house.

The kitchen was empty for a change. Teagen knew Martha would have turned in the minute Emily was safe in her bed. With everyone asleep, he decided to take a bath. He thought of drawing water and heating it, but it seemed like too much effort. He grabbed a towel and soap and headed out.

Stepping onto the porch, he heard Sage return. Before she reached the barn, he caught up to her. "You get rid of the kid?"

"Yes." She slid down and walked beside her brother. "But I fear he'll be back in the morning."

"You should be nicer to him," Teagen said in his usual ordering way. "He helped us out tonight."

"What?"

Before Teagen could answer, his little sister did what she'd done since she was old enough to walk. She tripped him.

He stumbled three steps but didn't hit the ground. Swearing, he picked up his hat and faced her. "I should have whipped you when I had the chance, Sage. You're going to break one of our legs someday doing that."

She laughed. "That's what you get for acting like I'm the only one mean to Roak. I try harder than the three of you do to talk to him. So don't go telling me to be nice to him."

Teagen looked at her. She was small, only slightly bigger than Jessie, but there was a world of difference between them. Sage was tough. He guessed she had to be to grow up around three big brothers. At almost twenty, she knew her own mind. She loved horses and the ranch, but she also loved doctoring people. She'd delivered half the babies born around here last year and helped the doctor who dropped by twice a year. He'd bet his boots the bags she brought back from Austin were full of books on how to heal both animals and humans.

"All right," he admitted. "I'll try to at least speak to the boy, but I got the feeling he's like a stray cat. He'll want to hang around the house and eat, but he's bone-wild and will turn on us one day."

"I don't know. Strange, how he brought Emily back. Seeing how he hates you, he could have just taken her to Elmo's place and left her. Someone would have seen her back here."

"He may hate me, but he loves you."

She shook her head. "A kid like that doesn't know what love is. He wasn't raised around caring folks. He's never had anyone who noticed if he lived or died. He may think he likes me, but if it came right down to it, I doubt he'd risk his life for me or anyone else."

She turned toward the barn.

Teagen tugged the reins. "I'll take care of the horse. You get some sleep."

"I don't mind."

"No, I need to ride down to the creek for a swim anyway."

Sage grinned. "Too many women in the house for you to bathe in the mud room."

"Something like that."

He rode toward the creek. The passing clouds revealed little moonlight, but it didn't matter. All his plans for the evening were gone. No ride to the east pasture. No talk with Jessie. In a moment he was back to being alone.

Telling himself that was exactly how he wanted it, Teagen stripped and dove into the water. Jessie and her daughters would be gone soon. It made sense to cut any ties with them now. Starting tomorrow, Sage could look after their company, and he'd go back to work.

He didn't need or want to be close to anyone. She'd just been interesting company, nothing more.

The warm summer air dried his body as he stepped out of the water. They'd had no rain since the day of the stage holdup over two weeks ago. The grass felt stiff beneath his feet as he dried off. If it didn't rain soon, he'd have to start worrying, but tonight all were home and safe. Tonight he could relax.

CHAPTER 15

JESSIE WATCHED HER DAUGHTERS SLEEPING. EMILY SO fair, Rose with her midnight braids, and little Bethie with auburn curls. They were as mixed a batch as a calico cat's kittens, but Jessie thought each one beautiful. She said a silent prayer for their safety. Here was her life. No matter what she had to do, she'd protect them.

She heard Sage climb the stairs.

"Good night, Jessie," Sage whispered as she paused in passing.

"Good night." Jessie liked having someone to say it to. "Sleep well, and thanks again for all your help."

Sage's smile was earnest, but exhaustion reflected in her eyes a moment before she turned and moved on to her room. She closed her door softly. The three bedrooms upstairs were exactly the same. Three rooms for the three boys who'd grown up here. Now, the little girls slept in the middle, safe and sound, with Jessie on one side and Sage on the other.

Jessie had never felt so safe in her life. Leaving here would be the hardest thing she ever had to do, but somehow she'd manage. Maybe Teagen would help her get to Austin, and she could find work there once her child was born and Teagen realized no relatives were coming. Sage had mentioned the capital was large enough to have three bookstores already, and it seemed to grow daily.

The house was quiet as she moved to her bed, but her nerves still vibrated with the echoes of fear. She tried to sleep but couldn't make her eyes stay closed. Too many thoughts of what might have happened flashed in her mind like strikes of lightning. Blinking away tears, Jessie swore she would not cry, not now, not when Emily was safe.

Finally, frustrated, she tiptoed down the stairs looking for something to read. Books had been a comfort all her life. It really didn't matter which one she picked up; reading would calm her.

She was well into the study when she realized Teagen sat in his big leather chair by a cold fireplace. He hadn't lit a lamp, but moonlight streamed through the window, offering a low glow to the room.

She stood stone-still, watching him. His eyes were closed. His hair shiny as if wet. The powerful man looked younger in sleep. Here was the man she'd called friend for half her life. He'd always been with her, even though he wasn't aware she lived.

She moved as silently as possible, not wanting to wake him. He'd shared her fears and panic today, and tomorrow she'd thank him. Right now, she wanted to let him sleep while he could. Teagen pushed himself too hard. Jessie guessed he always had.

She pulled a book from the shelf without even looking at the title.

Halfway back across the room, she glanced over her shoulder and saw him watching her.

"I'm sorry," she whispered. "I didn't mean to wake you."

"You didn't."

She took a step closer, thankful for the night. She hadn't slipped on a robe before heading downstairs and thought she must look like a ghost haunting the study. "Thank you for all your help," she said. "I don't know what I would have done . . ." Her voice broke at the thought of what might have been.

He watched her a moment, then asked, "Aren't we going to have my lesson in conversation tonight, Jessie?"

She had a feeling he was smiling, even though his face was in shadow.

"It's very late."

"True," he answered. "But you're not asleep. And from that book you just picked up, I'd say you plan to be awake for a little longer."

She moved closer. "I couldn't . . ." Her voice broke again as the fear she'd felt all afternoon flooded her mind. "I almost lost my Em." The tears she'd blocked all afternoon long piled behind her eyes. "If I'd stayed in Chicago? If I'd let her grandmother raise her? If I'd been strong enough to fight them? I wouldn't have put her in danger. She—"

"Stop, Jessie." Teagen's order reached her ears, but her emotions were too raw for her to hear.

"It's foolish to cry now," she said as she shoved tears off her cheek with her palm. "I don't know what's wrong with me. I seem to cry at every opportunity."

Her body shook as if a war raged inside.

"Jessie." Teagen leaned forward and took her hand. "Jessie," he said as he pulled her near. "It's all right now. Em is safe upstairs, asleep with her sisters."

His tone was still more order than comfort, but he was trying. She laughed at his effort. "I'm crying and laughing at the same time."

"I know." He sounded as confused as she felt. "Come here."

She crumpled into his embrace. Like a child needing strong arms to hold her, Jessie melted atop him and let the tears come.

For a while he just held her. Peace settled over her even while tears fell. When she stopped crying, she felt no desire to leave the comfort she'd found. Part of her had turned to Teagen a dozen times in her dreams. There, he'd always held her and told her all would be fine, just as he did now.

Jessie closed her eyes and savored the tender time.

She wasn't aware of how long she'd been in his arms. Maybe a few minutes, maybe an hour. Awaking from a dreamless sleep, she felt Teagen's slow breath brush her throat and realized he'd also fallen asleep.

If she was heavy on his legs, he showed no sign. One arm

rested over her hip, another braced her back. She cupped his chin with her hand and whispered, "Teagen, Teagen?"

He shifted. His arm tightened around her waist.

"No," he said more asleep than awake. "Don't leave yet."

She smiled. He didn't sound nearly so stern. She rested her head on his shoulder and promised, "I won't." They were both too tired to care that what they were doing wouldn't be considered at all proper. "Tonight, there is nowhere I'd rather be."

His arm tugged her against him. "Good," he whispered into her hair. "Then let me hold you for a while."

CHAPTER 16

TEAGEN WOKE AT FIRST LIGHT. HE SHIFTED, STRAIGHT-ening his leg that seemed to have fallen asleep during the night. Without opening his eyes, he knew why. Jessie's bottom rested on it. She'd spent the night in his arms.

Slowly he opened his eyes, hoping his slight movement wouldn't wake her. He studied the bundle of cotton and lace cuddled against him. She looked so young with her hair down around her shoulders and her cheeks streaked with the tears she'd cried last night. Even now, with her sleeping against him, he couldn't believe she'd come to him so easily. He'd lifted his arms, offering her a hug, and she'd climbed into his lap without hesitation.

There were grown men who crossed the street to avoid him, and Jessie cuddled right against his heart.

He frowned. He had no idea grown women did such a thing. Maybe none of them did except Jessie. She seemed far too unique to serve as his reference about how all women act.

The thought worried him that he didn't know if she needed him or just needed someone, and he happened to be near. If it was just someone the little widow needed, he could be that for her, but Teagen found himself wishing that it were the other.

He gently stroked her arm, wondering what it would be like to have this tender soul want him. No woman had ever wanted him. A few had acted like they did for the price of a tumble, but he knew they lied. He could see it in their eyes. When he'd been in his early twenties and it was safe to leave the ranch, he'd let himself believe what they said, but deep down he'd known the truth.

He'd finally turned away, not needing their kind of affection. He had more important things to do, like raising his siblings and holding the ranch.

By the time he'd thought of looking at any of the girls from around these parts, he'd hardened so much they considered him old and frightening. At twenty-five he'd been too old for the girls just growing into womanhood and too young to settle. So he'd done the only thing he knew. He'd worked.

Looking at Jessie, he realized now what he had missed. A wife. Children. A woman to fall asleep with. Something so simple seemed a strange thing to long for. He'd read all the great biographies where men wanted wealth and power. For him, could it be too little to dream of or too much to want, someone to sleep beside?

Teagen shook his head. He wasn't making sense. He'd been working too hard lately.

The memory of Jessie telling him that Eli had gone to the pub every night drifted into his thoughts. How could the man have preferred a room full of drunks to what now lay in Teagen's arms?

Eli had written grand letters, but the man must have been a fool to leave her alone.

Teagen brushed the cotton of her gown. He didn't even know how to touch her. She was small, almost fragile. Not the kind of woman he'd need.

He wrapped a strand of her hair around his finger, wishing she'd wear it down during the day. Swearing beneath his breath, he called himself an ass for letting his mind wander where he had no business going. She wasn't his. She'd never be. Even if she wasn't planning to go to California, she wouldn't stay out here. This land was raw and hard even on women born to it.

And he wouldn't want her anyway. It might be interesting to have a house full of girls for a few weeks, but not forever. He had all he could handle already. He had no time for a family.

"Not now, not ever," he mumbled as he let go of the hem of her gown.

She stirred and looked up at him.

He'd expected surprise or embarrassment or even anger. But Jessie just smiled a shy smile at him as if sleeping with him had been something quite ordinary.

"I'm sorry," she whispered. "I guess I fell asleep."

"We both did." He watched her carefully, waiting for emotion to fire her brown eyes. He wouldn't have been surprised if she yelled and blamed him for what had happened without either of them planning it to.

She stretched, unaware how he felt her body brush against him. "I meant to say good night, but I guess it's too late now." They watched the sun's first light sparkle into the room.

"We could act like it's not all that late." He set her feet on the floor in front of him.

Pushing against his chest to stand, she agreed to his game. "Good night, Teagen." Just before she straightened, she leaned in to kiss him.

Teagen turned just as her lips lowered, and their mouths touched. For a moment neither of them moved; then, before he changed his mind, he kissed her. Not a friendly peck or a light thank-you kiss, but a real first kiss, more promise than passion.

She pulled away, wide awake now. "Oh," she managed.

"Oh, what?" Teagen snapped, angry that he'd stepped over the line.

"Just oh." She touched her fingertips to her lips. Then, like a ghost at dawn, she disappeared.

Teagen sat in his chair. He could still feel the warmth of her on his lap. He'd slept sounder in the chair than he'd slept in weeks. Part of him wanted to run after her and demand what *oh* meant. She didn't look embarrassed or angry. He frowned. Or all that interested, either. If he didn't know better, he'd think she had never been kissed. But that was ridiculous. The woman had been married half her life. She had three kids and another on the way.

He tugged on his boots and headed out to ride the sunrise boundaries. Maybe the morning air would clear his mind.

Tattor Sims and Dolan Hatch stood on the bunkhouse porch drinking coffee when he walked out. They both fell into step when Teagen headed for the barn. With very few words between them, the men saddled up and began their first day.

By the time they'd covered the eastern border, the old Rangers knew what their jobs were. Both were good trackers. If anyone stepped foot on McMurray land, they'd be able to tell. Tattor liked to talk now and then, but Dolan Hatch never did more than nod that he understood.

When they circled back to the house, the men found their breakfast waiting for them in the bunkhouse. Martha said good morning but didn't waste a second being friendly.

Teagen felt the need to explain. He didn't want the men taking her curtness personally. She was an equal opportunity hater of men in general.

Before he could say more than a few words, Tattor waved him away. "We know about your housekeeper. When we rode with your brother, he used to tell us stories about her."

Dolan grinned, and Tattor continued, "Did she really toss out your meals if you didn't wash up before you went inside?"

"Yes." Teagen remembered being in his twenties before it occurred to him that everyone's housekeeper might not threaten to let them starve if they ever gave away all the carrots in the bin again, or used the washtub for target practice, or skinned rabbits in the mud room. He could name a hundred more, and it appeared his brother had done just that.

Both men looked at each other. "If it's all the same to you, McMurray, we'll be happy to eat our meals in the bunkhouse." Tattor might have voiced the words, but both men nodded.

Teagen headed for the house. "I understand completely," he mumbled to himself.

As he stepped off the porch, he heard Tattor Sims add in a whisper, "That Martha is one fine-looking woman."

Teagen couldn't be sure, but he thought he heard Dolan answer, "If you like porcupines."

He fought the urge to turn around and question Tattor Sims's eyesight. Never, not once, had anyone called Martha a "fine-looking woman," but then very few people had seen her over the years. To the boys she was just Martha, probably old enough to be their mother and meaner than a rattler on a hot day.

If Tattor wanted to look, let him look . . . but if he wanted to keep all his teeth, he'd better do so from a safe distance. Teagen almost laughed out loud. He could guess what Martha would do to the old ranger if he so much as winked at her. Tattor would think the badlands along the border were summer rain compared to the storm of Martha angry.

Walking across the yard, Teagen realized he hadn't had time to think about the way he'd kissed Jessie. He figured that once she thought about it, she'd have far more to say than "Oh." Only problem was, he'd have no answer about why he'd done such a thing. It certainly wasn't proper, he knew that much.

The only other fact he knew for certain was that he wanted to do it again.

He could hear all the girls in the kitchen when he moved onto the porch. Carrying two buckets of water, he stepped inside.

Sage held Bethie on her lap. His sister was the one covered in oatmeal today, but she didn't look like she minded. She made funny sounds to make the baby laugh.

Emily, for once, wasn't waiting by the door to go riding. He felt sure her riding days were over, at least until Jessie forgot some of the fear she'd carried last night.

Rose had crawled under the table and pulled the tablecloth low to the floor.

"Do you know what I am?" Rose saw Teagen first.

"No," he answered, guessing she didn't want to hear that she was a noisy little girl who asked far too many questions.

"I'm an Indian, and this is my tepee."

"Oh," he said, then caught Jessie's eye as he realized he had repeated the last word she'd said to him at dawn. He could see it in her stare. She was also aware of the parallel.

"Sit down, Teagen, or you'll miss your breakfast." Jessie

tugged her middle daughter out of her tepee. "Breakfast, my wild one."

Rose saw tiny fried apple pies on the table and started asking how apples could get in the pockets.

Teagen looked for an empty chair. The kitchen was almost full. If anyone else came home, they'd all be taking meals in the dining room.

Jessie helped Martha set the food on the table, then took the chair next to him. She only greeted him with a nod.

"Did everyone sleep well?" he asked awkwardly.

Martha raised an eyebrow. "Since when did you care, Teagen? I've been here for almost twenty years, and you've never checked on my slumber habits."

Teagen squashed the growl he felt rumbling up. Emily already thought he was a bear. There was no sense adding to her theory. He forced a corner of his lip into almost a smile. "Maybe I'm working on my conversation skills?"

"It's about time." Sage laughed, and Martha joined in.

Teagen thought of telling both his sister and the housekeeper what they could do with their gay mood, but before he could form words, Jessie's leg touched his beneath the table.

He forgot what he planned to say. He forgot to breathe. This wasn't an accidental brush or an impersonal pat. The lady was touching him on purpose.

Above the table, Jessie offered him more coffee in a proper voice. Underneath the table, her body rested against his, and all the clothes in the world couldn't have blocked the heat he felt.

"You're not eating much, Teagen," Martha commented. "Maybe you're not getting enough sleep."

He heard the giggle in her words, but he didn't care. "I slept better than I have in months last night." Forcing himself not to look at Jessie, he added, "It must be getting cooler."

Sage fed Bethie bites of egg. "I heard someone in Austin say that it may be an early fall this year."

"How would anyone know that?" Martha shook her head.

Sage and Jessie began to tell all the signs for forecasting the weather. Teagen stopped listening. He didn't care if it snowed tomorrow. Jessie's leg moved gently against his trousers.

Rose scooted off her chair and came to stand next to Teagen. "What do caterpillars taste like?"

"I don't know." Teagen studied the child. She had her mother's eyes. "Why do you want to know?"

She smiled, loving having an adult's attention. "I saw a chicken eat one."

"I see," he said. "Did the chicken look happy? Did she smile after she ate it?"

Rose shook her head.

"Then I'm guessing it didn't taste so good."

Rose accepted the answer and hurried off to find what had become of *her* egg basket. Martha had made her one special with a ribbon on top and deep enough so an egg didn't accidentally roll out.

"Those hens are not pets. Do you hear me, Rose," Martha yelled behind her. "And you remember to leave that setting nest alone."

Teagen shook his head. First they stopped eating the pigs, and it looked like the chickens would be next. Before long he'd be having dinner with the horses.

He stood, and Jessie did the same. She was so close they were almost touching. No one seemed to notice.

"Would you walk with me to the barn?" He tried to think of a reason in case she asked why.

"All right," she answered.

Teagen went out without a backward look. He heard Jessie tell Emily to help her sister gather eggs and ask Sage to keep an eye on Bethie for a few minutes. He was almost halfway to the barn when she caught up to him.

Walking in silence, he thought of what he needed to say to her. He wanted her to know that nothing about last night or this morning had been planned. If he had to, he decided he'd even say he was sorry, but the lie would probably taste a lot like a caterpillar going down.

It didn't seem right to apologize for something he wouldn't mind doing again. But he didn't want to have her think ill of him. It occurred to Teagen she might be the first person in the world that he cared about what she thought of him.

When they stepped into the cool shadows of the barn, she slipped her hand in his. The simple gesture rattled all thought from his brain.

Teagen pulled her into the darkness behind the barn door. A heartbeat later, she was in his arms. He lowered his mouth over hers and kissed her again as he had in the study. It might not have been a kiss of passion, but it was a hell of a lot more than friendship.

She gave no response, and after a few seconds he figured he'd be hearing "Oh" again real soon.

He raised his head, noticing Jessie had braced her hands against his chest. She'd been pushing on him, and he hadn't even noticed.

"Teagen," she whispered. "Put me down."

He lowered her to the ground and forced himself to take a step backward. The last thing he wanted was to frighten her; he'd done enough damage already. "If you're waiting for an apology, you'll have to give me time to muster that big a lie."

She smiled. "There is no need to apologize."

"Then why did you ask me to put you down?" He'd spent more time trying not to yell since he'd met her than he had in his entire life.

She looked down and walked toward the back of the barn with her arms crossed tightly over her blouse.

He waited. Whatever she said, he'd take it full-on.

Finally, she put her hand in his again and said, "Could we walk out the back door of the barn and look at the horses?"

Teagen almost said he had a full day of work to do and walking wasn't one of his planned chores, but he nodded his agreement. "I need to check to see if Roak brought the horse back."

"I thought he planned to have breakfast with us?"

"That's what he said, but the kid's a shadow. I have a feeling he's wearing all black these days because he figures he can move more freely at night. I wouldn't be surprised at anything he tried, but one thing I know, the boy will never bother our stock. He might steal everything else he could carry, though."

They stepped into the sunny pasture at the back of the barn. Watching Jessie, he knew this conversation wasn't the one she wanted to talk about. He had no idea how to bring up the kiss in the barn. She wasn't acting like she was mad at him, but a gnat could notice she hadn't welcomed his kiss.

When they reached the fence, Teagen propped his leg on the first rail and watched her as she stared at the horses. A week-old midnight colt danced around his mother, who ignored him as she grazed.

Jessie laughed at the sight, and Teagen relaxed. Whatever she planned to say to him couldn't be terrible, because it didn't seem to weigh too heavily on her mind.

"There's Glory," she shouted.

Teagen looked over near the trees and saw the palomino grazing as if she'd never left the ranch. Roak had kept his word. He'd brought the horse back. Growling, he realized he'd have to thank the kid again.

Jessie laughed as if she'd read his mind.

They stood, less than a foot apart, but very much aware of each other. There was something about being near her that made him feel like he should at least try to be a better man. He wondered if she had that effect on all people or just him.

The morning was still cool, the air dry. This time of year, summer took its toll on the land, making the days hot and rain scarce. The green of spring dried into shades of brown. In the fall this part of his land would be beautiful with color and cool days, but not now.

She leaned against the fence and looked at him. He didn't know what to do. He just stood beside her, feeling as big as a tree next to her . . . and about as bright. He could manage one of the biggest ranches in Texas, but he couldn't figure out one woman.

"Would you teach me to drive a buggy?" she asked.

"I said I would," he answered.

"Would you teach me to fire a gun? I may need the skill on the way to California."

"I will, if that's what you want."

Her next request came as a whisper. "Would you teach me how to kiss?"

Teagen looked down into her eyes. "You don't know?"

She shook her head. "This morning was the first time I've ever felt a man's lips on mine. I wasn't sure what to do. I felt like a fool. Most girls know something so simple long before they marry."

A hundred questions avalanched through Teagen's mind, but he didn't want to pry. Finally, he settled on one. "You figure you'll need that skill on the way to California?"

She laughed. "No. I don't think I'll ever need the skill, period. But I'd like to know what the romantics write about." She looked away, watching the colt again. "I need you to tell me how, and I don't want the kiss to come as a surprise. I'll need time to get ready for it, so I can do it right."

He wasn't at all sure he was qualified as an instructor, but he didn't like the thought that she might go in search of another teacher. "Fair enough," he said. "How much notice do you need?"

A minute seemed about right to him, but she whispered, "A day."

Before he could debate that a kiss didn't seem like something that should be planned, Rose and Emily exploded into the calm pasture.

"Look, Mister, look." Rose held out a toad. "We found him."

Emily followed her sister and added, "He's ugly, isn't he. Even uglier than mud, and Martha says that's ugly."

"He keeps wetting on me." Rose made a face. "He's so fat and slippery. Can I keep him?"

"No," Jessie said, staring at the toad.

Teagen squatted down and studied their find. "This toad has an important job. He's not a pet. All day long, he catches flies. If it weren't for him, those flies would be bothering the horses."

"He eats them?" Rose made a face.

"I'm afraid so. Loves them, from all I can tell." Teagen fought to keep from laughing.

"So you don't think he'd like to live in the house?" Rose sounded disappointed. "Do you think he could hop up the stairs to my room? We taught Bethie to climb up and down the steps. I guess we could teach him."

Teagen shook his head. "He'd hate it, but he probably wouldn't mind if you visit him every day. Toads like folks to wave now and then just to be friendly."

Rose lowered the toad to the ground. "I'll add it to my list of things I have to do, but he may not be easy to find."

As the toad hopped away, both girls followed behind him in a line. They jumped each time the toad jumped, looking so ridiculous, Teagen had to smile.

Jessie took a few steps to follow them, then turned and looked back over her shoulder. "Until tonight, Teagen."

He headed to the barn, wondering if she were giving him her one-day notice. The idea of performing on a time line didn't much appeal to him. But the thought of Jessie kissing him back this time would be something he'd wait all day for.

CHAPTER 17

THE DAY WAS FILLED WITH WORK. JESSIE AND MARTHA did the laundry and made bread. Sage took a few hours to take the girls on a hike up to Lookout Point. By the time they got back, the little ones were so tired they could barely eat lunch. Bethie fell asleep on her bread, and the butter made it stick to her face. Jessie cleaned it off and carried her upstairs without waking her.

"I used to sleep like that." Sage yawned when Jessie returned. "My brothers teased me that they gave me the downstairs bedroom in case I got fat and they could no longer carry me to bed."

Jessie smiled. "It must have been hard being the only girl."

"It was sometimes, but mostly it was grand." Sage added, "Did you have any brothers or sisters?"

"No. I was an only child of two people whose families were dead before I was old enough to remember even one of them. My parents were best friends as well as all the family they had. I don't think one would have wanted to live on after losing the other. I buried them within a week of each other, and I remember thinking that they must have walked into heaven together."

Sage nodded as if she understood, but Jessie knew someone surrounded by brothers could never know what being totally alone felt like. When she'd been thirteen and first realized she was all alone, she'd been too frightened to breathe. She'd left what had been her home with nothing but a change of clothes in an old pillowcase.

Sage was halfway through a story about growing up with brothers before Jessie pulled away from memories and started listening.

After the dishes were done, Sage rode out to check on a horse that had stepped into a hole. She promised not to be long, but Jessie had figured out the girl's schedule. Once she was on horseback, time didn't matter much to her.

Martha settled into the great room to quilt, leaving Jessie alone. She curled into Teagen's big chair with a book, planning to spend an hour reading, but the memory of last night was all around her.

She had no idea why she'd asked Teagen to teach her to kiss. It seemed a foolish thing to bother with when there were so many other skills she needed, but she wanted to know. Funny, she thought, all her life in the bookstore when she'd read a book and the writer described a kiss or a touch, it had always been Teagen she'd thought of touching or kissing, never Eli. For a time she'd called him her shadow man because, though she couldn't see his face, she felt close to him.

Her husband had saved her from the streets when she'd been a child. It took her a few years before she realized that he'd done it for himself, not for her. At first he'd tried to be kind, always making sure she had food and teaching her the bookstore business. Then, once he trusted her, he'd left, and she'd known that behind all his kindness had been his need to escape. As long as she was there, running the store, making it look right, doing the ordering, paying the bills, then to his family he was making a go of it.

When Emily was born, things changed. Eli began to resent them both. He stayed away later and later, then slept the days away. When he woke, he complained that she wasn't keeping up with everything as well as she once had. The only real fights they had were when Jessie tried to stop the drinking, and the only conversations they ever had were about changes that needed to be made in the store.

Years ago, with Eli cold and distant and no way to leave the store to look for companions, Teagen became her only friend.

He was the one she talked to. He was the one she always wanted to share her problems with. He'd been the one she thought of kissing. Not so much because he was real to her but more because he was all she had.

Jessie brushed the arm of the leather chair. Tonight, she'd cross the line from him being in her mind to being real.

She spread her fingers over her tummy. The baby would move soon. Then, for the rest of her life she'd live for her children. She'd be a mother until she was old and gray, and then she'd be a grandmother. But not tonight. For a few hours when no one needed her and all the chores were done, she wanted to know what it was like to be a woman, if only for one kiss.

The rest of the day passed in a haze. Jessie worked well with Martha. Since she'd had little time to spend in the kitchen and Martha had spent her life there, they bonded as instructor and pupil. Each day the housekeeper showed her another skill. She'd say, "You'll need this on the trail," or, "Once you're settled in a new place, this will make things easier." From how to keep the bugs out of the flour to how to make piecrust a dozen at a time, Martha taught, and Jessie learned.

The day passed in an easy routine of chores and talk. When she saw Teagen come in, Jessie was surprised it was almost dark.

He didn't look at her as he sat down at the table with Rose on his left and Emily on his right. They had egg sandwiches for supper. Teagen didn't say a word.

When Martha served his favorite chocolate pie, she said as if he'd complained about the meal, "We got too many eggs these days. I didn't want none of them going bad."

Teagen raised an eyebrow. "Mighty fine sandwich."

Sage broke the silence with a giggle. "Are you paying a compliment?"

"No," Teagen answered, "just stating a fact."

"Feel his forehead, Martha. My brother must have a fever. I think I've heard him voice two compliments in one decade."

Martha walked away. She never came between the Mc-

Murrays, whether they were fighting or teasing one another. It was none of her business, she'd often said.

Rose jumped out of her chair and stood beside Teagen. "Can I touch your forehead, Mister? Will it burn?"

"No," Teagen said.

Jessie set her fork down to watch. She knew Rose would never stop so easily.

"Why not, Mister?"

Teagen glanced at Jessie as if hoping for a way out, but she just let him suffer. "Because," he finally said, "I don't have a fever."

"How do you know? How do I know? Martha says folks can be knocking at death's door and not know it."

"I wouldn't quote Martha if I were you."

"Why? Could it cause a fever?"

The child planted her elbows on the table and studied him as if his head were a volcano, and he might explode at any moment.

Teagen tried to ignore her. Finally, he broke. "All right, you can feel my forehead."

Rose moved closer and lifted her hand. She touched one finger to his skin and then another until her hand rested above his eyes. "Nope," she said as if she'd been to medical school. "No fever."

"Thank you," he managed.

She nodded. "You're welcome."

Before Teagen could finish his pie, Bethie toddled over and wanted to give a second opinion. She crawled up on his leg and put her hand where her sister had, then mumbled something no one in the room understood. When she crawled away, Jessie noticed chocolate pie fingerprints just above Teagen's eyebrow.

Without a word he wiped them off with his napkin and finished his pie. For the first time in her life Jessie thought she could love someone like Teagen if she ever had the chance. He'd done so many good things for her, letting her come here, teaching her things, caring about all of them as if they were family, but the kindest thing he'd ever done was letting the girls feel his forehead for a fever.

When she found him in the study two hours later, she crossed silently to his chair and brushed her fingers over his temple.

He looked up from the book he'd been reading. His eyes seemed to drink her in, and she knew that, like her, he'd waited all day for this time.

She took the book, placed it open on the desk, then walked the few feet back to his chair and sat on the wide leather arm.

His arm settled around her back, but he waited.

"I'd like that lesson now."

"It's too late to go for a drive," he teased. "And target practice only works in daylight."

She liked the low rumble of his voice. "Tell me what to do, Teagen."

He tugged, and she slid onto his lap, bringing them nose to nose. "Tilt your head to the left."

She nodded, bumping his cheek.

"Now, open your mouth, just a little."

Licking her lips, she followed instructions.

"Now, come closer."

Slowly, she moved toward him. When their lips brushed, she closed her eyes, trying to remember the exact way a kiss felt.

His lips were softer than she'd thought they would be, and the slight touch made her feel warm inside.

She pulled back. "What's next? It seems hard for you to tell me what to do when we can't talk and kiss at the same time."

Teagen's big hand brushed her shoulder. "Do it again, only push your lips against mine. From then on, I'm afraid I'm going to have to show you, not tell you."

She nodded, bumping his nose with her head. They both laughed.

Then she straightened and took a deep breath as if preparing to dive. Slowly, once more, she drew closer and pressed her mouth to his. The sensation was not unpleasant. As she waited, his lips began to move over hers stroking, touching, applying gentle pressure. When his tongue brushed across the corner of her mouth, Jessie shook with pleasure, and his arm tightened around her waist.

She felt his chest press against hers as he pulled her to him. The second time he tasted her lips, his body took the shock of surprise from her. She liked the boldness and did the same to him, but his reaction came as a groan that whispered between them and made her smile.

Step by step he taught her how to kiss, and she learned about the powerful control she had over this man. When she ran her fingers in his hair, the kiss deepened; when she pulled away slightly, his touch turned soft as if he thought he might have frightened her. And when she kissed him boldly, his hands moved over her as if he couldn't keep them still.

When finally she broke the kiss, he stared at her with a hunger she'd never seen in his eyes. It would have frightened her, but his fingers gently stroked her back. He moved his head, his warm lips brushing her cheek.

She smiled. He kissed the other side, then moved in closer and tasted the corner of her mouth.

When he finally straightened away, she whispered, "That was nice, Teagen, very, very nice."

"Lesson over?"

She nodded. "But, if you don't mind, I'd like to practice what I've learned some other time."

His hand moved along her waist as though touching someone was newborn to him. "Anytime."

"Do you really mean that?"

"I'd consider it a privilege."

"Thank you," she said as if he'd just passed the butter. She rested her head on his shoulder and talked of her day. She found herself storing things away in her mind to talk to him about.

He asked questions, laughed at the tales of the girls, and encouraged her to say more, but all the while, he continued to rest his hand against her, communicating with his touch.

A half hour passed before they both grew silent. She knew

it was late; she should turn in, but she didn't want their time together to end.

"Jess." He finally broke the silence. "Would you mind if I lay my hand over where the baby grows?"

She couldn't answer. It was too embarrassing . . . too personal. Closing her eyes, she remembered that this wasn't some stranger. This was Teagen, the best and only friend she'd ever had.

She tugged his fingers from her waist and placed them over the small, rounded spot. Then she leaned back on his arm and lay very still.

For a while, his big hand didn't move; then, slowly, he measured the place. "It's not very big."

"She'll grow," Jessie answered. "Emily was small inside of me. Most of my customers didn't even know I was pregnant until the last few months."

"She?"

"That's all I seem to have."

His hand was so gentle she wanted to cry. She knew he was touching the baby, but he was also touching her.

"I'd like to touch this place again before you leave and see if the child grows."

"You can touch me anytime you like, Teagen. I don't mind." She sat up and kissed him lightly on the lips. "I have to go to bed. Tomorrow we have a busy day planned."

He helped her up and walked her to the stairs without a word, but she noticed something in his eyes and realized their time together had meant as much to him as it had to her.

"Until tomorrow," she whispered halfway up the stairs.

He didn't answer, but when she looked back, he was staring up at her.

CHAPTER 18

MIDMORNING THE NEXT DAY, JESSIE HEARD THREE shots echoing from the direction of the bridge. The quiet day shattered like the plate she dropped. Teagen told her that three rapidly fired shots were the warning for trouble. Her first thoughts were not of defense but of finding her girls.

She ran into the dining room and found them all playing under the table tent Martha had made from colorful quilts. They had tiny handkerchief dolls and were using the dinner napkins to make beds for their babies. Her daughters looked so happy, she hated to interrupt them.

Sage bolted past her, a rifle in each hand. Her eyes watched the windows as she spoke. "Until we know what's happening, it's best to take the girls to Martha. She always goes down to the root cellar. They'll be safe there."

Jessie didn't have time to answer before Sage was gone. She collected her daughters and met Martha at the trapdoor in the corner of the kitchen. The housekeeper had thrown together a box of supplies: water, cookies, an extra lantern, and an old blanket.

"Don't worry." Martha sounded as if nothing were out of the ordinary. "Heading to the cellar is only a precaution. There always seems to be one kind of storm or another hitting this place."

As Jessie lowered the girls down the narrow steps, they giggled, thinking they were having a grand adventure.

"I'm staying with Sage until we know something," Jessie

said more calmly than she felt. She knew she'd be little help to the McMurrays, but she couldn't hide away if they were in danger.

Martha agreed as Jessie handed her the box. "I'll watch over your babies. If trouble's coming, I don't much care to see it. We'll be fine. Just open the trap when it's over."

Jessie hated closing the door in the floor, but she knew she could be no help if she were worried about the girls. She'd been down to the cellar. It was full of supplies. The perfect place to play hide-and-seek. The girls would love watching the spiders making their webs and drawing in the fine dust. The kitchen floor had been built over the cellar with thick logs, making the space below almost soundproof. No matter what happened above, the girls would hear nothing.

As if to add another layer of protection, Jessie tugged one of the kitchen rag rugs over the trapdoor; then she ran to the porch.

Sage waited, both guns by her side, as she looked toward the bridge. "The Apache are gone. Packed up so early this morning no one saw them leave."

Jessie watched. The land looked empty near the bridge. She'd grown used to seeing them, even though the Apache never came near the house.

"There's a buggy coming." Sage shaded her eyes and added, "No, not a buggy, a carriage. A big one like I've seen in Austin. It looks like that old Ranger, Tattor Sims, is riding beside it."

"Could it be your brother, Travis, back from Austin?"

"No. Sims wouldn't have fired if it were family. He served with Travis and knew him well, so he wouldn't take my brother for a stranger."

Teagen swung over the railing at the side of the porch. The women had been so absorbed in watching the carriage they hadn't noticed him ride up at the side of the house. He had his rifle in his hand. His face looked hard, unyielding.

Jessie saw nothing of the gentle man who'd kissed her only hours before. The memory of his kiss was so thick in her head she could almost feel his lips pressed against hers. She'd lain awake late into the night reliving every moment of their time in the study.

As he passed her, his fingers brushed her side, a slight touch no one else would see, but Jessie calmed inside and wished she were in his arms.

Dolan Hatch came from the barn armed for a fight. He didn't say a word as he took up guard on the other side of the porch. There was a coldness in his stare. Whatever happened, good or bad, in the few minutes that followed didn't matter. Dolan was just doing a job.

Trying hard to breathe slowly, Jessie looked around, realizing what a fort Whispering Mountain must be. The hills in the back made it impossible to be attacked from that direction. The house had been set far enough from the bridge to give them time to arm, yet not so far that they couldn't see the dust of anyone riding in.

"Who is it?" she asked of no one in particular.

"I don't know," Sage answered, "but we've learned to welcome all uninvited guests fully armed. For years after our folks died we not only had to fight off raiders, we had to stand against fast-talking con men who thought they could talk us out of our land."

"You were a baby then, Sage," Teagen said without turning his eyes away from the carriage.

Sage made a face. "I know, but I remember some of it. I was four when you fired at one man who tried to force you to sign papers or he'd see we all went to the orphanage in Galveston. You were just a kid, but he turned around real quick."

"I was sixteen," Teagen corrected, "and the shot missed him by a foot."

"You hit the couple who came out claiming to be relatives of Papa's."

Teagen shrugged. "I only grazed him. I hit her bag, but she was the one who did all the screaming. I swear I could still hear her climbing into that canoe at the river. She was saying how glad she was not to be related to us."

The carriage was halfway to the house. Neither of the Mc-Murrays seemed all that worried, but Jessie couldn't think. She wasn't brave. She'd never been brave. Eli hadn't even owned a gun. Half the time he forgot to lock the bookstore door when he came in. She'd always considered strangers who walked into the store as customers. The knowledge that a threat might be coming terrified her. She picked up a rifle and held it close.

"You know how to use that?" Sage asked.

"Not at all, but whoever's coming doesn't know."

"I'm afraid this is the kind of trouble we can't fight with weapons, anyway," Sage decided. "If it were strangers, Sims would have stopped them at the bridge. They wouldn't be headed this way. If they meant us no harm, he wouldn't have fired the shots."

They all stood as the carriage pulled up and rocked to a halt.

Sims walked his horse to Teagen's side of the porch. "I tried to stop them," he said, "but they got a marshal riding with them. I don't know the other two, but the lawman is legit. I met him once down by Houston."

"You did the right thing," Teagen said, "but cover my back. Badge or no badge, this could be some kind of trick."

Sims waited near the house as Teagen walked toward the carriage.

Two men stepped out. One wore a tall hat and a wool great-coat like the rich men in Chicago wore. The other had a western-cut jacket with a badge on his chest.

Teagen offered no greeting. He hadn't invited them on his land, so he saw no need to welcome them.

A third man, almost too wide to push his way through the carriage opening, climbed out last. He was short and double Teagen's age. He had a wild mane of white hair that hung across the cape covering his shoulders. He was a man no one would accidentally forget meeting.

"Teagen McMurray," the fat man said as he fought for more than his share of air. "I'm Judge Frazier out of Austin, and I'm here to make sure all is legal in this matter that has come to my attention."

Teagen finally offered his hand but didn't say a word or lower his gun.

Frazier frowned. "You mind turning that rifle in some other direction? I don't favor staring down the barrel of a weapon."

"You're on my land uninvited."

The judge laughed a short bark. "I believe we are, sir, but we mean you no harm."

The lawman standing to the left of the judge looked bothered. "McMurray, I knew better than to expect a welcome from you, but Randell Frazier is a district judge, and you'd be wise to show a little respect."

Teagen propped his weapon on his shoulder, no longer pointing it at the visitors, but not following orders either. "Sheriff Brown, right?"

The sheriff, to his credit, offered his hand.

Teagen hesitated a moment, then took it. "I've heard of you. A little out of your territory, aren't you?"

"I was asked to follow this matter from the coast." The sheriff seemed to relax. "I know you don't like folks stepping foot on your land, and I can't say as I blame you, but this is official business, and it's nothing to do with you."

Jessie and Sage moved closer as Teagen answered, "If it's on my land, then it's my business."

The sheriff introduced the man in the tall hat as Mr. Andrew Wenderman, a lawyer from Chicago.

Teagen introduced no one.

Wenderman wiped sweat from his bald head. "Do you think we could get out of this sun? I can feel my skin blistering in this blasted heat."

Teagen didn't move. "You won't be here that long." He turned back to the sheriff. "Mind telling me what this is all about? We've wasted enough time. I have work to do."

Jessie watched Teagen's every move. This was the hard man everyone talked about. The head of the family. She was glad he stood between her and the Chicago lawyer. She could smell trouble, and if it wasn't about the McMurrays, then she feared it might be about her.

"Of course." The judge had captured enough air to draw up to his full five-feet-four height. "Mr. Wenderman has traveled all the way from Chicago on the trail of a young woman who kidnapped three little girls. It seems she had no money or family and is unable to provide for the girls, yet she took them from the loving arms of their grandmother." He paused as if reciting charges he found distasteful. "Mr. Wenderman's client is the children's grandmother and has papers from the Illinois State Court awarding her full custody."

The words began to sink in. Jessie's worst nightmare was happening, and she no longer had anywhere to run. She watched the sunny day go black and closed her eyes as she tumbled forward.

For a while, she felt nothing but black velvet surrounding her, pushing away all thought. Then, as if from far away, she heard Teagen say, "Jess, wake up."

She smiled. He wasn't ordering, he was asking, she reminded herself, although the two sounded pretty much the same to someone who didn't know the man.

The world came back along with the panic. The horror she'd feared since the day Eli died was real . . . was happening. They'd come to take her babies away.

"Jess," Teagen said again. "Can you hear me?"

She opened her eyes and saw his worried stare. She was in the study, curled up on the arm of the big chair he usually sat in. Sage stood in front of her with a glass of water in one hand and a towel in the other. Teagen knelt on one knee beside her chair.

"You gave us a fright." Sage smiled. "If I hadn't noticed you swaying like an elm branch, you would have hit the ground. Too much sun, I think."

"Too many people," Teagen corrected.

Jessie pushed herself into a sitting position and noticed Teagen's arm braced around her for support. "I'm all right. I must have fainted." She looked around the room. "Are those terrible men gone?"

Sage shook her head. "They're on the porch. Teagen didn't invite them in. With the noon heat coming on, the lawyer should be slow cooking about now in that wool coat."

"Good." She looked at Teagen. "The girls?"

"Still safe in the cellar. As soon as I know you're all right, I'll go tell the judge that this is just some big mistake. You're the girls' mother, and you have family coming to pick you up. The judge in Chicago obviously didn't have the facts."

Jessie met Sage's stare but couldn't say a word.

Finally, Sage said in a low voice, "Jessie has no relatives, Teagen."

"You're wrong. She's waiting for them."

Sage looked at Jessie for the answer. There could be no more hiding.

"She's right," Jessie said, remembering how it had only been a few days since she'd accidentally told Sage the truth. "I have no one coming. I have no living relatives. No one is coming for me."

Teagen stood and pulled away, leaving her feeling more alone than she ever had.

Sage touched Jessie's hand only a moment before she said, "I'll offer the men on the porch some tea. You two have some talking to do."

Silently, without looking up, Jessie agreed.

Sage almost ran from the room.

Jessie didn't want to face Teagen or the lie she'd told to stay, but she had no choice.

Teagen walked to the window and stared out, but she knew he saw nothing right now but her lie. How many times over the years had he written that he hated liars? For Teagen there was right and wrong and no room in between.

Lifting her head, she forced herself to begin. "I had to tell you I was waiting for relatives. You wouldn't have let me come if you thought I had nowhere to go."

He didn't answer.

"I didn't lie about Eli's mother. I knew she would take the girls from me. I had to run. There was no time to plan what I would do when I got to Texas. Once I was here, I thought if I could just rest a few days at the ranch, then I would think of something." Fighting back a sob, she added, "I never thought she'd find me here."

"A woman alone with three small girls wouldn't be hard to track." Teagen didn't look at her.

Long past tears, she buried her head in her hands and shook with fear. If she were brave, she'd grab one of the guns and kill the lawyer. But he was just doing his job, and Eli's mother would simply send another. She didn't even have the money to run, and it would only be a few months before the baby she carried would make it hard for her to work. If they found her all the way here, they could find her anywhere.

When she finally raised her head, Teagen was gone. She wasn't surprised. She'd lied to him. If he were this angry over one lie, she didn't want to think what he would be like when he learned that she'd written the last letter, or worse, if he ever knew that she'd written all the letters. Every single one. The friend he thought he had in Chicago all those years had been her, not Eli.

She forced herself to shove every fear aside as she stood and tried to think. The bright, sunny day might as well be a storm. Sheriff Brown stood out by the carriage with the carriage driver. Both men seemed to be passing the time of day with Sims. The lawyer had removed his hat and coat. He still looked uncomfortable sitting in one of the porch chairs. A half-empty pitcher of tea stood on the table beside him. He looked as hard as oak, and Jessie guessed tears wouldn't affect him. He was just doing a job. One he was paid well for if he were willing to follow her here.

It took her a minute to realize that the judge was missing. With his width, he wasn't the kind of man one could miss in a crowd, but none of the others seemed to notice.

Jessie turned as Sage came in. "I made you a glass of tea with cold well water. The day's already too hot for coffee."

"Thanks."

Sage glanced around the empty room. "Did Teagen finally calm down?"

Jessie shrugged. "He hates being lied to. I think right now he probably hates me."

"Probably, but he can just get over it." Sage joined her at the window. "You had good reason to do what you did. Three good reasons."

Jessie managed a smile. She had a feeling Sage would be on her side. "I can't let them take the girls. You don't know what Eli's mother was like. She spoiled my husband all his childhood, and when he turned out to be just what she'd made him, she disowned him. After buying him a little bookstore to keep him from starving, she claimed to wash her hands of him, but every year she'd come around to check on him and remind him of how dearly he'd let her down."

"But she must have loved the girls. She's fighting for them now."

Jessie shook her head. "Eli told me she stopped by when she heard I'd had a baby just to see if it might be a boy. I never saw her. Eli said she told him he couldn't do anything right, not even father a son. She blamed him, and he blamed me. The only reason she wants the girls now is because he's dead. But I can't give them to her. I can't."

"Of course not," Sage said without a second's hesitation. "They are your daughters. They belong with you. It's not right for that lawyer to even think of taking them back."

"When we got to the trading post, I only wanted to stay here long enough to rest. I was afraid Teagen wouldn't let me stay if he knew no one was planning to come after me." Jessie shoved a tear away. "So I lied about relatives coming to pick me up."

"That doesn't matter now. What matters is that man thinks he's got a right to the girls." Jessie turned back to the window. "I'm guessing Mr. Wenderman brought both the sheriff and the judge so there would be no mistake that he was within the boundaries of the law. He might have guessed we'd shoot him accidentally for a snake if he came alone." Sage touched the gun holstered at her waist.

"Would you?" Jessie whispered.

Sage shook her head. "Probably not, but Teagen would. He'd do whatever he had to do to protect family."

Jessie felt a lump in her throat grow. She wasn't family, but Sage had included her.

Both women turned as Teagen walked in with the round judge right behind him.

The old man nodded at both women, then looked around the room. "I'm not fond of tea, but I'll take something stronger if you have it, Mr. McMurray."

Teagen took a bottle from a cabinet and poured him a shot of whiskey.

The judge smiled with pleasure, making his cheeks as round as apples. "Delightful," he said as he took the glass. "I haven't had a drink all day."

No one in the room mentioned that it was still morning. They just watched as he downed the alcohol. His huge throat reminded Jessie of the toad Rose had found.

When he finished the whiskey, he wiped his mouth on his ham of a hand and smiled. "Now, down to business. Which one of you lovely ladies is Jessie Barton?"

"I am." Jessie stepped forward.

"Are you the mother of Emily, Rose, and Bethany Barton?"

"Yes." Jessie could see no point in denying it.

"The court papers that rattlebox of a lawyer carries say that you are a widow without family or means to support your children."

Jessie raised her head but didn't answer.

Judge Frazier looked like he could use another drink. Finally, he continued, "There's not much I can do in the matter if the facts are true. I understand from Wenderman that the grandparents are quite wealthy and can provide a fine life for the children." He shook his head. "But I don't cotton much to the law taking kids from a parent. It don't seem nature's way. Now, if you had family or were remarried to someone willing—"

"We'll be her family." Sage stepped beside Jessie.

The judge shook his head. "Saying you're family and being it is two different things. I talked to Wenderman about taking this lady back with the girls, but he swears the grandmother wants only the little ones. If your husband's people would take you in, they could be your family, Mrs. Barton."

Jessie stared at the floor. She'd never been welcome in their home, and she knew she never would be. Eli had married her, but he'd never treated her like family. She'd never spoken to Mrs. Barton until the week before Eli died, and then the woman hated her so much she wouldn't even say her name. It had taken Jessie a long time to figure out why. Finally she'd realized that because of her, Eli had been able to live the way he wanted to live. If she hadn't been around to run the store, he would have failed and had to go back to his mother.

Judge Frazier's voice lowered. "I'm real sorry. I don't always agree with it, but my job is to uphold the law."

Jessie couldn't move. She wanted to run, grab her girls, and head for the trees. She'd live on the land and eat berries and nuts. She'd build a shelter of twigs. She'd do anything, but she wouldn't give them up. She couldn't. They were her life.

For a minute Teagen's words didn't register. "Judge, did you say if she were remarried that would change things?"

The old man nodded. "If she were married to a man who could provide for the children, I don't see how the grandmother would have any rights."

Teagen spoke only to the judge. "Do you think I could provide for a family?"

"Of course you could." The judge studied Teagen. "Are you saying you'd marry Widow Barton?"

"I am."

Jessie stared at Teagen, but he didn't look at her as he added, "She can stay here until the baby she carries now is born; then I'll buy her a house in town and see that she has enough to live on. You have my word."

The judge looked suspicious. "That's mighty generous of you."

Teagen's face was hard. "I'm not doing it for her. I'm doing it for the girls and my one friend, Eli Barton. If he hadn't asked me to take care of his family, I wouldn't bother, but he was my friend, and to my way of thinking, I should put no boundary on his request. He must have known his mother would try something, or he wouldn't have written that last note."

The judge seemed to see Teagen McMurray for the first time, and when he spoke again, he said, "The child she carries . . ." He couldn't finish without being disrespectful.

"Is my husband's," Jessie finished. "If it's a boy, his mother will want it a hundred times more than she'll want the girls."

Frazier seemed to understand. He looked directly at Jessie. "If you marry this man, any child born of that marriage will be his, even if it's born a day after the wedding. Do you understand that?"

She nodded. "Eli's mother will never be able to lay claim."

The fat judge ran his fingers through his hair and handed Teagen the empty glass. "I need a drink. There are a few questions we'd better get through."

Teagen poured another whiskey and said, "The only question I have is, can you perform the ceremony? Make it legal?"

"I can," the judge answered as he tested the strength of the chair behind the desk, "but I don't do this kind of thing lightly."

Once he settled in, he seemed in his element. Behind the desk, he appeared taller, more powerful. "First, do you love this lady?"

"No." Teagen's words were cold.

The judge turned to Jessie. "Do you love this man?"

Jessie closed her eyes and admitted what she'd felt for years. "Yes."

"No, she doesn't," Teagen countered. "She's lying because she thinks the truth will mean you won't let her keep the girls."

"It doesn't matter, anyway." Frazier poured himself another drink. "Half the folks I marry don't even know what love is." He downed his whiskey. "Now, and more important, will you be true to this man as long as you live?"

"I will." Jessie knew she would.

"And you, Teagen McMurray. If you marry, even under these circumstances, will you swear to be husband to her for as long as she lives?"

"If I marry, I'll keep every rule of marriage."

Then Frazier motioned for them to step in front of the desk. "Are you agreeing to this, Jessie Barton?"

"I am."

"And are you agreeing to this, Teagen McMurray?"

"I am."

"Then I'll draw up the document. Ask one of your men to come in and witness it. No one would dare question a Ranger's word."

"That's it?" Sage finally spoke. "No wedding service, no vows, no kiss at the end?"

"Under these conditions, I don't think it will be necessary. Once I write up the paper, they are just as married as they would be in a big church."

Jessie ventured a glance at Teagen. He did not look happy. In fact, he looked like a man who needed something to hit. She knew he was still angry at her, probably always would be, but he'd offered her a way out, a way to keep the girls.

And he'd done it not out of caring but because of his friend's dying request.

A request written and signed by her.

CHAPTER 19

A MINUTE AFTER THE JUDGE SAID THEY WERE MAR-
ried, Teagen walked on the porch and told the lawyer the
news. To his credit, Wenderman took the development with
disappointment but grace. Teagen couldn't help but think
maybe a small part of the man didn't like the job he'd been
hired to do. He asked if he could be allowed to see the girls before he departed so that he could give a report of their well-
being to his client.

Teagen saw no harm in the request. "All right, but they are
not to know why you're here."

"Fair enough," Mr. Wenderman agreed.

Sage offered the men lunch, and everyone began moving
into the dining room of the house.

To his surprise, the sheriff looked happy about the marriage. He pumped Teagen's hand and wished him the best, then
kissed Jessie on the cheek. He'd be repeating the story when he
got back to Austin. The McMurrays were a well-known family
in Texas, and Teagen's marriage would be news.

Teagen told himself he felt nothing. He'd done the right
thing. He always did the right thing, no matter the cost to him.
The friend he'd had for years had asked him to take care of his
family, and he'd done just that.

He heard the women welcoming Martha and the girls out
of the cellar, but he was gone before everyone sat down to
lunch. He rode toward Lookout Point, needing to be alone.
Sage would tell them he had ranch business to see about. That

was what she'd told the few people who asked about him from time to time.

Once on the point, in the shade of the hills, he stood, looking over his land. The spread was big, one of the biggest in Texas, the land rich and perfect for pasture. He could breed twice the horses and ten times the cattle if he wanted to. Before he turned forty, he could be one of the most powerful men in Texas if he wanted to be, and no one could take this place from him. That had been his dream for years, not the power but the security.

Only why, now, did he feel so alone?

He'd always done what was right, done what he had to do. He'd never put himself first, and no matter how much it hurt, he'd always told the truth. Then why did doing the right thing hurt so badly deep down inside?

The marriage didn't matter. He'd never planned to marry, so if Jessie needed his name to be safe, it seemed a small enough gift. The girls would be fun to watch grow up. They already meant more to him than he'd admit.

So why did what he'd done eat away in his gut?

Teagen climbed back on his horse and began to ride. He crossed the hidden trail his father had been shown by the Apache thirty years ago. Only Teagen didn't follow the path. This time he wasn't riding to the trading post. He was riding away from the ranch house and as far away from Jessie as he could.

It was almost nightfall when he circled around to the summit of Whispering Mountain. He left his horse and climbed the last few hundred yards. Finally, after a few scrapes because of his own carelessness, he reached the summit where the land leveled out onto a flat plane. There, with trees surrounding him and the sun turning the sky to a pale red, Teagen stopped running.

He lay down in the grass and closed his eyes, feeling totally alone. For a long while he thought of nothing; then slowly, wandering thoughts seemed to drift past his brain like clouds in a night sky.

His mother moving silently in her moccasins. He must

have seen her run to his father a hundred times. They'd embrace at the end of each day as if they'd been apart a long time and were homesick for the sight of one another. For a while after they died, he wondered if when their spirits met on the other side they'd done the same thing. The reports coming back from where his father died at Goliad said the men's bodies had been dismembered and finally burned. His mother had bled to death in the bed where she'd given birth to Sage. But Teagen always saw them whole in his dreams. Whole and happy.

He remembered a Christmas when Sage had been about seven. He'd signed for the land that year, and they'd rebuilt the bridge. She'd been able to start school at Mrs. Dickerson's. That year she wanted to have a Christmas party for her friends, and Martha had talked him into it. All the kids arrived with their parents and had a great time. Teagen had watched it all from outside. He'd planned to at least stand around and watch from a corner of the room, but even the parents looked at him with worried eyes, as if he were some kind of monster or hardened hothead they feared. None of them seemed to understand that he'd done what he had to.

Mrs. Dickerson came out on the porch at one point to tell him that if he planned to make any friends, he had to stop glaring at people.

He'd almost told her of his friend in Chicago. He wanted to say that no one needed to fear him; he was still in his teens, and everything he'd done had been to protect the ranch. He wanted to say that he had one friend who understood.

But he hadn't told anyone. He'd just stood in the cold and watched, hardening inside until he didn't care if anyone liked him or not.

After that, he made sure he wasn't there when Sage had friends over. He told her it was because he didn't want to frighten them, but in truth, he didn't want to see the fear in their eyes.

He relaxed in the summer grass, thinking how Jessie hadn't been afraid of him. Not after that first day, anyway. Sometimes she'd lean over for no reason at all and touch him. She'd curl up in the chair next to him and talk to him as if she had no worry that he might turn and snap at her. And when he did grumble, she'd laugh like she thought he was making a joke.

Memories of the weeks she'd been on his ranch drifted in his mind. The talks, the rides, the kisses they'd shared. He'd enjoyed it all and stored away the moments because he knew she'd be moving on soon.

Only she'd lied. She had no family. Maybe the whole thing between them had been part of her game. She'd lied to him from the first, and now he didn't know what to believe.

She'd even lied and told the judge that she loved him.

Closing his eyes, for the first time in his life Teagen thought about what he wanted. Not what he needed or what was best, but what he wanted.

He wanted Jessie. He wanted her smile every morning at breakfast and their talks over supper. He wanted the feel of her near him. He wanted her in his bed. And most of all, he wanted her honest and straight with him.

And that, he decided he might never have. She'd lied.

As the sun set, he drifted into sleep, dreaming of her laughing. As the wind kicked up a cool breeze, his dream turned dark and stormy like an ink sketch curling up in fire and smoke. Her laughter turned to cries, and he stood frozen, able to do nothing but listen. He saw death's black hand move over Jessie mixed in dark red blood.

Teagen awoke with a start. He walked to the edge of the clearing and looked down. He couldn't see the house from this point, but still his eyes searched the night. All was quiet.

The dream had been just that, a dream. Jessie belonged to him now. She was his wife, if only on paper. He'd see that nothing happened to her. He'd not allow the nightmare to touch her.

He had no more answers than he did when he rode up on the mountain. As he climbed down, he knew what he had to do. He'd keep his word to Jessie. He'd buy her a house in town and see that she had a credit at the trading post for whatever she and the girls needed. But she wouldn't be his wife. Not in the real sense. He'd not allow her to hurt or manipulate him again. And in time he'd forget how he needed her, just as he'd forget the dream he'd had.

Long after dark, he returned home. When he stepped from the barn, he spotted Drummond Roak a moment before the boy fell into step beside him.

"Evenin', Teagen," the kid said as if it were perfectly natural that he'd be out strolling by the barn at midnight. "I'm probably the last person you want to see right now, but—"

"You'll have to get in line to be the last one I want to see. Several are ahead of you, Roak."

Drummond laughed. "You don't sound like a very happy bridegroom."

Teagen groaned. "She may be my wife, but I promise you it will be in name only." He stopped and faced Roak when he realized he'd spoken his thoughts. "What are you doing here? You're either way late for breakfast or way early."

Roak was too busy thinking about what Teagen had just said to answer. Finally, he pushed his hat back and stared at Teagen with a puzzled look on his young face. "That don't make any sense."

"What doesn't?"

"Well, I don't want to marry Sage, I just want to sleep with her, and you, you marry a woman and don't want to sleep with her."

Teagen didn't know which part of Roak's logic to attack first and, in truth, he was too tired to fight right now. He decided to just forget he'd heard the kid. "You want to come in for a meal? I'm sure Martha left me enough for two." He thought about adding that if Roak ever even thought of taking advantage of his sister, Teagen would kill him, but he knew Sage would get there first.

Drum smiled as he started up the steps. "You bet. I'm starving." He slapped his arm around Teagen's shoulder like they were friends, and Teagen shrugged it off.

The boy took no offense as they stepped into the kitchen,

and he took a deep breath. "Heaven must smell like this," he said.

They collected the food from the warmer, then agreed to split an apple pie Martha had left. Neither talked while they ate, but the silence was comfortable. From the way he shoveled food in, Teagen had no doubt that this was the boy's first meal all day.

Finally, when Teagen walked Roak back to the porch, he asked, "Why are you here? It's not like you to come so late when you know you're not going to get the chance to pester Sage."

Roak agreed. "I come with news, but I didn't want to run into all the company passing by your place today. So I waited until that big carriage went back to the hotel. I figured if I wanted to catch you alone, I'd better stay on the other side of the bridge until all was quiet."

"I guess you heard what happened."

Roak nodded. "Everyone in town did. That lawyer went back to the hotel and gave a detailed account. By the time it got passed from one ear to another a dozen times, I knew I'd have to check the facts myself."

"So you rode out, uninvited as always."

"I was invited to breakfast. Consider I'm a tad late. But that's not the reason I came. I wanted to fill you in on something I heard."

"What's that?"

"The raiders are still out there. They raided a place two days north of here a week ago, but it didn't get them much more than a fresh supply of horses, so they headed back this direction. They know the Apache left, and they know about the two men you hired."

"And," Teagen asked, suddenly on edge.

"And if I were you, I'd hire more men. From what the drunk told Maria, a girl I grew up with who works in the saloon, every man who rides in the raid has been promised a McMurray horse. She said the guy admitted that the boss of the operation wasn't interested in the stock as much as he was the land."

Teagen frowned, already ahead of Roak and not wanting to hear the rest.

"The boss of this band of cutthroats is planning to wipe you off the land like you was nothing but grasshoppers and claim it for himself. He figures he'll fight your brothers when and if they ever come back."

"What do you care if I die?" Teagen suspected Roak's sudden interest in the ranch.

"I don't. I tried to kill you myself not too long ago. But I don't like the idea of my woman being caught in the middle."

"Sage is not your woman, kid. She never will be."

For once Roak didn't take offense at being called a kid. He simply straightened and said, "She will be, McMurray, and when she is, I won't be fool enough to let her sleep alone."

Teagen closed his eyes and leaned his head back, bumping it against the porch post. He'd had one hell of a day, and Drummond Roak had just made it worse. Not only were the raiders still out there and planning an attack, he had to listen to advice from a boy who knew even less about women than he did.

When he opened his eyes, he wasn't surprised Drummond was gone. Something told him Roak's information was fact, but of late Teagen's ability to judge fact from fiction had come into question. He'd never questioned for a second when Jessie had told him her relatives were coming. Now, looking back, he should have known better. If she'd had a relative alive, she would have lived with them at thirteen and not hidden out in Eli's bookstore.

When he walked inside and headed down the hall, he found Jessie sitting on the third step of the stairs, waiting for him.

She looked so young and afraid in her white nightgown and bare feet. He didn't bother with a greeting. "You should be in bed. It's late."

She stood, holding onto the railing as if the house were a rocking boat. "I have to know something first."

"What?" He didn't plan on making it easy for her.

She closed her eyes, and he could see that tears already made her cheeks shiny. When she looked back to him, her brown eyes were canyon wide. "Will you be coming to my room?"

He could almost read her thoughts. She'd told him Eli had given her a room. She'd even told him how he'd come to her now and then in the middle of the night after he'd been drinking. When she'd said it, she'd looked sad, and he knew she'd hated those visits and the night alone that followed when Eli left for the pub.

"No," he said. "I'll not come to your room. Not tonight. Not ever. You can sleep without fear."

She nodded and climbed the stairs. He waited until he heard her door open and close before he went to the study and finished off the bottle of whiskey. Eli might drink because he slept with Jessie, but Teagen drank because he couldn't.

The days that followed melted together in the late summer heat. Slowly, she looked at him with only a shadow of sadness in her eyes, but she never came to the study for their talks.

He missed them, but he wouldn't say a word. He pushed himself hard, leaving early and returning late. When he did stay in because of a sick horse or shoeing to do in the barn, he saw the girls but never Jessie. On the rare occasion they sat down at a meal at the same time, she always took the chair opposite him, never beside.

Neither knew how to cross the cavern between them. He'd told himself she'd been in the wrong and he'd not make the first step, but as the days passed, he wondered if she would. If she didn't say she was sorry, how could he forgive her?

Without rain the grass dried to brown, and he had to move the horses to the upper pastures. Tattor Sims took over the job of picking up supplies and came home one day with three buddies from his army days. They'd been north moving cattle and were looking for work. One looked like he'd be little use in a fight. He didn't even wear a gun. But, like the other two, he was good with horses, so Teagen hired them all.

To his surprise, Sage asked them if they'd seen a Drummond Roak up North. When they said they hadn't, she looked relieved. Since that midnight visit Teagen hadn't seen him, but he hadn't expected to. He could feel Roak though. He knew the boy was somewhere watching like some kind of pesky guardian angel.

A month passed before he spoke to Jessie directly. He'd eaten alone and gone back out on the porch for a smoke before turning in when she joined him.

For a minute, he just stared as she walked out and took the chair next to where he stood watching the night. He didn't know what to say to her. He'd missed their talks, but he didn't want to be lied to again.

She leaned her arms on the railing and watched fireflies. Finally, when he'd about decided she'd never talk, she said, "The baby moved."

"Oh," he answered.

Silence again. For all their conversations they seemed to have nothing left to say. He'd gotten over being mad at her. He'd even reasoned out why she'd lied, but there seemed no way back from where they'd come.

He sat next to her, thinking it couldn't hurt just to be in the same place with her. After all, she was his wife, and he would have to deal with her from time to time. He'd find her a place before the baby came and, once she could travel, he had no doubt Sage and Martha would help her move. She and the girls could live in town where she'd be somewhat protected and the girls could go to school. When he went to town once a month for supplies, he'd stop in and see if she needed anything. Maybe she'd even offer him a meal or a cup of coffee. Then they'd talk about the girls.

Absorbed in his plan, he hardly noticed she stood until she moved in front of him. "Would you like to feel the baby again?"

Teagen watched her a moment before nodding.

She stepped closer and took his hand.

He spread his fingers over the spot that had grown considerably since he'd felt it before. She might have asked him if he wanted to feel the baby, but he realized he was also feeling her. And Jessie felt so good to the touch.

Suddenly, something pushed at his little finger. Teagen shifted his hand and felt the tap again on his palm. He laughed in wonder.

When he looked up at her, she smiled. "Teagen, I've missed our talks. Can we go back to being friends?"

"No lies."

"I'll never tell you another lie. I promise."

He realized how much he'd missed her. "All right. We can try." He'd never open up to her as he had before, but they could talk about things like the girls and the land. They might even talk of books.

She nodded as if she knew it wouldn't be the same for a while, maybe ever. The easiness between them was gone.

She curled back into the chair beside him, and neither said a word for a while.

Finally, he said so low he wasn't sure she heard him, "Jessie, you don't have to be afraid of me. Not now, not ever. No matter how angry I was, I would never hurt you or the girls."

"I know, Teagen," she whispered back. "I've always known."

After he'd thought about what she'd said, he stood and told her it was time for her to go to bed.

When she reached the stairs, she turned and kissed him lightly on the cheek. The gesture was awkward, but it was a start.

Teagen went to bed thinking they might never be as before, but at least there was a peace between them. Maybe that was the best he could hope for.

CHAPTER 20

JESSIE LAY AWAKE MOST OF THE NIGHT THINKING OF Teagen. She thought of how he'd kissed her the night she'd curled into his arms and wondered if they'd ever be that close again. She liked being close to him . . . the way he smelled of leather and earth and hard work . . . the way he touched her as if she were priceless and he had to be very careful . . . and how sometimes she saw a need in his eyes that only she could fill.

The next morning, she was surprised to see him at breakfast. In the month since they'd been married, he'd lost a few pounds. She knew he made coffee before anyone got up, and he ate supper after everyone went to bed, but she doubted he had anything in between.

Martha filled his plate with pancakes and handed it to Jessie to deliver. She touched his arm to let him know she was near before she set the plate in front of him. The muscles of his shoulder tightened, but he didn't look up.

When she sat down beside Sage, she overheard her say, "We've moved most of the stock, what else can we do?"

Teagen started to answer, then noticed Jessie. For a moment, their eyes met, before he said, "You don't look like you're sleeping, Jess. There are dark circles under your eyes."

"That doesn't matter." Jessie tried to ignore his observation, even though it was true. She'd felt a sickness deep inside from the beginning of this pregnancy. She'd blamed it on grief and fear, but deep down she knew something could be wrong. If she refused to face it, the problem might go away.

She changed the subject. "Is there a problem on the ranch?"

Teagen didn't say a word.

Sage poked him. "She's a McMurray now. She's got a right to know."

Both Teagen and Jessie faced Sage. It was obvious that neither had thought of Jessie as a McMurray. In the month since the judge called them man and wife, no one had referred to her by her new last name.

"All right," he whispered. "I might as well tell you both all I know. Trouble's coming as sure as fall. We need to make a few plans. I've already moved the stock, except for the breeding mares too close to giving birth to make the run."

"What about the cattle?"

"All but two milk cows are in the north canyon. They'll be all right. Anyone coming, if they plan to come fast with enough men to overrun us, will have to come from the bridge."

Sage glanced at Jessie. "Which means they'll have to ride past the house."

Jessie didn't have to hear more. They were telling her that they might have to make a stand at the house. If so, it wouldn't be a safe place to be.

Teagen waited until she looked up at him and then added, "We might want to think about getting everyone into town. It would be dangerous making the trip, but you'd be safer once you're there. Mrs. Dickerson would probably be glad to put you and the girls up."

"Whisper all you want to," Martha shouted from the stove. "I can hear every word, and I can tell you right now, Teagen McMurray, I'm not leaving this place. If trouble comes I'll go to the cellar, but no farther. I haven't stepped foot off this property since I arrived, and I'm too old to move now, so you best figure out a way to keep me safe."

"I'll stand with you and the men." Sage's tone held no argument.

"So will I," Jessie said, wishing she was half as sure as Sage. "The girls can wait out whatever happens in the cellar with Martha. If these raiders are planning to steal your land, they'll stop at nothing. I'd be in more danger in town than here. If they kill you and Sage, it makes sense they'd come after me next."

Teagen looked like he'd already had this discussion with himself. "All right, we all stay, but Sage, I want you to teach Jessie to shoot a rifle today. If trouble crosses the bridge, I want her upstairs in one of the windows where she'll be well protected."

They continued to whisper as Martha made more pancakes. When she finally called the little ones to breakfast, Jessie leaned back, too nervous to eat. Teagen and Sage lived in this world, but it was new to her.

She'd read his letters describing trouble on the ranch. It had always seemed like a grand adventure. Now it seemed only frightening.

When Teagen stood to leave, he looked at her plate and frowned.

Jessie lifted her chin. He might try ordering her to eat, but he couldn't make her keep it down.

He walked out without a word.

Jessie rubbed her hand over her belly. The morning sickness should have been over a month ago. She'd never been sick so long before. The baby had been moving for two weeks now, but she still hadn't felt a solid kick, just slight tapping a few times a day. Something was wrong; she knew it in her heart.

"Are you feeling well?" Sage asked as if reading her mind.

"I'm fine," Jessie lied. "Just a little tired." This family had enough to worry about without her problems piled on top. She told herself she'd get more rest, drink more milk, prop her feet up at least for a few minutes every morning. She'd take care of this problem herself, and in a few weeks she'd feel as perfectly normal as a pregnant woman can feel.

"Do you feel like learning to fire a weapon?"

Jessie nodded. "Martha's making gingerbread men this morning. When the girls are busy helping, we'll slip out."

Sage agreed, and an hour later the women laughed as they

slipped from the house and walked through the barn and out into the pasture beyond. Sage took her time showing Jessie each step in loading the gun and firing. It wasn't as easy as Jessie thought it might be and, after a half dozen shots, her arm and shoulder ached.

Sage talked her into firing a few more times, then they crossed back to the house. Sage stayed behind in the barn where Teagen had brought in a lame colt. Jessie returned to the house.

To her surprise, she found Tattor Sims in the kitchen helping with the baking, or at least trying to help. Jessie noticed that Martha didn't seem upset by his presence, so she passed through without comment.

The old Ranger was in the middle of a story about his wild days down on the Rio Grande. He didn't seem to notice her pass by.

Jessie tried to ignore the pain in her shoulder. She was turning into a bundle of aches and pains. She felt like the lonely old man who used to come in the bookstore every day with a new medical problem.

By noon her shoulder still throbbed. While Martha fed the girls, Jessie slipped into the downstairs bedroom and unbuttoned her blouse until she could push the material off her shoulder and examine her skin in the mirror.

Just as she'd suspected, between her throat and arm were bruises. Long blue lines the width of the back of the rifle.

"What's wrong?" Teagen startled her.

She tugged her blouse up and stared into the mirror as he walked through the doorway. "What are you doing here?" she asked.

"This is my room." He stared at her in the mirror, a more direct look in his eyes than he might have given her if they'd been facing each other.

Jessie knew that this room was now his, but he was here so little she seldom thought of this space in the house as a bedroom. Some nights the bed wasn't slept in, and no personal belongings cluttered the room.

"Oh," she finally said but still didn't turn around. His reflection was hard enough to stand up to; she wasn't sure she wanted to face the real thing. "I was just looking in the mirror at the bruises from my lesson."

He moved closer, reached over her shoulder, and gently tugged the collar of her blouse open.

She didn't have to look at him to know he was frowning.

Stepping up behind her, he said, "You should have kept the butt of the rifle snug against your shoulder."

"I know that now."

Still reaching over her shoulder, he pulled the material until he saw all the bruises. "I could give you some liniment to put on it to ease the muscle pain."

"I'll be fine." In truth, she no longer felt any pain. He hadn't been so close to her in a month, and the fresh, welcoming smell of him she'd grown used to in weeks past was better than any perfume ever sold at the fancy stores. He was so close behind her she could feel the heat of his body through both their clothes.

She expected him to step away, but he didn't. He rested his calloused hand lightly on her tender skin, letting the warmth in his fingers relax her.

A sigh escaped before she could stop it, and she felt herself wishing he'd never back away. He must have known what she wanted for his hand tenderly moved over her skin, pushing the blouse off her shoulder.

She swayed, and his other hand braced her as he continued brushing away the pain with his touch.

Long fingers moved from her throat down to her shoulder. Hardly able to stand, she took deep, slow breaths and felt his hand brush lightly over the swell of her breasts above her camisole. Closing her eyes, she smiled as he unbuttoned another button of her blouse and pushed the material wide. Then, as she knew he would, he went back to touching her. Starting at her collarbone, he feathered soothing strokes over her exposed skin. This big, hard man seemed to know how to apply just the right pressure so that her flesh warmed.

"I hate the blue marks," he whispered against her ear. "But you feel so soft, Jess."

She stepped back against him, and his hand lowered over her breast once more. Though she was fuller than usual and tender, her body ached for him to continue. It felt so right to have him touch her.

He lowered his face against her hair and tugged her camisole slowly away. She made a little sound of pleasure and rocked gently against him.

He replaced his hand where the lace had been and tightened his fingers. Jessie opened her mouth to cry out, but no sound came. He pressed his palm over her fullness, gripping her with tender pressure. She parted her lips to cry out again. If he hadn't been holding her, she wasn't sure she would have been able to stand.

He kissed her hair. "Jess," he whispered, his voice rough with need. "Open your eyes."

She forced her eyes open a fraction and saw his tanned hand molded around her pale flesh.

"Do you want this?" he said.

"Yes," she answered, knowing she should be embarrassed but unable to deny the way he made her feel.

"Am I hurting you?" he asked.

"No," she said, wishing she could put into words how wonderful he made her feel. "Don't stop."

His kiss against her forehead was tender, his grip over her flesh firm.

"Unbutton the rest of your blouse." His words drifted through her hair.

She fumbled with the last few buttons, then watched as his hands moved along her sides and pulled her camisole open.

"You're beautiful." His fingers moved over her once more. "You're the most beautiful woman I've ever seen." He traced the fullness of each breast with his fingertips.

She leaned her head back against his shoulder and moaned softly as he continued to caress her body as though he'd found a great treasure. He lowered his mouth over her bare throat and tasted where her pulse pounded as his hand tenderly branded its way from one breast to the other. Nothing had ever made her feel so alive. When he brushed his knuckles between her breasts, she whispered, "Please."

He moved to her ear. "Please what, Jess?"

She bit her bottom lip. Her breath came fast, rising and falling with the feel of him. "Please more," she whispered.

His laugh was low in her ear and his hands hungry for the feel of her.

The sounds from the kitchen reached them, and he reluctantly pulled away. Without a word, she began buttoning her blouse. When she looked up in the mirror, she saw his eyes and knew he'd watched every movement. His steel-blue gaze was full of longing and promise.

Turning away, suddenly shy, she finished the last button. When she looked up again, he was gone.

All day she thought of the way he'd touched her. When she closed her eyes she saw the hunger in his gaze. There were so many things he was—strong, good, stubborn—but today she'd seen something else. She'd seen a need in him. A need for her.

That night, when he didn't return for supper, she knew he was staying away because of her, and she understood; he didn't want to want her. He was a man who prided himself in needing no one.

She waited up for him until midnight.

He didn't return.

At breakfast, Sage commented that they both looked tired. Jessie promised she wouldn't wait up again, but the next night she was still awake when she heard him come in. It took every ounce of her determination not to run downstairs to him.

By the third night, her need to see him won out over her pride. She waited until he turned out the lamp in the kitchen and tiptoed down the back stairs, hoping to watch him walk to his room or study his silhouette as he smoked his cigar on the porch. She'd promised herself that just watching him, if only for a moment, would be enough.

Halfway across the dark kitchen, she realized her mistake.

He wasn't in the hallway or on the porch. He'd blown out the light and remained in his chair at the kitchen table.

She turned slowly, barely able to make out his outline.

He didn't move.

Like a deer caught by sudden light, she became a statue. Didn't breathe. Didn't blink. As if by remaining perfectly still, he might not notice her.

Closing her eyes, she thought of him. She knew he was too proud to come to her, that doing so somehow would admit a weakness, a need within him, but she'd seen the longing in his eyes, felt it in his touch.

Like a ghost, she moved toward him. Opening her eyes, she let her gaze study him. The hard set of his shoulders, the stiff way he waited almost as if he expected an attack.

He didn't move when she reached him, but her eyes had adjusted enough to the night to see his gaze devoured her.

She gently pushed her knee against his, and he opened his leg. She moved closer until his powerful thighs braced her legs. She leaned down and brushed her lips against his.

No response.

On the second kiss, she pressed harder.

If he'd said a word or asked her what she thought she was doing, she would have run back up the stairs, but he didn't move.

Frustrated, she slid her tongue over his bottom lip, then kissed him again. If he didn't like what she was doing, he was going to have to show some sign.

She felt the hint of a smile before his lips softened to her kiss. Then he kissed her back.

Gently, as if he feared she might break, his arms circled round her and lifted her up as he stood. "We'll continue this discussion in the study," he whispered against her mouth as he walked down the hallway.

The moonlight shone bright through the big windows. She saw his smile as he broke the kiss only long enough to make sure there wasn't a cat sleeping in his chair. Then she was cuddled into his lap again, and his kiss continued.

After a while, she straightened and pulled away. He didn't try to stop her. He simply watched as she unbuttoned her gown.

"Touch me again, Teagen," she whispered.

He ran his fingertips down from her collar until they rested between her breasts, then he gently tugged the gown to one side until a pink tip was exposed. She watched him as he studied her flesh, barely touching her with his hand for a long moment before he leaned down and kissed her breast with a tenderness that made her shiver.

She wrapped her arms around him and cried softly at the joy she felt. He held her to him and let her cry, stroking her back as her tears fell against his shoulder.

She had no idea if he knew how much his touch meant to her. This hard man who never seemed to say the right words was the only person who'd ever made her feel desired.

Before her tears stopped, he began kissing her. Gently, at first, as if not wanting to frighten her, then deeper and deeper until she gulped for air each time he set her mouth free.

Without allowing her time to calm her heartbeat, he wrapped his big hand into her hair and pulled her back to him again and again as if he needed to drink more of her.

Her mouth opened to him, and he took all she gave with each kiss, then backed away as if fearing he demanded too much.

She caught her breath and laughed, then he pulled her to him once more with renewed desire.

Once, he stopped long enough to whisper against her mouth, "I can't get enough of the taste of you, Jess."

"I'm here," she answered, letting her mouth play against his. "There is no hurry. Taste me all you want."

He crushed her against him and let out a low groan like an animal in pain; then his arms cradled her gently once more, and his kiss became tender, telling her how dearly he wanted her near.

When she finally pulled away, he made no effort to stop her as she fell back against his arm.

"I needed that." She laughed.

"Me, too," he admitted.

His hands moved over her gown, calming her, while she rested against his shoulder, feeling boneless in his arms. He brushed over her breasts as if he knew his touch would be welcomed, and his hand spread over her tummy. He seemed to be learning every curve of her, and she'd grown used to his boldness.

She let him touch her, welcomed it. When he lowered his mouth to hers again, the kiss remained tender. Long, slow kisses that made her feel like she was floating. Her lips, once bruised by his demanding kisses, now felt raw, sensitive to even the slight movements of his mouth over her. She relaxed in his arms as he pulled her against his heart.

He fell asleep with his hand over her breast.

Jessie enjoyed the slow beat of his heart until she knew he slept soundly; then she crawled from his lap and tiptoed back to bed. They hadn't talked tonight. Problems still lay between them, but something had changed. Something she wasn't sure either of them was willing to admit.

CHAPTER 21

TEAGEN WOKE ALONE. FOR A WHILE HE DIDN'T OPEN his eyes. He wanted to relive every moment with Jessie. She'd stepped into his arms so easily last night, asking nothing. He'd wanted her so badly he'd almost devoured her.

Yet, even when he'd kissed her hard and long, she'd welcomed him. He'd barely given her time to breathe. Her lips were probably bruised with his demands, yet she hadn't pulled away. She'd let him touch her, mold her, explore her so willingly he'd drunk her in like cool water on a hot day.

Even though he'd forced himself to slow down and kiss her with the tenderness she deserved, he knew he was only kidding himself. He wanted Jessie with a fire that might consume them both.

Before last night, when she'd come to him, he'd been convinced it would be better to stay away from her than torture himself with halfway passion.

But for once in his life he wasn't sure he was strong enough to do something. She belonged to him . . . belonged in his arms. And, he realized, Jessie belonged in his bed. He might never climb the stairs to her room, but he had no objection to her visiting his room.

His thoughts drifted to what might have happened if he'd carried her, not to the study, but to his room. His bed. Would she still have moaned with joy and stretched so willingly against the brush of his hands over her?

The vision he'd seen in the mirror flooded his mind. When

he had time alone with her, he'd let her know his door would always be open. Rubbing his thumb over his bottom lip, he thought of the way he'd kissed her. He grinned, remembering the way she'd kissed him back.

He had no doubt that he was the first man to ever kiss her. How could his friend have lived with her for all those years and never kissed her?

Teagen knew the answer. For some men the act of love-making was only breeding. He'd read that some religions even preach that it should be no more. But how could any man look at Jessie and want so little?

He stood and stormed outside to wash up at the stand by the well. With the dawn he had to shove the night and Jessie's touch away. He had work to do. He couldn't go around day-dreaming like some half-grown boy.

After dumping a bucket of water over his head to try to clear his thoughts, he shook his hair and heard a giggle.

Teagen looked up to see Rose watching him from the steps. "Why'd you do that?"

"It gets the sleep out of my brain," he answered.

"Martha says coffee does that for her. Maybe if you poured coffee in that bucket, you'd wake up even faster."

"Maybe," he answered as he pulled on a clean shirt and stepped on the porch. He didn't feel up to the kid's questions, but his frown didn't make her disappear.

"Em," she called. "Come help."

Before he could pull away, Rose grabbed his first two fingers and began to pull. He stepped forward, and she smiled, took another stance and pulled again. Emily hurried to his other side and, without looking up at him, began to push on his leg.

He moved another foot closer to the kitchen door, and they both relaxed for a moment, took deep breaths, and began again. If he'd wanted to, he could have ignored their efforts, but they seemed to be trying so hard, he took another step.

"What are you doing?" He leaned down to Rose, knowing he'd never get the answer out of Emily.

The little five-year-old put her hands on her hips as if she were dealing with a bothersome giant of a child. "Martha says you sometimes have a hard time stepping into civilization in the morning, and we all need to help." Without another word, she began tugging once more.

Teagen frowned at them and then suddenly laughed. They thought they were helping him, and from the look of it, both were willing to give it their all.

He let them direct him into the kitchen and push him toward a chair. Then Rose stood in front of him and stared hard. "Are you there yet, Mister?"

"I'm close," He ran his hand through his wet hair and finished buttoning his shirt.

Rose patted his hand. "You're trying, I can tell, and a try is only a step away from a can."

Martha walked in the room and raised an eyebrow. "Morning, Teagen," she said. "You're up early."

"I'm being dragged into civilization."

"About time."

He frowned at the old housekeeper, who poured him a cup of coffee and went about making breakfast.

Rose still stood at his side. "Mister?"

"Yes," he said fighting down a smile.

"Are you our father now?"

Teagen and Jessie had never talked about what they'd tell the children. He wasn't sure what she'd want him to say. "Do you want me to be, Rose?"

She propped her elbows on the table and shook her head. "Emily and me don't want another father. Our father was always yelling at us and he made Mom cry sometimes."

Teagen was starting to question his judgment in friends. Eli had seemed so logical, so reasonable, in his letters. How could the man be so different?

Drinking his coffee, he thought of his own father. He'd worked hard, but he'd never been unkind. "I called my father Papa when I was a kid. He never made my mom cry."

Rose frowned. "Did he let you talk to him?"

"Every night, and when it stormed, he'd take my brothers and me out on the porch. We'd curl up in a blanket and watch the storms roll in over the land. He'd tell us stories of growing up in Ireland."

"Where is he?"

"He's in heaven, I guess, with my mother."

"Our father is in the ground," Emily whispered.

Teagen almost reached out to touch the thin child on his right, but he knew he'd only frighten her. This conversation was way over his level of skill. He was glad to see Jessie walk into the room with Bethie on her hip.

She looked all proper and stiff with her hair pulled back in a bun and her black dress. Little remained of the woman he'd held in his arms a few hours ago. Perhaps her bottom lip was a little fuller from being kissed; maybe her cheek bore a hint more red from the blush that had burned in the shadows when he'd cupped her breast.

Teagen wished he were civilized enough to think of something to say to her. But, "I want you like you were last night," didn't seem right for breakfast conversation, so he just watched her.

She helped Martha and handled the girls with gentle guidance. Then, for the first time in over a month, she sat down next to him. She didn't touch him, but her simple gesture seemed to settle his world. There were things that needed to be said between them, but they could wait another day . . . another night.

Sage came in, complaining about the heat already being too warm for this early, and she and Martha wished for rain. Rose ate her breakfast and asked, "How come Sage can put sugar in her coffee, and I can't have sugar in my milk?"

They talked about the day, all that needed doing and all that would have to wait until tomorrow. When Teagen stood, Emily jumped from her chair and ran for her hat. She stood at the door without a word.

Teagen strapped on his gun belt and grabbed his hat, then finally turned to her. "What is it, Em?"

All he could see was the top of her head as she stared at her feet. "Can I ride out with you as far as the end of the corral? Sage has been teaching me. I'll turn around then and come right back, I promise."

"Look at me, Emily?" He tried to keep his voice low.

When she looked up, he swore she trembled as if a tornado were shaking the house.

"If you ride, you follow orders."

Her head bobbed.

"Then you can ride."

Sage laughed. "You see, Em, I told you he'd let you. Come on along, and I'll help you saddle up."

Teagen glanced back at Jessie but spotted Rose halfway between them. The middle child looked like she was going to cry.

"What's wrong?" he asked Rose as Sage and Emily hurried out.

"Who is going to help me count all the pigs? And gather eggs, and say hello to the toads, and . . ."

"How about Bethie?" Teagen tried.

"She can't count." Rose frowned.

"You could teach her."

Rose studied her little sister. "I suppose, but it's another job that will take me hours."

"I could let you have Sage's old chalkboard, and we could make a desk up," Martha offered.

Rose watched as Jessie wiped the baby's fingers and set her on the floor. She took her sister's hand and shrugged her shoulders almost to her ears. "All right. I'll do it, but I'll have to teach her to talk first, and heaven only knows how long that will take."

With her sister in tow, she followed Martha out of the room.

It took Teagen a minute to realize he and Jessie were alone. When their eyes met, he swore he could read her mind. She'd been smiling at her daughters, then slowly her smile turned into something quite different.

He watched as she crossed the room and stood a few feet from him.

"I want to touch you." He said the only thing on his mind.

"We can't," she answered.

"I know. But just tell me if you want it too?" He had to ask.

She looked down for a moment, then faced him again. "I do."

Teagen almost strangled the brim of his hat. He knew Martha would be back in the kitchen at any moment. Sage and Emily could probably see them standing in the doorway all the way from the barn. Now was not the time, but he swore he could already feel her in his arms.

"Until tonight." He crammed his hat on his head and stepped out before he proved to her just how uncivilized he was.

The old Rangers were waiting near the barn. Teagen wished his brothers were home, but these men were the next best thing. The three hired hands would take care of the herd, but the retired Rangers would stand with him, no matter how outnumbered they were in the fight.

Tattor met him halfway. He fell into step as Teagen moved toward the others. "Dolan found fresh tracks down by the river this morning. Looks like three riders swam over sometime after midnight."

"Any idea what they were doing?"

"Watching," Tattor said. "Just watching, like always. If this raid don't come soon, I'll be too fat from sweet Martha's cooking to set a horse."

Teagen glanced at him to see if the Ranger had hit his head, then decided to ignore the *sweet* comment. Surely he meant the food was sweet, for Martha was far more vinegar than sugar. Pulling his gloves from his back pocket, he said, "If they are hoping to catch us off guard, they'll have a long wait."

Tattor Sims shook his head. "That's just it. I ain't never seen outlaws hang around like this. Men who live by the gun tend to act first and think later. If there is a gang hiding out, that kind would be shooting each other by now. Whoever is in charge is either real smart or real mean. He'd have to be to keep trouble down."

"Got any ideas?" Teagen had already come to the same conclusion. He wasn't dealing with the lowlife who usually raided in these parts. This wasn't a man looking to steal a few head. Whoever planned this raid wanted all Teagen had and a half-dozen lawmen between here and Austin wouldn't be able to stop him.

"Nope, no plan comes to mind," Sims answered.

"We'll find one." Teagen knew it was up to him and his small army of old Rangers and broken-down cowhands.

He talked to the men, preparing, as always, for the unexpected. Over the years Teagen had learned from every Ranger who worked for him. He knew his grandfather would stop any attack coming from the hills. Men trying to run the river would never be able to get enough raiders across the water and onto Whispering Mountain land at one time to fight. Drummond Roak had been right; if the raid came, it would be from the bridge.

Teagen glanced over at the barn and saw Emily waiting. She looked so small next to Glory. So tiny and so determined to ride. The need to protect her choked around his heart, and he thought of how tough his father had been on him, always pushing him to do his best. Andrew McMurray had made his sons strong enough to stand what came after he died, and now that the girls were his, Teagen had to do the same.

He walked to the child and lifted her up. "If you're going to ride, Emily, you're going to fall off sometime. That's just a fact."

She nodded. "I know. Sage told me."

He patted her hand as she gripped the saddle horn. "When you do fall off, I don't want to hear a word unless you're really hurt. No complaining about little aches and pains."

Her head bobbed.

"That's my girl," he said and stepped up on his horse. "Now, ride with me to the end of the corral."

He didn't say another word, but when she looked at him with pride, he smiled.

As he turned to watch her riding back toward home, Teagen saw Sage standing at the corner of the barn, waving.

Fighting down an oath at the delay, he galloped toward his sister.

"Sorry," Sage said, "but I forgot to tell you, I ordered medicine that should come in on the stage today. It's what I need to help that colt's open wound heal. I could ride in, or we could send one of the men."

Teagen shook his head. The men didn't know about the secret pass through the hills to the post. His sister knew the shortcut, but he'd worry about Sage being alone in town. "If you'll stand guard, I'll go get it."

She looked like she'd already come to the same conclusion. "You can be back in two hours. I'll be armed and in the saddle until you get home."

He climbed down and stepped into the barn to grab a few burlap sacks. Knowing Sage, there would be more than one box to tie down.

Sage pulled a slip of paper from her pocket. "Martha had Jessie jot down a few things she needs."

He frowned.

"It's not much," Sage teased. "You can carry it all behind the saddle."

Teagen might have said something about Martha being able to wait until the end-of-the-month trip, but Jessie walked into the barn, and he forgot about being bothered.

Sage disappeared to help Emily water her horse.

His new wife glanced over her shoulder to make sure they were alone, then walked right up to him and kissed his cheek.

He bent and captured her mouth in a warm, friendly kiss he'd been hungry for all morning.

She put her arms around his neck and held on tight. When the kiss ended, she whispered low in his ear. "Touch me."

He stared at her as he tugged off his glove and spread his

hand over her breast. When she closed her eyes and smiled, he pulled her to him and kissed her again.

The second time he lowered her to the ground, she giggled and ran away. He could do nothing but watch. His Jessie was coming out to ask him to touch her; life didn't get much sweeter.

CHAPTER 22

Sage saw Jessie leaving the barn smiling, and when Teagen came out a minute later, his mood had improved. Whatever the little widow was doing to her brother should be bottled. He was a man who brooded his bad moods to perfection.

"I'll be back as soon as I can," Teagen said with a nod. "Keep your eyes open, Sage."

She waved even after he turned toward the hills. Then she walked into the barn to saddle her horse. In truth, she looked forward to a morning ride. In a few weeks, Emily would be skilled enough to go with her. Sage knew her brothers preferred solitary work hours, but she liked company, and having Jessie and the girls on the place made the days seem fun, even when she was tied to household chores.

Emily showed all the signs of becoming an excellent rider. She had one thing no amount of training could force: a love for horses.

Just as Sage reached for the first stall door, something dropped from the loft along with a dusting of hay.

She pulled her pistol and swung around, almost colliding with Drummond Roak.

"Hellfire, Drum!" She raised her gun as if it were a club she planned to use.

He laughed. "Glad to see me?"

She lowered the weapon but didn't put it back in the holster. "I should shoot you for scaring a year off my life."

He winked. "Sorry. Wouldn't want you getting any older on me, darlin'. I'm already picking fruit long on the vine."

"Stop calling me darling, and you're not picking anything." She waved the barrel of her gun at him. "I've told you before—"

He grabbed the weapon from her hand and tossed it in the hay. Then with swift strength, he caught her around the waist, lifted, and shoved her against the rough stall gate. His whole body slammed against her as his mouth found hers.

Sage fought, kicking and hitting as anger built. He was too strong. She couldn't get in a full swing to make her blows count. Finally, in frustration, she bit his lip.

"Ow!" he wailed. "You bit me!" He stepped away, letting her tumble to the ground.

She jumped up, ready to fight. With one swift kick, she hit his shin as hard as she could, then swung her leg and tripped him as he tried to stagger away.

He hit the ground hard and lay spread out like a gingerbread man.

She drew back her boot to kick his ribs.

"Just kill me!" he yelled without trying to defend himself.

She stopped in midswing. It was hard kicking a man when he asked for it. "You're lucky I don't, Drummond. I could break at least one rib."

He sat up and raked a hand through straight black hair a month past needing a cutting. "I'm sure I deserve it, trying to kiss you and all. I was just hoping you'd be in a friendly mood for a change."

She offered him a hand, and he stood. "I told you I'd shoot you the next time you tried to kiss me. What's wrong with you?"

"I don't know, Sage. I can't seem to help myself." He rubbed the blood from his lip. "But you do object strong enough to make me reconsider."

"You attacked me."

"I just wanted to kiss you."

She let out a long breath. In the rough world this wild boy came from, he probably thought that was how to approach a woman. She almost felt sorry for him. "What are you doing here, anyway?"

"I came to offer my help. I think the raid may come within the week. I wanted you to know so you wouldn't shoot me. When trouble starts your way, I'll cross the bridge."

"You'd fight with us?"

"Sure," he said. "You're all I got, Sage."

"You don't have me, Drum." She felt sorry for the kid. "I'm too old for you, and besides, you don't even know how to treat a lady." She reached in her pocket for her handkerchief and dabbed at the blood on his lip. "I thank you, though, for the offer to stand with us in the fight. This time you may be joining the weaker side. There's a chance we could be killed in this battle coming. I heard one of the Rangers say that the leader of this band may be the strongest outlaw in the state. Rumors are he has as many as fifty men."

"More like thirty, I'm thinking, but it don't matter. I'd die by your side," he whispered, and she rolled her eyes.

"If you die by my side, it's probably my gun smoking. Now swear you will never grab me, slam me up against a wall, and try to force yourself on me again."

"I wasn't forcing nothing." He pouted then yelped when his lip hurt. "I was kissing."

"Drum, folks don't kiss like that."

"They don't?"

"No. They hold each other gently and barely touch lips."

He raised an eyebrow in disbelief. "Show me." One side of his mouth lifted in challenge.

She knew she shouldn't; it was like petting a stray dog. But she felt bad for hurting him when he'd obviously meant her no harm. "All right." She stood on her toes and gently placed her lips on his.

He didn't move.

She pressed against his mouth ever so lightly.

He slipped his hand over her breast and squeezed.

Sage pulled away and swung, but Drum caught her fist. He had the nerve to look sorry. "That was wrong, right?"

"Right." She pulled her hand from his grip. "Where could you have learned such acts? Add that to your never-do-again list."

Drum looked confused. He didn't answer her question or swear never to do it again, but he did pick up his hat off the floor and step a safe distance away. "I'll learn," he finally said. "One day you'll be asking me to touch you, Sage."

She watched him move away and swore he turned a little more into a man every time she saw him. Soon she wouldn't be able to talk to him as a boy, and she wasn't sure how she'd react to the man.

He pulled Satan from a back stall and swung up. "I'll be close when you need me."

No matter how irritated she was at him, she admitted, "I'll be grateful."

CHAPTER 23

Teagen crossed through the secret passage, making good time. Though it was midmorning, the day didn't seem as hot as usual. A few clouds dotted the sky, and he hoped they were in for a break from the past week of hot sun.

He watched for any hint that a horse had passed along the trail as he carefully left no trace. His father had taught the boys well. No one would ever know of this trail into and out of McMurray land. It took less than half the time of going over the bridge and down the road. If he were lucky, no one watching would be aware he left the ranch.

At one point, he paused long enough to see the smoke from his grandfather's lookout camp. The Apache were always close, but even when it might have meant McMurray lives, his grandfather had not interfered. He taught them how to hunt and track. He'd even shown them ways few white men knew, but the old man believed his grandsons belonged to the white man's world and had to fight their own battles among their people. Teagen often thought, if all McMurrays were killed, his mother's people would come down from the hills and bury them.

Still, today the smoke from their fires gave him comfort.

Though he fought the distraction, his mind kept going back to the barn when Jessie asked him to touch her. He knew he'd have to be careful, but it was time for their flirting to be over. He wanted to lay her down on his bed and run his hand over her body. He wanted to feel the child growing in her, a child that would be his, even though not by blood. If it was a boy, maybe they'd name him Eli after his friend. Eli had always written of how he longed to live Teagen's life in Texas; now maybe his son could. If the baby was a girl, that would be all right too. Teagen had laughed more in the weeks they'd been on the ranch than he'd laughed before in his life.

It crossed his thoughts that he'd promised Jessie a house in town. Just because she kissed him and cuddled up a few times didn't mean she wanted to be his full-time wife. Being a true wife might be more than she was ready for. She hadn't married with any promises of such. Maybe she didn't want any more than they had now. With things comfortable between them, he wouldn't mind riding into her place a few times a month, and she and the girls could come for a long visit in the summers. With the girls and his brothers, their wives and babies, the house would be full of noise and laughter. Who knows, once Rose saw Duck, Travis's adopted son, she might decide to teach him to talk too. He and Jessie would watch them grow and laugh about what they did for years.

He knew if she took the house in town, he'd be settling for less than he wanted, but he'd settled all his life, and if it took that to keep them close, he'd buy her a place.

Teagen felt his whole body shift as if the earth had rotated backward for a heartbeat. He wanted more, much more. For the first time ever he needed something he'd never had. He wanted Jessie. She might not love him. She might never love him, but he needed her by his side and in his bed. He'd give her the house in town if she insisted, but he would be part of her life.

He galloped to the high point of his land and glanced back one last time before descending away from his property. For once the grand sight didn't fill him with pride. His mind was soaked with the memory of a smile on one very special brown-eyed woman. If she asked for his touch this morning, she'd ask again tonight, and he planned to take his time giving her what she asked for.

Smoke to the east caught his attention. Not the thin line from a campfire but the rolling black kind that could only signal a grass fire.

With a sudden jerk of the reins, Teagen turned his horse and raced back toward home, his mission to town forgotten. The horse's hooves almost drowned out one lone shot coming from the same direction as the smoke. Teagen pushed harder, leaning low as the animal ran.

When he reached the barn, Martha yelled from the porch. "We got a grass fire going on the east side!"

"I know," he said pulling his saddle from the lathered bay. "I saw it from the top of the mountain. I'll change mounts and be out there. Tell Sage to fire rounds to pull all the men in."

"They all know. She had Hatch load the wagon with both rain barrels and all the old blankets. The other two men are already there fighting it dry. Sims rode off in that direction to check the riverbank half an hour before we saw the smoke. He probably made it to the site first."

Teagen slapped his horse into the corral and began saddling a fresh one. The small herd they kept in the corral was circling nervously. They'd already smelled the fire.

A grass fire was normally somewhat controllable on windless days. But the land was dryer than usual, and guessing from the direction of the smoke, this fire appeared to be close to the place Travis was building in the woods. They'd need to get it contained fast, or the blaze would take not only the half-finished house belonging to Travis and Rainey, but the trees around it.

Jessie ran to the fence. "What can I do?"

He knew the more help they had, the better, but he didn't want her too near the fire. "Help Martha hitch the old wagon and load it down with buckets full of water." He looked directly at her. "Tell Martha not to drive the wagon within a hundred yards of the fire. I don't want the horses bolting on her. We'll see her and come to her."

He pulled the fresh mount past her and lowered his voice.

"You stay here. As soon as Martha comes close, we'll trade wagons and send her back. Refill the buckets as fast as you can."

Jessie nodded. "Em and Rose will help me."

He swung up without another word and headed toward the smoke. He wished he'd had a minute to hold her. The fear in her eyes worried him. Grass fires could be hell to fight, but they'd fought several over the years. By nightfall it would be out with hopefully only a few sections of grassland lost. The land would look dead and black until spring, but then any sign of the fire would disappear.

The heat hit him before the smoke did. A warmth like opening an oven washed over him, turning the already warm air to hot. He saw three men working thirty feet from the tree line. A tall figure that could only have been Hatch rode in, jumped from his horse, and joined them. With no wind, the fire was eating up the ground on the other side, but the wet blankets the men slapped against the earth seemed to be holding it away from the trees.

He saw Sage pulling a wagon along one side of the fire pushing the blaze into a triangle shape so that it would grow smaller. They were letting the third side of the blaze burn its way to the river.

To Teagen's surprise, Drummond Roak stood in the back of the wagon, hatless and dripping wet as he splashed bucket after bucket from the rain barrel. From the looks of it he was dipping deep, almost out of water. They'd be ready for another wagonload of water long before Martha could get to them.

Teagen rode toward his sister. The moment he tied his horse to the wagon, Roak tossed a dripping blanket at his head. Grumbling, Teagen went to work.

The air burned down his lungs, and his clothes turned black from the smoke, but he didn't slow. If the wind whipped up before this line of the fire was under control, it could head straight to the house. They kept the area around the house and barn free of grass, but he knew seeing the smoke coming would frighten the girls.

Sage yelled when she saw a wagon coming. Drummond dropped the last of the water out and jumped to the ground with a soaked tarp over one shoulder.

"I'll trade out the wagons and send Martha back," Sage said, already turning the team.

Neither man uttered a word as they continued to fight. At times, the fire seemed to circle as if playing a game of surrounding them. To Roak's credit, he knew how to work the flames. When the fire came too close, the men fought with their backs to one another. The blanket dried, becoming less effective with each swing.

Teagen raised his head. The men who'd been near the trees were working their way closer, and the smoke seemed less intense, but Sage was nowhere in sight. With clouds covering the sun and all the smoke in the air, Teagen couldn't see any sign of either Sage or Martha's wagon.

His lungs ached, and his knuckles were starting to bleed, but he didn't slow. The wind kicked up, sending the fire dancing but bringing whispers of rain to come. With no moisture in weeks, this would be the perfect day for an afternoon shower. Raising his head, he took a deep breath and smiled. Rain was in the air.

They worked for an hour before the fire was brought under control. At first, he'd thought Sage must have driven the wagon farther to the east. The buckets of water could be used on any side. But as time passed and the smoke began to clear, Teagen couldn't see her.

A worry fisted in the pit of his stomach, bothering him far more than the fire. He glanced at Roak just as the kid raised his head to look in the direction Sage had gone. Roak was worried about her too. She should be safe. She drove away from the fire. Once she traded wagons with Martha, she should have had a full load of fresh water.

"She's safe," Teagen shouted to the kid.

Roak glared at him.

Neither of them believed his words.

They worked on, the worry building. When Teagen and Roak

were within fifty feet of Hatch and the two hired men, Teagen yelled, "Have you seen Sage or the wagon?"

The Ranger shook his head even before his "No" reached them.

Teagen swore and fought down worry turning to panic.

Roak echoed his words from a few feet away.

"Have you seen Sims?" Hatch shouted.

"No," Teagen answered, knowing somehow the two missing people were connected. He reasoned that Sims could take care of himself, but Sage might try to take on more than she could handle.

Roak tossed the remains of what had been a good tarp on the ground and straightened. "I'm going after her," he said. "To hell with this fire."

For once Teagen couldn't blame the kid. In fact, he felt the same way. But Teagen stayed, thrashing away at the flames as he watched Roak head in the direction Sage had gone.

Thunder rattled above. For the hundredth time, Teagen prayed for rain.

Just before the kid disappeared into the smoke, Teagen thought he saw the outline of a wagon. He dropped his blanket and ran.

The shadow of the wagon was ringed in smoke.

The whole world seemed to darken. Teagen couldn't tell if it was from the smoke or the clouds gathering above. He didn't care as he slowed his steps, searching for any sight of the wagon he'd seen minutes before.

"Over here!" Roak yelled.

His words circled in a gust of wind, but Teagen spotted the wagon sitting in the middle of burned grass still smoking, even though the fire had died. He saw no one.

As he stepped over the wagon tongue, he guessed Sage must have turned the team loose. But why? If the horses were able to run out of the fire, why hadn't she ridden with them?

His boots crunched in the blackened remains of grass as he stormed closer. She shouldn't have been this close to the edge of the fire. Martha must have pulled the wagon too near. Or

Sage had been dumping the water herself and let the flames get too near.

His boot sank suddenly into mud. He looked down. A circle of water steamed around the wagon.

What he saw didn't make sense. Why would she dump water on the wagon to keep it from burning and set the horses loose? Why didn't she just get out?

No one was in the wagon. Half the buckets were still full.

Teagen ran around to the other side and froze. The sight before him stopped his heart.

There, on an unburned patch of pale grass, knelt Sage and Roak. Sage had used half a wagonload of water to save one small patch of ground.

He took a step closer as Roak stood and backed away. "I'll be back as fast as I can," the boy said to Sage as he turned, almost colliding with Teagen.

Teagen made no move to get out of Roak's way. He saw only one thing amid the smoke.

Jessie lay curled on the ground, her black dress only a foot away from the scorched grass. The spilled water had saved the one spot she lay on.

He moved closer and saw a flash of the white of her petticoats. Then, all that filled his vision was red.

Blood red everywhere.

CHAPTER 24

SAGE GLANCED UP AT HER BROTHER AND WISHED FOR a second that she could spare him the pain. He'd never allowed himself one day of happiness before Jessie came into his life, and even with her as his wife, he'd been slow to smile. But she'd made him happy. Sage had seen it this morning. They'd both been laughing at something secret between them when Sage saw them leave the barn. Something secret, something nice.

And now she would have to tell Teagen horrible news.

Teagen knelt. His hand went out to touch Jessie, but dirty, soot-covered fingers pulled back. "What's wrong with her, Sage?"

Before she could answer, he swore. "She shouldn't be out here. I ordered her to stay at the house where it was safe. Why would she drive the wagon out? Martha should have done that."

Jessie whimpered and moved as if trying to curl into a ball, and Teagen seemed to forget all his anger. He glared up at Sage. "What can I do?"

Sage nodded once, knowing that she'd have his help, and they'd need each other if they were going to move the little widow.

"She's losing the baby," Sage said plainly, knowing Teagen would want the facts fast. "She tripped climbing out of the wagon. By the time I reached her, blood was already flowing out, and I was afraid to move her."

Teagen looked up, and she knew he could fill in the rest. Sage had let the horses go, doused the area with water, and tried to help Jessie, even though they were in the middle of a grass fire.

"What can I do?" he repeated between clenched teeth.

Sage shook her head. "She's in so much pain she won't let me see. I need her to lie back so that I can see how far along with the delivery she's come. If you could hold her . . . comfort her . . . maybe I could see if we'd be safe moving her." Sage met his stare before whispering, "With this amount of blood, I've little hope we can save the baby. It will be too small to survive. Now the best we can hope for is to save her."

Teagen knelt at Jessie's head and hooked his hands beneath her arms. He pulled her gently up against him until he held her shoulders and head.

She whimpered in pain.

"Easy now, Jess," he said. "I've got you."

Her fingers closed around his arm, and she took a breath. "Teagen," she whispered. "You're here."

Sage moved to her skirts. "Jessie, you've got to let me look. Hang on to Teagen and try to relax enough so that I can have a look."

"Jess," he whispered as he pushed her hair away from her eyes. "Jessie, we're going to help you get through this."

She bit her lip against the pain, and he would have given his soul if he could have taken this torture from her.

"Jessie," he ordered. "Look at me."

She didn't move.

"Look at me."

Her eyes fluttered open. "All right, Teagen," she whispered.

"I'm right here with you." He closed his hand over hers. "I want you to relax and let Sage help you."

Jessie nodded and glanced down.

"Look at me, Jess. Look only at me." He didn't want her to see the blood.

"You're a mess," Jessie answered.

He smiled at her. "Ranching is a dirty job most days."

"I . . ." She glanced down as Sage lifted her skirts. "My baby?"

"Look at me, Jess," Teagen demanded.

She met his eyes. "An order or a request?"

"A request," he answered. "I like looking into those brown eyes of yours. I think of them sometimes when I'm alone."

"You do?" she whispered in pain as Sage gently pulled her legs apart.

Jessie seemed to understand what was happening for the first time. Tears rolled down her cheeks, but she did not break the stare. "I'll look only at your face if you'll look only at mine."

He tightened his grip. "I'll do that. We'll get through this together. Sage knows what to do."

Jessie bit her lip and nodded as Sage moved her hands beneath her skirts.

Teagen had to think of something to take her mind off what was happening. "Why'd you come out after I told you to stay at the house?"

"I had to," Jessie said, pulling her gaze back to his. "Martha was busy taking care of the Ranger named Sims."

"Why?" Teagen asked, still holding her tight.

"He rode in a few minutes after you left. He'd been shot in the leg." She bit back a cry of pain, and they heard Sage whisper an apology for what she had to do.

Teagen forced himself to keep questioning Jessie, even though all he wanted to do was ask Sage to hurry up. "Did he know who shot him?"

Jessie gripped his hand tightly and let out a little cry. It took her a few minutes to recover enough to answer, but she seemed to be fighting to continue. Teagen felt like they were both playing a game to keep from dealing with the reality of what was happening.

"Sims said someone shot from the brush along the river edge. He didn't see who."

Teagen swore, then forced himself to calm. "We'll deal with them later. If Sims was talking, he's probably not dying, and if I know the old Ranger, he'll be wanting to find the answers as soon as he can ride."

Jessie pulled his hand against her cheek. "Stay with me, Teagen. Promise me, no matter what happens, you won't leave me out here alone."

"I promise." He kissed the top of her hair. "Roak has gone after the other wagon. As soon as Sage checks you out, I'll take you home. Don't worry; you'll be in your bed in no time."

"Good." Jessie closed her eyes and seemed to relax a little.

He glanced down at Sage. His sister's hands were covered in blood now. She'd cut a piece of Jessie's petticoat away and was wrapping something.

"Jess," he whispered, but his wife didn't open her eyes. He moved his cheek along her face and felt the slow exhale of her breath. He didn't know if she was asleep or passed out. He didn't care, as long as she was alive.

They heard the sound of a wagon as Roak drew near. He'd wrapped the horses' hooves in wet burlap bags and blindfolded them so they wouldn't see the fire burning only ten feet away. He walked beside them, guiding them as close as he could.

Teagen rose to his knees without letting go of Jessie. "Can we move her now?" he asked Sage.

"Very carefully," Sage whispered as she stood cradling the tiny bundle in her arms. "She lost the baby."

Teagen had no time to worry about how he'd tell Jessie. Right now all he could think of was getting her out of the mud and blood. He lifted her gently and held her against his chest as he walked through grass still smoldering to the wagon. Without a word, he sat on the tailgate.

Sage climbed in beside Roak, and they headed back toward the house.

"Don't die on me, Jess," Teagen whispered against her ear. "Promise you won't die on me."

She was so still it frightened him. Halfway back to the house he felt warm rain on his skin, but he didn't care. All that mattered was in his arms.

Roak must have told Martha what had happened, because

she was standing on the porch with a quilt ready to wrap around Jessie.

Teagen paused without loosening his hold on Jessie as Martha tucked the blanket around her.

"The girls are playing in the dining room, so you should have no problem getting up the stairs with her."

"How's Sims?" Teagen remembered why Martha hadn't been the one driving the wagon.

"He'll live. I dug the bullet out and gave him half a bottle of whiskey to drink while the wound drained. I figured Sage would want to sew him up." Martha touched Jessie's forehead. "She's cold."

Sage walked up behind Teagen. "She's lost a lot of blood." She turned to Roak. "Wash up, then get Martha two buckets of water to boil, and I'll need another two upstairs, still cold from the well."

Teagen moved through the house. "I'm not taking her upstairs. She'll be downstairs, in my room."

No one argued. They all moved to follow orders. Drummond ran to wash and haul water. Martha hurried ahead to make out the bed. Sage went after her medicine box.

Teagen crossed into the room that served as his bedroom. One foot into the room he saw the mirror Jessie had been standing in front of only hours ago. She'd looked so beautiful he'd had to touch her. She'd smelled of vanilla and tasted of heaven.

He gently placed her on the bed and stepped back. She looked so pale in her black dress. All the warmth he'd seen in her cheeks was gone.

"Go clean up, Teagen," Sage said softly. "Martha and I have work to do here." When he hesitated, she added, "It's all right, and the way you look, you'll probably frighten her when she wakes. Go."

He didn't want to leave, but Sage was right. His skin was covered in black smoke, and he smelled of the fire. "I'll be right back," he promised. "If she wakes—"

"We'll tell her," Martha said in her no-nonsense way. The housekeeper was already unbuttoning Jessie's blouse. "Don't come back until you're called." She glared at him. "I mean it, Teagen."

"All right," he said, feeling useless. He thought of how he'd watched Jessie do the same thing hours before. He didn't want to see her flesh now. Not now, with her hurt.

He almost ran to the mud room.

Roak stood by the washstand, his shirt off, his body already scrubbed clean. Teagen almost told him to get dressed, then realized the shirt he had been wearing was now a rag.

He nodded. "Grab one of the shirts along the first row."

Roak looked around at the three rows of clothes behind him. "You giving me one of your brothers' shirts?"

"No. I'm giving you one of mine." Teagen pulled off his own shirt and began to soap up. "It eats at me that I have to keep thanking you."

Roak grinned. "I know. That alone makes even the sacrifice of my best shirt worth it." He tugged on the shirt two sizes too big for him.

Teagen dumped a half bucket of water over his head, and by the time he looked up, the kid was gone. He continued to wash, knowing that Sage and Martha would need time. They'd have to undress Jessie, clean up all the blood, and then pull a nightgown over her. He wasn't sure what else they'd do or if he wanted to know. Sage had asked for hot water and cold. The hot must be for a bath. The cold to slow the bleeding.

He didn't like to think of his Jessie hurting.

He dried his hair and changed into clean clothes. When he stepped out on the porch to watch a storm move in, he realized he had no idea what time of day it must be. The sky was twilight dark. The smoke and fires were out, but the land that had burned lay dark as if a cloud blocked even the moonlight from the earth.

Teagen watched Roak walk through the light rain with two

more buckets of water. When he passed Teagen, he said, "Martha told me to leave these outside the door. She said I wasn't even to bother them with a knock."

Teagen could stay still no longer. "I'll be checking on Sims if they need me," he said as he bolted off the porch and ran toward the bunkhouse.

Sims smiled when he entered. "About time someone came to check on me," he said as Teagen shook the rain off.

"We've been busy, but that don't mean you were forgotten."

Sims shrugged. "I'm too far past sober to complain. Martha took good care of me, and she's right, letting this wound drain a little will get all the black powder out of it." He lifted his glass. "I would like a cigar if you got one though."

Teagen pulled out the cigar he'd shoved in his pocket before he stepped onto the porch. "I brought you one," he lied as he lit a lamp to brighten the dingy room.

While Sims smoked, Teagen took a look at where the bullet had punctured the old Ranger's leg. It was a clean wound. Martha was right; it would heal fast.

Sims lifted his glass. "All these years, I've never been shot. To tell the truth, I'm tired of listening to everyone else tell stories of what it's like." He laughed. "Now I finally got a wound to show, but I got to work on a more interesting story than being shot from the weeds."

"Did you see or hear anything?"

Sims shook his head. "I've been thinking, and I've figured out that someone crossed the river and set the fire. He must have just finished and ran back for the river when I came along. If I was betting, I'd say it was a kid or a drunk because from that range, a man who was any kind of shot couldn't have missed my heart."

Teagen thought about what he said. "Maybe the trespasser didn't want to kill you?"

Sims gulped down the last of his drink. "No, I think he did. He was close enough to the water that I'd never been able to get to him before he was in the water. Maybe I surprised him. Maybe he was nervous, but if he took the time to keep gunpowder dry while crossing the water, he meant to shoot."

Teagen nodded. "You're lucky."

Sims shook his head. "If I'd been lucky, he would have missed."

The other men came into the bunkhouse. If possible, they were even blacker than Teagen had been. The hired hands said they wanted to clean up before going back out, but Hatch just checked on Sims and walked outside.

Teagen followed him. "You want to wash up?"

The Ranger shook his head. "Rain'll wash me. I'll ride guard in this storm."

Teagen thanked him and moved back to the house. When he reached the porch, three little girls stood blocking the door.

"Is this a storm?" Rose asked.

Teagen smiled. "I'd say we're in for a good one." He glanced up at the lightning show above.

Emily took his hand and led him to the bench.

Teagen raised an eyebrow but sat down where she patted. Emily sat on one side, Rose on the other. Bethie raised her hands for him to lift her onto his lap.

Emily jumped up and darted inside.

Rose said, "Martha told us Momma is sleeping, so we decided to come out here with you."

Emily appeared with her blue blanket he'd bought her that first day. She spread it over them all and returned to her seat beside him.

"What are we doing?" Teagen asked. He knew the girls well enough by now to guess they were up to something.

"We're watching the storm roll in with our papa," Rose said simply.

Teagen leaned his head back against the house and smiled. For a man who always thought he had no heart, discovering that he was wrong shook him to the core.

Bethie leaned against his chest and fell asleep, while Rose

asked questions, and Emily pressed her face into his shoulder every time it thundered.

Hours later when Sage said he could see his wife, Teagen sat beside her bed and told her all that had happened. She never woke, but he had a feeling she heard him.

CHAPTER 25

Jessie woke slowly, pushing the pain away an inch at a time. She felt weak and hollow inside. She opened her eyes to a shadowy room lit by one lamp burning low. It took her a moment to realize she was in Teagen's downstairs bedroom. Sage's full-length mirror stood in one corner; her hope chest rested beneath the window.

Jessie remembered the last time she'd been here. Teagen had touched her as she stood in front of that mirror. He'd acted as though she were priceless, and for a moment, she thought she was.

She twisted slightly, ignoring the soreness from her waist down. Teagen sat in his favorite leather chair beside her bed, his chin resting on his chest. He must have moved the chair and set it beside her bed without waking her.

Pieces of memory drifted into her thoughts. The fire. Fighting with the horses, trying to get them to stop before they were too close. The fall. The pain. Teagen holding her.

She moved her hand across her abdomen and knew the baby was gone without anyone telling her. She felt the loss in her heart.

Teagen had been there with her through it all.

Jessie studied him. He must have picked her up and carried her back here.

The door sounded. Sage tiptoed into the room and grinned when she saw Jessie. "You're awake."

She started to move around the bed, but Jessie shook her head. "Don't wake him."

"He'll want to know," Sage answered, still smiling. "He's been worried about you."

"How late is it?"

Sage glanced at the window. "It's almost dawn. I just started the fire for breakfast."

Jessie looked at Teagen. "He's slept in that chair beside my bed all night."

Sage nodded. "Every night for almost a week. He works all day and comes in worried about you. Martha told him she thought you'd be fine, but he insisted on being here by your side every night."

Jessie studied him. He looked a bit thinner, and she could see the worry lines and dark circles beneath his eyes even in the shadows. She glanced back at Sage. "Could you give us a little time alone?"

"Sure." Sage took a step backward. "But I should tell you—"

"I know," Jessie whispered. "I lost the baby." She fought not to cry. Almost every woman she'd ever known had lost at least one child. She had to think of the three alive now. "What was it, a boy or a girl?"

"A girl." Sage silently cried tears Jessie couldn't let fall. "Not yet two pounds, I'd guess. She was so beautiful, and when we wrapped her in a tiny blanket, she looked like she was sleeping."

"Where is she now?" Jessie asked, needing to know.

"Dolan Hatch made her a pine box with a rocking horse carved on the lid. We buried her next to my mother up on the hill. I hope you don't mind."

Jessie smiled. "When I'm better, I'll visit her there." She wanted to say that someday she'd be buried there also beside her daughter, who would have been named Anna if she'd lived. For as long as she'd remembered, Jessie had thought that Whispering Mountain would be as near to heaven as she'd ever get. She even thought of asking Eli if he'd cremate her and have her ashes sent here. But Eli would have thought her a fool.

"Thank you for taking care of her." Jessie's arms ached to have held the baby one time, but she knew it was not to be.

Sage patted her hand. "I did all I could. We were so worried about you, Jessie. Martha thought Teagen might lose his mind with worry. He'd sit in here for hours and talk to you, even when we knew you had far too high a fever to hear a word he said."

Sage glanced at her brother and seemed to remember she'd been about to leave. "I'll bring you both breakfast in an hour."

She was gone before Jessie could answer.

Jessie waited until the first light glowed from the window. Then she reached and touched Teagen's big, scarred hand.

He shifted slightly.

She brushed his hand again.

He opened one eye. "Are you awake?" he grumbled, half asleep. "Or am I dreaming again?"

"I'm awake." She smiled.

He opened the other eye. "Good." For a moment he just stared at her, then he added, "Do you need anything, Jess?"

"Yes," she answered. "I need you to hold me."

"Sage said not to move you." He leaned forward. "But I'd like to do just that."

"Then lie down beside me," she whispered. "I won't move."

He hesitated, then slowly unfolded from the chair. As slowly as he could, he slid atop the covers beside her, and Jessie rolled into his arms. He tugged the covers around her and held her gently.

Neither said a word. She spread her hand over his heart, and he placed his on top of it. She breathed in the scent of him and drifted back to sleep, the nightmare of the fire and the pain no longer in her mind.

When Sage woke them, the sun was bright. She tapped on the door and said, "This is your third call to breakfast. If you sleep any longer, I'll be serving lunch."

Teagen gently settled Jessie against the pillows and told his sister to come in. He sat back in his chair and ate breakfast, watching every bite Jessie took.

When he stood after barely eating, he walked to the door and ordered, "Make sure she rests today, Sage."

Jessie smiled. "I can hear you, Teagen. Stop ordering your sister around."

Sage came in, laughing. "Teagen, she's going to be all right. The fever is gone, the bleeding has almost stopped, and she's eating. It's my medical opinion she'll be up and about in a few days."

Teagen turned to Jessie. "Do everything Sage tells you, Jess."

"I promise, but you have to stop worrying about me. I'm weak as a kitten, but I'll be right here when you get back."

He frowned like he wasn't sure to trust her and walked out of the room.

Jessie leaned back and smiled up at Sage.

"My brother's not very friendly on his best day."

"I've noticed, but he doesn't fool me. I know he cares about me, if only a little."

"A little?" Sage laughed. "The man is nuts about you. I think he may have driven us all crazy if not for the girls. They settled him even in his darkest moods when we all feared you might die." Sage tucked in the covers around Jessie. "Speaking of the girls, they're outside waiting to come in. Do you feel up to seeing them?"

"Definitely," Jessie answered, and a moment later the room was filled with their voices.

They stayed with her for an hour, then Sage talked them into playing on the porch while she and Martha helped Jessie bathe. Once she was tucked back into bed, Jessie slept the rest of the day away.

When she woke just before sunset, Martha brought her a dinner of soup and corn bread. Jessie ate as much as she could while asking questions about all that had happened. She learned of Sims's fast recovery and how it rained for three days after the fire. When she asked about her new nightgown, Martha told her that Teagen had picked it and several other things up for her weeks before but didn't know how to give them to her. She showed Jessie a robe and slippers as well as a wide bonnet and material in several colors.

"He told me to keep them until you needed them, and I figured you needed them now." Martha took the tray. "Sage will get the girls to bed. She's had no trouble since she started telling the stories about her grandfather the chief."

The housekeeper stopped at the door. "Get some sleep. You'll feel better tomorrow. I'll be on the porch having a cup of coffee with Sims if you need anything."

Jessie drifted back to sleep but awoke when she heard Teagen enter the room. He tugged off his boots and sat down in the chair.

"Evening," she whispered.

He seemed surprised to find her awake. "How'd your day go, Jess?"

She pulled herself up on the pillows. "I'm better, Teagen. You can stop worrying about me. I stayed in bed today, but tomorrow I think I'll be able to get up and at least sit in the kitchen for a while."

He frowned.

She laughed. "Stop trying to bully me, and come to bed. I've missed you holding me all day."

He raised an eyebrow. "I don't know."

She smiled. How could he not know that he was the medicine she needed? "You don't have to be afraid of me. I'm only planning to sleep with you. I'll save attacking you for another night."

A slow grin spread across his face. "I don't know if I can trust you."

"You'll just have to take a risk," she dared him. "Now, come to bed."

He lowered himself beside her. "Then I guess the question is, do you trust me?"

"What do you think?" She liked this teasing Teagen.

"For tonight," he whispered as she moved into his arms. "I wouldn't mind being close." He kissed her head.

They both fell asleep smiling. The next night, he didn't wait for an invitation and the third night, he climbed beneath the covers, saying the night had a chill to it.

Now the rules had changed, even though neither had said a word. She could feel the warmth of his skin beneath the layer of his shirt, and when he rolled near and tugged her back against his chest, she felt his need for her, even though he still wore his trousers.

Though she hadn't said a word, Martha and Sage both knocked before entering the bedroom, giving Teagen time to move back to his chair before he growled, "Come in."

She couldn't tell if he didn't like being interrupted or if he hated pretending that he wasn't sleeping beside her. His grumbling made her smile, but as soon as they were alone again, she wanted him close. He seemed to feel the same.

On their fourth night, she didn't fall asleep for a long time and guessed that he was awake also. Finally, she could stand the silence no longer. She rolled over and faced him, aware that her unlaced breasts brushed against the wall of his chest.

"Teagen," she whispered. "Are you asleep?"

"Not likely," he answered.

She didn't know how to say what needed to be said between them.

Finally, he broke the silence. "Do you want me to leave?"

"No," she said, surprised at his thoughts. "I was wondering if you could bring yourself to kiss me."

"I don't want to hurt you."

"You won't."

"Is this one of those things you're just wanting to experience?"

"No." She laughed. "I was just remembering how you kissed me and thinking it would be nice, since we're not doing anything right now and we're not asleep, if you might be willing to kiss me again."

"Hush," he whispered as his mouth found hers. "You don't have to talk me into it."

The kiss had a hunger to it that surprised her. She wrapped

her arms around his neck and pulled him close, loving the way his tongue explored first her lips and then her mouth.

She heard herself make a sound of pure pleasure, then she pressed the top of her body against his chest, loving how much more exciting kissing was while lying down. The two layers of cotton between them did nothing to hide the feel of him against her.

A low rumble of a hunger having nothing to do with food echoed in his kiss as he threaded his hands in her hair and turned her head just right so that the kiss deepened. He teased her tongue into playing a game that pleased her.

When he finally raised his head, she stared at him in the shadows and noticed he was smiling.

"Is that what you wanted, Jess?"

"Yes." She moved slightly, and her lips touched his throat. "That was very nice." Her words brushed against the dampness left by her kiss. "But not enough, Teagen. Not nearly enough."

He tugged her mouth back to him as she knew he would and kissed her so tenderly he took her breath away. When he pulled back the second time, he rolled her gently from her side to her back and slowly moved his mouth down her throat.

He braced his chest a fraction of an inch above her so that each time she breathed, her breasts brushed against him. The slight contact warmed her. She stretched, begging now for more.

Answering her silent request, his touch grew bolder, his kiss deeper. When his mouth finally returned to his journey down her throat, she sighed softly with need and felt his laughter against her throat.

She turned her head away, giving him free range of her neck. The tip of his tongue playing lightly over the flesh he'd just kissed drove her wild. She felt his fingers fumbling with the buttons at her throat and closed her eyes as she waited for the pleasure she knew would soon come.

Her gown was open to her breasts when he kissed her ear and whispered, "Do you want this? I'll stop if you don't." His finger rested at the last button.

She pushed against his cheek until she found his lips. "I want you to touch me tonight." Her words were lost in his mouth as he kissed her again, hard and wild. His hand spread feather light over the cotton of her gown, making her nipples peak with need.

"Tell me," he muttered. "Tell me what you need."

"You," she whispered. "I need you."

His big hand closed over the cotton clinging to her breast.

Her body shook, and he cradled her close, but his fingers continued to grip her tender flesh. She settled beside him as he kissed the corners of her mouth. Without understanding the words he whispered between his kisses, she mumbled yes again and again. He tugged her lips apart and kissed her deep and hard.

When he backed away, she gulped in deep breaths.

He tugged the gown to her sides as if opening a grand gift. He watched as her chest rose and fell a few times before he molded a hand over one bare breast.

"Easy, Jess." His words brushed her cheek. "I'm just going to touch you tonight. But someday we'll do far more, and I promise you'll like it just as much as you do this." His hand tenderly circled round her flesh, feeling of it as though he'd never felt anything so perfect.

She lay still, drifting in paradise as he moved to the other breast and did the same. When his mouth returned to kiss her, his hand remained on her flesh, molding her gently. He felt and caressed and explored with his hand while his mouth made her forget everything but him.

Slowly, she relaxed in his arms. He'd begun to make her his as he became hers. She learned what he wanted in a kiss, and he learned to please her.

When he finally stopped and buttoned her gown, he pulled her back against him. She let him slide his hands along the length of her body and mold her against him. When she whimpered for the need of another kiss, he placed one hand over her breast and teased it gently as he tugged her hair back and whispered a kiss in her ear. She wasn't sure what he said, for the touch of his lips and the warmth of his breath sent liquid pleasure flowing through her.

"Go to sleep, Jess," he whispered as he rubbed his chin against her hair. "You need your rest."

Jessie closed her eyes and melted into him, loving the warmth of his body beside her. "All right," she said, smiling at how his words had sounded like an order, but his hand still spread over her.

Late in the night, she awoke as he rolled her to her back.

"Jess," he said with an urgency. "I have to have another taste of you before this night ends."

She didn't open her eyes but smiled as he leaned down to part her lips once more. His mouth pressed gently over hers, then his tongue brushed her lips, and he drank long. There was a wild hunger in him that seemed to surprise them both. She stretched her arms above her and sighed softly as his kiss moved down her throat.

"I love the taste of you," he said.

She stretched toward him in answer and felt his laughter against her skin.

He unbuttoned her gown and spread it apart, then continued kissing her. His beard tickled her tender flesh when he kissed one breast and then the other. When he took her nipple in his mouth, she almost bolted upright.

Rising above her, his fingers combed through her hair. "Easy now, Jess, I'm not going to hurt you." He kissed the corners of her mouth.

"Teagen," she whimpered. "Do it again."

"Are you sure?" His hand fisted in her hair. "I . . ."

"I'm sure," she answered.

He kissed her softly, then as he had before, he traveled down her throat. When his mouth circled over her peak once more, she held her breath a moment to allow melted pleasure to wash through her body.

His hand covered the breast he'd just tasted when he looked up. In the moonlight, his face was in shadow, but she knew he smiled. "You all right?" he asked, already knowing the answer.

She nodded.

Slowly, he buttoned the gown back in place and lay on his

back beside her. "Thank you," he whispered when she was almost asleep. "I think I've satisfied that hunger I seem to have developed for you. At least for a little while."

"You're welcome," she answered, already drifting into dreams.

He shifted to his side and moved his hand over her side. "Jess, when the time is right, will you come willingly to me as a wife?"

His words blended in her dream.

When she awoke at dawn, he was gone, and she wished he'd touched her once more during the night. For the first time since the fire, she dressed and joined everyone in the kitchen.

Sage and Martha thought she should go back to bed, but Jessie needed something to do. It was time to step back into life.

Martha gave her the sit-down work. Every time she tried to lift something, one of them was there to help or try to stop her. So she passed the day doing mending and reading to the girls.

Teagen sent word that there were problems in the back pasture. The hired hand who brought the message asked Sage to help him pack for a summer camp. Sage rounded up the equipment.

No one was surprised when Teagen didn't return that night. Jessie lay awake, thinking of how tender he'd been and wishing him near. Deep down she knew he wouldn't be away if the ranch and maybe even their lives weren't at stake.

Her friend was turning into her lover. Jessie was afraid to even think something so wonderful lest it vanish like so many of her hopes. Teagen came to her that night in her dreams. When she woke without him near, her body ached with longing, and she couldn't help but wonder if he was somewhere beneath the stars feeling the same.

She pulled the pillow he'd slept on to her and slept curled around it until first light.

Little by little Jessie felt herself grow strong. Without the morning sickness, she ate well and put on a few much-needed pounds. Each morning and evening she'd sit on the porch and watch for any sign of him. She knew he was watching over her; she could feel it.

As the days passed, Martha spent an hour each morning checking on Sims, then just before dark she'd step over to the bunkhouse porch and drink a cup of coffee with him. Jessie and Sage watched but neither commented.

Sage worked awhile every afternoon in the barn, and Jessie took on her share of the load. They talked of the canning to be done now that fall grew near. Martha brought out a bolt of material of hunter green and said it was time the girls all had new dresses. The women cleaned and washed and baked, but no one spoke of Teagen being gone. Martha left him a meal each night and tossed it to the pigs in the morning.

Jessie couldn't tell if Teagen being gone was unusual, or if Sage and Martha feared voicing his absence might bring on worry.

Nights were Jessie's only time to dream. She'd imagine, if Teagen came in early, that he'd carry her out on the porch after the girls were in bed. They'd talk and laugh. Then, without a word, they'd undress and crawl into bed. Some nights he just held her to him. Some nights they would explore each other.

She'd whisper how she loved sleeping next to him almost as much as she loved waking up to the feel of him touching her. He'd learned her body.

In her fantasy, one night he'd ask if she were ready, and when she said yes, he'd make love to her.

In the waking hours, she'd blush at her dreams. Surely if he missed her as dearly as she did him, he would make it in at least one night. She feared she was making more of their few nights together than he was.

Jessie needed to talk to someone about her feelings. She needed to talk to her best friend. She needed to talk to Teagen.

CHAPTER 26

At sunset, as he'd done the three previous nights, Teagen walked away from the campsite and looked in the direction of the ranch house. Twice last night, while asleep in his bedroll, he'd turned over and reached for Jessie. It bothered him that she had moved under his skin so easily. He told himself not to let her matter too much. She had only married him to keep her children. He wasn't about to start wishing for more than she planned to give.

Their last night together had been magic, and he reminded himself that he was rooted in reality with no time for feelings to clutter up his mind.

A man doesn't get used to a woman after a few nights in bed. He'd slept alone all his life. It seemed he should be more natural alone, but asleep his body craved her, even if he wouldn't let his mind admit it.

As the night darkened around him, Teagen opened and closed his hand, swearing he could feel her. The need to touch her was a physical ache within him. But he couldn't go to her. Not yet. Not till he knew the ranch was safe. The way he felt about her, raiders would be on the porch before he noticed, if he were in her bed. Better to stay away and do his job.

"Evening, Teagen. Dreaming of home?" Roak's voice shattered his thoughts.

"Something like that." Teagen faced the kid. "You just drop by to chat?"

Roak shook his head. "I come to tell you the little news I

know. Word is that the band planning to take over your operation is waiting for more arms."

"I'm beginning to wonder if there is a band. All we've seen are a few tracks."

"Someone set the fire and shot Tattor Sims."

"That could have been a lone horse thief thinking he'd cause a distraction with a fire so he could take a horse. Sims just got too close, so the thief shot him."

Roak shook his head, but said, "Could have been."

"You seen more than a few of the outlaws you claim are waiting to attack?"

Roak shook his head again. "Just the two who come in for supplies and drink at the little cantina. They usually wait around for the stage. I've seen them pick up a package now and then. I followed them once and got close enough to see their campfires."

"Did you go in?"

"Couldn't get close enough without being shot at." Roak pointed to the east. "They're camped on the other side of the river about five miles into that worthless rough land. Ground's so rocky out there a man's lucky if his horse don't go lame crossing it. I hunted out near there as a kid. If their camp is in those rocks, you can bet they're not sleeping in comfort."

Teagen swore. It didn't make sense. An outlaw doesn't hang around for a month waiting to raid. It's not in their nature. "Why do you think this gang is waiting to attack me?" he asked, not expecting Drummond Roak to give him an answer. "Maybe they just think they've found a place no one will look for them. The leader might like a hard place to spread a bedroll."

The kid smiled. "Maybe he's planning to drive you so crazy worrying that you'll kill yourself."

Teagen swore again and muttered, "It's a short drive to crazy these days. I could probably walk."

Roak didn't bother to argue. He just checked his gun and said, "You ready to ride over and take a closer look? There's no moon tonight. If we were on foot, we might get within sight of the camp. Then we could quit guessing how many men are out there; we'd know."

"I'm ready as I'll ever be." He almost added that memories of Jessie would keep him up all night anyway, so he might as well be out scouting.

Teagen moved toward the horses, thinking that it was funny the turns life takes. He'd never liked the kid, but Roak was the only man who could go with him where he was headed tonight.

Most men would consider it suicide to even think of sneaking into an outlaw camp, but if anyone could get away with it, Roak could. He'd offered to go alone, but Teagen insisted on backing him up.

They rode in silence to the river, then climbed off their horses and swam beside them. Roak's horse Satan took to the river without slowing as if the chore were nothing new to him. Teagen's bay balked but swam once she was forced in.

The current was not as strong as it could have been. During the heavy rains of spring Teagen doubted either horse or man would make the far bank. But even with the rain the night of the fire, the river was still low and fairly calm.

When they reached the far bank, both men collapsed in the tall grass while their horses rested.

"Now tell me again why we didn't use the perfectly good bridge a mile downstream?" Roak said in a low voice that barely reached Teagen's ears.

"They could have someone watching the bridge."

"Like you do?"

Teagen frowned. He hadn't mentioned the man he kept near the bridge since the day Sims had been shot. But, in truth, he wasn't surprised Roak knew about the guard posted.

"How often are you on my land anyway, Roak?"

"Often enough to keep an eye on Sage. I don't give a damn about your land or all them horses you McMurrays have. As far as I'm concerned, the only thing of value is Sage."

"Then why are you helping me?"

Roak sat up and dumped his gear from the sack he'd tied to Satan's saddle. "I figure Sage would be real unhappy if something happened to you. Though for the life of me, I can't tell why all those women you got love you. You're the meanest man I know. You tied me up in your barn and would have turned me over to the sheriff just for borrowing a horse. He would have hanged me."

"Well, I didn't turn you over, and he didn't hang you." Teagen had wondered many times if he would have gone through with turning in the boy. He'd decided he probably would have tried, but after some arguing, he would have let Sage or Martha talk him out of it.

He stood and grabbed his own gear. "So, we might as well get on with the business of getting us both killed tonight. My sister might be sad at my passing, but she'll be relieved to be rid of you."

They were both grumbling and not speaking to each other as they strapped on guns and pulled on boots.

"When I get back," Roak mumbled to himself, "I'm going to kiss your sister right in front of you."

"Like hell you are." Teagen answered in the same low whisper.

"You think you can stop me?"

"I won't have to. Sage will. If you kiss her, you'll be running from flying lead."

Roak dried his horse with the sack he'd carried. "I don't much care. It would be worth it. I feel like I'm dying every day from wanting to. If I kissed her, she could only kill me once."

Teagen fought down a laugh. "Knowing my sister, she'd think of a way to double kill you."

They saddled and rode to the last stand of trees before the heap of rocks blocked all vegetation from the land.

Without a word, they tied the animals and began moving low and slow across the uneven ground. They made it a quarter of a mile before Roak spotted the first guard. His rifle rested in his lap, and his head almost touched his chest.

"He's asleep," Roak guessed.

Teagen knew they were risking their lives on that guess. He motioned for Roak to follow, and they both moved silently forward, keeping a close eye on any movement the guard might make.

As they passed out of sight of the guard, Teagen knelt down. In the darkness he felt more than saw how the brush had been broken down. "They must have brought a wagon along here."

Without debate, Roak began to follow the path. It stopped a few feet short of a boulder twice his height. "The trail just disappears."

Teagen studied the ground, moving his hand a quarter of an inch above the dirt like his father had taught him. The tiny wave in the dust told him what he needed to know. "The wagon turned around here."

Roak didn't move.

Teagen stood and brushed his fingers over the wall of rock. "I'm guessing they lifted supplies up and over this rock."

"You're good, McMurray. Must be that Indian blood you got in you."

"Nope." Teagen smiled. "Just logic."

Roak swung a rope he'd brought until he caught a jagged edge of a rock above. He braced his legs and began to climb, walking the rock with ease. When he reached the top, he shook the rope, telling Teagen it was his turn.

Teagen braced himself as he'd seen Roak do, but the kid was more than ten years younger and sixty pounds lighter. Pulling the rope as he walked up the rock was hard work.

When he reached the top, he dropped beside Roak. "You've done that a few times."

"Nope," Roak lied. "Just using logic."

If Teagen had had the energy, he would have knocked the kid off the rock. By the time he was breathing normally, Roak had already disappeared into the night.

Teagen followed, figuring if there was a hole between the rocks, he'd follow Roak right down. The thought crossed his mind that his one regret before he fell to his death would be that he hadn't had another night with Jessie.

Finally, after about five minutes of walking, he saw the

flicker of a fire. Halfway between the light and him lay Roak. The boy was so flat against the rock the men below wouldn't have seen him if they'd looked.

Teagen crept close and lowered himself beside Roak. For a while they were silent. Then Roak whispered, "There's no way in. I'm guessing it's a forty-foot drop from here, and we couldn't do it without waking half the camp up."

"In daylight we could probably see another way in. All those men and horses didn't just drop down."

"In daylight they could see us." Roak slid back. "There has to be a way into that place."

Teagen studied the camp. He couldn't tell how many men slept around the fire. Thirty, forty, maybe more. From the looks of the place, they'd been here awhile. It had been a natural basin lined by trees on one edge. Most of the trees were now stumps, probably used for firewood. The gang had cut down the only protection they had if they were invaded. A few men with good rifles could probably pick half the gang off before the rest could saddle up and leave. He'd bet the way in on horseback was a narrow one.

He searched the rim. It might only take two men to attack, but those who escaped would be headed right for his ranch. What good would it do to kill half the gang and have the other half attack his ranch while he was gone?

There was no more he could do tonight, and until he knew these men were a threat to him and his, Teagen knew he wouldn't be within his rights to fight.

He also saw no sign that they planned a dawn raid. No horses were saddled. No weapons laid out in ready.

"Let's go," he said as he backed away.

Roak nodded and followed, retracing their steps back to the horses.

The boy rode with him to the river, then waved him good-bye. Teagen swam across alone.

When he reached the shore, he turned toward home.

It was an hour before dawn when he made it in. He'd

thought he'd just curl up next to Jessie and sleep awhile with her. He knew he'd be welcome. She'd made that plain. He'd have to be careful not to startle her though.

Rain tapped on his jacket and hat as he walked from the barn. The sky was dark and brooding. He'd be riding in mud tomorrow, but for the next few hours all he wanted to do was sleep.

Pulling off his boots on the porch, he silently moved down the hall and slowly pushed the door to his bedroom open.

He wasn't the only one she apparently welcomed in her bed.

Three little girls, looking like angels in their gowns, were circled around their mother. He heard the rumble of thunder, but none of them moved. They were where they knew they'd be safe.

Teagen smiled and lowered into the leather chair beside them. He watched them until he drifted off to sleep, thinking he'd have his midnight with Jessie later, but right now the sight of them sleeping offered him a peace he'd seldom felt.

CHAPTER 27

"Momma," Rose whispered. "Momma, there is a bear in the room."

Jessie awoke and patted her middle child. "Go back to sleep, Rose. It's only a dream."

"Momma! I'm awake, and I can still hear the bear."

Jessie opened one eye. A gray, watery dawn greeted her with the rhythm of rain against her window. One by one the girls had all come downstairs to her room last night. Emily was frightened of the thunder. Rose said it was too noisy upstairs, and Bethie just followed without voicing a reason.

Now, her youngest slept curled against Jessie's back, Emily lay sideways across the bottom of the bed, and Rose rested nose to nose with her.

Listening, Jessie heard the bear. For a second she almost believed her daughter; then she made out the shadowy outline of Teagen sleeping in the chair in the corner. His low rumble of a snore made her smile.

"Rose, you know the story Sage told you about how her grandfather had to face a bear to become a man?"

Rose didn't look too happy. "Yes," she whispered.

"Well, I think it's time you faced the bear."

"Do I have to fight him like Sage's grandfather did?"

"I think so."

Rose's face wrinkled. "All right, but I'm not naming him."

"Don't worry." Jessie fought down a smile. "I'll be right behind you."

The five-year-old shoved the covers aside and stood on her knees before turning toward Teagen. Without hesitation, she jumped into his lap.

Teagen reacted like a warrior blindly attacked in his sleep. He flung the child halfway across the bed. She tumbled into her sister.

As Emily cried, rubbing her eyes, Teagen woke up enough to realize what he'd done. "I'm sorry. I didn't realize . . ."

Emily began to scream for Jessie, but Rose stood like a brave little David facing the giant. "I'm not afraid of you, bear," she yelled. "I come from a long line of people who eat bear for breakfast, and I'm feeling mighty hungry this day."

Teagen shook his head, and his hair, in need of a cut, shadowed his eyes. "That's what my grandfather said once . . ."

Jessie laughed, realizing he'd figured out Rose's game. When he roared, Rose put her hand on her hips and faced him. Emily stopped crying long enough to watch.

"I'll pick my teeth with your bones, little Apache," Teagen said, stumbling over the words as he obviously tried to remember the story.

Rose jumped again, and he swung her round and round while her fists flew about his head. "Take that, bear. And that!" she yelled.

When he tossed her into the covers a second time, she giggled and stood on the bed, bouncing enough to finally wake Bethie. The baby looked up at Teagen and said, "Papa. Papa."

Teagen was so distracted by the baby's chatter he almost missed catching Rose when she bounced off the end of the bed. He held her high until she giggled uncontrollably, then he set her down beside Jessie. "I give up, brave Apache."

"No." Emily scrambled to her knees. "Swing me. I want to fight the bear too."

Teagen held his arms up, and Emily hesitated only a moment before leaning into them. He swung her in the air, then lowered her gently. She didn't giggle, but she did smile up at him.

Next came Bethie, who wanted to do everything her big sisters did. When she let out a grand squeal, Martha hit the door in a run.

"What's happening!" she shouted as she charged into the room ready to fight anyone trying to hurt the girls.

Rose answered, "We're fighting the bear. I won."

Martha looked from one of them to the other, stopping at Teagen. "Does the bear want breakfast?"

Teagen lifted Rose on one arm. "Since I can't eat brave little Apache, how about a half-dozen eggs and any unnamed meat you've got available."

Martha lifted Bethie off the bed. "I'll get them dressed first. With the rain this morning, there's a chill in the air. Sage has already started the coffee. It'll be boiling in a few minutes." She looked down at Jessie. "You can sleep awhile longer, if you like."

Jessie shook her head. "I'll be fine."

The girls followed Martha out, and Jessie stood slowly. She slipped on her new robe and ran a brush over her hair, very much aware that Teagen watched every move she made.

"How are you, Jess?"

"Better each day." She figured he already knew, because every day since he'd been at the camp, he'd sent a man on some errand with instructions to get a report on her condition before he headed back to the camp.

"Good," he whispered so close she could feel his breath.

"You were wonderful with the girls," she whispered. "And with that beard, you do look more bear than man."

He moved up behind her and without a word fisted a handful of her hair.

She closed her eyes and waited for him to touch her.

He didn't disappoint her. His big hands moved from her shoulders down her body with a loving touch.

"I missed you," he whispered as he turned her to face him.

She expected him to say more, but he simply tugged her arms over his shoulders and pulled her against him in a hug.

His face brushed against her cheek as he moved his hands down her back.

There was a boldness in his touch that she'd grown used to. His hands covered her hips and pulled her to him so that she knew exactly how dearly he longed for her. When he moved to her waist, she leaned back, breaking the contact.

Frowning, his hands slid down once more to her hips and drew her harder against him.

She didn't pull away the second time he fitted her against him.

When his hands returned to her waist, he held her gently and kissed her. This was the way he wanted her, she realized, and she was more than happy to comply to his not-so-subtle request.

She felt his need for her and couldn't decide if she were more frightened or excited.

He smiled down at her as if he could read her mind and knew what the final decision would be. With a gentle stroke he moved his fingers inside her robe. His hands teased the sides of her breasts, pushing them together slightly as he studied their outline beneath her gown.

Then he slipped his hands under her arms and lifted her up. Slowly, as he lowered her, she felt as if she were raining down on him. His face slid over her body as if he were drinking her in. She brushed against him on her way to touch ground. He paused long enough to press his face against her now-flat stomach. He stopped again at her breasts, tasting each through the layer of cotton. When his mouth reached her throat, he once again took his time kissing all the way to her ear.

Her knees buckled, and she would have fallen if he hadn't held her up. They were both clothed, but his actions left her feeling as if they were bare with not even air between them.

When her feet finally touched the floor, his fingers fisted in her hair, tugging her head back so that he could kiss her deep and hard like he liked . . . like she loved.

When Martha called them from the kitchen, he loosened his hold and smiled down at her.

"How do you feel now, Jess?" he asked as if he hadn't been devouring her a moment before.

"You know quite well how I feel," she answered. "You seemed to have felt most of me."

He patted her bottom. "I plan to do a great deal more if we're ever alone."

She let him tug her into the hall. "Oh, don't worry; the girls will be grown in twenty or so years."

He didn't have time to answer before they were within hearing range of those in the kitchen. She'd expected him to step away as they entered, but he locked his fingers in hers as they walked in.

If she planned to ignore him this morning, she'd have to do it one-handed.

The girls didn't notice, but Martha raised an eyebrow as if she was a proper chaperone, and they were being far too friendly.

A few minutes later, Jessie fought the urge to reach over and kiss him as he growled while Bethie giggled and smashed scrambled eggs in his week-old beard.

Rose ran back and forth from the window giving weather reports every few minutes. "Still raining," she shouted. "Can I go out and see if the chickens are standing on their porch?"

"No," Jessie answered. "It's raining too hard."

Sage looked up at Teagen. "At least we won't have to worry about a raid today. The way it's coming down, the river will be bucking its banks in an hour. Even if they could cross the bridge, they'd never get the herd rounded up in this storm. If the raiders couldn't run them back across the bridge, they'd never be able to push them into the water."

Martha set a plate of ham in front of Teagen. "If you're not afraid of getting wet, you could go into town after those supplies I asked for last week."

Since the fire, Teagen obviously hadn't given a thought to the grocery list she'd handed him. "Get Jessie to write it again while I saddle a horse as soon as I finish. This storm doesn't look like it's going to get anything but worse. I might as well get wet now."

He turned to Jessie and quietly added, "I've seen well-trained mounts go wild in a storm like this, so try to make Emily understand that she can't ride today."

She smiled and nodded as if she understood.

He had no idea how attracted she was to him, and the one thing that made her love him most was the way he'd lost the great battle with the little Apache this morning.

His touch might make her heart race, and his kisses made her crave more, but his kindness melted her heart.

When Teagen finished saddling his bay, he turned and saw Emily standing by the barn door. She'd used her blanket to protect herself from the rain, but they were both dripping wet.

"Em." He moved toward her. "Didn't your mother tell you that you couldn't ride today?"

"Yes, sir," she whispered, staring at her feet.

"Then you'd best get back in the house."

"I come," she started. "I come . . ."

He knelt down so that he could see her face and waited. "What is it, Emily?" Unlike Rose, Em never talked unless she had to.

"I come to ask you something."

"All right." He could think of lots of questions he wasn't prepared to answer.

"Is this my home? I mean my real home."

Teagen smiled. An easy one; he could handle this one. "Yes. This is your home."

"Am I a McMurray like Momma?"

Teagen frowned. "Yes, if you want to be."

"I do," she whispered.

"Then you are."

"Forever and ever?"

He figured he could handle this worry. "Forever. Even when you marry and move away, this will still be your home."

She didn't move.

"Is there something else?"

She nodded. "If there is trouble, I want to stand and fight for my home."

Teagen started to say no; then he saw it in her eyes: a determination, a will that wouldn't be easily broken.

"You told me your brother Tobin was only six when the three of you fought for the ranch. I'm seven. Sage let me help clean the guns. I can load, even if I can't fire. I can help."

Teagen wasn't sure what to say. If he told her she could help fight, Jessie and Sage would both probably kill him after Martha got through. But, he couldn't break her spirit.

He tried to guess what bothered her so. "You're worried about the horses, aren't you, Em?"

She nodded. "Martha says that's why the raiders may come. They want to take the horses away."

"We won't let them have a single one, will we?"

"No," she answered.

"Right." He smiled. "But we also have to keep Rose and Bethie safe. If trouble comes, will you do me a great favor and help Martha get them to the cellar? Then when I need you, I'll call. If trouble comes, we may need all the McMurrays on the porch."

She squared her shoulders. "I'll be ready."

He lifted her up with one arm and stepped into the saddle.

She pulled the blanket close as he rode into the rain toward the house. She might be a shy child, but she had a warrior's heart. His grandfather was going to love this grandchild.

When he set her down, he whispered, "I'm proud of you, Em. You're a fine McMurray."

She smiled.

"You'd better get into some dry clothes."

"All right, Papa," she whispered and ran inside, almost colliding with her mother.

"The grocery order," Jessie said as she handed him Martha's list. "Hope you can read it, I was writing fast, and Sage said to remind you to look for a post from Austin."

Teagen touched his hat. "I'll be back before you miss me." She grinned. "I doubt it."

He would have leaned down to kiss her, but she jumped back when the brim of his hat dripped water. They were both laughing when he rode out.

CHAPTER 28

No one was at the trading post but Elmo when Teagen walked in, shaking the rain off him. A few old men, who looked like they'd been sitting on the porch so long they'd petrified, didn't even notice when he passed by them.

"Shake outside," Elmo ordered. "I don't want to have to mop again."

Teagen removed his hat and said, "Sorry."

Elmo raised an eyebrow. "Oh," he managed. "I didn't know it was you, Teagen. I think you got mail back there somewhere, but I didn't figure you'd be in for another week."

Teagen handed Elmo the list addressed to him and began rummaging through the boxes stacked in one corner of the post. Some boxes waited for weeks to be picked up, and Elmo felt no need to organize them. Any newspaper mailed that was less than six months old was considered new. Folks usually untied the twine, read it, then rolled it back up. If they weren't picked up promptly, the paper would be in shreds by the time they were claimed.

"McMurray?" Elmo yelled as if Teagen were half a mile away. "Can you read what Martha wants here? My sight tends to fade when the sun ain't shining."

Teagen took the note. Usually he or Sage printed the list, but Jessie had written in a clear hand. As Teagen read aloud, something nagged at his mind as if he was piecing together a puzzle, but he had no idea what the picture would be.

Elmo wandered off to collect the last few things, but Teagen continued to stare at the writing. Something familiar. A style he'd seen a hundred times. A script he'd read as often as he had his own bold writing.

He focused on Elmo's name. The *e* had an extra curl at the top and a smooth slash into the *l*.

Teagen froze. It couldn't be. Somehow the note had been written in Eli's hand.

That couldn't be. Eli was dead.

He walked out to his saddlebag and pulled the letter Jessie had brought from his friend that first day she arrived. The *e* and the *l* on Eli's signature and the first two letters of Elmo's name were exactly the same. One could have been laid over the other and copied.

Comparing other letters, he had no doubt that the same hand had written both. The same script had written him letters for years. He would have known Eli's writing anywhere.

He grabbed the bag of supplies and headed home without bothering to say good-bye to Elmo.

At first he tried to tell himself that maybe Eli taught Jessie to write, but that didn't make sense. He taught both his brothers to write, and their signatures were nothing like his. Mrs. Dickerson put up her students' papers around her classroom, and no two of them had ever looked alike. Eli's writing had always shown a flair. Teagen had assumed it was because his friend had been schooled for years longer than many of the children growing up in the West. Most folks he knew in Texas considered themselves educated if they'd made it four or five years in a school.

But Eli hadn't written the grocery note. Jessie had. Her hand couldn't look exactly the same. It couldn't.

Halfway home, he came to the only conclusion that made sense. Jessie wrote both the letter from Eli she delivered and the list. He knew without checking that the writing would be the same on all Eli's letters he kept stored in the office drawer.

She'd written them all.

She'd lied. He'd told her how he hated lies, and she'd lied again.

He dropped the supplies in the mud room and stormed into the kitchen an hour later. All three women turned around and stared, but he only spoke to his wife.

"Jessie!" he yelled. "We have to talk right now!"

She reached for a towel and said, "All right," as if he'd asked nicely.

Sage stepped between them. "Lower your voice, Teagen. The girls are upstairs. You're causing more racket than the storm."

"I'll yell if I want. What I have to say is between Jessie and me, so stay out of this, Sage. I'm warning you."

To his surprise, his little sister didn't move. "No," she said. "I know you. When you get angry, we all get out of your way, but not this time. You'll not bully Jessie."

Martha raised a skillet. "I agree. For once, I'm stepping in. Teagen, calm down or get ready to hit the ground." She raised the pan like a weapon.

Teagen had never been so frustrated. He had no intention of hurting Jessie, but he did plan to have it out once and for all about her lies, and no one, not even these two misguided crusaders, was going to interfere. "Get out of my way," he growled.

To everyone's surprise, Jessie stepped to his side. "Teagen," she said with a smile, "calm down. If you want to talk, we need to go someplace where the girls won't hear you yell."

She took his hand and tugged him toward the cellar. "Martha says she can't even hear gunshots down here, so maybe they won't hear you shout."

Teagen glared at his sister and the crazy housekeeper. "Lower the door," he said as he started down the stairs. "What I got to say is between my wife and me. You two stay out."

Martha wiggled the skillet. "If that girl comes out crying, there'll be a dent in this pan and you'll be eating burned gravy while your head heals."

Sage didn't say a word, but he got the feeling she felt the same as she slammed the door, almost hitting his head.

He stumbled down the last few steps and moved to a spot where he could stand without hitting a beam. The place was cool and damp and silent. Even as a kid he'd never liked it here, but he was surprised at how organized Martha kept everything.

Jessie sat on a barrel and waited.

He pointed his finger and said the first thought that came into his mind. "You should be afraid."

"Of you?" She watched him with tenderness. "I know about your temper, Teagen. No matter the volume, I could never be afraid of you."

He wished he didn't know the truth. He wished he could go back to the way it was this morning. But she'd shattered all that. She'd lied. And this wasn't some small lie about nonexistent relatives. This was big. This was about his best friend.

He pulled the letter and the grocery list from his pocket and handed them to her.

Jessie's gaze changed from trusting to questioning.

"You said you'd never lie to me again." He surprised himself by not yelling, but his words still seemed to cut her deeply. "Did you write both these?"

She didn't look away. "I did."

"You wrote all of Eli's letters?" He wished he could turn away and not have to look at her as pain filled her face. "Every one?"

"You've figured out that I did. I see no point in denying it."

"Did Eli even know of them . . . or of me and Texas? Did he say he wanted to come here? Did he send you with his last breath?" Teagen didn't have many people in his life, and all he thought he knew of one had simply vanished.

"He saw the first few letters, but he never read them." She tilted her head. "I never saw him interested in corresponding with anyone. As for Texas, I'm not sure he knew or cared where it was."

"And this friendship I had with him all these years. My one friend, the one person I thought I could be totally honest with . . . but it was all a lie."

A single tear ran down her face. "Not all. I was there, Teagen. I was your friend."

Anger boiled in his blood. "And then when Eli died, you signed his name to use me. You knew I wouldn't say no to his last request, so you lied again."

"Yes."

"To use me?"

"No," she answered. "To be with you."

Teagen slammed his fist against the post between them, sending dust showering from the rafters above. He hated being deceived. For the first time in his life he'd opened himself to someone, and she'd twisted any truth he thought he knew. It had all been a lie. His friendship with Eli, his belief that someone understood him. She'd come here looking for a way out of her trouble, and he'd believed it all. Even when he'd discovered the first lie, he'd been willing to forgive, to understand. But not this time. It was too much. A lie that covered a lifetime was simply too much to forgive.

He slammed his fist against the wood again, not caring that his knuckles bled. Jars of canned fruit clattered off the shelf behind him.

Sage opened the trapdoor. "Teagen!" she shouted as she made it down three steps before she saw Jessie sitting quietly on the barrel. "Oh, I thought you might be hurting her."

She noticed his hand. "But I see you're just hurting yourself." She looked at him as if her big brother had just turned into the village idiot. "Want to tell me why you're looking like you might kill someone, Teagen?"

"No. Get out." He paced like a trapped wolf. "I have nothing to say to you or anyone, including my lying wife." He would have stormed out of the cellar if she hadn't been blocking the way.

Sage folded her arms. "Have you gone mad? Correction, even madder than usual? I'm not leaving until you tell me why you're making such a ridiculous claim. If you've got rabies, I might as well shoot you now before you bite someone."

Silence hung in the air for a few minutes before Jessie broke the standoff between the McMurrays. "Teagen just found out I wrote all the letters he thought were from Eli."

"All of them?" Sage's eyes widened. "For all those years? The post that came as regular as the seasons was from you?"

Jessie nodded. "For over ten years. I found the book order from Whispering Mountain among a stack of forgotten mail when I first started working at the store. I sent the next stack of books and every order since."

Sage sat on the steps as if a great drama drew her like a big city stage show. "And you never mentioned you were a woman to Teagen?"

Jessie shook her head. "I signed all Eli's correspondence. Then, when the letters became more than just orders, I didn't know how to tell Teagen. He thought he was writing Eli, and I saw no harm in continuing. I never thought there was even a tiny chance that we would meet."

"So you lied." Teagen snapped. "With every letter, you lied."

Sage stared at her brother. "Let me get this straight. You're mad because Jessie turns out to be this best friend you've had for as long as I can remember." She raised her voice. "Your wife is your best friend." She threw her hands in the air. "I'm hammering the trap door closed, Teagen. You've obviously gone nuts."

She stormed out and slammed the door. In the silence after the echo, they both heard the latch being shoved closed.

"I guess we're down here for a while. When Sage gets mad, she tends to stay that way."

Jessie just watched him.

Teagen forced his breathing to calm. If Sage had been a man, he swore he would have beaten her senseless for being so right. He turned to Jessie. "I hate being lied to. I won't stand for it."

She nodded. "I know."

He realized she did. She knew all about him. She knew his dreams and fears and thoughts since he'd been little more than a kid. For years he'd written everything about his life in letters to not Eli but her.

It was a moment before he looked down and noticed she'd moved to his side and was wiping the blood from his hand with a dish towel. As far back as he could remember, men stepped aside in the face of his anger, but not his Jess.

"You knew I wouldn't hurt you?"

"Of course I did," she answered.

"Apparently, you know me better than my sister or Martha."

"Teagen, my greatest fear, before I saw you, was that you would not be the wonderful, caring man I knew from your letters. I came here because I knew if you were half that man, I'd be safe with you."

"But I don't know you," he realized. "I don't know you at all."

He sat on the step and fought the need to pull her close. "Tell me about you, Jessie, and don't lie. Don't leave out a single detail if you want me to ever believe you again."

She closed her eyes. "There's not much to tell."

Teagen waited, then ordered, "I want it all, including what Eli was like. I thought I knew the man. Since I was wrong, at least let me see who he really was."

She hesitated so long, he feared she wouldn't speak, then she whispered, "I used to hide in the store at night when I was thirteen, because I had nowhere else to go. My parents were good people, but their illness took all we had, and I found myself on the streets. Eli was in his late thirties and drunk most of the time even then. He'd taken a profitable store and run it to the ground by the time I met him.

When he found me, he offered me room and board if I'd clean the place up and run things so he could go out in the evenings. After I learned all he knew, he pretty much stayed gone at night and slept most days. The rest of the time, he read."

She leaned against Teagen's shoulder and continued, "The store began to make a profit. When I was almost eighteen, Eli knew I'd find other work eventually, so he told me he wanted to marry me. He was sick by then, pasty white and weak from drink. He said I could have the store after he died if I stayed. He told me he didn't want a wife, just someone to work. His greatest fear seemed to be that he'd lose the store and have to go back to his mother's house. He told me once that he'd live on the streets first, but I don't know if he meant it. He said a lot of things he didn't mean."

Teagen listened and tried not to notice how warm her body was against his.

"We married, and I worked hard to make the store the best around. All seemed fine; I had a home and books to read. We'd eat a meal together now and then with our books on the table. I never remember talking to him about much of anything but the store."

She straightened and said in a voice so low he barely heard, "Then one night he came in early and saw me taking a bath. He didn't say a word. He just looked at me and went to his room. I was too embarrassed to even mention it. I thought he'd forgotten about me, but a few weeks later, he climbed the stairs."

She stopped.

Teagen wasn't sure he wanted to hear more, but he knew he had to. He'd asked for this. "Go on."

Jessie looked up at him with a sadness that twisted his heart. "He pulled the covers off my cot and shoved my gown to my waist. Then he climbed on top of me and hurt me. When he finished, he staggered to his feet, buttoned his trousers, and called me a whore. The next morning he left more money than usual in the cash box. I don't know if it was because he was drunk or if he felt sorry for what he'd done. I took the cash and hid it under my bed. I don't know if he meant it for me, but in a strange way it seemed a way to get back at him.

After that first night, I thought it would never happen again. But it did. We never spoke of the nights he came to me, but the memory hung between us. When he found out I was pregnant, he slapped me so hard I passed out. I woke with my mouth bleeding. He was gone and didn't return for almost a month. When he did, he looked weaker than ever, and I remember thinking that somehow it was my fault.

"Eli didn't bother me for almost a year after Emily was born. He even stayed in some nights and ate meals. My life settled into a routine, and I remember thinking I could be happy with the store to run and a daughter to raise.

"Then the visits started again. Not often, and never a word of warning. I'd just wake feeling him pushing my gown up and bruising my legs with his grip. Sometimes he'd say he was sorry. If he was very drunk, he'd call me names and say it was all my fault for tempting him. Sometimes Emily would wake and cry, then he'd leave.

"When he died I took all the money I'd hidden under the bed. I knew the store wouldn't be mine, even though he'd told me it would be. I think I always knew; maybe that was why I tucked away money. I came here because I had nowhere else to go."

Teagen waited until she finished before he touched her.

When he opened his arms, Jessie crumpled against his chest. "Don't you see, Teagen? You were my only friend too."

She cried so hard he felt her whole body shake. "I'm sorry I lied," she whispered. "Don't hate me."

At that moment Teagen hated himself more than anyone. He shouldn't have made her tell him the details. He'd made her relive the hell she'd survived in for years.

"Stop, Jessie," he ordered. "I don't hate you. Not anymore. Not ever." He kissed her hair. "You could have told me the truth from the first."

She shook her head.

He guessed she was right. He'd lived his life in black and white and never seen the gray until today in the cellar. She'd lied, she'd hid money, she'd survived.

Wiping her tears away, he looked down at her. "Swear you'll tell me the truth about one thing."

"All right."

"Did you marry me to save your children?"

"Yes," she answered.

"Then you lied about loving me when the preacher asked?"

"No, Teagen, I've loved you for years."

He frowned. He wasn't comfortable with the word *love*.

When said between a man and a woman, it seemed to come with far too many hooks and strings.

She smiled as if she understood his thoughts. "I've had years to love you, dear, but I'll be happy if you just find me tolerable to be around."

He fought to keep from smiling. "I could do that."

She patted his cheek. "Now you have to get your sister to let us out. It's almost lunchtime. Rose is probably already asking questions about where I've gone."

Teagen didn't move. "Swear you'll never lie to me again, Jess."

"I swear."

"And," he ran his fingers through his hair, "I find you more than tolerable. I don't even mind if you call me dear when it suits you." He frowned. "But no other names. You wouldn't believe some of the foolish things Tobin's wife calls him. Liberty seems to think he's her own private pet that she has to rename every day."

"All right."

They sat for a while, holding one another in silence; then Teagen banged on the door, and Sage let him out. They didn't say a word, but he nodded once to his sister, silently thanking her for standing up for his wife, even if it was against him.

Sage smiled and sat down at the table with the girls, who were playing toss the biscuit behind Martha's back.

Jessie hurried to help with lunch. Teagen intercepted the crumbling biscuit and ended the game before Martha noticed. Rose frowned at him but didn't say a word. Emily wouldn't face him, and Bethie was too busy licking the butter off her biscuit to notice the game had ended.

His wife ate next to him without looking his way. Teagen let the conversation flow around him. With this many women in the room, he never noticed a pause in the talking long enough for him to say anything.

He finished his meal, grabbed his hat, and started out.

Jessie caught up to him on the porch. She didn't say a word;

she just kissed his cheek and went back inside. Teagen tried to remember how mad he'd been at her. They had a great deal of talking to do, but he had a feeling she'd be doing it in his arms.

He stepped into the rain that had slowed to a drizzle.

CHAPTER 29

THE AFTERNOON PASSED IN A BUSY HIVE OF ACTIVITY. Jessie couldn't seem to stop smiling. No lies lay between her and Teagen. She didn't have to worry about him finding out about the letters. He knew and understood. The man she'd dreamed of lived in more than letters; he existed.

The sun was almost to the horizon when Sage shouted from the porch, "Riders coming in from the bridge."

Jessie glanced out the window and saw two big men riding full-out toward the house and Sage running to meet them. She didn't have to ask; she knew they were Teagen's brothers. Travis, broad-shouldered and dark-skinned; Tobin, thinner, younger. Both men rode like Teagen . . . like they'd been born in the saddle.

By the time Jessie reached the porch, the brothers had jumped from their horses and were swinging Sage around as if she were a doll. Jessie could hear her squeals of joy. The bigger one, Travis, finally stopped long enough to grab his saddlebags and toss them to Sage to carry while he pulled rifles from a long leather bag tied to the back of his horse. The markings on the leather left no doubt that it had been made by his grandfather's people.

Tobin, who wore moccasins laced to his knees, took the horses and headed to the barn.

As Travis and Sage walked toward the house, they talked of people Jessie had never heard about. She knew Travis, the

Ranger, had married a woman named Rainey, and Tobin had married Liberty, but Teagen had said very little else.

Tobin hurried from the barn, his shoulders loaded down with his saddlebags and two rifles. He dropped them on the porch out of the rain.

Minutes later they were all laughing when they hit the kitchen.

Sage introduced Jessie as the newest Mrs. McMurray.

Tobin nodded without a word and offered his hand.

Travis lifted her off the ground in a bear hug. "Welcome to the family," he shouted. "Big brother must have had to tie you up to get you to come home with him." Travis glanced at Sage. "Is she deaf? It'd be a big advantage around Teagen."

"No," Jessie smiled. "I'm not deaf, and he didn't drag me here. I happen to be quite fond of your brother."

"I'll thank you to put my wife down," Teagen ordered as he entered.

The kitchen exploded in laughter.

For a moment she couldn't tell if the men were hugging or fighting. She felt like a mouse in a buffalo stampede.

"We heard you married, Teagen, but no one who'd ever met you believed a word of it." Travis slapped his big brother on the back, sending rain flying across the kitchen floor.

Martha hurried down the stairs. "Quiet down, you boys, I've got babies taking naps." She frowned down at the three men from her perch on the second step. "You're all three dripping onto my clean floor."

Travis raised an eyebrow. His stare would have frightened a gunfighter. "We're a little old to strip on the porch."

Martha shook her head as she headed down the hall. "I give up. If I couldn't civilize you three, wives don't have a chance." She turned her back to them. "I better get a fresh pot of coffee on."

"Any chance we could get a bite to eat? We've been riding hard in rain since before dawn." Travis spoke to Martha's back.

"You weren't here for lunch. This ain't no restaurant. I serve supper at six. If you want to eat then, your boots better be under the table."

Teagen grinned. One thing about Martha, she was constant. "We're hoping a few chickens drown before dinner." He slipped Tobin the cookie jar, and they moved down the hall.

"Word is trouble's coming," Tobin said more seriously. "So we left our brides in Austin and rode in as fast as we could." He crammed two cookies in his mouth and passed the jar to Travis.

The mood sobered as the McMurrays gathered around the dining table to talk. Sage tossed each a towel, then joined them. To Jessie's surprise, the men dried their weapons first, then their faces and hair.

Tobin touched Jessie's arm when she poured coffee and said, "Welcome to the family. My Libby said she can't wait to meet you." He tugged something from his saddlebag. "She sent you this as a welcome-to-the-family gift."

He handed Jessie a present wrapped in white paper. While the men talked, she slipped back in the kitchen and opened it. A deep blue shawl with long fringe tumbled softly into her hands. "Look," Jessie whispered to Martha, "Tobin's wife sent me a gift. It's made of the softest material I've ever felt."

Martha was too busy peeling potatoes to give it more than a glance. "She's like that. Kind and thoughtful. Not at all uppity like you'd think she'd be with her dad so powerful and rich."

Jessie brushed her fingers over the gift as if it were breakable. In a month it would be cool enough to wear it, and she could hardly wait.

As she set it high on a shelf, Martha handed her another pot of coffee. "If I know them, they'll be needing this. When they've got planning to do, they drink coffee as fast as I can boil it."

When Jessie walked back into the dining room, Travis stood and offered her a seat. "You're a McMurray now; you'll need to join us."

She glanced at Teagen, and he nodded his agreement. When

she took the nearest seat, she spotted Rose peeping around the door.

Teagen saw her too. "There's more you need to meet." He grinned at his brothers. "Rose, bring your sisters in if they are up from their naps."

The five-year-old came in first, fascinated by the big men. She shook Travis's hand. "You look Indian," she said. "I'm Indian every day until noon; then Martha says she has to fold all the blankets. How come if you're younger than my papa, you look bigger? Martha says you have a son named Duck. That's not a proper name, but I'm good with names. I'll help you think of a better one."

Travis smiled down at the child. "Duck is going to love meeting you."

Teagen agreed. "Duck never talks, and Rose never stops. They should be great friends."

While Rose continued asking her new uncles questions, Emily slipped into the room. She looked about to faint with fear. She glanced around like a trapped animal, then suddenly darted to Teagen.

Jessie watched as she tried to hide behind Teagen's arm. He tugged her gently around and set her on his knee. Emily fisted her hands in his shirt and held on as if her life depended on it. Teagen's big hand rested on her shoulder.

"It's all right," he said softly. "These are my brothers, Em. They are not nearly as frightening as they look. In fact, you'll probably like Tobin; he's part horse."

Tobin stood, walked the length of the table, and knelt down by Teagen's chair. "You like horses?"

Emily nodded, then buried her face in Teagen's sleeve.

"I do too," Tobin said. "In fact, I'm bringing a horse from back East that is so small you can ride it without needing a step to climb up." He looked at the others. "Libby and I figure with all the kids around the place, a few ponies might make sense."

"Does he have a name?" Rose asked.

Everyone laughed.

Bethie waddled into the room. Tobin made the mistake of picking her up. A sticky hand patted his cheek, but he'd had enough practice with little ones to not let it bother him.

Martha rushed in, nodded to the men as if she had nothing to ask them about in the months they'd been gone. She gave her full attention to Bethie. "Sorry, the baby is sticky. She got into the honey again."

"She's always sticky," Teagen commented. "We're thinking, when she grows up we'll have to marry her off to the first fellow she dances with, because he'll be stuck on her."

Teagen glanced at Martha, and she seemed to understand. She nodded once and circled the little ones. "We'll be in the kitchen if you need us. I got a feeling what needs to be talked about in here ain't something for little ears."

Jessie wanted to go with the girls, but she knew that what was about to happen was not just conversation. The dining room had become the war room, and plans needed to be made.

She moved to the chair beside Teagen. He took her hand under the table as he leaned forward and filled his brothers in on all that had happened. Some of the things he said were problems he hadn't even shared with her.

As he talked, his thumb rubbed gently across her palm as if to remind her that everything was going to be all right.

Travis said he'd been in touch with the Ranger headquarters in Waco. They thought the man who waited outside Whispering Mountain was probably an old ex-soldier from Santa Anna's army. A dangerous man, hungry for power and believing he had a right to land in Texas. His men called him General, even though the Rangers doubted he'd ever made near that rank during his army days. Those under him were riding for the money they'd been promised.

Tobin added that word was, the General had raided ranches along the border for almost twenty years. He even ran a widow out down by San Antonio after her husband was killed, but her ranch wasn't big enough for him.

"He's never come this far north." Travis swore. "But he must think this place is worth the trouble."

Jessie had heard Sage and Martha talk about how large Whispering Mountain Ranch was, but she'd never thought of it as more than Teagen's home.

Tobin's voice was lower, slower than his brother's, as if he thought about each word before speaking. "If he saw us ride in today, and I'm thinking he did, he'll either give up the quest or hit fast and hard before more men come."

Both brothers agreed.

"The ranch near San Antonio came too easy," Travis said. "So he thinks he might as well try for more."

Teagen shook his head. "And so now he thinks he can just move in and take Whispering Mountain."

"That's about it. When you were here alone, he must have thought it would be easy to ride in and kill you and claim you died after you sold him the land," Travis guessed. "There are enough crooked lawyers in this state that he could make up a bill of sale."

"But," Tobin added, "you confused things by marrying." He turned to his sister. "One man and his little sister must have looked like easy pickings. I'm surprised he didn't try to take the ranch the day he got here."

"He didn't have the men." Sage finally jumped into the conversation. "Roak said he's been recruiting for over a month. Half the men he found were strays from the forts or trail drivers down on their luck. Word is he had to arm them and train them before they'd be any good in a fight."

Travis ignored all but the first of her comments. "That kid, Drummond Roak, still around?" he asked.

Teagen stood, and Sage's answer died on her lips. "First things first," he said as if calling a board meeting to order. "When I turned eighteen, I put the ranch in my name, but we've all known it belonged equally to the four of us. Travis, draw up the papers. Four McMurrays will be harder to kill if this general is planning murder. Second, I'm tired of waiting for him. I say we take this discussion to the general."

Jessie felt her entire body turn cold. All four of the McMurrays were talking at once. Defending their ranch was one thing, but going out looking for a fight was another. She couldn't breathe. When she heard Bethie cry, she bolted from the room.

At the door she glanced back. None of them seemed to have noticed she'd left. They were all talking about what had to be done.

Jessie hurried to the kitchen and cuddled a fussy Bethie to her. She'd thought she belonged here, but now she wasn't so sure. She could learn to fire a gun, but she knew there was no way she could raise it and kill someone. She wasn't like them. Fighting wasn't in her blood. Jessie had read a debate once where one man claimed all the strong Americans were heading west, while another man said only the foolish and lawless were dumb enough to leave the safety of their homes for the wilderness. Right now she felt like she was surrounded by strong, foolish, wild men.

"I'm not brave enough to be a McMurray," she whispered.

Martha shook her heard and seemed to read Jessie's thoughts. "Or crazy enough maybe. They're a wild bunch, no matter how they try to act civilized. But you married Teagen. I reckon that took a wagonload of bravery. That man can frown and frighten bark off a cedar."

Jessie didn't see the Teagen they all seemed to know. She'd run to him because of fear, never thinking of him as some kind of bear of a man to be avoided. "I should leave," she said thinking of the few dollars she had left in her bag. More than the fear of getting killed, she couldn't bear to think about how he would look at her when he found out she was a total coward. If she'd been brave, she wouldn't have put up with Eli; she wouldn't have run when he died. Teagen deserved a wife who could stand by his side in hard times, not a mouse of a wife who wanted to set up housekeeping in the cellar until all this blew over.

"I wouldn't give much thought to leaving," Martha said as she vigorously smashed boiled potatoes. "He'd come after you. McMurrays don't let go of nothing. That general coming in better have a hundred men riding with him if he plans to take one handful of dirt."

"You're not worried?"

"Outlaws don't scare me. I came from worse. When a sheriff in Austin told me about a need for a housekeeper up North along the frontier line, I used every dime I had to get here. Every soul I ever cared about had died or disowned me. I just wanted someplace to be alone and keep my hands busy. The three untamed boys and a baby I saw here needed me, so I stayed. They were fighting to hold the ranch then, and I saw my job to keep them fed. I didn't want much in this world, and I found my place when I came here. I'm never leaving this land."

"You love all four of them, don't you?"

Martha shook her head. "They didn't need love; they needed to grow strong and survive. I did my part to see they had that chance. Now, as grown men, I guess they do need love in their lives, but it's not a fighting woman they crave, it's a caring one. All three of them boys need a woman's tenderness 'cause they never had it growing up, but not one of them would admit it if you asked him." She looked at Jessie. "A warrior needs something worth fighting for."

"You love them," Jessie said again, and this time Martha didn't deny it as she turned back to her cooking.

Teagen stepped into the kitchen a moment later. "We're riding out to make sure everything is quiet for the night. Martha, we'll have to eat supper in shifts."

"All right."

"If you hear gunfire . . ."

"I know what to do."

He looked at Jessie. "Keep the girls close to the house till bedtime. It might not be a bad idea to have them sleep in the cellar for the next few nights. If trouble comes riding in, we won't have long to wait."

He didn't need to say more; she understood.

Without a word, she followed him out to where the others were already mounting.

"Teagen?" she whispered not knowing what to say.

He leaned down and kissed her hard and fast. "It's all right. I'll be back in a few hours. We're planning to all get some sleep tonight, then Travis and I will leave at first light to see if the general and his men are still camped out in the rocks."

She wanted to hold on to him and not let him go. Even if she tried to tell him, he'd never believe how much he meant to her.

Darkness crept across the land as she watched them ride away. For a while, she stood on the porch listening, but all was quiet. The air smelled newborn after the rain, but lightning still flickered to the north. It seemed the threat of a raid had been a cloud over the ranch almost since she'd arrived.

Part of her wished for the quiet days of the bookstore, when all adventure came from books. But that life had been without Teagen's touch, and deep down she knew that was the one thing she couldn't live without. Somehow, she'd stay, no matter what the danger.

Almost three hours passed before he returned. He looked tired and dusty from riding hard, but he barely touched his food as he sat alone at the table. When Jessie asked him how things were, he simply said, "Fine," but the deep creases along his forehead told her he lied.

Sage stood guard on the porch. Teagen took his coffee and spelled her so she could check the last of the mares still in the corral. Danger might be riding toward them, but they still had a ranch to run.

Sage poked her head inside and asked if Jessie minded if Emily went to the barn with her. "She's big enough to be a great help with the animals."

Emily was out the door before Jessie had a chance to say yes. Bethie and Rose were already asleep on beds in the cellar. Martha had agreed to sleep with them, but Emily wanted to stay upstairs with her mother. The child might not say much, but she sensed things. Whenever Jessie was unhappy or worried, Emily always seemed to lean close against her, silently comforting her.

Jessie filled her fifth cup of hot coffee and joined her husband on the porch. She knew as long as the others were out, she'd stay awake. At the first sound of gunfire, she'd send Emily to the cellar, but if possible, she planned to remain with Teagen.

She tried not to think about what might happen. What might go wrong. If Teagen was hurt, she would help. If he died, it would be in her arms. He'd been a part of her soul for years, and she had to be strong enough to help him if he turned to her. If she lived to be a hundred and loved her children's children, none would ever be a part of her like Teagen was. No one would, no one could.

He didn't seem to notice she was by his side for a while. He studied the night. Finally, he took a drink and said, "You should be in bed."

"An order," she whispered, knowing requests came hard for the man.

He turned to her. "A request." His tired eyes seemed to drink her in.

"I belong here, beside you." The truth of her words hit her fully.

"Because I'm your husband?"

She nodded. "And because I care."

She knew he wasn't comfortable with words, but she needed to say it. "I want to be at your side, dear."

"When?"

"All the time."

"Now, in the fight?"

"Always."

The silence between them seemed thick as a muddy river. Finally, he added, "In my bed."

She didn't move. "Yes."

He slowly set his cup down, then took hers from her and placed it beside his. Without a word he moved behind her and gently slid one arm around her waist. When he tugged her against him, she went willingly.

She could feel him breathing, feel his heart pounding, feel his warm breath as he leaned over her to kiss her hair. "I want you to be my woman, Jess, forever."

"I'm already yours." She leaned her head back and let him kiss his way down her throat.

In the distance they heard Sage and Emily coming back from the barn.

His words came in a low whisper against her ear. "In a few hours, I'll turn in for some sleep. I want you next to me."

"But you'll need sleep."

"I'll have it, but I'll have you against me first."

She trembled, and his grip tightened slightly.

"Will you be there?"

She nodded and slipped a few inches away as Sage and Emily grew close.

Sage thanked Em for her help, then turned to her brother. "I'll get a few hours' sleep, then spell you so you can do the same. Travis and Tobin will also take turns."

Jessie picked up the cups and followed Sage inside, leaving Teagen on guard. She knew this was not the time for Teagen to court her, but whatever happened, they both needed to be alone together if only for an hour.

CHAPTER 30

Teagen rode to Lookout Point. Everything was quiet. The cool midnight air made him almost believe his land was blanketed in peaceful sleep. He knew Tobin covered the west side at the riverbank, and Travis watched the east. They had two men on the bridge tonight, and Tobin would be there long before dawn. One man, alone and well-trained, might be able to move onto Whispering Mountain land, but not the army it would take to run the McMurrays off. He'd never lost a battle, and he had no intent of losing this one. Travis was right; it was time to ride over the bridge and see what was rumor and what was fact. He was tired of worrying about when trouble might come.

The land to the road from the bridge was clear and safe. A few miles north, the terrain turned rocky and spotted with brush and trees, not fit for farming or raising anything but goats. Teagen had tried to buy the section of ground more than once because he didn't like the idea that someone could move in on the other side of the river, but whoever owned it had refused to sell. In fact, he couldn't even find out the name of the heir who'd inherited it from the old man who originally settled there.

He'd seen the outlaw hideout there. It would be impossible to get close without the men knowing they were coming. No one else was around to notice they were camped there, much less run them off. He knew he'd be stepping over the line if he demanded they leave. They might think they had as much right to be on that worthless strip of land as he did.

Teagen didn't care. He wanted to live in peace for a change. He wanted to sleep in his house with his wife and not see worry in her eyes.

Thoughts of Jessie moved him toward home. He made one last circle of the house and barns, then turned in for a few hours' sleep. After washing in the mud room and putting on clean clothes, he walked through the silent house. Travis and Tobin, if they slept, would do it under the Texas sky. Travis liked the trees down by the river. He'd wake if one horse splashed ashore. Tobin would bed down close to the bridge.

Pushing his bedroom door open, he smiled at the sight of Jessie curled on top of the covers. She wore her white night-gown, buttoned all the way to her throat, and she'd tucked her feet beneath the hem. A book lay beside her as though it had tumbled from her hand when she'd fallen asleep.

He walked silently to the far side of the bed and lay down beside her. When his weight shifted the mattress, she rolled into his arms. He'd planned to just rest beside her. That would be enough, he'd thought, but when her soft body pressed against him, he wanted more than sleep.

Moving his hand lightly over her gown, he touched her middle, missing the baby that had grown there. "Someday," he whispered against her hair, liking the idea of another child growing within her. If she ever carried another baby, it would be his from the beginning.

He liked the way she'd given him permission to touch her whenever he liked. She had no idea how little he knew of touching a woman or how much the gift of having her near meant to him. He wasn't sure he'd ever be able to tell her, but he promised he'd always be gentle with her.

She made a sound in her sleep when his hand moved over her breast. Stretching, she leaned into his warmth. The full-ness of her breast filled his hand.

"Jess," he whispered. "Open your eyes and look at me."

Sleepy brown eyes met his. She smiled as his grip tight-ened slightly.

"I want you to know it's me," he whispered. His lips brushed her cheek. "Now, open your mouth."

She grinned as his kiss gently claimed her. It took a few seconds before she awoke enough to return his advance; then she opened to him, and he tasted the sweet depths of her mouth. He liked the shy touch of her tongue on his almost as much as he loved the way she silently pleaded for more when he hinted of pulling away.

His hands moved over her in tender caresses as the kiss deepened. His need to know every curve of her grew with each touch. They'd settled it in the cellar this morning. She was his . . . she wanted to be his wife.

But he'd go slowly. He wanted her, and someday he'd take her hard and fast, but not tonight. The first few times he touched her, he'd force himself to go easy, so slow she'd be begging for him before he moved inside her.

He loved hearing the soft sounds of pleasure she made when he stroked her breasts. She'd come to his arms and his bed willingly. Tonight he'd please her. If she had any idea of the hunger pulsing through him, she might be frightened even more than she had been this afternoon with the talk of a fight.

When he finally settled her against his heart, he thought he'd let her rest and grow used to him beside her, but she'd discovered the hair on his chest and kept running her fingers over it.

"Jess," he ordered. "Stop that and go to sleep." He wasn't surprised when she ignored him.

She giggled. "I never knew you were so hairy. Maybe you are part bear."

He caught her hand as it slid over his nipple. "What are you doing?"

She rose to one elbow. "I'm exploring you." She kissed his throat. "You belong to me, you know." She tugged his shirt aside and undid the first few buttons of his trousers.

He'd never thought of it, but in a strange way, he didn't mind if she claimed him. He kind of liked the idea of being her man. "Oh, so you think the beast is yours," he growled low against her ear.

"Yes," she answered. "All mine."

When she ran her hand along his stomach to below his unbuckled belt, he almost jerked out of the bed.

"Easy now," she said, pushing her fingers an inch lower. "I'm just getting used to the feel of you. Be still until I've had my chance to explore."

"I don't know if I can do that, but I'll try." He'd felt so few touches in his life. Most of the time he'd told himself he didn't need such foolishness, but Jessie was proving him wrong. Her touch could quickly become an addiction.

He tried to relax as her hand played across the muscles of his chest, and each time she reached his belt, she pushed a little further as if she sensed how greatly she affected him.

"I like the feel of you, dear," she whispered, almost asleep. "Almost as much as I like you touching me."

"Are you finished?" he asked, catching her hand over his heart.

"No." She laughed. "I plan to touch you so often you won't even notice my hands sliding over you."

"I doubt that will happen in this lifetime, but I'm willing to test the theory."

She wiggled, turning her back to him. He shifted to his side, pressing his need for her against her hips. He wanted to strip off her gown and feel her bare body against him, but he knew he needed to erase the past one touch at a time.

"Jess," he whispered. "You're mine. I want you here with me like this every night."

"In my dreams, I've been here with you for years," she whispered. "In my dreams I always fall asleep with you holding me."

"And touching you?" He moved his hand over her hip.

"Mmmm," she mumbled as he stroked her again.

She was already too near sleep to answer. He tugged the ring he'd picked up at Elmo's weeks ago from his pocket and slipped it on the third finger of her left hand. "I meant to give you this before, but I wanted to know you came willingly to me."

When her eyes didn't open, he lifted her hand and kissed the ring. "Tomorrow I'll remind you never to remove the ring, but for now, I'll let you sleep while I learn the feel of you."

While one hand held her close, the other reached around and unbuttoned her gown. "Jessie," he whispered as his hand slid from her throat to below her stomach. "Jess, I'm just going to touch you tonight. You keep dreaming, darling. I'm not going to hurt you."

"All right," she answered in sleep. She shifted slightly as his hand moved lower.

He couldn't be sure if she was awake or sleeping, but she moved as he slid his hand over her body and began to stroke her most private part. When his fingers pushed inside, she let out a little sigh and rocked onto her back.

"Sleep, darling," he whispered. "Sleep and dream of me touching you."

He continued exploring as his mouth gently took her breast.

Her sighs were the music to his movements as he worshiped every inch of her body. He felt the way her breathing changed when his fingers played inside her and the soft way she begged him to kiss her breasts again and again. She rocked with need when he took her soft mound deep inside his mouth.

Her body grew warmer to his touch as he learned her every curve and tasted the damp moisture along her body. She rocked with pleasure in his embrace.

When she began to move faster, he rose and kissed her deeply. He captured her cry at the moment she lost complete control. Her body tightened, then melted as she sighed in contentment.

He stilled, not believing what had just happened. When he raised his head, all he saw were her big brown eyes sparkling.

He cupped the back of her head in his hand. "Are you all right?"

She nodded as if she didn't trust herself to speak.

"Are you angry?" He didn't think she could be. She was still warm and molten in his hand.

She shook her head slightly.

He needed to know what she felt, but it wasn't something he could demand. Kissing her cheek, he whispered, "I wish you understood how much I love touching you."

She pulled away, paying no attention to the fact that her gown was open. Once above him, she leaned down and kissed his cheek just as he had hers, then she whispered, "I do."

Without another word, she cuddled back into his arms.

He pulled the covers over them both.

He thought of touching her again. Of asking her to touch him. Of pulling off all their remaining clothes and making love to her.

Then he smiled.

They had a lifetime of nights together. He planned to savor each moment to the fullest. She'd liked his touch; she'd like the next step even more. And there would be a next step, and then another and another. The ache he had for her would take years to ease.

Closing his eyes, he slept soundly.

CHAPTER 31

THE SOUND OF GUNFIRE WOKE HIM AT DAWN.

Jessie moved first, running for the door. He caught up to her by the time she reached the kitchen. Both had buttoned to presentable.

"One shot," she said. "I heard one shot."

Teagen tugged on his boots. "It's almost light. I should have been in the saddle an hour ago." He strapped his gun belt around his waist as Sage rushed up the porch steps. "Teagen. It's Tattor Sims. I think he's been shot again."

When he and Jessie stepped outside, Teagen made out the old Ranger's horse coming toward the house with Sims fighting to stay in the saddle.

"Get ready for him. I'll ride out and see he makes it in."

Teagen didn't glance back at Jessie. He knew she was probably terrified, her big eyes round as saucers. She'd told him more than once that she hated the thought of anyone hurting.

If he turned to her, he'd see reality. He wasn't ready to let go of the memory of the way she'd felt in his arms when he'd satisfied her as a woman. He'd loved the way she'd jerked against him in pleasure and how she'd held onto him as if she feared she might drift away.

He forced his mind from the night as he stepped up on Sage's horse and rode out to Sims at a full gallop.

The old Ranger was swearing a blue streak. He'd been hit in the left thigh this time and, from the blood dripping out both sides of his leg, the bullet must have passed right through.

"I thought it was still dark enough to walk the river's edge. I figured if I didn't get some exercise my wound would never heal up. Some blasted son of the devil must have seen me." He swore a while and then added, "I'm getting mighty tired of being used for target practice."

By the time he reached the house, he'd stopped swearing and started claiming he was dying. Sage and Martha took over, moving him to the downstairs bedroom.

"I'll see to him," Sage yelled when Teagen looked like he planned to follow her into the house.

He glanced toward the kitchen and saw Jessie, now in her robe. She was busy starting the stove and putting water on to boil. He had to force himself not to step inside for one kiss. He had a job to do, and if he didn't do everything right, they might all be in danger. Plus he knew one kiss would never be enough.

He ran for his horse and had the mount halfway saddled when he remembered how she'd said he was hers, like she claimed him. When there was time, he planned to do some thinking on that. He swung into the saddle in a hurry for all the trouble to be over and well aware that he had to shove Jessie out of his mind if he planned to be at his best.

His best and nothing less, he thought, for all their lives depended on it.

Before breakfast two more men had been shot at, but neither was hit. Teagen pulled the riders to a safe distance from the river, but he couldn't find Tobin. Travis told him not to worry; Tobin was used to doing things his own way.

"It bothers me someone can stand across the river and fire at our land." Teagen had been fighting the urge to fire back since dawn.

Travis shrugged. "You can't buy all of Texas. We're safer here than most ranches. As soon as we know Sims is going to make it, we need to figure out how we plan to get to them. I'm thinking we could cross downstream and ride behind their camp. We could be on them before they saw us coming."

It was a plan, but Teagen didn't see, even with the advantage of surprise, that the two of them would have much chance against thirty or more. Travis knew as well as he did that they couldn't take more men. If they did, they'd be leaving the ranch unarmed.

He was standing on the porch thinking things couldn't get any worse when an old buggy rolled across the bridge. He swore, knowing who it was by the ragged fringe and broken-down mule. Mrs. Dickerson. The old schoolteacher had a way of butting into their lives. This time she'd be lucky if she didn't get herself killed.

Knowing her, she'd heard about their trouble from some-one in town and came out to check on them herself. The only way they'd welcome her was if she came armed to the teeth, and he somehow doubted that would be the case.

"Sage," he yelled from the barn. "Get rid of her."

Sage stepped out. "I've got my hands full with Sims. You'll have to talk to her, big brother."

He looked around for someone else to pass the chore to, but Travis had vanished, and Dolan Hatch wouldn't talk to her even if he wasn't watching the herd. The three other men he'd hired were probably sleeping, since they'd stood guard all night.

Teagen walked to the center of the yard and waited, his rifle braced across his shoulders.

Mrs. Dickerson's rig rolled to a stop. Her mangy mule looked like he might drop dead any moment. Besides being the ugliest animal Teagen had ever seen, the old lady had put a bow in the mule's mane. That had to be humiliating, even for a mule.

"Morning, Teagen," the teacher said as if he were still a child. "Help me down, young man."

"Mrs. Dickerson, we got no time for company today." That was the most polite thing he could think of, but he knew it fell far short of proper. "Do you think you could come for a visit some other day?"

"I know all about your trouble. Drummond told me."

"How do you know the kid?" He offered his hand as she

wiggled from her buggy. He could never quite tell if she was fat or simply wore a dozen layers of clothes. Her four husbands probably died of exhaustion trying to undress her. Just the thought made him want to slam the butt of his gun against his head to knock the image out.

"Never mind that. How I know Mr. Roak is none of your concern," she said. "And for now, I won't discuss how I expect your new daughters to be in school next month. I've more pressing things that must be dealt with at present."

Teagen spotted Travis coming from of the barn. He almost made it back out of sight before the old schoolteacher spotted him. "Travis McMurray, I'll be needing to talk to you also. Come over here."

The hardened Texas Ranger who now served as a lawyer at the capital followed orders and stepped forward with a polite, "Yes, ma'am."

Teagen fought the urge to shove the bundle of p's and q's back into her buggy, but in truth, he respected the old lady. She'd been the one person in town who'd kept up with them when their parents died. For years she'd sent reading lists and nagged Teagen to keep up his brothers' studies. She had even given him the address of a bookstore in Chicago and Eli's name. Whatever she came out here for, she must think it important. He could spare a few minutes, then send her flying back to town as fast as her half-dead mule would take her.

"Would you like to join us for breakfast?" he asked, not missing the frown Travis gave him.

"No, thank you, but I will have a cup of Martha's coffee." Mrs. Dickerson walked inside. She took time to meet Jessie and talk to each of the girls before settling down at the table. Emily was shy as always, but Rose seemed fascinated someone had appeared who might know the answers to all her questions. Bethie grabbed for the glasses dangling around the teacher's neck. Instead of telling the baby no, she simply explained that these were her glasses and only she could touch them.

Bethie, if she understood a word, showed no sign.

Teagen, listening to their chatter, stepped down the hall to where Sims lay on the same bed he'd shared with Jessie only hours before. The seasoned Ranger looked pale and older. He'd weathered the first shot well. He might not be so lucky this second time.

"How is he?" Teagen asked Sage.

"I've almost got the bleeding stopped, but he's already got a fever. Also, the fall has opened the old wound."

Teagen knew black powder poisoning killed more men than bullets. "Anything I can do?"

Sage's smile was wicked. "Talk to Mrs. Dickerson."

He frowned and headed back to the kitchen. Travis stood by the stove, watching the old teacher fuss over the girls. She was a Pied Piper. Children loved her. There would be no stopping Emily and Rose from starting school this fall.

Teagen took the time to pour himself a cup of coffee but didn't sit down. He waited, knowing the woman would tell him why she came in her own good time.

"I thought I heard shots while I was heading this way," she finally said when the girls seemed more interested in the chalk she'd brought them than in any adult conversation.

"You did. Someone is across the river taking shots at my men. You'd be wise to leave before they charge the ranch. One of my men, Tattor Sims, was hit. Sage is seeing to him now."

The old woman had lived through far too much to be frightened by words or even a few shots, for that matter.

"I've made the acquaintance of Mr. Sims twice, once in Austin at a funeral and last week when he rode in for supplies. How is he?"

"He'll live if we can keep the fever down."

She nodded in understanding. "I lost my first husband to fever after a gunshot wound." She took a sip of coffee and announced, "You need to get those terrible men off that land. This kind of thing is just not to be tolerated."

He looked up, surprised she'd voiced his plan.

Travis answered. "We're thinking of heading over and doing just that, but we don't own that slice of land. Legally, they've got as much right to be there as we do. And we've no proof they are the ones shooting."

"Of course you do. Mr. Sims's bullet holes should count for proof. And who else would be out there foolish enough to shoot at a McMurray but some stranger to this part of Texas."

"You've got a point. But they still got rights."

"Not if I say they don't," she said in her most teacherlike voice.

Both men stared, but Travis got his question out first. "Why do you say that? Do you own that land, Mrs. Dickerson?"

"My second husband did. When he bought it, he was afraid they wouldn't let me have it if he died, so he put my name on the deed. Though I go by my middle name of Etta, my mother named me after the doctor who delivered me. I was Floyd E. Bradly before I married Mr. Hayes, before I married Mr. Dickerson." She turned to Travis. "Is the land still mine, even though I remarried?"

"I don't know if it would stand up in court, but right now you got more claim to it than anyone." Travis knelt down beside her chair. "And if you want us to run those men off, we'd consider it the neighborly thing to do."

"I do," she said just as gunfire exploded outside.

Everyone ran for the windows. Travis took one look and knew what they'd feared was happening. A line of thirty or more riders was forming on the other side of the bridge, ready to storm across. In minutes they'd all be on McMurray land riding straight toward the house with their guns blazing.

Teagen picked up his rifle. "Jessie, you and Martha get the girls to the cellar." He glanced at the schoolteacher. "Will you join them, Mrs. Dickerson?"

"I will not," she said, "but I will sit with Sims so Sage can fight with her brothers. If I know that girl, she'll not want to miss a fight, and Sims and I will have a nice visit."

"Done," Teagen said and ran through the door without another word.

If they'd had time, the McMurrays would have met them at

the bridge, but with so many men, they needed the cover of the porch as an advantage.

Travis had rifles lining the railing when Sage joined them. "Where's Tobin?" she asked as she lifted her gun.

Before anyone could answer, Roak ran around the side of the house and swung up on the porch. "Morning," he said as if all hell wasn't about to break loose. "I was afraid I'd be too late." He winked at Sage. "Need another gun?"

"Yes," she managed and handed him a second rifle.

His hand covered hers for only a second, but Teagen thought he saw something pass between them. An acceptance maybe, or the beginning of a friendship.

Everyone stared at the outlaws just beyond the bridge. They were too far to shoot, but once they charged, the McMurrays would need every loaded rifle on the porch to get them all. Even good shots couldn't hit a moving target 100 percent of the time. That would leave half or more of the men making it to the yard before the McMurrays had time to reload. Maybe the outlaws would even be close enough that the fight would turn to hand-to-hand combat.

Travis wore a long knife on his belt; Teagen kept one in his boot. If he survived this day, he swore he'd buy a cannon and mount it at the bridge with a sign that anyone coming within range might find themselves buzzard meat.

"Where's Tobin?" Roak whispered.

No one answered as the yell to charge echoed from the bridge. From the way they came, there was no doubt that a military man planned the attack. Ten men hit the bridge with another dozen right behind.

Teagen and the others raised their guns in silent readiness. Seconds ticked by in slow motion. This was what he'd trained all his life for. This was all he'd ever been. Like lightning flashing against midnight sky, the image of Jessie sleeping on his bed crossed his mind, and Teagen realized if he died today, he'd known one more thing. He'd had the promise of her. If it turned out that was all he got in this life, it was enough.

He molded his finger around the trigger and held his breath. Every shot had to count. He would not fire until they were within range.

Suddenly, an explosion shattered the wooden bridge as if it were no more than a toy. Men and horses flew in every direction. Pieces of wood showered the land and splashed into the river. A thunderous roar rumbled, then echoed off the hills behind them.

The family watched in silence as black smoke cleared, leaving a gaping hole where the bridge had been. The few men who had made it across the bridge gathered the wounded and dove into the rapid current to try to swim away. The outlaws on the other side turned tail and rode away, leaving one man shouting orders to no one.

As if nothing out of the ordinary had happened, Travis said calmly, "Well, at least we know where Tobin was."

"If the general can catch what's left of his men before they make it back to Mexico, he'll have a hard time getting here without the bridge." Roak rested his rifle on his shoulder. "And I was all fired up for a fight."

Travis set his guns down. "In a few hours I'll take a couple of men and ride over to make sure they are not planning to regroup." He looked at Roak. "You want to ride with me?"

"Sure." Roak smiled. "You bet. Any chance we're having breakfast first?"

"That and lots of coffee. We'll have to swim the river."

The boy laughed. "No problem."

"We do have another problem, gentlemen," Sage added.

All the men looked at her.

"Mrs. Dickerson is on this side of the bridge."

A groan came in harmony.

"I could blindfold her and take her through the pass," Teagen offered.

Sage shook her head. "She can't ride. Bad back. Her buggy would never make the trip through the passage."

No one answered when Drummond said, "What pass?"

"Well." Travis shrugged. "I guess she's staying for dinner till fall."

Teagen frowned. The longest he'd ever been able to stay in the same room with the old lady had been five minutes, and he was about to have her around for a month or more.

Another problem crossed his mind. Roak had heard them speak of the passage through the hills. They'd have to kill him or marry him into the family. Teagen didn't want to even think how the vote would go.

CHAPTER 32

Tobin didn't return until noon. When he'd fired the powder beneath the bridge, the blast threw him in the river. He drifted with the rubble for a mile or so before swimming out and walking back to the house. He had several cuts Sage doctored as she lectured him on trying not to get killed.

Tobin didn't say a word; he just sat at the kitchen table next to Travis and drank coffee while he tried not to flinch as she pulled splinters from his hands.

Jessie watched, knowing that Sage's anger at her brother was out of love. She might be six years younger than him, but as she did them all, she mothered him. Teagen might be the head of the family, but Sage was the heart.

When Tobin took off his shirt, Rose saw the terrible scar on his chest and began asking questions.

After Tobin told her all about being shot as a child the first time the bridge blew, she went around the house asking everyone if they had scars. Jessie could almost see her little mind cataloging each account so she could check on them later.

When Rose wandered into the downstairs bedroom and saw Tattor Sims, questions exploded from the five-year-old. Martha ran her back toward the kitchen, claiming that no child should see a man's bare limbs. So Rose asked her mother all about men's limbs while Jessie tried to get a meal ready alone.

As soon as Sage finished caring for her brother, she grabbed her hat and hurried out. There were horses that also needed doctoring.

Tobin tugged on his shirt and stood. "Don't tell my wife I was hurt," he said to Jessie as he dropped his coffee cup in a pan of soapy water. "She'll have a fit."

Jessie paused in her chore of peeling potatoes. "All right, I won't. But she's bound to notice the bandages. Maybe you should stay away from her until you heal."

He shook his head. "If I know her and Travis's Rainey, they've already hired a coach and are waiting to head this way. I made her promise not to start until I sent word that all was clear." He looked miserable. "Travis and I left Austin less than a week ago, and I already miss her. We're going to have another baby. Liberty says a girl this time, but McMurrays tend to produce boys."

"Which do you want?"

He shrugged. "I don't care. I just wish she was here."

Jessie remembered Teagen writing about Tobin's marriage last year. She also thought he said his brother never talked. Maybe he'd just had little to say before he married.

Rose circled through the kitchen once more, wanting to know where Emily was. "Martha said she thought she seen her following Sage to the barn, but she didn't tell me she was leaving."

Tobin reached for his hat. "I'd best go help. The men found three horses near the bridge. They were all cut up and bleeding. We need to do what we can to patch them up, even if they're not ours."

"What about men?" Jessie didn't like the idea that even an outlaw might be hurt and left to die.

"I saw a few bodies in the river," Tobin admitted. "Dolan Hatch found two dead on our land. He said from the blood trails to the river it looked like several more were hurt and running for their lives."

"I hate thinking about them hurting," Jessie whispered.

"They would have killed you and the girls if they hadn't been stopped," Martha cut in as she stepped from the hallway.

"Men like that don't put no value on life. Look what they did to poor Mr. Sims, and he was a Texas Ranger who never did nothing to them."

"I know," Jessie managed, "but I do care about anyone hurting. I think we should help them if we can."

No one else in the room said a word.

Jessie thought of the days when adventure and danger could be escaped by closing a book. The dangers in this land frightened her, but she felt more alive here. She'd thought she liked the silence, but she loved all the noise of the McMurray house much more. She took her first stand as a McMurray. "Who'll go with me to check?"

"Not me," Martha said in her flat tone, "but I'll stay here and finish up lunch. Appears you got a fine stew going."

Travis, who'd showed little interest in what was happening, now looked up at her from the table. "If Teagen were here, he'd be throwing a fit about you even thinking about stepping outside this house. We won't know until we search if they're all gone. There might even be one who made it across and is hiding in the trees near the bridge."

There was a hardness in Travis's face that left Jessie with no doubt he spoke the truth, but that didn't change what needed to be done.

"I can face Teagen. If I had a guard, I'd be safe. We can't just let someone who is hurt out there bleed to death."

Both brothers looked at each other and smiled.

"Did you hear that Tob? She can face Teagen." Travis let out a yell.

"I did." Tobin laughed. "If she's that set on going, I guess we both better go along to see that nothing happens to this brave little woman. Teagen is never going to find another wife like her."

They were pulling their hats down when Teagen came back into the room.

He took one look at them and said, "What's going on?"

Both younger brothers fought down smiles. Finally Tobin said, "Ask your wife."

Teagen turned to her. "Well?" he said, obviously bothered everyone else in the room seemed to know something he didn't.

"I'm going down to see if there are any wounded outlaws." Jessie untied her apron. "Tell Sage I'll bring any back that I find for her to doctor."

She ignored the fact that her husband looked like he might explode with unsaid words as she walked out of the kitchen.

The brothers scrambled to follow her.

Halfway to the barn, they all heard Teagen roar from the porch. "Watch out for her!"

Jessie grinned. He was angry at her, but he didn't try to stop her. Teagen was learning. Tonight she'd tell him just how wonderful he was.

Tobin pulled the wagon round for Jessie, and they rode beside her all the way to the bridge. Hatch had already taken the two bodies away, and Jessie saw for herself that there were no wounded. Because of the shattered bridge, they could go no farther, but she stood in the wagon and looked anyway as both brothers stood guard.

Then, knowing she'd tried, she turned the team and drove back to the house.

Teagen met her at the barn.

She wasn't surprised both brothers found something to do. The oldest McMurray looked like a one-man war party.

"Jess," he said low and deadly. "We need to talk."

She headed for the cellar.

"Stop, Jessie," he said.

She remembered telling him that was all it took to get her not to leave. So she stopped and turned to face her angry husband.

He caught her hand and held it. For a moment he just stared down at her, his eyebrows pushed together in a frown. "Ride with me to the lookout." It was an order, not a request.

"Of course." She could tell he was still upset, but his touch was gentle when he lifted her up onto his horse.

They rode to the lookout in silence. Because she sat in front of him, his arm brushed the side of her breast with each turn, and she made a point of not trying to stay out of his way.

By the time they stopped and she turned to face him, a fire that had nothing to do with anger burned in his eyes.

"I love you," she said before he said something that would make her hold the words back.

He showed no sign of having heard her. He swung off the saddle and lifted her to the ground. "We need to get something settled. I want you safe. I don't want you leaving the area around the house when it's not safe. I want . . ."

She smiled. "You want me," she finished.

He frowned at her. "Don't change the subject."

"You didn't want me to go because you care about me, and I think it frightens you more than the raiders did."

He remained stone, and she knew he couldn't lie to her, but he wouldn't admit the truth.

She moved near the mountain's cool shade and away from the cliff that provided such a grand view. "You know what I want, Teagen. I'd like to talk about what happened between us last night."

He remained in the sun. "I don't think folks talk about such things."

"Why not?"

"I just don't think they do. It's too private."

"But—"

"Stop it, Jess. You're starting to sound like Rose." He turned away from her, staring with blind eyes at his land. "We need to talk about you having enough sense to be safe, not about things that belong only in the bedroom."

"I'll not stop," she said. "What happened in my dreams last night has never happened to me before, and I want to talk to my only friend about it."

"All right," he said without turning around. "Then we talk about you following orders and staying safe."

She leaned against the rock wall behind her and whispered, "Last night, I felt like I was floating toward the sun. I was weightless and growing warmer with every touch."

He twisted his head and squinted to see her in the shadows. "You liked it?"

"Did you?"

He took a step toward her. "You know I did, Jess."

"And is it something a man would do more than once to his wife?"

He joined her in the shadows. "It's something this man would do to his wife, but Jess, you know there is more."

She raised her head. "I know. But, if I asked . . . if I begged . . . would you . . ."

He closed the distance between them and he pulled her to him. "That's enough talk."

His mouth came down on hers. The kiss was long and warm, with his body pressing her against the solid wall of rock behind her. When he pulled a breath away, he whispered, "You'll never have to ask or beg. If you want me to make love to you, all you'll ever have to do is unbutton the top button of that very proper gown, and I'll do the rest."

"You'll still want me when you're mad at me?"

He laughed. "I have a feeling I'll still want you when I'm in my coffin."

"Tonight?"

He crushed her to him. "Every night."

Widening his stance, he lifted her to her toes and pressed against her. Even fully clothed, she felt the warmth of his body. "It's about time we started this marriage. I got a feeling we're going to be far more than friends, and that dream you had last night may be a recurring one."

She laughed and shoved his hat back. "I think you may be right."

He kissed her until she felt mindless, then she rode home in his arms. They didn't say a word until he lowered her to the side of the porch. She could see shadows listening from the kitchen.

"Now, have I made myself clear about you keeping safe," Teagen said in his usual cold voice. His fingers slid along the side of her breast in a caress.

"Yes, dear," she answered.

He touched his hat and smiled. "Until tonight."

She didn't answer. Her midnight dreams had almost come true in broad daylight.

CHAPTER 33

SAGE WALKED THROUGH THE LATE AFTERNOON SHAD-
ows of the barn. She wanted to check on the injured horses that
had been left after the raid. Tobin had warned her not to release
them in the pasture with any McMurray horses. They didn't
have the breeding, he'd told her. If their wounds healed, Tobin
planned to leave them with the blacksmith near Elmo's place.
Her brother said the blacksmith could use them as loaners.

Brushing them, she felt sorry for the horses. They'd probably spend the rest of their lives penned in the blacksmith's
small corral. Most didn't look like they'd ever had the proper
care.

A dusting of hay from above caught her attention, and she
looked up. "Drummond." She tugged the hay out of her hair.
"What are you doing up there?"

"The bunkhouse is full, so I thought I'd bed down here for
the night, since I'm trapped on the ranch."

She frowned at him. "You're not trapped here. You've been
swimming that river for months."

"Years," he corrected.

"So go home." The minute the words were out, she regret-
ted saying them. Everyone in the area knew Roak didn't have
a home.

He stared down at her, reminding Sage of the wounded
horses. He was lean and hard, even though not fully grown.

Suddenly, he winked. "I was hoping to stick around for another kissing lesson."

"Well, you can forget that," Sage answered. "And there's no use your coming back here. I decided today to take the offer Liberty's father made me. He said since I was Tobin's sister, I could use their place in Washington. I plan to go there and study to be a real doctor."

Roak swung down from the loft. "Is that far?"

"Hundreds of miles, so don't stay around waiting for me. They say it might take up to two years to become a doctor. I might like it up North so much that I decide to stay." She knew she was lying, but she had to say something to make the boy stop hoping for what would never be. Her heart was buried on the hill with her Ranger.

She expected him to pout or get angry, but he just shrugged. "Suit yourself. You're right. I can't wait around forever for you to decide I'm old enough to be your man."

His words rang cold. She started to snap back, but then she saw the hurt in his eyes. Hurt, as a boy, he couldn't manage to hide. She had a feeling that in two years when she came back, he'd be different, colder, harder. This land had a way of turning men to oak.

He shifted when she looked too close. "I'm thinking of heading back to Austin when Travis goes. He was telling me this afternoon that when all this trouble is over, he's riding that way, and if I wanted to go along, he'd introduce me to a few of his friends in the Rangers. He seems to think the Rangers might need a man like me."

"You are not thinking of being a Ranger?" For a second, she saw the image of his dead body lying in a buckboard.

"Maybe I am."

She put her fists on her hips. "You're not old enough."

"I'm only a few months younger than Travis was when he joined up."

"It's too dangerous."

Roak shook his head. "Like life around here isn't." He smiled. "If I die, will you bury me up in that little cemetery?"

"No," she snapped. "Never come back here, dead or alive.

I don't want to ever see you again." The last thing she wanted in this lifetime was to have to bury another Ranger.

She whirled around and ran to the house. Drum was just trying to hurt her, and she wouldn't stand by for another blow.

When she stepped onto the porch, she almost collided with Teagen.

"What's wrong?" he asked.

"I hate Drummond Roak. I swear he says and does things just to make me mad. We should have turned him over to the marshal last year and let him hang."

Teagen nodded as if he totally understood and then said calmly, "Would you consider marrying him?"

"What? Are you insane? I wouldn't marry him if he were the last single man alive."

Teagen shrugged. "I was afraid that would be your answer."

Travis walked up with fresh horses.

Teagen turned to his brother and yelled, "Go shoot Roak before we make our rounds."

Travis looked from Teagen to Sage. "Sure," he mumbled and tied the reins to the fence. He pulled his gun from its holster and began checking the chambers as he turned toward the barn.

"You are *not* going to shoot him," Sage snapped.

"But he knows there is a back passage." Teagen looked like he was fighting down a smile. "If he doesn't become part of the family, we'll have to kill him."

Sage glared at her brothers. "You two had better think of something else, because I'm not marrying him, and you're not going to shoot him. Understand?"

Before they could answer, she stomped into the house.

Laughing, Teagen walked to the horses. "I had a feeling it wasn't going to be so simple."

Travis grinned, put his gun back, and climbed into the saddle. "We'll think of a third plan, but I told you an hour ago that Sage wouldn't be that easy to marry off. She must like the kid a little, though, if she won't let us shoot him."

"For some crazy reason the kid likes her. If he'd marry her, it would save some other poor fellow from being miserable." Teagen frowned. "You should have seen how fast the last single man ran from this place."

As they rode rounds, Teagen told his brother about the preacher.

CHAPTER 34

Dinner conversation was explosive from the moment the brothers stormed the door. Jessie found it interesting that, like her, Drummond watched more than participated. Teagen took his usual place at the head of the dining table; Travis balanced the other end. Tobin pulled Jessie's chair out for her and then did the same for Sage. Drummond followed his lead and held Mrs. Dickerson's chair.

Teagen's frown made Jessie laugh. It was obvious he'd never thought of the courtesy.

Martha helped put the food on the table, then said she'd sit with Sims so Sage could eat with the family. All the women had taken turns with the old Ranger, hoping to have some improvement to report, but all day he hadn't moved.

The conversation turned to ranch business. Teagen said all he wanted was the general gone, but Travis claimed they should chase him all the way back to Mexico. He didn't like the idea of the outlaw picking on some other ranch.

Halfway through dessert, the men agreed to leave the ranch separately so anyone watching would not see what they were planning. Teagen would ride out before dawn, taking the trail through the hills to Elmo's place, then crossing back to watch for any sign the outlaws headed in that direction. Travis would circle to the east and cross the river to do the same. Roak would wait one day and then cross by where the bridge had been and head south. They all agreed that, once they joined up, if the outlaws had traveled any direction but south, the McMurrays would know it.

Jessie listened, finding herself wishing that she could talk to Teagen, but her husband seemed totally focused on what needed to be done. He was a strong leader, but she didn't miss the fact that whenever one of his siblings talked, he listened. In the end, any plan made had to have a majority.

The old schoolteacher sat between Rose and Emily, showing little interest in what the men had to say. Drummond remained silent, and Jessie couldn't help but wonder if any of the McMurrays even noticed he was there. He missed little, though, as he watched everyone at the table.

After dinner, Mrs. Dickerson moved into Jessie's old room upstairs. Jessie moved in with Sage, and Teagen stormed out to the bunkhouse with his brothers.

"I swear," Jessie heard him mumble as he packed up his saddlebag, "come next spring, I'll build a wing onto the house so I can at least sleep under my own roof."

When he noticed her watching him, he added, "I don't like being around myself most days, much less a half dozen men."

She followed him out the door, fully aware that he knew she was just behind him. He slowed his step as they walked, but he didn't turn around until they reached the bunkhouse porch.

Laughing, Jessie offered him little sympathy when she handed him towels and soap. "It's only temporary, dear."

He took the towels and said, "Is it such a crime that I want to sleep next to my wife? It seems a fairly small thing to ask for."

This powerful man reminded her of a pouting child. "I know," she answered so no one in the bunkhouse could hear. "I'll forget the feel of you by the time the bridge is rebuilt and all the company leaves."

He tugged her against him and would have kissed her if he hadn't noticed Travis staring at them. "What?" he growled at his brother.

Travis grinned. "I still can't believe you found a woman who likes you. She's even pretty and seems to be in her right mind—about most things, anyway."

Teagen looked like he might clobber his brother, but Jessie's gentle touch calmed him. She had a way with him, and she loved knowing that she did. She spread her hand along his back and felt his muscles tighten. Then, because they were not alone, she pulled away.

"How long will you be gone?"

"A few days. A week maybe," he said without meeting her eyes. "I'll be back as soon as this is finished."

She wanted him to hold her, but now was not the time or the place. Others were watching, and she had girls to get to bed.

Just before dawn the next morning, Jessie watched from her upstairs window as Teagen loaded supplies while Travis saddled up. She told herself if he even glanced toward the house, she'd run down and hug him good-bye.

He never looked. His mind must have been on his work and not her.

Jessie thought she would be too busy to notice Teagen was gone. After all, they'd only shared a bed a few times. But the first night he was off the ranch, when all were asleep, she found herself missing him. The men were somewhere south of here, searching. She didn't have to ask, she knew they were in danger, but Teagen already had Travis with him and by tomorrow night he'd also have Roak.

Tugging on her robe, she walked out onto the porch. She stood in the shadows, hugging herself and staring at the remains of the bridge, wishing Teagen could cross the distance between them and come to her. A thousand words needed to be spoken between them. They seemed to have left so many things unsaid.

He'd touched her with such tenderness, but she still wished for the words. She'd felt them in his caress. She knew he cared about her. He must. He could have never held her so without loving her. Could he?

Frustrated, Jessie went inside. In the first study drawer she found paper and pen. If she couldn't talk to Teagen, she'd write to him. Somehow, even if she had nowhere to mail the letter to, just writing would make her feel closer to him.

The memory of Teagen leaning against the bunkhouse wall last night came to her mind. From the kitchen window, she'd looked out just after blowing out the last downstairs lamp and noticed him. He seemed so alone. The tiny flash from his cigar lit his strong jaw for a moment. He was staring at the main house, frowning.

Just as she took a step toward the back door, he slammed his hand against the wall and turned away. For a second, she stood frozen, feeling as if he'd turned away from her.

Jessie decided he couldn't have. He was angry at something else, maybe even at leaving. He couldn't have seen her standing in the kitchen.

She decided they'd laugh about it in a few days when he got back.

After writing her thoughts in a letter, Jessie crossed the hallway to relieve Martha, who had taken the first shift of caring for Sims.

When she reached the bedroom door, she was surprised to find Martha crying. The old Ranger lay on his bed, mumbling out of his head. With his gray hair and skin, he appeared to be fading away.

Jessie hugged the housekeeper close. "What's wrong?" Sims had done so well the first time he'd been shot, but not this time.

Martha shoved her tears aside with her palms and straightened as if ashamed that someone had seen her cry. "He's dying. We've done all we could, but I don't think he's going to make it. I think he's reliving every gunfight he ever fought in. It's like he's counting up all he's done before he meets the Lord."

Jessie brushed his forehead with her hand. Tattor Sims was burning up. "Do you want me to get Sage?"

Martha shook her head. "She told me an hour ago that there was nothing she could do for the man. The fever has to run its course. Sage said the best we can do is keep him comfortable."

Jessie swore she could smell death on the man. "Maybe he could use a bath. That might make him comfortable."

Martha shook her head. "It ain't healthy to bathe the sick. It'll only bring on more trouble."

Jessie offered to get Martha a cup of the tea she liked so much. While she was in the kitchen, she put on an extra kettle. What if they did invite more trouble? He could only die once, and being clean seemed a better way to go than with the smell of rotten flesh surrounding him.

After handing Martha her tea, Jessie said, "I've read about this health movement started by a minister named Sylvester Graham. The followers are called Grahamites."

Martha showed no interest in her story. She just stared at Sims as if her will could make him open his eyes.

Jessie tried again. "I think Mr. Graham started preaching health about twenty years ago. They don't eat meat or anything from an animal, and take no medicine. Graham believes that to stay healthy a man should bathe at least three times a week in winter and summer."

Martha snorted. "That can't be healthy."

"Maybe not, but the followers claim they've never felt better. The Reverend also doesn't believe in spices, so he developed a cracker made from whole wheat and honey so his followers would have something tasty now and then."

Martha frowned. "What are you saying? We need to send for some kind of cracker to help Sims? It'll never get here in time."

"No." Jessie leaned against the windowsill. "I'm saying we try giving Sims a bath."

"Cold water would kill him for sure, and hot water would only make him hotter."

"Water that's not hot or cold might work," Sage said from the doorway behind them. Teagen's sister walked into the room, excited at the idea of doing anything more than just watching.

"It might," Jessie agreed, even as Martha shook her head.

Sage leaned over Sims. "I've heard of using water to cool a fever. If a cold rag on his head can help, why not a bath?"

Martha stood. "No. It'll kill him."

Sage put her arm around the older woman. "He'll be dead by morning if we don't do something. His body can't stay this hot without hurting his mind. I have a feeling he'd want us to fight, not watch."

Martha nodded once. She had no faith in the cure, but she knew they had to do something. "Maybe it'll help wash out the wounds."

The women moved the tub beside the bed. Jessie helped Sage haul water, mixing hot with cold until it felt room temperature.

Sims wasn't a big man, but he was solid as lead. It took all three women to lower him into the water. Martha made sure a towel remained over his private parts. "It ain't proper for no woman to see a man naked. My mother had eight kids, and she never once saw my dad in the total."

Jessie looked at Sage, and they both smiled.

Sims groaned when they moved him, but once in the water, his body seemed to relax. He tried to come around a few times, but his efforts were unsuccessful.

Sage put a wet towel over his head. His shoulders and arms were out of the tub on one side, and his stocking feet on the other. Jessie added warm water so that he didn't shiver, and Martha carefully cleaned the dried blood away from his wounds, then she washed them with lye soap.

After fifteen minutes, Sage whispered, "I think he's cooler."

"Maybe we'd better get him out before he catches a cold." Jessie realized it had taken all their strength to lower him into the tub. She wasn't sure they could get him out without reopening all his wounds.

"I'll get Drummond," Sage said as if she read Jessie's mind. "If I go to the bunkhouse, I'll wake everyone up, but the boy is alone in the barn."

Without a word she left. A few minutes later, a sleepy Roak appeared at the bedroom door. "Holy cow, what do you ladies think you are doing to this dying man?"

Sage glared at him. "Doctoring, of course. Now, help us get him out."

Without another word, Roak lifted Sims's shoulders slowly

out of the water. Jessie and Sage each took a leg, while Martha kept the towel in place.

Once he was in bed, Sage bandaged the wounds, which looked better now that they were well cleaned. When they finally tucked him in, Sage whispered, "His skin seems cooler, and he's not talking out of his head."

Jessie tugged off Sims's wet socks. "We may have to do it again."

"I hope not. My back can't take it." Martha straightened.

They all sat around waiting for an hour, but the fever remained low. Finally, Roak helped Sage carry the tub out. As they dumped the water, she said, "Thanks for helping."

"You needed me tonight."

She couldn't deny the truth. "I did."

He glanced up at the stars. "In a few hours I'll be leaving, and I don't know when I'll be back. If Travis has his way, we'll chase the varmints all the way to the border."

Sage stretched, feeling exhausted. "Say what you're thinking, Drummond. I'm too tired to guess."

He propped the tub against the wall. "I'm saying, or rather asking, if I could hug you before I leave. I don't want to leave with you hating me. Since you're going back East soon, and I plan to go on with Travis to Austin when all this is over, I don't know when . . ."

"All right," she said knowing he'd never stop talking if she didn't give him a hug.

He didn't move.

"I said all right," she snapped. She'd been up almost all night and was in no mood to be polite, but she did owe him something for all his help.

She'd expected him to give her a quick bear hug and be gone, but he didn't. He stepped up to within an inch of her and gently brushed her shoulders with his strong, lean fingers. She closed her eyes, thinking his touch felt good caressing her tired muscles.

He moved his hands along her arms all the way to her

fingers. Then he raised her hands to his shoulders. Circling her waist, he tugged her toward him. He was almost a head taller than her, and the softness of his cotton shirt felt good against her cheek. She leaned into him.

Neither moved. He wasn't trapping her in an embrace, or even hugging her. She could have stepped away. They were simply two people standing very close. The warmth of him relaxed her, and for once she didn't feel the need to shove away.

Finally, he brushed his cheek against her hair and whispered, "Sage, don't get mad this time, but I got to say it before I go. Someday you'll need me, and I swear I'll be there."

She was far too tired to argue. "Good night, Drum."

"Good night," he said as he let her step away.

She thought she heard him call her darling as she stepped back into the house, but she couldn't be sure.

CHAPTER 35

Jessie FILLED THE NEXT FEW DAYS WITH WORK. TATTOR Sims slowly began to improve. Everyone was thankful when Mrs. Dickerson offered to read to him in the afternoons, but Martha still insisted on sitting with him at night until she was sure he'd fallen asleep. Sage commented that Sims was the first man Martha had ever found tolerable.

Mrs. Dickerson loved telling bedtime stories to the girls and would continue her story until all three were asleep. Though she talked of her home and complained that her garden must be dying, she seemed to enjoy the constant chatter around her.

With Teagen and Travis gone, Tobin took the rest of the men north beyond the pastures each morning to cut enough trees to rebuild the bridge. Jessie noticed, as the days passed, he had less and less to say. Sage wasn't worried, but Jessie saw a sadness about him that made her feel sorry for him. He avoided everyone, saying he didn't have time for supper, and ate breakfast even before Martha was up.

Jessie thought she knew how he felt. He missed his wife just as she missed Teagen. Only she had the girls, and all Tobin had was work.

The second week she was alone, Jessie feared Travis might have won the argument, and they were chasing the outlaw out of Texas. Martha reminded her that the ranch was the most important thing in the world to the McMurrays; it had been since their father died. Each one of them would ride to hell and back to protect the land.

Jessie tried to understand but couldn't. She'd fight to the death for her children, but not for land. She could love this ranch, but not the way she loved Teagen. She came to the conclusion that he didn't feel the same about her. He'd never said he loved her, but he'd been willing to die for a piece of dirt. She lost sleep wondering if she could be happy settling again without love . . . even in Teagen's arms.

Finally, she decided she could. Being with Teagen was a world apart from being Eli's wife. Most of all, she loved Teagen. She loved the strong, bossy, bull of a man who fought for what he thought was right, and she loved the tender man who let Rose push him around and played the bear in the girls' games and touched her so gently when they were alone. Even if he never loved her in return, they could build a good life together. Her love would have to be enough.

The next morning, after Sage left to cross through the pass to pick up supplies, Mrs. Dickerson took over entertaining the girls. Jessie sat on the porch with her mending. She somehow felt closer to Teagen when she was watching the bridge being built. In a few days it would be open again, and they would be connected with the world.

Strange how it didn't really matter all that much to her. This place had become her world. Maybe Teagen's philosophy was rubbing off on her.

Fall was in the air, and she drifted to sleep in the peace of the morning. As always in her dreams, Teagen was with her. He was silently telling her that he loved her with every touch.

Sage woke her with a yell. "Jessie! Look what I found in town."

Jessie stood as a tall woman in a chocolate-brown riding suit rode into the yard. She was followed by a boy no bigger than Rose, handling his own horse and two pack mules.

Sage jumped down from her horse. "Jessie, I'd like you to meet Liberty, Tobin's wife, and my nephew Duck. They rode into Elmo's place yesterday with a company of soldiers heading north." Sage giggled. "Liberty said she was about to ride out to the other side of the bridge and throw rocks until Tobin swam over to get her."

Liberty dismounted slowly from her horse. Tobin had said she was pregnant, but no sign of it yet showed. She walked up to Jessie and hugged her as if they were old friends. Suddenly all three women were talking at once.

To Jessie's surprise, the fine lady had a pack on her back made of leather and bent wood. She tugged it off and lifted a cloth to reveal a baby sound asleep. "I know I should have waited and ridden in the wagon with Rainey, but I couldn't. She'll be here tomorrow or the next day, but I can't wait any longer to see Tobin, and Duck was driving everyone crazy wanting to ride. When the soldiers passed us on the road, I talked them into letting me ride with them. I knew the baby would be fine in the carrier Tobin's mother carried all three of the boys in. And sure enough, he hardly made a sound."

She tugged her firstborn from the cocoon and handed him to Sage. The chubby infant wiggled and laughed. He was less then a year old but already bigger then Bethie.

The girls hurried out, all wanting to see the baby as soon as introductions were over. When Sage set him down, they surrounded him.

Bethie tugged on his hand, but he didn't stand.

Emily tried lifting him, but he just sat right back down.

"What's wrong with him, Aunt Liberty?" Rose asked.

Liberty knelt to her level. "He's not a year old yet. He hasn't started walking." She brushed Bethie's curls. "He'll walk by the time he's as old as his cousin."

Rose studied him. "I guess I'll have to teach him. You wouldn't believe all I have to do around here." Her long-suffering sigh made all the women laugh.

The sound of a horse coming fast made them turn around in time to see Tobin jump off without slowing and run to Liberty. He lifted her off the ground and swung her around, then kissed her soundly without saying a word.

Liberty laughed. "I've missed you too."

Jessie saw it in Tobin's eyes. Liberty was the one thing he hungered for. The one thing he couldn't live without.

Suddenly the house seemed to have doubled with people.

Duck wasn't like any child Jessie had ever seen. He never said a word, but he climbed and jumped on everything. Travis had found the boy tied up like an animal at a raider's camp. They'd probably planned to use him in trade. When Travis brought him home, he was far more animal than boy. The McMurrays fell in love with him, and when they couldn't find his parents, they made him a McMurray.

Rose constantly ran in with reports of what he was doing. She seemed to think him some kind of strange creature she should teach to behave. He obviously had other plans. Unlike the girls, who stayed in and near the house and did what their mother told them to, Duck pretty much did whatever he pleased.

Since Travis and Rainey were not there to keep him in line, no one else took on the task. He ate cookies for breakfast, slept in the rafters, and most days disappeared into the barn for hours. With Tobin's help, he saddled any horse he wanted to ride and shot out of the barn for parts unknown whenever he wanted.

Martha's favorite saying became, "I'm going to tell your parents when they get here."

Tobin and Liberty took long rides in the evening and retired early with the baby to a bed they'd rigged in the study. Jessie could hear them talking when she passed on her way upstairs. Apparently Tobin didn't have any trouble talking to his wife.

She couldn't help but envy them a little. Though Teagen had said he needed her, even wanted her, she knew he'd been trapped into marrying her by honor. He'd even told her once that he only helped her because of his friendship to Eli. Would he have felt the same if she'd told him right away that it had been her who wrote the letters? Or would he have left her at Elmo's Trading Post?

She went to bed wanting to dream of him holding her, but doubts had begun to build like clouds in her mind. She wanted him, she'd always wanted him, but had she manipulated Teagen? She wished, just once in their talks, that she'd asked him if he was happy before she came. In his letters he seemed to be. She'd added so much more responsibility on his shoulders. Finally, she fell asleep wishing she knew what he'd say if she asked him what he truly wanted.

Sims slowly recovered enough to sit on the porch during the day, but he liked to take his meals in his room. Jessie didn't miss the fact that Martha often joined him. He told everyone who would listen about a dream he had while near death. He swore he dreamed he was laundry being washed and left on the line to dry.

Things seemed to be changing around Jessie, but the longing for Teagen never lessened.

Since the bridge was made of whole logs lined on a sturdy brace, it was built faster then Jessie thought it would be. Three days after Liberty arrived, four long wagons pulled across the new bridge.

Rainey brought lumber and enough men to build a second wing onto the house. They unloaded the wood and went right to work finishing the cabin Travis and she had started last summer and never completed inside. Once Rainey spent a few hours saying hello, she rode down to her cabin to oversee the finishing, and Duck went with her. Rainey had become his mother, and not only did he mind her, the boy seemed protective of her. They'd come back for supper every night, then disappear to sleep in the only finished room of their cabin.

Liberty and Sage wanted Jessie to plan the new wing of the ranch house, but she couldn't. She and Teagen had never talked of her staying here forever. She couldn't design a home that wouldn't be hers. The only time they'd talked about a house was when he said he'd build her one in town.

She found one excuse after the other not to start the project, finally saying she wanted to ask Teagen what he wanted. Her sisters-in-law gave in and agreed to wait. There were plenty of other things to do as fall blew in.

Rose, who'd complained constantly about Duck, was bothered by his absence and talked Sage into taking her to see the boy. An hour later, Sage brought Rose back. The five-year-old announced that she absolutely hated Duck and he should have been named Squirrel.

Jessie felt like she lived in a city. The kitchen was always busy with cooking, children, and talk. She enjoyed Liberty, but she found she identified with Rainey. They'd both come from the streets and known what it was like to be hungry and alone.

Each night, after she put the girls to bed, Jessie sat on the porch and waited for Teagen. She had a hundred things to tell him. Bethie was starting to put sentences together. Mrs. Dickerson left to get ready to start school but agreed to come for Sunday dinner every week. Tobin brought Rose and Duck each a puppy from town. And most of all, she wanted to tell Teagen that she missed him.

By the third week, everyone began to worry about the men, but no one said anything. If she hadn't had the girls, Jessie felt she would have gone mad. Once school started, she drove the girls into town every morning and returned early enough to check the mail before she picked them up. The long drive gave her plenty of chances to practice her skill with the team.

No mail came, or if it had, it was hopelessly lost in the mountain of papers and boxes Elmo called the mail room.

Martha tried to make Jessie feel better by telling her how Teagen was a man who always did what was best for the ranch, and if he thought finding the man who called himself General was important, all other worries went out of his mind. Teagen would know that his brother was taking care of things at the ranch. He wouldn't be worried about them, so they shouldn't worry about him or Travis.

The housekeeper's logic offered Jessie little comfort.

The fourth week Travis sent word to Rainey, saying he'd be home soon, but Teagen planned to travel to Mexico with several Rangers to testify against the general.

Jessie waited.

September blew into October. Travis wrote for Rainey to meet him in Austin. He said he could wait no longer to be with her. Rainey glanced at Jessie when she read the letter, and Jessie didn't miss the sadness her sweet sister-in-law felt for her.

No word from Teagen. No hint about how he felt.

One windy afternoon, Jessie left the ranch early to pick up the girls. When she walked into the trading post to pass the time, Elmo yelled, "Afternoon, Mrs. McMurray."

"Good afternoon," she answered, loving that he called her Mrs. McMurray.

The storekeeper moved around the counter. "No stage today, so you've no mail to go through." He shook his head. "He'll be home soon. Your man isn't one to be gone this long from his land."

Jessie did her best to smile. "I know."

Elmo looked like he had something sour in his mouth. "When he gets in, I got something to tell him. He told me last time I saw him to let him know right away if a place in town came up for sale."

A chill passed over her. "A place?"

"A house," Elmo corrected. "I didn't pay much attention to his request 'cause we ain't got that many houses. This one is brand-spanking-new, but small. That new preacher had it built for his mother, but she can't stand Texas. Imagine that."

Jessie didn't care about the preacher's mother leaving; neither would anyone in town, she guessed. "Did Teagen say what he wanted the house for?"

Elmo's face wrinkled like an old piece of rawhide. "I sure hope he wasn't planning on surprising you. I'd hate to ruin that, but he said he wanted to buy you and the girls a house."

Jessie fought to hold every emotion in place. "I knew about his plans," she managed. "He promised me a house on our wedding day." That day, that promise seemed like a million years ago.

The old man relaxed. "Well, good then. I thought I'd better tell you because a nice little place like this won't last long. The preacher's mother is even leaving her furniture. She says it will cost more to haul back than it's worth."

"How long ago did Teagen ask you to keep an eye out for a house?"

Elmo shrugged. "It's been a while. If you want to take a look at the house, it's tucked in between the church and Mrs. Dickerson's, so you'd be safe."

Jessie said good-bye, knowing what she had to do. Teagen was a man of his word. If he wanted her to have a house, she'd move.

She talked to Sage and Tobin about buying the place, and they agreed, with winter coming on, it might be safer for her and the girls to stay in town on school days. Everyone tried to be light, but a sadness hung in the ranch.

With the lumber for the new wing stacked beside the ranch house, Jessie packed her few belongings while the girls were in school. Tobin had taken care of everything. He'd bought the house and set up an account at Elmo's to cover anything Jessie needed.

Martha stepped out, carrying a load of quilts. "Best take these. It gets cold in town."

Jessie knew better than to ask her to visit. "We'll be back Friday."

"I don't see why you're leaving. Wouldn't hurt to wait another week or two."

"It's been almost ten weeks," Jessie said. "This is what we agreed on when we married." If Teagen hadn't told Elmo to look for a house, she might have stayed, but he'd set this course in action, not her.

How many times had he told her he didn't like being around people or that he hated company?

Though she'd relived his every touch, she also couldn't help but remember the night he'd turned away from her. She'd thought of it over and over, trying to find some clue. They'd been so happy; he'd said he needed her. He'd kissed her wildly, passionately. But in his letters he'd always written that the ranch came first with him. Had she somehow threatened that?

CHAPTER 36

Aﬁﬂﬂﬂﬂﬂﬂﬂﬂ
AFTER A FEW DAYS THE GIRLS LOVED THE IDEA OF
having two homes. They hated getting up before dawn for the
hour of bumpy road to school, only to have to repeat it again
that afternoon. In town they had their friends to invite over, and
every Friday they looked forward to going back to the ranch.

Rose kept a list of things she had to do when they got to the
ranch each Friday, and by Saturday night, she was making another one for things she had to do when she got back to town.
Emily spent her weekends riding and helping Sage with the
horses. Martha cooked and spoiled Bethie. The weekends
were always fun for Jessie, the weekdays lonely. She filled her
time with sewing.

By the end of October, Jessie agreed to help Elmo organize
his tiny mail room. She was hard at work one Tuesday morning
when a cold wind blew in suddenly along with a tall, broad-
shouldered man.

She almost turned away. The man seemed familiar, but he
was too thin, too hairy to be anyone she knew.

A moment later she heard a thunderous roar that could have
only been one man. Her husband. "Jessie!" he shouted.

He was staring right at her, so she saw no reason to say
anything. She moved around the counter to the main room as
he took off his hat. He looked more like a mountain man than
a rancher. If steam could shoot from a person's ears, the room
would be foggy.

"Yes, dear," she managed, telling herself Teagen would

never hurt her. And somewhere, beneath all his hair and dirt, had to be the man she loved.

Elmo moved to shield her. "Welcome back, Teagen. It's good to see you." The old man looked nervous even while trying to be friendly.

"Get out of my way," Teagen ordered, and Elmo took a step backward. He hadn't lived to be sixty by interfering in private matters.

Teagen stormed toward her and didn't slow until he was an inch away. Then, without a word, he grabbed her hand and turned to the door.

"Teagen." Elmo mustered a bit of courage. "Don't you think you should at least say hello to her before you drag her off?"

"I'm taking my wife home," he said between clenched teeth. "Stay out of this, Elmo."

Jessie looked back at Elmo's worried stare as Teagen pulled her out the door. "I'll return after lunch, Mr. Anderson."

"No she won't," Teagen shouted without slowing down.

In the middle of the road, he finally stopped. "Which way is this house you bought?"

Jessie thought of telling him to let go of her, but he didn't seem in a listening mood. She pointed to the cute little house that sat nestled between the church and Mrs. Dickerson's place.

He showed no sign of noticing anyone passing as folks bumped into each other to get out of his way. He headed for the house, and she ran beside him to keep up with his long strides.

A minute later, if Jessie hadn't reached for the handle, he might have kicked the door in. When he hesitated, she almost laughed. "Come in, Teagen."

He stepped into the frilly room packed with lace and cushions and slammed the door closed. Before the sound faded, he whirled her in front of him.

"You've got some explaining to do."

"Me?" Jessie managed as he began stripping off his coat.

"I thought you said you loved me." He stopped long enough to point at her. "That better not have been another lie, Jess." He unstrapped his gun belt and hung it on the nearest chair. "I come home, and you're gone. You're not walking out on me without a word."

"Me!" She took a step backward. She didn't seem to be able to get more than one word out.

He tugged off one boot and tossed it in the corner. Suddenly the small living space that had been just right for her and the girls seemed tiny.

"I have a few things to say to you before you start leaving." Trail dust flew off of him as he moved. And she couldn't help but notice that his socks were almost as muddy as his boots.

"I do love you," she finally yelled back. "I'm not the one who left. You did. You left that morning without even saying good-bye. And you told Elmo to find me a house in town."

"That was months ago," he snapped. "Things have changed between us since I asked that favor."

"You never said so, Teagen. You have to talk to me. I have to know how you feel, where we stand."

"You're my wife. That's where I stand, Jess." His voice turned low. "Maybe it's time we got that clear."

Her back bumped up against the wall, and she knew she could go no farther. "I know I'm your wife, Teagen. But you left without even looking in my direction. I was watching."

He pulled off his other muddy boot and sent it flying. "I didn't see you."

She stared as he began unbuttoning his shirt. "You think I could have left that morning if I had seen you? I couldn't have held you like I wanted to, anyway. There's not a single room in that house that didn't have family in it. I figured the wing would have a roof by now, but Sage said you slowed the builders down."

"I wanted to wait and see what you wanted."

He frowned. "I want it done the way you'd want it. As long as you don't paint it pink and put these funny-looking string things around, I don't care." He lifted one of the doilies the preacher's mother had left.

She grinned.

When he unbuckled his belt, Jessie finally asked, "What do you think you're doing?"

"I've had three months to think about it, and I've decided I'm sleeping with my wife. There's not going to be two houses, Jess. You said you wanted to be mine, and we've wasted enough time talking already."

Jessie backed toward the door. "What if I don't want to go back to the ranch? It's a long drive for the girls on school days. Before long we'll be starting the trip before dawn and getting back after sunset. It's too hard."

"Then we're living and sleeping together here."

"What if I've changed my mind? You were gone a long time and not even a word."

He brushed the tip of his finger along the side of her cheek. "You haven't changed your mind. You've loved me for years, remember. I wasn't gone long enough for you to forget the way I touched you. I can see it in those big brown eyes. The feel of your skin next to me has haunted me every hour I've been away."

Anger melted as she saw the memory of their last night together flood his mind. "I've been to hell tracking down a man so he'll never bother me or my family again. I want to live in peace with you. I want to sleep with my wife and not worry about being invaded."

"Teagen, you can't just come in here storming around like a tornado, making demands. That's not how it's done." His words stopped her heart. The hunger for her was a need as dear as life in his eyes.

He pulled his pistol from his holster and handed it to her, handle first. "I want to sleep with you, Jess. If you don't want the same thing, shoot me now. All I wanted was to be with you. I've ridden from Austin without sleep because I didn't want another day between us. Where is the bedroom in this place?"

"Not like this." She straightened, knowing she'd have to face him as an equal. "Not with you yelling and bullying me."

"I'm not pulling chairs out for you or making pretty speeches about how much I love you." His stubborn jaw hardened. "I'm not that kind of man, and you know it."

Jessie smiled. "I'm not asking you to."

"Then tell me, Jess. Tell me what you want."

She stared at his chest, knowing that this was hard for him. He'd always fought for what he wanted, never asked. "You're thinner," she said, the first thing that came to mind.

When he didn't answer, she took a step toward him and brushed her fingers over the hard wall of his chest.

He raised one hand and touched her hair. "I'm not doing this right, am I?" Leaning near, he closed his eyes and took a deep breath. "I can run a ranch. I can defend it, but I don't know how to court my own wife."

Jessie could only imagine the scene he'd caused at the ranch.

"You need a bath and a shave, dear. I need time to think."

"I'm not leaving until we clear up a few things." He jerked slightly as she moved her fingers along his ribs. "I don't think I can walk away from you a second time."

"All right. Would you like some coffee while we talk?"

"No," he grumbled and then added, "thank you."

She didn't know what to do. She'd known from the first he'd never harm her, but what he said could hurt her far more. He'd written her his feelings for years. Why couldn't he tell her now how he felt? Why couldn't he look at her and say what she needed to hear?

"Teagen, just tell me how you feel. Tell me honestly from your heart like you did when you wrote to me. I know you love your ranch. I know it will always come first. I understand."

"No you don't," he said, sounding tired for the first time. "That's just it. You know how I felt, not how I feel now."

"All right. Tell me."

"I know you thought I was putting the ranch first when I left, but it was you and the girls that made me leave, kept me on the trail until justice was done. I couldn't stand the thought of seeing fear in your eyes or having Em worry about someone hurting the horses."

"But the last night. I saw you slam your hand against the wall of the bunkhouse."

"I was fighting not to cross to you." He brushed his calloused hand against her cheek. "I love the ranch, but I love you more."

She moved into his arms, and he held her gently. She could feel him taking deep breaths of her as his hands moved over her back.

After a long while, he said, "I guess I finally said something right. I got you in my arms."

"I guess you did." She fought back tears. "Say it again, Teagen."

He held her face in his hands and looked into her eyes as he repeated, "I love you, Jess."

"I love you too, dear."

"How about I go get a bath and come back. Maybe we can start over."

"We have all day before the girls get home. I asked the preacher's mother to watch Bethie while I helped Elmo today. I told her I'd pick her up when the girls got in."

He leaned away from her. "What are you saying, Jess?"

"I bought a tub big enough for all three girls to bathe in. It should hold you."

"And what do you plan to do while I wash up?"

"Watch." She smiled. "And there will be no towels until you're ready to dry off."

Teagen raised an eyebrow and began unbuttoning his trousers. "Whatever you say." He grinned and looked around. "On second thought, we may want to keep this place. I can think of some good uses for it from time to time."

She pushed him into the kitchen and heated water while he pumped extra buckets.

As he splashed into the heated tub, he heard her lock the door and pull down the shades. A few minutes later, she walked into the kitchen with her nightgown on.

He started to tell her she didn't need it; then he saw the top button. Unbuttoned.

When he stood, she handed him a towel. He felt her gaze as he dried, then walked toward her.

She stepped easily into his arms just as she always had. He lifted her up and walked through the house. As he laid her on the bed, he whispered, "I do love you, Jess."

"I know," she answered as he kissed her. "Now stop talking and sleep with your wife."

He raised above her. "I have plans to do much more than sleep."

She laughed. "I certainly hope so."